CHARRED ROOTS

THE GREATEST SIN BOOK 6

Published by Tangled Sky Press
www.tangledskypress.com

First printing, July 2019

CHARRED ROOTS

THE GREATEST SIN BOOK 6

ERIK KORT
LEE FRENCH

TANGLED SKY PRESS

ACKNOWLEDGMENTS

ERIK KORT

There are times when creating a fictional world and populating it with characters crosses the line between the-fun-space-in-my-head and into the-real-world-feels-scary-and-this-feels-real-too.

When that happens, I tend to crawl into a cupboard and refuse to come out, even when bribed with ginger cookies.

This book happened at such a time, and I owe everything to those around me who supported me through it. To Alex, who never failed to let me wail and then picked me up again. To Lesla, who came and cleaned my house (!!!!!) when I couldn't string two sentences together in order to ask for help. And to Beth, who let me snarl and bark at them when I was too far into my feels (and work), and still let me hug them afterward.

We all need a clan around us, even when we're as prickly as Chavali. Thanks to mine, from the bottom of my heart.

LEE FRENCH

Thank you, Mom.

BOOKS BY THE AUTHORS

The Greatest Sin Series

epic fantasy

The Fallen

Harbinger

Moon Shades

Illusive Echoes

A Curse of Memories

Charred Roots

ERIK KORT

(as Erik Marshall)

Wards of the Thicket

adventure fantasy

Children Without Faces

Children Without Voices (coming soon)

LEE FRENCH

www.authorleefrench.com

In the Ilauris setting

standalone fantasy tales

Damsel In Distress

Al-Kabar

and much more...

Tilzam
THE CREATOR'S DIVIDE
Cladrum
Grippa
Cloverdale
Cliffside City
Shappa
Todan
North Cascain
Ket
Harbor City
Milpo
South Cascain
Silverpeak
Mecalle
Nataille
N
W E
S

CHAPTER 1

The last page of an idiotic story, one of many in a book of similarly idiotic stories, taunted Chavali with all its words. She used the fingers of one hand to keep her focus on one word at a time on the smooth, worn page while she moved her mouth to form the sounds in her head. Despite the brevity of the inane drivel, the effort exhausted her.

Hand-drawn, full-color illustrations on the pages should've helped her understand the story. Her inability to see color meant they showed only nebulous gray cloud shapes.

Colby sat across the small round table from her, watching her with an infuriatingly bemused smile and holding her tea hostage. With his hand covering the mug to keep it warm, she couldn't even smell the soft, soothing blend with a hint of mint she'd come to appreciate over the months since waking from death as an agent of the Fallen.

Frustration simmered in her belly as the exercise took longer and longer to complete. The more time she spent in Colby's room, the more tongues wagged in the tower. Every one of these irritating busybodies, of which the Fallen included a distressingly high number, wanted to know everything about her. They chattered about what she did, how often, with whom, without whom, and anything else they could mine for tidbits of entertainment. Half the time, they made up details to fill in the gaps.

Skulking between their personal rooms at odd hours allowed Chavali to sleep in Colby's bed most nights without notice. Colby, of course, refused to sneak in any way. No matter.

He had a much-larger bed to match his much-larger person.

Standing nearly a foot and a half taller than her meant his feet hung off the end of her regular-sized bed.

At the moment, she wanted to throw the book across the room and lie on that bed, secure in Colby's embrace. He wouldn't oblige her until she finished the story. At least he didn't demand that she attempt to read the entire vapid tome in one sitting.

"This one," she tapped a word near the end and shifted the book so Colby could see. "Hone-sty?"

Colby almost choked trying not to laugh at her. "Close. Honesty." He coughed. "A word you'd naturally not recognize."

She took back the book without rising to his obvious bait. Once she reached the final words, Chavali shoved the open book aside. Violence directed at the book would solve nothing and damage something he valued.

"I don't understand the story." Sitting back in her chair, she crossed her arms and glared at the offending tome.

"But you can read it." Colby grinned.

She beckoned for her mug, demanding its return. "Not well enough to understand it. Why would a frog do any of these things? It makes no sense. What madness drove someone to write it?"

He snorted and released his hostage. Honey, herbs, and mint drifted into the air. "I love that you can ignore success to focus on the worst possible part of the whole exercise. Chavali, you can read. Five months ago, you couldn't. Not even letters."

Taking her tea, Chavali shrugged with contained exasperation. He wanted to speak about feelings. His body language told her, and he used that one blighted, obnoxious word casually.

Love.

The way he shifted his hand toward her, inviting her to touch him and take his thoughts, spoke volumes.

Anything she could do to avoid that subject suited her.

"What good is reading if it means exposure to this kind of idiotic tripe?" She'd elected to learn this skill because most people of Tilzam picked it up as children. Her clan had never seen value in reading or writing.

The spirits knew all the stories. As such, Chavali knew all the stories.

Writing them down meant opportunities for others to steal them.

Reading, on the other hand…

She wanted to know things. Everyone else wrote things to record them. Her healer had recorded a number of prophecies Chavali had spewed without knowing it. That book awaited her.

As soon as she could read it.

A knock on the door interrupted whatever answer Colby intended to offer along with his chuckle. He answered the door, holding it close to his body so the visitor couldn't see into the room. For her, he did that. Because she'd asked him to do it.

Someone in the hall murmured a question. Colby sighed and pushed the door open all the way.

A young woman in a servant's uniform, dark pants and a light shirt with a touch of silver ornament, flashed Chavali an uncertain smile. "Princess Aislynn would like to see you in her office, ma'am."

Chavali's lip curled. One more person had found her in Colby's room. This servant would undoubtedly report at some point about her whereabouts. Worse, Aislynn called for her, expecting her to run downstairs like an obedient dog.

"I'll go see her shortly." Chavali sipped her tea. Warm herbs and mint with a dab of honey always soothed her temper. The servants had a hard enough job without her yelling at them for doing it.

The servant held up a hand, preventing Colby from shutting the door. "Actually, ma'am? She asked me to bring you down."

Chavali turned her body to the side to make clear her intent to ignore the summons, at least temporarily. "I know where *Eldrack's* office is."

"If I were you," Colby told the servant, "I'd find another duty to handle for now." He shut the door, then turned and leaned against it with his arms crossed. "He might not come back, you know."

"Don't be ridiculous. Of course Eldrack will be back." Chavali stood with her tea, intending to take it with her. "Aislynn's presence is only temporary."

"The charges against him are serious."

"And fictional." She waved as if she could dismiss them at any time with a flick of her wrist.

Colby remained in her way. "And political."

She stopped in front of him and could tell he wanted something from her. "Will you allow me to leave?"

"Will you at least try to be diplomatic with Aislynn? Whether Eldrack returns or not, she's a princess of the kingdom we're sworn to serve. She won't become queen, but she has and will have the monarch's ear and trust for her entire life."

She'd expected him to require a display of affection to let her pass. Instead, he offered her pragmatic reminders.

Curiously, this made her want to offer such a display. She'd think about that impulse later.

Chavali nodded. "I'll keep that in mind."

He opened the door for her. "She's not an enemy right now. Don't turn her into one."

"I don't intend to." On her way out, she ran her fingertips along his arm, stopping short of touching his skin.

As she strolled down the stone hallway, one of many in the tower, she nodded to another Fallen who failed to suppress a grin at her. Busybodies, all of them. Worse than a gaggle of elder women trying to set up matches among their grandchildren.

The austere corridor of doors to other rooms like Colby's spilled into a wide spiral staircase connecting the levels of the underground tower. The central column spanned at least fifteen feet in width, and each quarter turn reached a new level. At the landing for Colby's floor, level eleven, Chavali paused and considered returning to her own room on the next floor up to make Aislynn wait longer.

Several Fallen and servants passed on the stairs. After over five months as an agent, Chavali recognized most residents on sight, though she knew less than a quarter of their names.

"Chavali!" One of her least favorite Fallen bounded down the stairs. Sean's bright, cheerful smile invited murder. He may have dispelled a number of ridiculous rumors about the source of her powers, but that didn't mean she wanted him to see her doing anything with or near Colby.

Chavali turned her back on him and headed down, hoping to outpace him.

"Oh, Chavali, you need to turn that frown upside down!" Sean looped his arm around hers. "I heard another agent woke up, and that's lovely news. It wasn't Harris, though. I mean, I know you're fond of him."

"I consider him a friend," Chavali said. She ground her teeth to avoid throwing her tea in Sean's face. Only twenty-six more steps down to level thirteen and Eldrack's office. If she could have done it without touching his skin, she would've pried Sean's hand off her arm.

"Exactly. I don't think I met him, but he sounds charming, in a sort of rough-and-tumble way. His death was, of course, quite distressing to everyone. I mean, how it happened. So much nasty business. Such a relief you took care of all that. Oh! I also heard we took in another body, which doesn't happen every day. You've brought in a body or two, haven't you?"

"One." She tugged on her arm. "Excuse me. I need to see Aislynn."

"Really." Sean's eyes gleamed. He let go. "What for?"

"No idea." She turned her back on him and stormed down the corridor.

"Good luck with whatever it is, then!"

She raised her hand to wave him off without looking. As she neared Eldrack's office door, it opened. A servant stepped through and stopped when he saw her. He glanced inside with uncertainty painted across his face.

"This is horsecrap and you know it," Railan said inside. Eldrack had trusted her as his second-in-command, and Chavali had worked with her more than enough to agree. Railan had helped Chavali a great deal with harnessing her telepathy. True control lay outside her grasp, but Railan's instruction had otherwise proven invaluable.

"This isn't a debate," Aislynn said. "The body is here, and I expect you to help my people find a healer to perform the ritual."

The servant met Chavali's gaze, sighed, and shrugged. He left.

Intrigued, Chavali waited outside the open door, hoping to hear more about Aislynn's people.

"Don't hold your breath. They have to want to do it. Willingly. You can't order someone to sacrifice her fertility to bring back some random person just because you said so. Eldrack would never accept a body under these circumstances."

"Eldrack isn't here," Aislynn snapped.

A chair scraped against the floor. "That's completely clear."

With the argument over and Railan ready to leave, Chavali stepped into the small waiting area outside Eldrack's office and shut the outer door behind her. The inner door stood open, revealing Aislynn sitting behind Eldrack's desk.

The Shappan princess wore her hair pulled away from her face in a tight bun with every hair perfectly in place. Her clothing always included some form of livery declaring her stations, and never showed any sort of rumpling or wrinkling no matter how many hours she spent poring over reports. She oozed the kind of arrogant authority Chavali found grating.

None of Eldrack's collected trinkets and knickknacks remained on the shelves behind her, not even the stone dragon Chavali had sacrificed so much to bring home from Harbor City. Instead, a stack of boxes dominated the back half of the office. Papers and folders covered every surface. Eldrack had kept the office tidier with more chaos.

Railan stood at the inner door, on her way out. Intriguing scars decorated her face, caused by the manner of her death. She otherwise dressed to blend and wore no sign of her station among the Fallen.

As Railan's gaze caught Chavali's, she flicked her eyes to suggest wariness around Aislynn.

Chavali needed no such warning about anyone, especially the princess who'd usurped Eldrack's position. "You sent for me?"

"Yes." Aislynn gestured to the pair of chairs opposite her. "Railan, you should stay for this."

Before turning to face Aislynn again, Railan glared at the wall. She took a moment to smooth her expression. "Of course."

"What do you want?" Chavali asked as she sat. She sipped her tea, expecting some vapid complaint or request for information she would obviously deny.

"I have a mission for you." Aislynn picked out a folder in the middle of the stack to her left and opened it on her desk.

Chavali raised her brow. She twisted to check with Railan, standing behind her, who shrugged. "You're sending me alone?"

"No, of course not." Aislynn flipped a page and seemed more interested in the contents of the folder than anything else in the room.

"Then why did you summon me alone?"

Aislynn looked up. "You're a mission leader."

"I see." Chavali took another sip of her tea. In Eldrack's chair, she saw a woman accustomed to competence and obedience. While she would find the former, the latter would elude her among the Fallen.

The entire investigation that had brought the princess here—to find a killer among them—had proven this. Chavali herself had never told Aislynn the full truth of what happened, and she knew Railan hadn't either.

They didn't trust her because they didn't know how much information she passed to the king or others.

"Is there a problem?" Aislynn asked, though her tone didn't invite a positive answer.

"Many, but none I expect to intrude upon this conversation." Chavali gestured with her cup. "Do go on."

Aislynn's mouth twitched with annoyance. "We have a retired agent with a situation. His handler has requested help."

No one had ever explained to Chavali all the options when a Fallen agent's five years of required service expired. She hadn't asked, either. Why bother? She'd barely begun.

Of course, Colby would finish his service before her. Perhaps she needed to know.

Because she enjoyed tweaking Aislynn's nose, she twisted in her chair to address Railan. "Retired?"

Railan held up three fingers. "When you finish your five years, you have three options. One, you can continue as an agent as long as you want. Two, you can take a different role in the organization, such as regional handlers, servant staff, archivists, recruitment investigators, spies and observers, and similar kinds of duties. Three, we can wipe your memory and set you up with a new life and history. The agents who take the third option are referred to as 'retired.' Handlers keep track of them and make sure they stay as safe as we can reasonably guarantee."

Having her memory wiped sounded like the worst punishment imaginable. To not know about her clan...Chavali shuddered at the prospect. When the time came for her to choose, she had two real options, not three.

"I've handled all the retirements personally for some time." Railan looked to Aislynn. "Who is it?"

Aislynn checked one of her papers. "A man named Torrel, living in a city called—"

"Palmia Basin. In Tila. I remember him." Railan delivered the words with a bite. Aislynn had offended her.

"Yes. His handler sent a report. She needs someone to come help sort out a mess he's gotten himself into. I'd like you to take a newly awakened agent and a mentor for him, because I doubt this will—"

"May I see it?" Chavali held out her hand, expecting to receive at least one page.

"See what?"

"The report sent by the handler."

Aislynn blinked at her. "What for?"

"To read it."

"You can't read," Railan said.

Chavali rolled her eyes. "In fact, I have learned. Everyone seems to think I mean something entirely different when I say Colby has been giving me reading lessons."

Railan huffed a subdued laugh. "Congratulations. It's a useful skill. I'm glad you've picked it up."

"I still wish assistance with writing up reports, but I can do more of the work now. So, may I have the report?"

Waving her off, Aislynn turned over another page. "My people have already picked it over. There's nothing of value in it. The new agent's name is—"

"Regardless, I wish to see it."

Aislynn met her gaze with a frustratingly neutral expression. "No." She consulted another page in her folder. "I've assigned Sivry as the mentor agent, and you can also take Portia and Colby. Get going as soon as possible.

Railan can give you information about locating Torrel. Dismissed."

As she stood, Chavali considered tossing her tea at Aislynn. For a moment, she would have the immense satisfaction of expressing her opinion of Aislynn's leadership style. Then the liquid would hit all the papers and folders. She imagined Eldrack's disappointment when he saw the mess she'd made. And then she thought of Colby's reminder to play nice with the princess.

Chavali paused to purge the venom from her words. "What is the handler's name? Where are we to meet this person?"

"You won't." Aislynn raised a hand and shooed her. "There's no reason to meet with her."

Of course not. Why would they want to meet with the one person who had information about the situation?

"I wish to make clear that I do not approve of you withholding mission-related information from any agent, regardless of how insignificant you might consider it." Chavali strode out without allowing a response.

Behind her, the door shut. Chavali slowed. Railan fell into step beside her. They climbed the stairs together.

"Watch yourself, Chavali. She has her own telepaths. They'll do what she wants. Our ethics codes are harsh, but have a lot of wiggle room."

"You should also watch yourself. She has her own telepaths." Chavali glanced aside and knew she didn't need to repeat the rest of Railan's words back to her.

Railan sighed and nodded. "Your options for this mission are to deal with the trouble or extract Torrel. Extracting Torrel means bringing him here. I'll have to wipe his memory again and implant a new history. We'll have to set him up someplace else. And every time someone is wiped, there's a chance they lose pieces of who they are. The important pieces."

She laid a hand on Chavali's arm and stopped. "Chavali, I looked this man in the eye. I told him I'd take his nightmares and give him a new life. I promised to watch over him. He doesn't remember that, but I do. Whatever he's gotten into, please do whatever you can to fix it. I don't know that Aislynn will let me handle it if you have to bring him back, and I don't trust her telepaths to rebuild him right. They didn't know him."

"But you did." Chavali nodded her head back toward Aislynn's office. "She told me next to nothing. Who is Torrel?"

"A man who makes the best of his situation. He's a leader, but not the usual kind." Railan sighed and shook her head, amused by something she thought. "He's like you. Competent and capable. Doesn't suffer fools. I guarantee the trouble he's in is about him trying to resolve some injustice. Hopefully, it's just about some gang in the neighborhood and nothing deeper."

He sounded like someone Chavali would've gotten along with. "Why Palmia Basin? How do you choose a location for such a thing?"

One side of Railan's mouth quirked into a smile. "He chose the location before I wiped him."

Chavali nodded. "I'll do whatever it takes to keep him there, and I'll make sure the others understand."

CHAPTER 2

Chavali waved as she approached the front door of her clan's farmhouse. Warm sunshine baked the worn, comfortable building settled on the land like an elder horse too tired to care if its coat needs brushing. Most of the clan worked outside, digging holes to accommodate a fence so they could keep goats without infuriating their neighbors. Everyone paused to return her wave.

She plunged inside and found the rest of the clan, two women and one child, in the warm, inviting kitchen. The room, not quite large enough to hold all nine of the clan's current members for a meal, smelled of yeast, chicken, and comfort.

If they wanted to share a meal as a full clan, they'd have to spill into the sitting room across the hall. Later, when she had time, Chavali would bring up this subject with all the adults to decide how to handle it.

Penny cut vegetables at the counter beside the cabinet housing their magic-powered oven. Though she appeared brittle with age, Chavali knew well how sharp she remained. Her strength clunked the knife she wielded against a wooden board, chopping through roots with practiced ease aided by the arcane power in her veins.

At the large round table in the center of the room, Kelly, Chavali's healer, kneaded bread dough. She looked up and smiled at Chavali without breaking her rhythm. How well she fit into the clan already, after her induction only a few days earlier, proved the rightness of the decision to bring her in. Something inside her had needed a deeper, closer community than the sisterhood of healers had provided.

Chavali certainly hadn't helped. Other Fallen agents actually shared their troubles with their healers.

Four-year-old Haizea stood on a stool next to Kelly, using a wooden spoon to mix batter in a large bowl. She showed great enthusiasm for her task, though not much skill. Gobs of the thick, light-colored mixture decorated the table and floor, as well as her clothes, arms, face, and hair. Like the other two children outside, Haizea had true clan blood. Chavali knew they all shared the same red-brown hair and olive toned skin, even if she couldn't see the colors anymore.

No matter how many outsiders Chavali welcomed into clan, and no matter how dear these others became to her, these children would always stand apart as the last remnants of her blood kin.

"I see you've usurped my healer." Chavali kissed Haizea's soft curls and ran her fingers through them.

Kelly grinned. She wore her light-colored hair in a loose ponytail and had chosen a plain dress for the day instead of her healer's white robes. Her choice to cleave to clan made Chavali wish she could stay for a while. "It gets boring down in that tower, especially when my Fallen almost never comes to visit me."

Ignoring the mild reproach, Chavali reached for a bowl holding berries.

Haizea smacked her arm. "Those are for after dinner," she scolded in the clan tongue.

"Spoken like your mama." Chavali stuck out her tongue at the little girl, happy to use the near-dead language in front of clan, even if they hadn't learned it yet. "But I won't be here for dinner." She swiped a berry.

Haizea stopped stirring and pouted. "Do you have a mission?"

"Yes. Colby's coming with me, so you can't pester him while I'm gone." Chavali popped the berry into her mouth and bit into the sweet, juicy little fruit.

"But you can have sex with him."

Chavali half-choked on her berry. She coughed. The girl didn't need to know the reasons she wouldn't bed Colby anytime soon. Explaining how the inability to shut off his thoughts made prolonged contact troublesome could wait until Haizea was older.

The girl would need to know eventually. She would someday succeed Chavali as the clan's seer.

"No, Haizea. That's not appropriate for missions. We'll be working."

"Are you all right?" Kelly abandoned her bread to thump Chavali on the back. "What are you talking about?"

Penny's wrinkles turned to creases as she tried not to laugh. "I still don't know all the words, and they speak it much too fast, but Chavali has a mission, and Colby is going too."

"I'm not sure you should still work missions with him," Kelly said. "You're not supposed to let them assign you together anymore."

"Bah." Chavali waved off the concern. "I can focus well enough for a mission with him around. Besides, I refuse to dignify all the swirling rumors about us. It's none of their business. Worse than a pack of old men who think they're in charge."

The front door opened and shut. The wooden floor creaked and chain armor jangled. "Marcus said Chavali is inside?" Colby called into the house.

"Interesting timing," Penny said with a knowing glance for Chavali.

Chavali ignored her. "Yes, I'm in the kitchen."

"If you won't have time on your mission," Haizea said, still using the clan tongue, "maybe you should bed him before you leave."

Grateful no one else present understood the little imp, Chavali flashed Haizea a half-hearted glare. She fled the room to intercept Colby and ran into him around the corner for the hallway.

Colby caught her before she fell and pulled her close. Her gaze met his. He brushed his lips against hers, his warm breath betraying a liaison with his favorite snack, blueberries.

::You're lovely.::

The moment deserved savoring. Chavali wished the mission could wait until morning. She touched his cheek, clean-shaven as always.

"The bed in the back room is big enough to hold him," Haizea said.

Chavali turned her head to see Haizea peeking around the corner and pointing down the hall with her mixing spoon. Batter dripped from the spoon to the wood floor.

::I don't know what she said, but I feel like I've been caught stealing cookies.:: Colby cleared his throat and set Chavali on her feet. "We should get going."

Under his thoughts, the thread binding his soul to the spirit inhabiting his horse's body pulsed with amusement. Their connection didn't allow for the sharing of fully-formed thoughts, but did keep them aware of each other's emotional state.

"Yes." Chavali let go of him much sooner than she preferred and herded Haizea back into the kitchen. "Be good for Kelly. She's clan now."

"I like her," Haizea said.

"Good." Chavali looked to the women and switched to Shappan to speak to them. "As usual, I have no idea how long we'll be gone. Perhaps a few days, perhaps longer."

Kelly nodded. "Take care with yourself, and we'll see you when you get home. Right?"

Chavali understood the question. Kelly wanted to do her job, which involved keeping Chavali in good health, both mentally and physically. "Yes, of course."

She left the room with a wave, then gestured for Colby to precede her out of the house. On her way out, she picked up the travel pack she'd left by the door. Karias, Colby's enormous white horse, waited on the front path. Colby climbed into the saddle and helped her settle in front of him.

Colby had no idea the horse concealed an intelligent spirit. Karias preferred he and the rest of the world remain unaware of his true nature. Chavali had no trouble keeping one more secret. At times, though, his observations made this task challenging. Often, such as now, she preferred not to touch him and hear his thoughts while riding with Colby to reduce the chance of accidentally responding to him.

Up the road, Chavali saw three horses with riders approaching at a leisurely walk.

Colby squeezed Chavali's waist and let go to take the reins. "I like not having to hide anything around clan."

"Yes, it's refreshing."

"I would also like not having to hide anything around other people."

Chavali's smile faded. "I don't think—"

"It's fine, Chavali. Theo agrees with you there's no rush, because keeping this quiet—"

"Who?"

"Theo. One of my sparring partners. His opinion—"

"Why does he have an opinion on this?" Chavali twisted to see Colby's face. She thought he seemed confused. "He would have to know to have an opinion."

She straightened and glared at the road. "And he knows because you told him."

"He's a friend. I trust him."

"You have a healer! We all have healers. Gretchen's entire job is keeping your secrets."

Colby sighed and rubbed his eyes with a finger and thumb. "Just once, can we have a mission together that doesn't start with an argument?"

"Apparently not." Chavali crossed her arms. "We agreed. You said you could handle it for a while."

"I said I'd be discreet until you're ready. I've been discreet."

Portia waved as the trio approached. She wore her dark hair in a loose braid with messy bangs. Most of the time, Portia's bright, open smile could disarm Chavali the same way her little sister had once excelled at brightening her foul moods.

Perhaps if she'd brought tea, Chavali could let Portia soothe her into ignoring Colby's gross breach of confidence. The man needed to learn how to keep his mouth shut.

For Portia's benefit, Chavali smoothed her scowl, forcing a veneer of bland, pleasant neutrality across her face. She returned the wave.

"How is telling your friends discreet?" she snapped, keeping her voice low.

"One friend. No one else."

Sivry rode alongside Portia. Dark metal wires spiraled through the lobes of her pointed elf ears and snaked into her skin at her jawline. Chavali had yet to ask about the unusual adornments. Something always managed to distract her, and she had no idea how private the explanation might prove.

The third person, an average everyman able to blend into most crowds and avoid recognition by most people, surprised Chavali. She remembered bringing his body to Eldrack from Ket. His duty of spying for a corrupt minor noble had both brought him to Chavali's attention and caused his death. She groped for his name and couldn't remember it.

"Jaris," Colby said as he extended a hand to shake with the spy. "Good to see you on your feet. You probably remember Chavali."

Jaris beamed at them both as he shook Colby's hand. "I'm not sure if I should thank you or curse you, but at the least, yes, I do remember you."

Portia grinned. "That's how most of us feel about Chavali at first."

Chavali rolled her eyes.

When Colby let go, Jaris offered his hand to Chavali. She flashed him a smile and didn't touch him.

"Did they tell you?" Portia asked. "The woman who killed you is dead."

Karias turned to take the lead and set a quick pace.

"Yes, thank you." Jaris took up his horse's reins and didn't seem bothered by Chavali's refusal to touch him. "They didn't tell me who killed her, though."

"Chavali," Portia said. "She looks harmless, but that stuff about stealing souls? It's all true."

Chavali grinned. "Quite."

Sivry laughed. "Just don't ask how she knows things, because she won't tell you. But I hope she will tell us where we're going?"

"Did no one say?" Chavali shifted her gaze from person to person, dismayed by all the shaking heads. "How idiotic. Aislynn wouldn't even give me the report we're investigating. We're going to a small city in Tila."

"I can't wait for Eldrack to come back," Sivry said.

"With the way everybody talks about him," Jaris said, "neither can I."

While the horses carried them up the forest road with birds too used to riders to shut up as they passed, Chavali offered the scant details of their mission.

"That's it?" Colby growled in the back of his throat, the sound vibrating in his chest. "I thought you'd have a briefing. Aislynn handles operatives all the time. She should know better. I have half a mind to turn around and demand more."

"It is possible," Sivry said, "she doesn't know anything and doesn't want us to know she doesn't know anything."

"Is that worse than withholding information?" Jaris asked. "It sounds worse, but is it really?"

Portia laughed. "There's a reason why we brought you back with us, Jaris."

As Chavali shared in the laughter, she noted the towering stone obelisk in view ahead. Made of smooth black rock, the hollow Creator's Tower rose hundreds of feet into the air, topped by a crystal Chavali remembered from her childhood as a deep, rich blue.

Only after her death, in random conversation, had Chavali learned the crystals could change color. If Shappa ever raised an army intended for offensive purpose rather than defensive, the crystals in all of Shappa's towers would turn black. If any country elected to pursue war with Shappa, all of Shappa's crystals would turn blood red. The same held true for the crystals in the other countries.

If only the memory imprinted on everyone at birth, of the Creator abandoning them all, could serve such a useful function. As far as Chavali had seen, it did nothing more than cause trouble. No one knew what horrible sin had driven the Creator from them. The quest to discover it had spawned zealots.

With one hand, She prevented wars, and with the other, She gave out reasons to fight them.

Followers of the Creator's Path stood guard at the base, wearing plate armor with full helms. They carried out an inscrutable duty to watch over those who used the towers. And, of course, like any Order, they profited off anyone they could.

As usual, the Fallen dismounted, showed their rings to the guards in lieu of paying the fees, and led their horses inside. They walked onto the rough map of the known world carved into the stone floor.

From this spot, they could travel to any of the other twenty Creator's Towers scattered across the world.

Marking each location except their current one, small crystal levers jutted from the floor. At their current location, a star had been etched into the floor instead.

Chavali studied the map and realized she didn't know which lever to choose. Checking a map for the small town had never occurred to her. Tila had three towers, with three more near its borders.

Eldrack would've included which tower to use in his packet of mission information.

"Pick one in Tila, I suppose," she muttered.

"Of course we don't know where we're going," Colby groused. "It's not like we need any details to do our job." He stalked back out and conferred with one of the guards. When he returned, he stepped on the lever for the northernmost tower in Tila.

Light flashed from the crystal five hundred feet above, blinding everyone. Chavali gritted her teeth against the expected and unpleasant sensation of pulling and twisting, dragging and tossing. Horses grumbled. The light faded.

They stood inside another obelisk with the star at a different location on the map. It otherwise could have been the same place. Two more guards in the same armor watched from the same two spots at the entrance to the tower. The garden beyond them used the same layout, though they grew a similar selection of plants with minor differences. Even the weather matched Cloverdale despite the mountains between the two locations.

With directions from a guard again, the group traveled a short distance through a forest to reach a bustling town on a wide river. There, Chavali hired a boat to take them all upriver. According to the guards at the Creator's Tower, Palmia Basin lay halfway between this town and the barren mountain peak they could see in the distance.

Two oxen, urged onward by a tender, walked on a wood and leather treadmill in the center of a wide barge. According to the boat's captain, the treadmill connected to paddles beneath the boat to propel it against the river's swift current.

Portia stood at the railing, heaving the contents of her stomach into the river. Chavali stayed with her, rubbing her back and keeping her from falling off the boat.

"Someday," Portia said, her voice rough, "I'm going to find a way to use magic so this doesn't happen anymore." She spat into the water. "You'd think that would be easy, but you'd be wrong."

"We could have Colby hit you in the head."

Portia chuckled and glanced behind them. Chavali followed her gaze and saw Colby. He stood beside the door to the watertight cargo cage they'd insisted upon loading Karias and the other horses into. The reasoning had something to do with weight distribution and safety. Chavali had left him to sulk there because she didn't want to argue about anything else.

Sivry and Jaris sat on the deck, chatting and playing cards in the sunshine.

"I think he'd rather see you than me," Portia said. She groaned and leaned over the side again.

Chavali held Portia's arm but watched Colby and saw the tension across his broad shoulders. "I hate the rumors."

Portia coughed and cleared her throat. "Everybody hates the rumors."

"Sean likes them."

"He likes knowing things. So do you. The difference is he likes to talk about those things and you don't."

Chavali sighed. "You remind me of my little sister."

"I'll take that as a compliment."

"It is one." Chavali remembered Pasha taking her hand and dragging her to the fire so they could dance together. Echoes of her laughter rang in Chavali's ears. "I miss her a great deal. She was a bright light."

"Didn't you have a husband or something before you died?"

"Bah." Chavali waved off the idea. "He was just a man."

Portia wiped her nose, covering her face enough that Chavali couldn't see her expression. "Is Colby just a man?"

Chavali turned toward Colby again as he watched their progress upriver. The wind ruffled his clothes. Sunshine painted him as a striking, heroic figure. She thought of his hands, rough and calloused from years of hard work and swordplay. Most would consider him handsome for the air of justice about him.

"None of your business."

"Mmhmmm." Portia nudged her with an elbow. "I'm fine, you know. There's nothing left in my stomach, so it's just dry heaves at this point. I won't fall overboard from that."

Chavali shrugged. No matter how attractive Colby seemed from across the boat, she knew what would happen if she left Portia to join him. Without understanding why, Chavali wanted to pick a fight with him. At the same time, she wanted to stand in his shelter. The conflicting impulses made no sense. She chose to ignore both.

"Ensuring your safety is no hardship."

CHAPTER 3

The small city of Palmia Basin covered both shores of a lake at the base of a wide waterfall at least one hundred feet tall and dominant enough to block any view of the mountain's peak. Ferns and vines grew among thin trees with wide, glossy leaves and threatened to overtake thatch-roofed structures.

Unlike the downriver town, damp heat swaddled this city within the sheltered, bowl-shaped valley.

Boulders flanked the river mouth, the only obvious entrance into the city. Buildings with spinning, splashing mill wheels clustered near the mouth on both sides of the lake.

At the far end, Chavali noticed curiously regular, unmoving sparkles of some kind in the midst of the waterfall, and unusually rounded structures at its base. She had no idea how to interpret either and hoped they didn't have to stay long enough to find out.

The oppressive warmth already sapped her strength. She wished they'd known to expect it. To survive this mission, they'd all need new clothes. Her boots seemed especially ill-advised. Open-toed shoes would serve them all much better.

Wide, concrete piers lined a wide section of the southern shore. People in loose-fitting uniforms of lightweight fabrics with sandals swarmed over boats and the nearest buildings. Twin cables ran across the lake, from one side of the city to the other, pulling small boats anchored to it in each direction. On the northern shore, much smaller wooden docks hosted a flotilla of rafts and similar craft.

Their barge angled for the near end of the southern docks. Half a dozen people in those same uniforms scrambled from a different pier to theirs, running with their heads down as if exhausted. Two carried long hooks. The rest dove for and prepared ropes. A woman, also in uniform and wearing a wide-brimmed hat, hurried up the pier with a clipboard in hand.

At the far end of the docks, Chavali thought she saw men in less regimented clothes sneaking boxes out of a building through a large window. No one else seemed to notice. She didn't know what to make of it.

As soon as the boat's captain and the pier's workers allowed it, Chavali assisted Portia onto their dock. The mage trembled and lowered herself to one knee to wait for the others and the horses.

The woman with the clipboard approached Chavali. Her gaze flicked from person to person, then her eyes widened. Chavali turned to see Karias marching out of the cargo hold, his coat gleaming with sweat in the bright sunshine.

"What is the purpose of your visit, and do you have any cargo?" She stammered as if she'd never seen such a large white horse. Her hand gripped her pen so tight against her clipboard that her knuckles turned pale.

Chavali noticed four people emerge from a building further up the docks, all with the practiced gait and weaponry of soldiers. Their uniforms fit them close, with a much different cut than the dockworkers and clipboard woman. They headed toward the group.

For some reason, Karias had spooked them.

She hadn't thought about their cover story and couldn't consult with anyone else. Vagueness had never failed her. "We are scouting a business opportunity for our employer, and no, we do not. Unless horses count?"

The woman gulped. Her shoulders tensed. She continued to watch Colby escorting Karias off the boat. "What kind of business?"

Surprised by the woman's reaction, Chavali chose to change the subject. "Our employer is considering expanding his operations and wishes to know more about your lovely city. Is the weather always this pleasant?"

Instead of relaxing, the woman seemed to tense more. "I really would like to know what kind of business your employer runs?"

The soldiers arrived and blocked passage off the pier. Another soldier exited the same small building, this one carrying his own clipboard, and headed toward them.

Chavali smiled, hoping to disarm the woman. "We are well paid for discretion, among other things." She leaned close to take the woman into confidence. Placing one hand on the woman's, she nudged it to remove the nib of her pen from the paper.

The woman's thoughts streamed to her. *::Strange accent. Weird feather. Panic. Well-armed. That horse is huge. Why do they need it? Attack? Which side? Is she a mage? Who are these people? Why is an elf here? Why is that man wearing armor?::*

She'd intended to deliver a veiled threat. Under the circumstances, Chavali thought it wise to instead offer an inoffensive trade option. Later, she would discuss this woman's gross overreaction with the rest of the team. "But confidentially, he is a distributor of fine spices and flavorings. He wishes to avoid his competition discovering his interest here."

::That doesn't explain the horse, but I suppose that man would need a large mount.:: "I see." *::One, two, three, four horses, four people, and one elf.::*

Chavali filed away the slight against Sivry to lean closer and murmur, "Rumors suggest there may be a unique spice in the plants here."

Had she known to expect prejudice against elves, she might have tried to use illusions to mask Sivry's appearance. It might have helped, or it might have backfired. Chavali still had a great deal of difficulty with skin tone. Making it move properly with Sivry also presented an extra dimension of challenge she hadn't practiced much yet.

The woman's tension drained, though she remained wary. Chavali saw no reasonable way to continue contact and withdrew her hand.

"I'm going to need all your names and the name of your employer."

The soldiers parted to let the man with the clipboard through. "How many weapons are you bringing into the city?"

"My name is Chastity." Chavali didn't want to give any of the other information. She also had no interest in an interrogation. "Is there a problem? Does my subordinate exceed some unknown size limitations?" She gestured to Colby.

Both the soldier and the woman shifted their attention to Colby, standing several feet back with the horses and the rest of the team. He smiled and raised his hand in polite greeting.

"No, of course not," the soldier said. "That's ridiculous. We'll need to search everything you brought with you." He peered at the woman's clipboard. "Trade, hmm? You didn't bring much for traders."

Chavali raised an eyebrow. "I've heard most people will accept a somewhat rare yellow metal in trade for a great many things."

Both her clipboard interrogators stared at her. Neither seemed amused.

"Let's see those packs," the soldier said. "Line them up on the pier. Right here."

"For what purpose? So you can see if we have extra swords hidden inside them? Or do you merely enjoy rifling through ladies' underclothes against their will?"

The woman blushed. The soldier shifted his weight and worked his jaw.

Annoyed by these two, Chavali pushed. "We have come with a fair amount of money, intending to leave it with people in your fair city. If you prefer that we turn around and take this money to instead part with it downriver, we can do this. The people of that small town at the bend seemed eager enough to cater to us."

At worst, she figured they could take the boat partway back, pay the captain a ridiculous bribe, and ride overland to return.

"Just let them through," the woman murmured.

The soldier jabbed the end of his pen at Chavali. "If you so much as look funny at anyone while you're here, you'll regret it." He turned his back on her and walked away.

His soldiers stood aside and continued watching.

Chavali waved for the team to follow her into the city. What had made a place with so much natural defense paranoid about invasion, of all things?

She wondered if they'd find Torrel at the center of it, or on the fringes. One retired Fallen probably hadn't caused that much trouble, but she had no doubt he'd gotten involved somehow.

Once they passed the soldiers, everyone mounted their horses and the team rode into the city. Ferns and flowers with wide leaves grew along the sides of narrow roads. Vines clung to whitewashed buildings and thatched roofs.

An excessive number of trees for such a large population center leaned into the gaps and shaded everything. Insects buzzed and birds squawked. The horses' hooves clinked on grooved tiles better suited to sandals and the paws of large, short-haired dogs and llamas pulling carts.

"This place is amazing," Colby said. "They've managed to arrange the flowering plants so their colors form geometric patterns. Look at that detail work." He pointed to a tall house visible through the flora. Intricate cutouts of flower shapes and curves decorated dark strips of wood surrounding the windows and hanging from the porch railing. "It's called gingerbread trim. It was popular in parts of Grippa about a century ago."

"I think we'll need to ask for directions," Chavali said. "I have no idea how anyone finds anything here. There are no signs, or maybe the plants devoured them."

Colby chuckled. "At least we know what we're looking for."

"Indeed." Chavali pointed to a pair of guards. They wore the same uniform as the soldiers at the docks.

Karias stopped beside the two guards without Colby asking.

"Excuse me," she said to the guards.

Both soldiers looked them over, noticed the other three horses and riders, and put their hands on the hilts of their swords. "Can we help you?" one asked, her tone thick with suspicion.

"We are lost? The place we're looking for is called The Flour Garden. It's a bakery in the northwest quarter."

The soldiers glanced at each other. Both shrugged. Neither relaxed.

One pointed. "The northwest quarter is that way. I haven't heard of that bakery."

"Are you familiar with an inn called Flower Beds?"

"Ah. Yes." The guard gave them directions and nodded as they continued on.

People passing on the street watched them with caution, fear, or hostility. Several stared openly at Sivry, and Chavali saw no elves among them. Many residents scurried along as if expecting attack around every corner. Sheets of wood covered a window here or there.

The more attention Chavali paid to the condition of the city, the more she noticed little things. Errant rags covered in grime decorated the edges of the street. Small rocks in random piles looked like rubble. Dead fronds clung to a scattering of plants.

On first blush, the city gave the impression of an improbable tropical paradise nestled in craggy hills. With closer inspection, Chavali suspected this city had many of the same kinds of problems as other cities, and perhaps some unique ones as well.

Flower Beds offered a collection of small cabins slathered with flowers and boasting excessive quantities of floral-themed gingerbread trim. Stone paths wound through wild gardens restrained by minimal fencing, connecting each cabin to a larger main building and a long, one-story outbuilding. Boards covered two of four visible windows on the main building. Fine netting hung in the other two instead of glass.

Colby made Karias stop and let Chavali down at the front door. The horse swung his head to look at her. Despite his lack of facial expression, she knew a demand when she saw one. He had something to say and expected her to listen.

She'd visit him later, when they could chat without putting on a show for Colby or anyone else.

She turned her back on them and climbed two creaking steps to enter the main building. As expected, the large room inside offered tables, booths, and a bar in the back. Several customers occupied the tables and bar stools, filling the air with amiable chatter. Painted flowers decorated the walls and tables. The young man who smiled and approached wore an apron with flower-shaped pockets.

"Hello and welcome to Flower Beds. I'm Iker. Are you here for dinner or the night?"

"I need rooms, please. Enough for five people, plus stabling for four horses. We'd also like dinner tonight. I'm not sure how long we'll stay. At least three nights, I think. Perhaps as long as a week." Chavali followed him to the bar.

"Wonderful. Would you like to stay in the cabins or the rooms upstairs? The cabins cost more, but they can fit up to four people each. The rooms can sleep two at most."

"Two cabins should be fine."

The door opened. Sivry and Jaris laughed as they entered. Portia held a hand over her forehead, betraying how badly she needed food and water. Colby undoubtedly still fussed over Karias.

Chavali waved to them and returned her attention to Iker. She saw the man's eyes widen. To her surprise, several of the patrons also seemed distressed by Sivry, Jaris, and Portia.

"Are those your companions?"

"Yes, plus one more who's quite attached to his horse."

Iker froze. "I don't want any trouble here. Maybe you should go someplace else."

"Trouble?" Chavali frowned. "We've just arrived in town for business and this inn was recommended to us."

Iker narrowed his eyes. "By who?"

"Our employer." Chavali covered Iker's hand to offer the illusion of comfort. "What trouble do you fear from us?"

Iker pictured men and women with cruel smirks and flashy, middling-quality clothes all of a similar style beating his mother, the owner. The older woman still recovered from a broken arm. Later, he'd discovered all the windows broken and had no idea who'd done it. *::Dear Creator, please don't let any of them see these people.::* "I just think you should go someplace else."

Chavali wanted to know what kind of vandals and thugs she faced. Railan had suggested this inn for its proximity to The Flour Garden. If some group threatened Flower Beds, it probably also threatened Torrel. She considered playing coy or wheedling, but Iker's intense fear pushed her to directness.

She couldn't ignore such misery, not even in a random stranger. Especially not this kind.

"Who attacked your mother?"

Iker blinked at her. "I didn't say—"

"I know. Who is responsible for that attack?"

::I don't want them to come back. They already demand too much from us. We can barely keep up with the payments.::

The Blaukenev clan may have swindled people, but they'd offered happiness and entertainment in exchange, not pain and suffering. They wouldn't have interfered in this sort of thing, of course, unless it also affected clan.

Colby, though, would never stand by and let this happen to anyone. She had sworn to watch his back, and if that meant meddling, she would meddle.

"Who is extorting you for protection money? You failed to pay enough once, yes? Then they beat your mother almost to death. And now they charge more, I imagine. So you told the guards because you have nothing left to lose, and they did nothing, or maybe they broke the windows. They might even have told the gang."

Iker's mouth fell open. Tears welled in his eyes. *::How could you know that?::* He covered his mouth.

"Listen to me, Iker." Chavali leaned in and kept her voice down. "I came here for other reasons, but if we accomplish nothing else while we're here, my friends and I will take care of this gang, and you will never have to deal with them again. Tell me everything you know about them." She handed Iker far too much money to pay for even the most extravagant rooms in the largest cities.

"What if you can't handle them?" Iker whispered.

Chavali growled in the back of her throat. "There is very little in this world that my friends and I cannot handle."

CHAPTER 4

"The gang calls itself Withered Fists. They moved into the area recently," Chavali said as she dipped bread into a mild soup and nibbled it between pieces of the story. Portia sipped tiny spoonfuls of the soup, taking her time to fill her belly. Jaris and Sivry both nodded along. Colby had already finished his food and sat with a cup of cool ale. All four grew grimmer with each new piece of information.

"They come for payment once a week, and should be back in four days. Iker doesn't remember dealing with another gang before they arrived, so if there was a battle of some kind for control, it didn't happen here."

"We should check on the bakery before we get some sleep," Colby said. "Torrel might be in a similar situation. He might've gotten hurt like Iker's mother with no one to help take care of him."

"I'm not sure what help I can be tonight," Portia said. Her voice still sounded rough, even after soup and a cup of chilled cider. "I'm exhausted. That river ride was long, and I think I lost every meal for the past week."

"Stay and rest," Sivry said. "I doubt we'll find serious danger."

"Can we talk about the state of this city, though?" Jaris asked. "Something stinks here like rotten cabbage."

Chavali finished the last of her dinner and smiled to herself. She'd made the decision to bring Jaris's body to the Fallen. His competence reflected on her judgment.

"The people are scared," Chavali said.

Jaris nodded and leaned toward her. "They don't see the guards as a source of security."

Chavali grinned, pleased he'd seen the same things as she. "Corruption plagues the docks."

"Multiple gangs are bankrupting honest people."

"At least one guild is boosting profits with unnecessary regulations."

Sivry leaned forward and opened her mouth.

"Probably two." Jaris echoed Chavali's grin as he cut off Sivry.

"I expect to find a thriving black market," Chavali said. "The guards know about it and look the other way."

"Kickbacks. Definitely kickbacks. They're in on the action."

"Whoa." Portia raised a hand between Chavali and Jaris, breaking their eye contact. "Slow down, guys. You're making some insane leaps from one ride through the city."

"Perhaps." Chavali shrugged and shared a knowing smile with Jaris. "I doubt either of us will be proven wrong."

"But that's not the whole picture." Sivry tapped one of her pointed ears. "I haven't seen any other elves, or any halfbreeds. That's unusual for a city of this size, even one as remote as this."

"Why were the guards so jumpy about us?" Portia asked. "We're lucky they didn't arrest us and impound our stuff."

Chavali huffed. "That was not luck."

Portia stuck out her tongue at Chavali and leaned her head on her hand. Her eyes fluttered as she struggled to stay awake. "Whatever you want to call it. The ones on the docks and those two you asked for directions all acted like we planned to attack them on sight. Do people not walk around here armed?"

"I've seen swords on people other than guards," Colby said. He shifted with discomfort and his shoulders bunched more than usual. Chavali couldn't guess why and that bothered her. Perhaps he disliked having so little to contribute to a discussion, though he'd never shown any such concerns before.

Sivry nodded her agreement with Colby. "We stick out. We look foreign because we're dressed for cooler weather. Whatever reason they hate foreigners may also explain the lack of elves."

"Or it could be unrelated," Jaris said. "Maybe they're afraid of foreigners exposing all the corruption. People with a good system in place don't like things that upset the cart."

Waving to dismiss his idea, Sivry said, "I doubt it's that concrete. Indirectly related is more likely. These things don't exist in a vacuum. They feed off each other."

"It's a good thing we had plenty of information before we came here," Colby grumbled.

"You know," Jaris said, "I hate to be the one who points out that Aislyn might not be as terrible as you all think, but is there someplace in the tower one of us could've looked up information about Palmia Basin?"

"She gave me the impression of urgency." Chavali shrugged because she should've done that, or asked Colby to do it. He, Jaris, or Sivry could've skimmed the available materials to determine the climate.

If they'd had a reason to suspect something unusual, which they hadn't.

Eldrack had always given them enough information. She'd come to expect this and didn't know what to look up. The thought hadn't even crossed her mind.

"Never mind the pointless griping," Portia said. She rubbed her temples. "I'm too tired and it's too hot for that. You've all noticed things about the city, but the underlying causes are what matter. We'll have to get a better feel for the city to figure those out." Portia stood with a hand on the back of her chair. "Tomorrow."

Chavali also stood. "Agreed. This is a good time for the rest of us to go check on our baker."

As she passed Chavali, Portia whispered, "That thing with Jaris looked like flirting. Watch yourself."

Chavali blinked and checked Colby. He watched Jaris with a hint of wariness around his eyes and mouth. "Thank you," she murmured. Somehow, she hadn't noticed the object of his discomfort. Perhaps Kelly had a point about a potential Colby-shaped blind spot.

She gestured for Sivry to lead the way. Jaris flashed Chavali a grin and followed Sivry. As Colby approached her, Chavali took his hand and headed for the door.

His thoughts bounced, scattered and half-formed. She couldn't grasp any of the pieces. They reached the door and stepped into the warm evening air before he managed anything coherent.

::When we get back, I want to talk to you.::

"Of course," Chavali said. "I do not expect to pull a blanket over my head and fall asleep in an instant."

He imagined her wrapped in a blanket with her feather sticking out.

She laughed and let go of his hand. A few paces ahead of them, Jaris glanced back, then put his head together with Sivry.

People walking on the street parted for the four of them, giving them plenty of space. Chavali noted their furtive glances and suspected Sivry had the right of it. Chavali stood out everywhere. The rest of them didn't. Jaris especially had a knack for blending, and he couldn't here. She doubted he'd blend even on his own. They needed local clothing.

One of the several dogs pulling carts up the road barked at Colby and Chavali. A dark llama carrying a load of sacks on its back spat a cloud of saliva at them, forcing Colby to wipe his face. Chavali noticed a pair of patrolling guardswomen watching them. Ordinary people watched from windows on upper floors.

At least they provided entertainment for the locals.

Jaris turned and walked backward. "You're a telepath?"

"Maybe you should shout it," Colby said. "I don't think they heard you across the water."

Jaris blushed and slowed to close the distance. "Sorry." He lowered his voice. "I just— I remember you threatening to steal souls, and I believed you."

"Thank you," Chavali said as she swatted at a passing cloud of tiny bugs. "I appreciate the compliment."

"So you don't steal souls."

Chavali snorted. "No. Neither do I eat babies, consort with demons, or any of the other ridiculous things people in the tower whisper about me."

Sivry sniffed the air and cocked her head to one side as they continued up the street. "I smell burnt sugar and...is that cinnamon? How much farther is the bakery?"

"Two more blocks," Colby said, "one this way and one to the left. I think we should hurry."

The air pulsed with an explosion Chavali felt more than heard.

They ran up the street. At the next corner, they found a row of buildings with shops on the ground floor and apartments above. Smoke belched from the broken windows of one in the middle. Both neighboring buildings appeared unaffected. A few people watched from their front windows on the second floor. Several more stood in the street, watching.

Running toward the roaring disaster, Chavali recognized the name of the shop to the left as the one Iker had noted as the bakery's neighbor.

She grabbed Colby's sleeve. "It's the bakery!"

Colby stopped short. He watched the evidence of fire like he expected the smoke to form a fist and smash him into the ground.

"Does that sound like screaming?" Jaris stood in front of the bakery, holding up his arm to shield his face.

Sivry cocked her head to one side. "Maybe, but there's definitely someone inside. We need some kind of protection to go in there. Chavali, can you do that?"

"No." Chavali pointed at someone watching through their window. "You! Do you have a blanket or a large towel? The baker is still inside!"

The woman hesitated for a moment, then she disappeared.

Colby stalked to the front of the building, grim and resolute. He glared at the flames.

His death, Chavali knew, had come during an attempted rescue of children trapped inside a burning building. He'd failed those kids. Death hadn't assuaged his guilt or eased his shame.

In the set of his shoulders, she saw his determination to face the failure he hadn't yet resolved.

A man covered in soot ran out of the shop, bent over and coughing. Colby caught him and forced him to sit. Sivry rushed to help.

Tension eased from Colby's entire body. He didn't want to go into the fire, and now he didn't have to. Chavali didn't want him to go into the fire either. She didn't even want to get close enough to feel the heat.

"Is anyone else still inside?" Sivry asked.

The man nodded.

Without taking a moment to think, Colby left him and sprinted through the open front door.

Chavali covered her mouth. Her heart stopped. She heard nothing but the angry growl of crackling flames and ringing static.

Something soft landed on her. A thick blanket. For a moment, she stared at it, unable to comprehend anything.

Karias charged the building. He stopped at the doorway and tried to smash the frame with his front hooves.

"He's going to bring down the building!" Jaris took the blanket from Chavali and hesitated. "Do you know how to stop him?"

Sivry circled to the horse's other side with her hands up and approached Karias's flank.

Karias's panicked whinny startled Chavali out of her own distress. "Stop!" Chavali yanked the blanket out of Jaris's hands and ran at Karias. "Get out of the way!"

When she reached the horse, she slapped his shoulder. "Idiot, you'll kill him!"

He stumbled to the side.

Chavali darted past him to get inside.

Like an idiot, Colby had charged into a burning building. Like a different kind of idiot, Chavali followed him.

Broken glass littered the bakery shop. The stench of burnt sugar dominated the room. Flames licked around the edges of the open doorway the back room. So far, the fire hadn't affected the shop much. Both the display cases still had their glass coverings, and the pastries and cakes inside them seemed fine. The explosion she'd felt must have blown out the windows and caused little other damage.

Another man lay on the floor, unconscious or dead, with a shallow gash across his forehead. Colby shouted from the back room, the roaring fire too loud for her to understand him. Someone else laughed with a cackle. A clang of metal sounded like swords clashing.

"Sivry! Come help!" Chavali took the unconscious man by the arm and dragged him toward the front door. He moaned.

Flames crept across the ceiling. Sivry ducked inside and took charge of the semi-conscious man.

Chavali turned and rushed into the back room, holding the blanket over her head and her sleeve over her mouth and nose.

Flames engulfed a kitchen with a wooden block table in the center. Smoke seeped through the floorboards. Metal shelves stocked with sacks, bins, and jars lined one wall. Pots, pans, and a wide variety of baking tools hung on hooks or sat on counters. On one side, a large sink stood between burning wooden cabinets. A burst sack crackled on the floor, its edges smoldering.

Colby stood over a simply-dressed, soot-covered man lying on the floor and held off two attackers, both women. Another person, this one a man, knelt on a trapdoor in the floor in a pose suggestive of prayer. All three of these other people wore practically-designed, tailored clothing of fine linens with embroidered flourishes in mushroom shapes. They used matching blades.

Most importantly, the trio repelled flames. Fire bent away from their bodies. Soot avoided them. They had no trouble breathing either.

Colby had to avoid flames, protect the man on the floor, and endure the smoke while fighting in close quarters. He couldn't manage it for long.

Chavali wouldn't provide much help by stepping to his side. She darted to the sink and turned it on. A stream of clear water thumped into the metal basin. To start, she soaked the cuffs of her sleeves and the corners of her blanket. With a container or solid flat thing, she could attack the fire.

As she spun to check for an object to help, the doorway to the shop collapsed with a thundering crash, cutting off any escape. Flaming timbers fell between her and Colby. She cringed backward.

The woman on the center table lunged. Colby grunted. Something thumped.

Chavali drew her dagger. With a dripping sleeve over her mouth and nose, she took a step toward the man on the floor. Between them, a sheet of flames rose to the ceiling. The intense heat forced her back.

The second woman held out a hand to stop the first. "Leave him. He's down."

No, Colby was not dead. That woman did not mean dead, she meant down, as in lying on the floor, having difficulty standing. The heat and smoke had overcome him enough without killing him.

Clinging to this obvious, hopeful truth, Chavali stepped toward the center table.

The second woman shifted enough to notice her. When their gazes met, Chavali knew she'd made a terrible mistake in following Colby. She should've run for the back of the building with Karias. That daft horse probably couldn't do anything coherent through his blind panic.

Sivry and Jaris wouldn't get Karias to do anything either. She had no idea if they could think of something brilliant to solve this.

"Hurry up," the second woman snapped. She gestured for the first woman to move toward their man.

To reach Colby, Chavali would have to clamber over the center table. Doing so would earn her the focused attention of those two women. If Colby couldn't handle them, Chavali certainly couldn't either.

She would have to move fast.

Throwing the blanket over the burning debris, she scrambled to stay as far from the enemy as possible. Flames licked her dress. Steam rose from the corners of the blanket. She flung her body across the table and off it to land beside Colby in a crouch.

He sat with his back to the table, holding his side and wheezing for breath. He sword lay on the floor. He'd pulled the man Chavali assumed to be Torrel closer to keep his feet out of the fire.

"Are you hurt?" Chavali touched his hand.

::Just bruised. There's no way out. We're going to die.:: Colby tried to speak and fell into a coughing fit.

Under his thoughts, the thread of Karias's panic fluttered and floundered like a bird with a broken wing.

"No. We're not going to die today. This way." Chavali pointed at a wooden door with flames rippling up the surface to lick at the ceiling.

::Yes we are. It's blocked.:: He tugged on her arm, pulling her close. Fear, shame, and guilt dragged him down into a vast abyss of despair. Karias and his thrice-damned terror didn't help. A steady anchor might have kept

him from surrendering, but he didn't have one.

She resisted the urge to slap him. It wouldn't help. Slapping the horse would've helped. "Colby, you swore to defend your clan and Seer. You do not give up. Not now, not ever."

::You can't lie to fire until it spills its secrets or agrees with you.::

"Get up."

::I'm beaten.::

Tiny wisps of flame danced in the air. Chavali swiped her hair over her shoulder to keep it close and leaned toward him, intending to urge him to crawl.

Colby wrapped his arms around her. *::At least this time I'm not alone. If I have to go, it's with you.::*

The back wall blasted in. Colby tensed and pushed Chavali's head down, protecting her from flying splinters and chunks of wood. The heat evaporated and the fire quieted. A man roared his anger. Metal clashed. People grunted and swore. Someone cried out in pain.

The voices and sounds of battle stopped. Someone panted to catch their breath. Sandals slapped the floor.

"Let her go," a woman said. She had a light, lilting voice. "Is that one dead?"

"Yes," a man with a deep voice said. "This one's not."

Chavali squirmed. Colby let her go. When Chavali popped her head around the side of the table to see the new people, Colby coughed loudly enough to attract attention.

Two new people stood over the bloody corpse of the first woman and the unconscious form of the man. She saw no sign of the third woman.

These new people had nothing in common with the attackers.

The new man had dark skin and long dark hair in braids held together at the nape of his neck. He wore a thick shirt with no sleeves, leaving his muscled arms bare to reveal a pattern of darker tattoos with geometric and curved shapes on the right side. He wore linen pants to his knees with a battle skirt made of leather strips and, like everyone else in the city, sandals.

Standing in the hole they'd made in the back wall, a woman with lighter skin broke off from surveying the room to see Chavali. She wore sandals too, along with close-fitting linens with a stiff, high neck. Her light hair perched atop her head in an elegant swirl with metal bands holding it in place. She held a crystal-tipped staff.

If they had to stay here for more than a day or two, Chavali wanted sandals.

As she watched, the man shifted his weight and directed his attention to the potential threat presented by Colby's coughing.

Chavali raised both of her hands into view. "I am not your enemy. There are two injured men here. One is the owner of the building. The other is my companion."

The woman nodded to the man and waved for him to lower his sword. "There should be a healer among the guards present by now. Rowan, I'll watch our prisoner. You help these men outside." She raised her hand and directed a magical blast at the debris blocking the inner doorway.

Rowan wiped his blade on the corpse and sheathed it. "Are you injured, miss?"

"Chastity," Chavali said. She checked Torrel while Rowan helped Colby to his feet. "Are you her husband?" She already knew the answer from the way he deferred to the woman and followed her commands. He served as some kind of subordinate to the mage. The question, though, seemed likely to disarm him.

A disarmed bodyguard might tell her many things.

Torrel groaned as she helped him sit up. His thoughts declared him half-awake and disoriented. Chavali shifted to avoid touching his skin.

Rowan blinked at her. "No. I'm Korrya's mlinzi."

Chavali thought she knew that word, mlinzi. It seemed familiar yet she couldn't place it.

With a grunt of exertion, Rowan heaved Colby to his feet. Colby couldn't stop coughing. The raven squawked and took flight, leaving Rowan's shoulders free to support Colby and guide him at a slow shuffle through the shop.

Though she wanted to know more about Korrya, and also wished to fuss over Colby, Chavali focused on Torrel. He regained his senses slowly.

"You're safe," she repeated several times.

Rowan returned with members of the Guard. They helped Torrel stand and took control of the unconscious prisoner.

Freed of her burdens, Chavali picked up Colby's sword and hurried outside to find him.

CHAPTER 5

Guards flooded the street. At least two dozen spoke to neighbors and kept people off the property. Another handful tended to the man who'd flown through the window and the one Chavali had evacuated. More tended the other two men who'd been in the building.

Sivry and Jaris lurked on the fringes of the property, acting like curious spectators. Colby sat to one side with his back to the shop and a blanket over his shoulders, speaking to a guardswoman while a man with a light-colored armband held a hand over Colby's neck.

On first glance, as a guardsman helped Chavali navigate the damage at the front door, she didn't see Karias anywhere. The giant white horse had an uncanny ability to remain unseen when he wanted. Then she caught a swish of his tail behind Sivry. The horse kept his head down and took small, slow steps away, as if he wanted to melt into the scenery. She'd never seen him try so hard to remain unnoticed in a crowd.

"Do you know who those people were?" Korrya asked Torrel. "Have you ever seen them before?"

Torrel shambled under the guidance of a pair of guards to sit where Colby had been only moments before. He shook his head and covered his mouth while he coughed. "No. Those two, though," he pointed to the initial two men Chavali had encountered, "are from the local gang. Withered Fists, whatever that means. Stopped by for their weekly shakedown.

"Those other three people came in while we were...negotiating their rates, and started the place on fire. They prevented me from leaving. She and her friend," he gestured to Chavali, "ran in and tried to help, but if you hadn't come along, we'd all be dead."

Chavali glanced around the scene for Colby and couldn't see him. He didn't normally disappear and had no skill at blending.

A guard pressed a cup of water into her hands and urged her to drink. The water had a curious hint of mint and berry. It refreshed her and soothed a scratchiness she hadn't noticed in her throat until it disappeared.

Korrya flicked her gaze over the crowd, settling on the area where Karias retreated. She paused and watched, possibly noticing the riderless horse. A small group of teenagers lurked in that area, which also could have attracted her attention.

The guard glanced at Korrya as if asking permission to continue, then asked another question. "Can you think of any reason someone might target you?"

"No?" He wheezed while the man with the armband touched his neck as he'd done for Colby. "I run this bakery, but I don't stock or offer anything exotic or expensive. If they just wanted money, they were too late, because these Fist kids take most of what I've got already."

The guard frowned and turned his attention to Chavali. "Do you often run into burning buildings?"

"Yes, this is a cherished hobby, one I look forward to practicing at every opportunity, along with poking dangerous animals with sticks." Chavali rolled her eyes at him. "Of course not. The fire didn't seem so bad when we arrived, and we heard someone inside."

She still thought they could have found a way to escape if Colby hadn't surrendered. He could've handled crashing through the door. Any burns would've proved minimal.

His accursed issues with fire needed sorting. During a mission wasn't her preferred time to tackle such things.

"Where are you from?" Korrya asked. "Your accent is unusual."

"Elsewhere." Chavali shrugged. She remembered the wariness she'd roused at the docks, and sought to avoid that. "We are in the city on behalf of our employer, a spice merchant."

"Did you know or recognize any of the attackers?" the guard asked.

This second round of questioning by two different people

representing two different interests intrigued Chavali. Though she preferred handling one opponent at a time, the staggering level of corruption—or incompetence—obviously at play here roused her curiosity.

"No. We arrived in the city a few hours ago. Do you also work for the Guard?"

Korrya tore her gaze from Karias's direction. "What? No, of course not. I work for the Consul and the high mage of the Spire. How did you know to come here?"

"We did not. We came across this by chance. Some run from danger and others to it, yes? We are the latter type." Chavali wished she could touch Korrya to avoid asking basic questions. At least she could use them to deflect. "Who is the Consul?"

"The leader of the city," the guard said. "Thank you for your help, ma'am."

"Yes, you can go." Korrya waved absently at Chavali and seemed to have lost interest in her.

Though she wanted to annoy Korrya with more questions, Chavali inclined her head in polite respect. "Thank you."

Torrel sat by himself, staring at nothing and holding a cup. Soot covered his face and simple clothing. His initial burst of coherence upon waking had faded.

"We did not meet in the chaos." She offered him a hand to shake. "I'm Chastity."

He directed his blank stare at her hand and didn't seem to know what to do with it. "Torrel."

She withdrew her hand and pointed to the bakery. Though she wanted to press him for long-term plans, he wouldn't have any yet. In another day or two, she'd have more luck asking such questions. "There's much damage. Where will you sleep tonight?"

He pointed to the upper floor of the building. A wooden beam chose that moment to fall with a crunch, sending a cloud of ash puffing through the windows. Chavali wondered if he'd considered the destruction and its consequences prior to her question. Probably not. "My apartment," he said in a small, lost voice.

"We are staying at an inn nearby, Flower Beds. Let me get you a room for tonight and tomorrow." The Fallen would cover his expenses, at least in the short term. Besides, this way, they'd know where to find him.

Blinking, he tore his gaze from the bakery. "What?"

Chavali stood and offered Torrel a hand to help him stand. "You need rest. Come with me."

"Oh. Yes. Rest." Torrel let her help him. He leaned on her as they walked down the street.

After they turned the corner, Jaris appeared from nowhere and slipped under Torrel's other arm. Sivry played lookout and made sure they didn't get lost. At the inn, Chavali paid for meals and a room in the main building for him. They helped him up the stairs, then into bed.

Jaris shut the door as they left his room. "Now what?"

"Now, we also rest." Chavali led them down the stairs. "In the morning, we discuss the situation." She hoped Colby had returned so she didn't have to try to find him.

While Sivry and Jaris headed for the cabins, Chavali checked the pub. She asked after Colby and no one had seen him. Expecting nothing, she hurried to the cabin she'd claimed for them. As she reached the door, she overheard Jaris on the path ahead of her.

"Wouldn't it make more sense for Colby and me to share one cabin while you three share the other?"

Sivry chuckled. "Only if you don't know Chavali."

Chavali smirked and unlocked the door. One wide bed and two smaller ones occupied most of the structure. Floral-themed decor also surrounded a dresser, desk with a chair, and small washroom. Aside from the exterior, it bore a strong resemblance to any other room at a luxury inn.

This particular room, however, also held Colby.

He sat with his back to her on the edge of the large bed, his shirt off and his head in his hands. Bandages covered his left forearm, his right bicep, and a diagonal stripe across his chest. Soot streaked his skin.

She hadn't seen his bare back before. Scars rippled down the left side, showing how flames had once licked his skin. A thin line of marred flesh slipped around his side. Seeing his death marks made her lift her own wrist and rub her fingertip over the knife scar.

An echo of the queer pain of stabbing herself for freedom made her shiver. She slipped into the bathroom to wash her face with cool water. Colby needed her. Her accursed memories could wait.

Her accursed memories *would* wait.

When she left the washroom, she took a clean, damp towel to him. Standing in front of him, the top of his head at the height of her nose, she brushed his shoulder with the towel. She didn't need to touch him to know his thoughts. Colby rode a swirl of shame and despair, wallowing in his death and failure. Nothing she said would convince him to break free. So she said nothing and touched him with only the towel.

She took one hand and wiped it clean. He lifted his head enough to watch her work. When his hand seemed clean, she set it aside and took the other.

"I'm sorry," he murmured.

"There is nothing to apologize for. You have already been forgiven for these things."

"I almost killed us."

"Perhaps." She set his other hand aside and used the towel to lift his chin until he met her gaze. Any idiot could see the pain inside him. "I cannot recall ever seeing you do anything more foolish than running into that building, but I understand why you did it."

He closed his eyes while she brushed the towel over his face. "I thought..."

"You thought you could defeat the memory by saving them this time."

"But I didn't. I can't. I—"

She wiped the towel across his mouth to make him stop. "You were tired and taken by surprise. You feel your death must be settled, because it happened two years ago. But this is not so very long as it seems. And just two weeks ago, those memories were churned."

He put his hands on her hips and pulled her closer. "How do you always know everything?"

"I am the seer. This is my job." She swiped the towel down his nose.

A tiny smile teased the corners of his mouth. "I wish I could see things the way you do."

"No, you don't." Chavali tossed aside the towel and settled her arms on his shoulders so her sleeves protected her from his thoughts. "You wish you could impress me with your observations like Jaris did."

Leaning his forehead against her chest, he sighed. "It shouldn't be hard to watch that, but it was."

Part of her wanted to slap him for daring to feel such possession over her that another man's interest would rouse jealousy. But she knew Colby didn't truly feel that. He didn't want to own her. "What will you do when I flirt with someone intentionally to get information?"

"I don't know. Will I be able to tell it's fake?"

"Of course not."

He chuckled. "You sound so offended."

"I love you, Colby. This gives you no power to see through the skill I have spent more than a decade perfecting."

For a long few heartbeats, he said nothing. Then he pulled away enough to meet her gaze. In the tightness around his eyes, she saw need, perhaps desperation. "Say that again. You don't say it often, and I want to savor it."

"Which part?"

His mouth twitched. She'd disappointed him.

He had no right to press her like this. Those words stuck in her throat most of the time. Once in a while, they felt natural and right. Every other moment, they beat frantically in the back of her throat, promising horrors if she set them free.

She leaned forward and kissed him instead. Three silly words proved her a coward.

::Is it really so hard?:: His thoughts shifted to the curve of her hips and the warmth of her skin. He remembered holding her in the bakery, expecting to die again and knowing the last thing he'd see was her. Karias's frantic panic had battered him as much as his own.

Chavali pressed close. He broke off the kiss and held her. They both needed this. She hiked up her dress and sat on his lap. His arms gave her a steadiness she hadn't known she craved until he'd first offered it. With him, she could bask in acceptance and the knowledge he expected nothing more than she was willing to give.

Not much more, anyway. Nothing he wanted from her felt possessive or demanding.

With her mouth close to his ear, she forced herself to let the horror free in a whisper. "I love you, Colby."

The Seer of the Blaukenev clan was no coward.

CHAPTER 6

The next morning, Chavali sat at a small table in the inn's common room with Torrel, watching him pick at his breakfast. While she sipped tea, he ate tiny bites, chewed them far too long, and spent minutes selecting and spearing the next bit of egg, fruit, or sausage. The full weight of his trauma had yet to hit.

When he saw the charred husk of his home and bakery, she suspected he'd show the qualities that had once made him Fallen.

Everyone else had eaten already, including Chavali. She'd seen Torrel plodding down the stairs as they finished and stayed behind to accompany him. In addition to finding the tea quite pleasant, she wanted to learn more about his particular situation.

"These Fist kids." Torrel shook his head as he broke the friendly silence between them. "At first, I didn't pay. They didn't scare me. Then they came through and smashed everything in the shop. Took me days to clean it all up and get going again. When they came back, the amount didn't seem unreasonable compared to the damage, so I paid it. That was a mistake I've been regretting for about six weeks now."

"With no one to back you up, you had little choice."

Torrel sighed. "No one else wanted to stand up to them."

She didn't blame the ordinary folk for caving to the demands. "This is how gangs happen, yes."

"I guess I can relax for a while. They won't bother me without a shop." He stabbed a bite of sausage and ate it with small violence. In the act, Chavali saw a resolute determination to deal with the gang, no matter the cost.

Railan's plea to spare him from another wipe of his memories made her want to help him. Iker's plight made her want to help him. These Fist people acted with crass impunity. If the guards had opposed the gang, she doubted she would have so much interest in the matter.

"Are you sure you wish to stay here? Someone with your skills and contacts can doubtless find employment or opportunity elsewhere."

He scowled at her, showing offense at the idea of leaving. "I've lived here long enough that this is my home."

In the months since she woke from death, Chavali had begun to understand the notion of attachment to a place. She still found it awkward, but could grasp the concept. Finding the destroyed wagons of her clan a few weeks earlier had made the comparison easier to comprehend. She missed those wagons. The creaking of wood, the jangling of chains, the layers of paint, the markings from her ancestors—all lived only in her memories now.

"Please rest for today. Let us see what we can do here first." She stood to go consult with the rest of the team.

"Why?" He sounded one part confused, one part suspicious, and one part lost.

"I may or may not have been entirely honest with the guards about our purpose in the city."

For several moments, he stared at her blankly, then he cracked a small smile. "I hope you can do something where the rest of us have failed. Good luck."

A short time later, Chavali leaned against the wall in the second cabin, listening to the discussion about how to proceed. Everyone else sat on the beds. Colby seemed in brighter spirits for the day. At the least, he'd found a way to set aside his issues. No one said anything about his behavior the night before.

So far, Chavali had refrained from sharing her opinion. She didn't trust it.

This desire to dive in and fix everything made no sense. Caring about Iker's plight in a real, visceral way also bothered her. Certainly, she disliked thieves and vicious swindlers, and preferred justice to injustice. Wanting so badly to solve all these problems for all these strangers seemed...suspiciously like Colby's thoughts on the subject.

As the mission leader, she thought she ought not to side with him from the start or behave like a tyrant demanding fealty.

"Chavali is usually the one to point this out, but you seem curiously committed to neutrality this morning," Portia said with a raised eyebrow for Chavali, "so I'll do it. A gang acting like a gang outside of Shappa isn't our problem. Our mission is to investigate the situation and extract Torrel from anything he can't deal with or escape. It's not to solve all his problems for him. Or, for that matter, Palmia Basin."

"He gave everything to the Fallen," Colby said, "including his memories. Doesn't he deserve more from us than a couple of nights at an inn?" In the past, Colby had taken such suggestions as attacks. This time, he seemed unruffled by it. "I think we owe him at least an attempt at resolving this gang situation."

"Gangs don't operate in a vacuum," Sivry said. "The conditions allowing them to grow and operate are usually ugly. The kinds of corruption or prejudice might differ, but they're always part of it. If we decide to look into this, we should expect things to get complicated and dangerous."

Jaris nodded. "We should also go into it knowing that we might accomplish nothing better than creating an opportunity for a worse gang. Unless there's someone else to fill the void, that's what always happens. Always."

Everyone looked to Chavali. She shrugged, pleased she could accommodate everyone, at least for the moment. "We're here and our rooms are paid for. I see no harm in at least spending the day investigating. The situation may be simple." She considered their various skill sets and gestured to Sivry. "You and Jaris and skulk about. Take opportunities if they seem reasonable to you. The rest of us will act like representatives of a spice merchant. Find out whatever we can and meet in the common room for dinner?"

Sivry nodded and stood. "Sounds fair to me. I haven't had a chance to skulk since Harbor City."

As she left with Jaris, he said, "We should get some new clothes.

Local stuff that blends better."

"Good idea. I like the look of the sandals they wear here."

The door shut.

"Should we try to blend?" Portia asked.

Chavali grinned. "I do not blend."

Colby stood. "I'll meet you by the stable. I want to go armed, and I think we should take Karias."

"You want to take one horse?" Portia frowned at him. "Colby, I can appreciate you're nervous after last night, but that horse stands out more than Chavali's eccentricities."

Though she agreed, Chavali saw the distress on Colby's shoulders. She knew why he wanted those two specific things. He needed security. Comfort.

Besides, Karias had made clear his distaste for spending missions locked inside a stable. After the fire, she expected him to find it even more frustrating than usual. They'd have to come up with a way to deal with the horse.

"His presence will draw attention. If you want to bring him, then you ride him, and Portia and I will take advantage of you as a distraction."

Colby nodded and flashed her gratitude as he left.

As Chavali moved to follow, Portia touched her arm and stopped her. "You can't let your feelings for Colby get in the way here, Chavali. You know that, don't you? There are reasons why Fallen aren't supposed to work missions together when they're in a relationship."

"Are you suggesting my judgment is impaired?"

Portia turned to look at the door. "I'm suggesting you wouldn't have let him bring the horse in Harbor City, even after he faced something like that fire. And, like I said, you waited to say your piece about Torrel. Which isn't like you."

Chavali frowned at the wall, considering everything that had happened so far. She didn't think she would've opposed Karias's involvement before, but couldn't be sure. "Aislynn laid the responsibility for this mission at my feet alone."

"Which was dumb, and not how Eldrack does things."

"True. Perhaps this has affected me more than I think."

Portia squeezed her shoulder, and they left the cabin. "I miss Eldrack too. I've always liked the man's style. Aislynn is fine, she's just different. You've had a bigger adjustment than most, so this change so soon after you've gotten used to the last one is probably harder on you than the rest of us."

With anyone else, Chavali thought she'd dismiss their thoughts. "I'll keep this in mind. If I seem to forget, please say something."

"Of course. How could I possibly resist the chance to tell Chavali she's wrong?"

Chavali snorted at her. They reached the outbuilding and checked inside. Several stalls, each much too small for a regular horse, lined both sides of a clean four-foot wide hallway. It smelled wrong, like wet dogs and clean goats. Through open half-doors in the wooden walls, Chavali saw several llamas and large dogs, some sharing space.

Colby hadn't arrived yet.

"Where does Karias even fit in here?" Portia asked. "You couldn't stuff half of him into one of these things."

A grumpy whinny answered them from the end of the hallway. When they reached him, they discovered Karias lying on the floor with his neck curled as much as possible. He had the largest box available and couldn't lie properly. With the low ceiling, he couldn't stand either. Chavali thought she could sit with him if necessary, but it would feel crowded.

"Do you know how to saddle a horse?" she asked Portia.

"Yes, but not that brute. His saddle probably weighs more than I do. Let Colby handle it. I suppose we could put on the bridle, though." Portia hauled open the bottom half of the stall door.

Karias shoved his nose at Chavali. She raised her hands by instinct. He shoved her backward until he'd extended his neck fully.

::I wish to complain about the accommodations, I'm incredibly bored, and you have Colby twisted in knots he can't understand. If you could rub my neck, though, that would help a lot.::

Chavali patted his nose, then rubbed his neck on one side. Karias wanted his nature kept quiet from everyone, including Colby. With Portia around, she couldn't answer him directly. "You're just a big puppy. I don't have anything for you now, but I'll bring something later."

::I suppose that's better than being called a baby. And I expect to see you later, with or without tr—I take that back. Bring treats or don't bother coming.::

Chavali stifled a laugh. She slid her hand down to his neck and pretended she needed to keep him calm.

"He really is a giant puppy." Portia brought the bridle from the next stall down and looped it over his head. "Good thing he likes you. It'd be bad if he decided you're a rival for Colby's attention."

::She's right. I could cause all kinds of problems if I wanted to keep him for myself. That would be kind of awkward, though, since I'm not attracted to him.::

"The center of attention, as usual," Colby said as he stepped inside the stable. He wore a light shirt of chain armor and carried his sword strapped at an angle across his back.

Karias tossed his head and whinnied in greeting. *::Yes, absolutely. As it should be.::*

Chavali's smile faded. She wanted to share what Karias said with Colby. Perhaps Karias would consent someday. "I wonder if the guard has any mounted officers? We could disguise you as one."

::I haven't noticed any, which now that you mention it, is interesting.::

"We should've known that before we got here." Colby beckoned for Karias to come closer. "C'mon, boy, I can't get in there."

Karias wriggled across the floor with an annoyed huff. *::I hate this city. Fix it already and let's go home.::*

Colby collected his saddle from the next stall and settled it on Karias's back. Karias stood and kept his head down.

"That's not completely fair," Portia said. "Anyway, maybe we should have Chavali ride. She's more obviously foreign than either of us."

Colby handled the saddle and its straps with the practiced ease of an expert. "No, Karias is actually more noticeable with a smaller rider. I look natural there, like he was made for me. I'm just a man on a horse with a sword. Put Chavali up there and she looks like she stole him."

Chavali sniffed. "I would never allow myself to be mistaken for a common horse thief."

"Karias is hardly common," Portia said.

::By my tally, Portia is beating you in the Always Correct department today. Are you feeling ill, by chance?::

Chavali shook her head at them and gathered her thick hair into both hands. She smoothed the feather back with her hair and wrapped a string around the mass. The style lifted her hair off her neck, which cooled her more than she expected.

"Does this help?" To make sure she got Karias's opinion, she set her hand on his nose as if she needed to keep him from feeling ignored.

Portia, Karias, and Colby all looked her over as if inspecting merchandise.

"I like that," Colby said.

"It works."

::That makes you look...ordinary. Which is extremely disturbing.::

She let go of Karias, worried he'd overtax her ability to swallow laughter. "We're watching for people in those same outfits," she said for Karias's benefit, "and people acting suspiciously. Anything else either of you can think of?"

"Guard behavior," Portia said. "I'd like to watch the docks for a while."

Colby led Karias out of the stable. "I think you two should pay attention to anyone watching me. I'll ride around and keep track of you." As soon as they reached the outside, Colby climbed onto Karias's back. The horse took a moment to stretch all four legs and his neck, then clopped up the road.

"Do you think he'll notice anything useful?" Portia asked as she and Chavali followed at their own pace.

"No, but he thinks he will."

"Then why are we letting him range about on his own?"

Chavali smirked at her. "He will flush the quail for us."

"Hm. Has anyone ever mentioned you're kind of devious?"

"I think you have."

They strolled up the street, heading toward the water. Chavali let her gaze wander, taking in the state of the neighborhood. Every building had at least one step up to reach the front door, and most of those doors stood open. Small debris, including broken glass, leaf litter, and wood shards, huddled along the sides of the tiled road in low clumps. Fungus colonies clung to everything with reliable shade. Every narrow building had a second floor, where Chavali assumed the shop owners lived. Netting and awnings covered some upper windows, while others had open glass panes.

She read the signs made of painted tile or wood, pleased she could do so. Each used small, simple words she could decode as they strolled past. Several had more decorative names she ignored as too difficult to puzzle out in such a short time.

Portia stopped her to go inside in one store where they purchased sandals. Though they had to carry their boots in sacks the seller had kindly offered, Chavali much preferred the fresh air on her toes.

Most adults on the street moved with purpose though not haste. They wore clothing with obvious repairs but not too many. These people neither suffered nor prospered greatly, yet they held their jaws with grim determination. Perhaps they worried about ordinary matters, or perhaps the city's rot had infected the lives of average, law-abiding citizens.

Children scampered and laughed with wild abandon, as they should. In many cases, medium-sized dogs chased them, or perhaps they pursued the sporadic flocks of free-roaming and boisterous chickens.

Few horses and no carriages used the roads, making Colby and Karias stand out more than usual. Chavali hadn't noticed that fact while riding. She'd seen the dogs and llamas without noticing the lack of horses or donkeys.

Chavali picked out a trio of young men who stood with the arrogant assurance of youth certain no one would punish them for anything. They lurked at a corner, watching people give them a wide berth and avoid the clothing shop they stood in front of. She recognized one face among them from Iker's memory. Once she noticed that, she noted the fact they wore wool sashes around their waists as belts.

As far as she'd seen, no one native Palmia Basin wore wool or used it for anything. They had no sheep and no need for fabrics suited to retaining heat.

"We should do something about them." She nodded toward the group.

Portia shook her head. "I think we'd be better off following them to their home base."

"We could ask them politely to take us to their leader."

"Politely?"

"A knife to the neck is polite, yes?"

Portia laughed. "Let's keep moving. They don't look like they're going anywhere for a while."

Karias and Colby passed them. Up the street, Chavali noticed two people take note of the horse and rider with more interest than most. Unlike the three gang members, they didn't seem out of place in the area, or otherwise notable. Colby wouldn't see them. Karias might.

Chavali nodded toward them. "Those are two people I want to follow."

Portia glanced in that direction twice before saying, "I don't see anything."

"Exactly."

CHAPTER 7

Hours later, with lunch behind them, Chavali leaned against a wall, chatting with Portia. Colby stood nearby, offering Karias local fruit. They'd followed a number of different individuals and small groups, including guards, and talked to a variety of shop and market stall workers. At this point, Chavali felt she had a good idea of how the city worked.

The Riverway Guild managed the docks and boats, in addition to handling all cargo in and out of the port. They did this for every city and town on the entire river. When the group had arrived, the woman with the clipboard had been their representative. Her job demanded she take control of cargo.

The guard didn't trust the Riverway Guild. Thus, they sent their own man with a clipboard to question all those entering the city.

Added to this, the city had at least two named gangs jostling for power. So far, they'd heard the names Withered Fists and Dragon Talons. Many people believed other, less organized groups also competed.

People knew the Dragon Talons well. The gang had operated in Palmia Basin for several years without causing much stress for ordinary folk. According to gossip Chavali had plucked from a young man working his mother's vegetable stall in the market, their leader had fought a dragon, or some similar such nonsense. Some regarded them as borderline heroic for acting when the Guard failed.

These Withered Fists, on the other hand, had first arrived within the past few months. No one saw them as anything other than a blight. The guard and the Riverway Guild both worried about new members of the Withered Fists bolstering the gang from outside the city. This had caused their reactions to the group on their arrival.

The building across the way and down the street bordered on the docks and seemed to serve as a local hub for some kind of questionable activity. Watching the place for a short time, Chavali had seen several different people come and go with a furtive quality to their behavior, including uniformed guards and Riverway Guild members. The team needed to find a way inside.

In her peripheral vision, Chavali saw movement near Colby. She turned to see him ducking behind a tree too small to hide him.

"Hot damn!" A tall, muscular woman rushed Karias and slapped his thigh. She wore the uniform of the Riverway Guild.

The horse jumped enough to bump into a passing llama and turned his head with his mouth open to snap. He saw the woman and stopped. The offended llama spat at Karias's head, making him sneeze.

"I'd recognize this horse's ass anywhere. Where's your master, Karias?"

Behind the tree, Colby grimaced, then revealed himself. "Hello, Daria."

"Someone from his first life?" Portia murmured.

Daria dove to hug Colby. He seemed somewhat awkward, though the embrace looked familiar and worn, like that of an old friend or former lover.

"I think so." Chavali weighed their options. None of them knew the city's major players on sight, so leaving their vigil outside the building wouldn't hurt them. They had no good ideas for getting inside that building, or how to deal with what they'd find. She wanted to know as much as possible about this Daria person.

Her interest in Daria, of course, had to do with the safety of clan and Fallen. She didn't care about women from Colby's past.

"What are you doing here, of all places?" Daria held Colby at arm's length, looking him over.

Colby glanced at Chavali.

She swooped in to rescue him. "Hello, I'm Chastity. Are you a friend of Colby's?"

Daria shook Chavali's hand with a big, friendly smile. "You could say that." She thumped Colby's shoulder. "We go way back." Her thoughts showed Chavali a relationship more intimate than mere friendship. "Nice to meet you, Chastity."

Chavali didn't try to prolong the contact. Meeting one of Colby's former lovers didn't bother her. Not much, anyway. But seeing it as a rapid series of private moments in someone else's head did grate on her nerves.

"What kind of crazy, noble quest did Colby rope you all into?"

Colby wore a fixed, fake smile. His tanned cheeks glowed with a mild blush. He crossed his arms and adopted a strange, wide stance. Chavali had never seen him quite so uncomfortable.

"We are here on business for our employer." Again, Chavali wanted to remain vague but worried it would create unnecessary concern or tension. "A spice merchant."

"Oh, someone looking to expand here? You'll need to talk to my boss. Actually, maybe you should come with me. It's worthwhile to know in advance who's really in charge, right?"

"Yes, quite. That's kind of you to offer."

"Bah. Anything for Colby. C'mon." Daria grabbed Colby's arm and dragged him across the road.

Chavali glanced at Karias, thinking he seemed annoyed, then Portia, who shrugged. They followed Daria and Colby.

"I heard you were dead," Daria said. She seemed to have two modes —loud and louder. "But I didn't really believe it."

Colby glanced at Chavali again. The man had no idea what to do or say. She mouthed some words for him.

"I got hurt," he said. "It was bad enough to send me home." He'd read Chavali's intent well enough.

"That's terrible, but it's better than being dead, right?"

"Yes. I don't really want to talk about it."

"Of course not. I bet it was awful. How did you hook up with a spice merchant, of all things?"

"Oh, you know. Things happen."

Daria burst into laughter as they reached the questionable building. She turned to wink at Chavali. "He's a terrible liar, you know."

Chavali nodded. "Yes, we've noticed."

"I bet. This is the place. Try not to get too touchy. There are armed people inside. As long as everyone stays calm, everything stays fine." Daria wrenched open the door and hauled Colby inside.

Colby turned and begged for help with his eyes.

For a moment, Chavali considered letting him go on his own. He'd fumble the entire situation, probably cause a major problem, and set back all their efforts. If she could've watched, and if she hadn't already made promises to Torrel and Iker, she thought she'd let him flounder for once and see what happened.

Portia followed Daria, so Chavali did too. They entered a small front room with no windows and one door. Two large, beefy men in city guard uniforms flanked the door. Racks on the wall held one sword, three daggers, and a pair of shoes with sharp, pointed heels.

"My name is Daria, I'm here on Nora's behalf. Someone should be expecting me." She shook hands with one of the guards and clapped the other on the arm.

Chavali shrugged at Karias, then shut the door. The horse would have to find something to do without attracting attention.

One guard nodded. "Who are the rest of these people?"

"They're with me," Daria said.

Chavali put effort into appearing harmless.

"You need to leave your weapons behind if you want to see Guyre." He pointed to the rack on the wall.

Colby sighed and unbuckled the harness keeping his sword strapped to his back. Portia raised her hands to show she had nothing. Chavali snapped off the sheath for her dagger from its spot on her belt at the small of her back and set it with Colby's sword.

They let everyone through and pointed them to a back room. Chavali took an extra moment passing through the door to get a closer look at the guard uniforms. She suspected they were fake, but didn't know the real thing well enough to spot proof. Which meant they'd put effort into it.

On their way down a dark, narrow hallway, they passed closed doors. The floor creaked. So did the ceiling. Colby's boots echoed in the cramped space.

Daria opened a door at the end of the hall. Voices murmured, then stopped. The group trooped down a half-flight of stairs to reach the floor of a large, pleasantly chilled room with soft globes of light provided by floral-scented oil lanterns. The light scent almost covered the damp, concrete dankness. Plush chairs and couches with signs of wear littered the floor. Enough thick curtains hung that Chavali couldn't see the walls. One man and three women occupied this room.

The tall, thin man sat at ease in the middle chair, projecting calm, confidence, and control. From the subtle smile on his lips to the dragonscale pattern on the wide leather bands of his sandals, he clearly considered himself heroic and the center of attention.

Chavali thought his pretty face needed a good slapping.

Behind him, one woman stood with her arms crossed, tapping her bare foot on the bare floor. She had the air of one who considered herself a power behind the throne without any sense the man ceded anything to her. Chavali doubted she wielded much more power than a secretary in this room, and thus dismissed her as no more useful than the furniture. Perhaps she served the man as his lover and had some administrative skill he prized.

The other two women sat on opposite ends of a long couch. Both wore the typical loose linens and sandals common to the city and would blend on the streets without difficulty.

The younger of these two, a woman near Chavali's age, sat furthest from the man with tension across every line of her body. She wanted something she doubted she'd get, or had a complaint. This woman would probably challenge the man for dominance the moment she felt he would lose. For whatever reason, that moment had not yet come.

As for the final occupant, the woman within arm's reach of the man, she bore the subtle wrinkles of middle age and the quiet dignity of an experienced mentor or teacher. Her gaze took in the details of Chavali and every member of the group with a sense of weighing, judging and digesting.

From the way they all shifted and fell quiet, Chavali assumed they'd interrupted business. Though the older woman and the man displayed keen interest in them, the would-be usurper huffed, sat back and tried to hide a sulk. The lover feigned disinterest with no skill whatsoever.

"Ah, friends from Riverway." The man gestured for them to approach. "What does Nora want?"

Daria strode into the midst of the chairs and stood where Guyre had to crane his neck to meet her gaze. "Guyre." She nodded to him in a gesture of politeness. "She wants to negotiate. This whole thing where we butt heads isn't working."

Guyre grinned. "It's working for me."

"Really? I'm pretty sure we snatched two of your people trying to steal from a warehouse this morning. And by pretty sure, I mean I was there and chased one down myself. We're holding them."

Chavali could see what had attracted Colby to Daria. They had a lot in common. Given the same mission, he would approach it the way she did.

Guyre's grin slipped. "I see. I assume Nora will release them as a gesture of good faith upon conclusion of these negotiations?"

"Yes."

Colby crossed his arms again. He had an idea what they'd walked into and reacted predictably to it. So long as he kept his mouth shut, Chavali could work with the situation.

"Before we get into that, who are these other people?" Guyre waved to indicate Colby, Chavali, and Portia.

"This is Colby. He and his friends work for a spice merchant who wants to expand into the city."

"Very well." Guyre waved to the cushioned chairs. "You three can sit and wait while I discuss matters with her. Pardon me, ladies, but this is rather time sensitive."

Chavali took a seat while Guyre gestured for Daria to begin.

She paid more attention to the much more interesting older woman than to the negotiation. The woman took care of herself and ate well. Her hands looked soft, and her gaze held none of the horror of recent hardship. Something about the way she watched everything gave Chavali the impression she'd found a kindred soul, of a sort.

Portia sat as close to Chavali as possible. Colby stood behind her.

"Nora wants to make a deal. We won't mess with you if you won't mess with us is the basic idea."

"We already have that deal," Guyre said.

"For the boats and piers, yes. Not for the warehouses. The Guild has worked hard to build our monopoly and you're jeopardizing it. For what? A little smash and grab? We'll pay you to protect the docks instead of steal from them, and we'll back your claim on the city. In exchange, we expect real security, not the sham the guard provides."

Chavali turned her head enough so she could see Guyre and Daria without letting everyone know she watched. Not that it mattered. Everyone watched and listened to them, including the older woman who applied the same approach as Chavali.

Guyre stroked his chin and stood at an angle to her. "I want to use warehouse space."

Daria shrugged. "Then we pay less because we're leasing you the space." Nora had prepared Daria well for this encounter. She seemed at ease and unsurprised.

"Access to the logs?"

"No, but we can notify you if you're looking for something or someone specific, so long as you pledge not to steal it while it's in our hands."

Guyre nodded, everything about his posture radiating satisfaction.

"How can you talk about that when you're hurting people in the city," Colby burst out, "like that bakery your people lit on fire last night?"

Everyone stared at Colby. Chavali jumped to her feet and stuck an arm in front of him. She had no hope of restraining him physically, but he wouldn't push past her for anything less than a threat of death.

"Excuse me for his impatience," Chavali said.

Guyre flicked his gaze between them. "My people didn't burn anything last night. We don't do that."

"One of our concerns," Chavali said, "is the state of security here. It was not clear to us who caused the fire, only that it was done intentionally.

Places where this happens with impunity present a risk not present in other locations."

Guyre's lover leaned close and whispered to him. He narrowed his eyes at Chavali. "Who do you really work for? The Spire? The Consul?"

"No. As I said, a spice merchant. He is based in Shappa."

"Of course." Guyre lifted his chin and looked down his nose. "Daria, I think you should be more careful about who you associate with. Miss Spice Merchant Pet, you and your coworkers can leave. Now."

Chavali flicked her hand at Colby. Portia stood and led the way to the stairs. Colby definitely wanted to strangle Guyre, but he restrained himself.

"Perhaps I can arrange to speak with you on my own," Chavali said, keeping her voice down so Colby didn't overhear. "I can see you hold a great deal of sway here, and that I would be in no danger while in your presence."

Guyre flicked his gaze behind her, then down and up her body. "I think I can work with that."

"Thank you." Revolted by his obvious ogling, Chavali inclined her head and left.

CHAPTER 8

Chavali took her time leaving. She had until she reached the street outside to curb the urge to slap Colby for putting her in that position. He knew better. His mouth should have remained clamped shut. The discussion formed in her head.

He'd claim Daria distracted him, she'd ask why he let that happen, he'd stumble and fail to come up with a good answer. The other option she expected involved his indignant outrage on Torrel's behalf.

By the time she snapped her dagger's sheath onto her belt, she had a solid handle on herself. The door at the end of the hall opened and shut. She turned to see Daria strolling toward her, all smiles and sunshine.

"Colby hasn't changed a bit." She opened the front door for Chavali.

Colby and Portia stood beside the door, waiting with Karias.

"Where are you guys staying?" Daria asked as she followed Chavali outside. "I'd love to catch up."

"Flower Beds," Colby said.

Chavali gained a fresh urge to slap him. He needed less of Daria, not more. The woman brought out his idiocy.

"Nice place."

Up the street, Chavali noticed a young woman wearing the wool sash belt of a Withered Fists member. Three other people, each unremarkable in appearance, escorted her to the Talon building. The girl, sullen and walking awkwardly, kept her arms behind her back. As they drew closer, Chavali noticed a rope. They'd taken the girl prisoner.

"It's nicer than I expected from the name," Colby said.

The girl noticed them. Her gaze bounced from one person to another and lingered on Daria.

Daria laughed. "Of course you'd think that. How long will you be in town?"

Chavali stepped away from the door and toward Karias. Portia also moved out of the way for the prisoner escort.

Colby shrugged. "We're not really sure. A few days, probably."

"Are you free for dinner tonight?"

One escort reached for the front door. Another shooed Colby and Daria aside.

The girl took advantage of their distraction to bolt. Her escort lost his grip on the rope. He turned and chased after her. The other two escorts swore and joined the chase. Their prey disappeared around the corner.

The incident seemed odd, but Chavali didn't know why.

"Damn. That was unexpected." Daria gestured in a different direction. "I have to report on my negotiation, but I'll stop by the inn later."

"Actually," Portia said, "I wonder if we could meet your boss? We still need to learn the lay of the land."

Though she preferred to never see Daria again, Chavali nodded. "Despite some things said inside, we appreciate the introduction you gave. This is challenging for outsiders."

Daria thumped Colby on the arm. "Sure! Why not? For old times' sake, right? Nora likes a good laugh and a good mystery, so she'll enjoy meeting you anyway. It's this way. On the docks, of course."

Portia beamed at her. Daria looped her arm through Colby's. Chavali set her hand on Karias's flank.

::Don't screw this up, Colby. Just don't— Ah. As I'm sure you've noticed, this is incredibly awkward. If he can't manage to answer your questions about her, come see me. I'll tell you everything.::

"I appreciate that," Chavali muttered.

::Did that little kerfuffle with the girl seem odd to you?::

Portia fell into step beside Chavali. "Did that thing with that Fist prisoner seem strange to you?"

"Yes," Chavali said to both.

"I almost got the impression the Talons wanted her to escape."

Chavali snapped her fingers. "Yes, this is the thing. They should know better than to let people distract them this much."

::Of course. That one is a classic. The Talons want her to report something to the Fists, so they let her see it and let her escape without her thinking she's been allowed to escape. The Talons are savvier than they seem on first blush. The question is, what did they let her see?::

Portia squinted at Daria's back. "Either they wanted her to know something that happened before they reached the building, in which case we'll never know what it was, or they wanted her to see a member of the Riverway Guild leaving their base. Or both, I guess." Though she couldn't hear or understand Karias, she clearly had thoughts along the same lines.

"And now she will also report about us." Chavali frowned. "I would have preferred to maintain a less obvious role in this mess."

::As if you've ever been able to do that. At least we're not being deputized by the local authorities this time.::

"You're terrible at less obvious." Portia patted Chavali's shoulder with a grin she failed to suppress. "It's just not who you are."

They reached a small building marked as the Riverway guildhall, but Nora wasn't there. Daria then took them to city hall, a quaint structure surrounded by a plaza and visited by a steady stream of people carrying papers and folders.

Fearless birds and small animals waddled across tiles painted with floral designs, fighting over crumbs of food with a storm of chirps and chitters. Excessive amounts of the gingerbread trim lined every door and window of the building, as well as the railing for the balcony on the upper floor. Short, squat plants with fern-like fronds grew at the base of the building and in hanging pots scattered up the walls. In a curious nod to practicality, trees with large, feathery leaves provided shifting oases of shade.

It struck Chavali as the kind of place nobles and the wealthy might squabble over for the right to hold a fete or wedding there.

Guards flanked the high double doors at the front of the building, each wearing the same uniform as the men and women patrolling the city. They heaved opened both doors for the group, suggesting they had no interest in barring passage to anyone other than obvious threats.

Though Karias could've fit through the doors, he stopped in the plaza. Colby turned and pointed for him to stay while they continued inside.

As Chavali passed the guards, she took a moment to inspect their uniforms. The patches on their shoulders looked somewhat different than the ones worn by the Talons. She expected to find no other discrepancies.

They crossed into a large, airy courtyard full of statuary depicting people dressed in the typical loose clothing of the city, and small animals she'd seen on the streets. Murals of similarly mundane subjects decorated the walls between office doors. Daria strode through the room to a wide set of stairs on the other side. Framed portraits of women in poses suggesting power lined the stairwell.

At the top of the stairs, a hallway ran right and left. Daria used the door directly in front of them. It opened into a large room with no windows. Despite this, cool air laced with a touch of mint flowed through the doors and washed over Chavali in a gentle, refreshing wave. Globes near the ceiling glowed with soft light. One extra globe dripped infrequent sparkles, pointing to it as the source of the pleasant temperature.

A rectangular table, its surface littered with papers, folders, mugs, and pens, dominated the room. Women sat at each of the twenty seats. Functional hairstyles and serious expressions suggested actual work happened here.

All deferred to the middle-aged woman with an air of comfortable authority seated at the far end of the table.

"I believe you left alone, Daria." The woman who spoke sat to the authority figure's left side. Unlike the rest of these women, she displayed the crass trappings of wealth on her person. Jewelry of dubious quality draped across her fingers, head, and neck as if she worried someone would steal it from her home. "Who are these other people?"

Daria gave the woman at the head of the table a polite bow and received a nod of acknowledgment. She turned to the woman bedecked with jewelry before speaking. "Nora, everyone, this is Colby and his team. They represent a spice merchant interested in expanding into the city. Since they're friends of mine from Grippa, I thought I'd introduce them around." Daria gestured for the group to stay near the door while she approached the speaker.

"Guyre took the deal with the changes you expected, except that he wanted limited use of transport in and out of the city with no questions asked. I gave him a discount on fees when he wants to use it."

Chavali knew she hid her surprise better than Colby. The Riverway Guild apparently conducted their corruption with the full knowledge of the Consul.

"He's always been such a good little soldier boy," Nora said with a smirk. She opened a folder and pushed it where Daria could see it. Her accessories winked and gleamed in the light with every tiny movement, calling attention to her. "Good work. How much did you get him to discount his extortion for using our warehouses?"

Daria lowered herself to one knee, putting her head below Nora's and Consul Shore's in an act of obedience and fealty Chavali hadn't expected from her. She had to hold her back straight and head high to see onto the table. "Half."

"Excellent." Nora handed Daria a pen, then looked to Consul Shore. "He won't do a damned thing without us knowing about it."

Consul Shore nodded her satisfaction. "Captain Faillit, go ahead and implement the procedures we discussed for this deal. Keep your arrests and raids sporadic and they shouldn't make the connection."

"Yes, ma'am," another woman said with a curt nod. Captain Faillit wore a guard uniform with an extra sash and a scattering of pins across her shoulders. She had all the bearing of a longtime officer. She also held some disdain for Nora, visible for a moment as a flick of her eyes and a flare of her nose.

Chavali didn't blame Faillit for her opinion of a showy twit like Nora.

The short exchange caused Chavali to reconsider everything she'd seen and deduced about the city guards. The Riverway Guild and the city worked in concert to craft an image for the benefit of the Talons in an effort to use them until they became obsolete. How many guards had she seen so far? Compared to other cities, not many. The throng at the bakery stood out as an anomaly for an emergency.

She wondered if the guard had its own factions.

A different woman raised her hand and pointed at Colby. Younger than every other person present, she fit into the group without seeming like a part of it. "Your employer is based in Grippa? What kinds of spices do they deal in?" She had a curiously uneven Tilan accent, as if she tried to suppress some other accent and only succeeded part of the time.

Chavali took a step forward to field the question. "He is based in Shappa." She didn't want to answer the other half of the question, so she looked to the Consul. "May I ask why you don't tackle these gangs in a more direct manner? They seem like a problem."

The Consul nodded as if the question didn't surprise her. "We— Excuse me, what was your name?"

"Chastity."

"Chastity, we lack the resources. If you or your employer haven't heard, we had some difficulties with the previous consul a few years ago. When he was removed, he left and took a significant number of loyal guards with him. We're remote enough to make replacing them a long-term prospect."

"Guyre was one of mine before that," Faillit said. "He knows to leave ordinary people alone and keep his crime to relatively harmless enterprises, like a black market for evading Riverway fees. The thefts his people commit don't have a measurable impact on safety or health, and they've been helping the Guard fill the gap."

Chavali glanced aside and saw Portia step on Colby's foot. Good. As long as these people didn't feel overtly judged, they appeared amenable to explaining curiosities about the city. Spice merchants needed their fears soothed, of course. "What about the other gangs?"

"That's something he's supposed to keep in check," Shore said with a frustrated sigh, "though he's been lax lately. This new deal is, among other things, an effort to remind him to do that job."

Faillit shrugged off the subject. She clearly wanted Chavali to leave as soon as possible, which Chavali considered fair. One petty merchant didn't deserve this level of attention from the city government. "By the time your employer has anything serious set up here, the situation should be under control.”

Nodding and projecting innocent, friendly interest, Chavali asked, “We appreciate the reassurances you offer. Is there someplace in the city we can learn more about your history? This sounds like an interesting topic, and I wouldn’t wish to take so much of your valuable time.”

“Nora.” Faillit smiled at Nora like a viper trying to tempt a baby chick closer. “Why don’t you help her with that while you show her out?”

Nora twitched her mouth to protest. She glanced and Shore, who nodded and flicked her hand toward Chavali. With a stifled sigh, Nora flashed a smile as real as her jewelry and stood. “Of course.”

“It was nice meeting you, Chastity,” Shore said with a polite, less fake smile. “I hope your employer chooses to invest in our city.”

“We shall see. Thank you for your time,” Chavali said with a polite bow of her head. She gestured for Colby and Portia to leave with her. They offered polite respect to the room and left.

Chavali waited for Nora, who accompanied her out of the room and closed the doors behind them.

“You’re not really interested in our history, are you?” Nora asked. She gestured down the stairs and took them at a slow pace with Chavali, keeping her hands clasped in front of her so Chavali had no excuse to touch her skin.

“On the contrary, I am exceptionally intrigued by a situation wherein the consul was removed yet not killed. This is an elected position, is it not?” Chavali doubted Nora would prove a valuable ally in any way, yet she might offer interesting information if treated with polite respect. The contrast from Faillit and her other peers should prove too flattering to resist.

“Oh, that.” Nora huffed. “Yes, the position is elected, but it’s a lifetime appointment. Almost everyone who matters here follows the Order of Spilled Blood.” She tapped her chest with an effete, snobbish lift of her nose to indicate she included herself in that group. “Consul Shore and the last consul both do, as does most of the council and, as it happens, Guyre.”

“Ah.” The adherents of that order refused to kill. As Chavali had learned in Ket, this didn’t prevent them from choosing excruciatingly and horrifically unpleasant punishments for criminals, but they stopped short of execution.

"Captain Faillit is Strong Arm, but she has no power to set policy and follows orders." Nora sniffed her disdain. "Mostly."

The rift between Nora and Faillit probably had jealousy as its root cause. Chavali doubted anything Nora said, did, or wanted played a major role in the city despite her obvious desire otherwise. Consul Shore's dismissal of her at Faillit's suggestion pointed to this.

"This previous consul was exiled, then?"

"Yes." Nora sighed, displaying some fondness for either that leader or the conditions under his regime. Perhaps she'd had more freedom to act without council oversight. "This all happened a few years ago." She leaned toward Chavali and lowered her voice. "Faillit said Guyre was one of hers, but that's not true. They were equals. The last consul went mad, and Shore was one of his councilors. When they deposed him, the old captain left with the consul, Shore won the election to replace him. She picked Faillit over Guyre to take the captain's place even though Guyre had been her most vocal supporter."

Chavali feigned surprise at such a scandalous choice on Shore's part because Nora definitely wanted her to. "Why would she do this?"

Nora grinned and her eyes sparkled with delight. "So many rumors to choose from. I think she seduced him and used him, then threw him away when she got what she wanted. He's so young and dumb."

"I can believe this happened. Men are so easy to manipulate."

"They really are."

They reached the bottom of the stairs. Nora shook hands with her, allowing Chavali to see she'd made a good impression.

"I appreciate your time, Nora. Thank you." Chavali afforded Nora a polite, shallow bow. She didn't deserve it, but the gesture made the woman happy and ended their audience without awkwardness.

Nora left with a pleased smile and a bounce in her step.

Portia and Colby waited for her by the door.

"This city—"

"Shut up, Colby," Portia hissed. "Wait until we're clear."

"Yes," Chavali said. Again, she felt the urge to slap him. She clasped her hands and followed them out the front door.

The sight of a giant white horse standing among the plaza statues with a swarm of pigeons and other small birds settled across his head and back eased her temper. Karias shook his head and sent the birds flying in every direction, chirping up an angry storm. He whinnied in greeting.

Chavali stopped and shielded her face from the mad birds. Colby and Portia did the same.

"Karias, what were you thinking?" Colby sighed. As the birds settled or moved on, he headed for the horse.

"Karias is a very strange horse," Portia murmured to Chavali.

"Yes."

CHAPTER 9

Colby climbed into the saddle and left the women behind. Chavali preferred this so she had more time to compose herself.

He hadn't changed and wouldn't change. If she couldn't deal with his most infuriating habits, she couldn't deal with the rest of him either.

She and Portia strolled down the road, taking their time on the way back to the inn. Though their clothing didn't match any of the many people they passed on the road, few people looked at them askance. Chavali suspected they chose to overlook some eccentricities because of the sandals. A woman could wear anything in Palmia Basin so long as she selected proper footwear to accompany it.

"Is it my imagination," Portia said, "or is Colby acting dumber than usual?"

"I have also noticed this."

"Since you know everything, how does he know Daria?"

Chavali's lip curled. She didn't mean to let it show, yet she did. For a long moment, she gave her attention to an elder man sitting on a front stoop, watching the world pass by while slicing leaves off thick, meaty stalks and letting them fall into a basket between his feet. She'd eaten those plants before, on several of her trips through Tila. They tasted like grass on their own but soaked up other flavors like a sponge.

Once they passed the man, she had to answer Portia or face prodding. "He fell in love with her and they had an amicable parting."

"Chavali." Portia leaned close and whispered, "Are you jealous?"

"No," she snapped.

"Of course not. You're just irrationally annoyed about running into his former lover, which is obviously completely different."

"Shut up."

Portia laughed while a flock of gabbling chickens crossed the road under the care of a pair of girls.

"I'm not jealous. I'm..." Chavali groped for a word that better explained. She didn't care about his past love life. This woman didn't represent a threat to her. Colby wouldn't drop everything to run off with Daria. The woman probably knew things about Colby that Chavali would benefit from learning. "I'm frustrated with him."

"I'm not surprised. You hate stupidity and incompetence, and he caused a problem with Guyre. That kind of thing really bothers you."

"Yes, exactly. And we have argued about things recently." She shut her mouth to avoid revealing anything important. Portia reminded her too much of her little sister.

"You argued with someone? I'm shocked. Stunned."

Chavali rolled her eyes and batted Portia's arm. "Shut up."

Portia laughed again.

As Chavali heaved a long-suffering sigh, she noticed two muscular guardsmen across the street. Their movements pitted them against the flow of traffic.

One dragged the other into a narrow alley bedecked with vines, ferns, and wide-leafed shrubs.

People nearby shied away from them. They stole furtive glances without looking directly at either man or the alley.

Nothing about their behavior struck Chavali as overtly antagonistic. A superior could've needed to discipline a subordinate.

Despite this, she couldn't shake the impression one man threatened the other and wanted to find a place to avoid witnesses. Perhaps one man worked for the Talons and the other for the Guard.

Her curiosity piqued, Chavali waved for Portia to follow and ducked across the street. She threaded her fingers through the spirits and covered the alley mouth with an illusion to block sight of them from passersby. She raised a finger to her lips and led Portia in a slow, careful creep down the alley.

"You won't get away with it." The first speaker sounded dazed, like he'd suffered a rap to the skull. Low-hanging branches and large leaves blocked them from view.

"This is the only warning you're going to get, Wray," the second man spat.

Something heavy hit something solid. Someone groaned.

"We know where you live, and that pretty little wife of yours doesn't deserve the pain you'll bring down on her."

"You're a blight." Wray had to gasp for breath. He sounded like Colby confronting injustice. "How do you even—"

The second man hit Wray again. Chavali rushed forward. Like Colby, Wray would stay ensconced on his high moral ground and turn a warning into a beating or death.

Portia cursed under her breath.

Chavali burst through the foliage to find the two men. One sat on the ground, recovering from a blow. The other stood over him, ready to deliver another. Both had the genuine patch of actual members of the Guard.

As she'd learned to do over the past few months, Chavali kept running and slammed her body into the attacker's before he registered her presence. They tumbled to the ground together.

He kicked her aside and rolled to his feet. She slid across damp leaves. Portia jumped in front of Wray. The attacker snapped his gaze from Chavali to Portia to Wray and fled. Chavali scrambled to her feet and knew she couldn't catch him.

Wray sagged and groaned. "I'm not sure if I should thank you or apologize."

Portia offered him a hand and helped him stand. "We'll settle for the reason one guard would attack another."

Nodding, Wray leaned against the wall. "That's fair. His name is Valen. Used to be a friend." He swiped a sleeve across his mouth, smearing a daub of blood across it. "My partner. I caught him taking a bribe. Who are you?"

"Dangerous foreigners," Chavali said as she brushed leaves off her dress.

Portia snorted. "I'm Portia, this is Chastity. We're trying to help a friend deal with the Withered Fists."

"That's who's bribing him." Wray rubbed his jaw and winced. "He's not the only one. I don't know what all is going on, but I'm trying to figure it out. My family has a shop, and the Fists have tried to extort my parents for protection three times in the past month. So far, I've shown up every time by chance, but I'm not sure how long my presence at random times will hold them off."

Chavali rubbed her arm to soothe the ache she knew would come. Her palm and elbow stung with mild scrapes. "I've noticed too few guards patrol the city regularly. Is this bribery matter the reason why?"

"No." Wray groaned and held his side. "It's not the only reason, at least. Captain Faillit won't hire more. She says there isn't enough money, even with the extra we get from the capital. Who knows what she's doing with her budget, but it's not hiring more people."

Intrigued alongside her disgust for these revelations, Chavali offered Wray a hand. "Can you walk?"

He waved off her help. "In a minute, yes. Watch yourselves. If they think you're involved, they'll—"

"We're not afraid of them," Portia said.

Wray sighed. "Please take this seriously."

"We are," Chavali said. "I suggest checking on your wife now, not later. Perhaps convince her to visit family elsewhere for a short time?"

He grinned. "Mara only seems harmless. If I ask her to leave for her own safety, she'll beat me up. But you're right. I should warn her they've escalated." With one hand on the wall, he straightened and shifted his weight. "I think I'll be fine. Thank you for the rescue, Portia and Chastity. Good luck and watch your backs."

"To you as well. We'll let you leave first." Chavali watched him limp to the end of the alley. She remembered the illusion she'd woven and dispersed it.

"This city is..." Portia shook her head. "I don't know what it is, but it's something."

"Excessively complex in its corruption for its size."

Portia nodded. "Yes, that covers it. Shall we?"

They left the alley and returned to the inn.

At the door to Chavali and Colby's cabin, Portia patted her shoulder. "Go easy on him," she murmured. "He didn't mean to run into her."

Chavali nodded. "Thank you for the reminder." She slipped inside.

Colby sat at the desk against the far wall with his back to the door. His armor and sword lay on one of the two smaller beds. He set down a pen and turned to face her with a small smile. It fell into a frown. "What happened?"

"Local color." She slipped into the washroom to clean her elbow at the standing sink. As promised, several tiny scrapes with tiny dots of blood decorated both it and her palm.

"You can't see color." He stood and joined her.

Chavali chuckled and ran water over a washcloth to clean the minor injuries. "We broke up a fight. It's nothing."

He took her hand and ran his thumb over the back, then lowered it so he could run water over her palm. *::I'm sorry about Daria. I haven't thought about her in years.::*

The cold water stung. She bit back a hiss and focused on what she wanted to say to him. "This is not something you need to apologize for. The part where you told her which inn to find you at, or the part where you blurted your morality into a meeting with a local crime figure? Those are things to apologize for."

His touch gentle, he shifted to wiping her elbow with the washcloth. *::I'm not sure why I did either of those things.::*

"You trust her and want to impress her."

::I don't want to impress her.::

She raised an eyebrow at him.

He frowned again. *::I was transferred and couldn't see her anymore, so we called it off. Maybe it wasn't as final as it could've been.::*

"And I am challenging, so part of you wishes for the simplicity you remember."

Colby paused and turned over her words in his head.

Chavali tugged her hand loose and dried both it and her arm with a fresh towel. "There is a truth I learned many years ago. Women are not meant to know what men think."

"I'm not interested in her anymore."

"I know. It isn't fair to you that I can't shield myself from your thoughts."

He backed out. She heard the bed creak as he sat. "You sound like you're ready to give up."

"Not at all. We are discussing the fact that I cannot handle your thoughts for more than a few minutes at a time." She checked her sleeve and discovered a dark smear. Once she'd brushed off the tiny bits of plant and dirt, she judged it good enough for the moment. Washing it could wait.

She stepped out of the bathroom and found him sitting on the edge of the bed. His gaze rested on the wall, but his eyes lacked focus.

"I'm hungry. Will you share dinner with me?"

Colby blinked and sucked in a deep breath. "Yes, of course." He offered his hand to her.

Looking at his hand, she wondered what he thought she'd just told him. "Say it out loud."

He frowned and let his hand fall to his side. "You're right."

Chavali shrugged and opened the door. She didn't need to read his thoughts to know that. "Take your time. I intend to have tea." She headed for the common room and didn't stop to check if he followed. If he needed another few minutes to sort his thoughts, she wouldn't fault him for it.

Inside the inn's common room, she found Portia already sitting in a booth in the back corner. Other customers chattered through their evening meal in the cluster of tables in the center, offering Portia's chosen table a measure of privacy beyond the three walls surrounding it.

The smell of something familiar yet strange, a sharp, tangy spice that reminded Chavali of the past without conjuring it, drifted through the room, accompanied by the aroma of roasting poultry and herbs. Her stomach growled.

She stopped at the bar to order tea, then nodded to one of Iker's waitstaff on her way through the room. With luck, the young man could extract himself from his other customers soon to come take her order. Whatever Iker's cook had prepared for the evening, she wanted some as soon as possible.

Portia raised her wine glass as Chavali sat beside her. "Do you think any of those guards Wray warned us about will show up?"

As Chavali stole a thin slice of bread from Portia's otherwise empty plate, the front door opened. She tensed. Sivry and Jaris entered the room with no pursuit, and she relaxed. "Perhaps."

The two spies wore local clothing and sandals they must have gotten from a second-hand shop. Jaris's loose pants had a dark patch on one knee. The fabric of Sivry's dress and the scarf over her head, covering her wire ornaments, seemed tired and worn.

They slid into the booth together. Sivry sat in the outer seat, leaving a gap between them wide enough to suggest a small amount of friction. They sat together, though, so the problem had a minimal impact. Perhaps they'd discovered a significant difference of opinion on some subject not critical to the mission.

"Where's Colby?" Sivry asked as she untied her scarf and let it rest around her neck.

Chavali shrugged. "Thinking too hard for his own good."

Portia snorted wine through her nose. Chavali handed her an extra napkin.

"Of course he is." Sivry raised a finger to attract a member of the waitstaff. "He can catch up later, then. We found out some really interesting stuff today."

"The Fists are new in town," Jaris said. "They're based in the capital, Cliffside City. Apparently, they're pretty big and have a strong grip on the warehouse district there."

Sivry nodded. "Reading between the lines, I'm sure they've got a deal with the authorities in Cliffside City, and are happy to use dead bodies as part of their enforcement plan."

"The group here was sent to colonize. They heard it would be easy to carve out a domain here." Jaris snorted and shook his head. "It hasn't been. At least, not as easy as they thought it would be. Another gang, the Dragon Talons, is pretty well entrenched."

Chavali raised her brow. Someone had to start a rumor about the state of the city. For it to travel so far, this someone had made an effort. "We encountered the Talons."

"I'm not surprised," Sivry said. "They're hard to miss. But there's another group operating here too. Qanafe Furies. They seem more like a cult than a gang, and they're the ones responsible for the fire at Torrel's bakery. They've destroyed several buildings already, and people are scared of them."

"Qanafe is a local plant," Jaris said. He seemed like he would leave it at that, then he glanced to the side and continued, "They use the whole plant for one thing or another. Flowers are nice and have a light fragrance. Grind up the seeds for a spice. Eat the leaves raw. Cook the roots with meat. We tried some of the various options. Delicious. I think our spice merchant will want some of that."

"This cult—" Sivry coughed and cut herself off as Jaris nudged her with an elbow and Iker stopped at their table.

Iker set a steaming mug in front of Chavali, which she appreciated. "Are you all here for dinner?"

"Yes," Chavali said. "Plus one more, please. The big man will join us soon."

He pulled over a chair from a nearby, unoccupied table, then left.

Sivry waited a few beats before resuming the discussion. "The Furies are agents of chaos. No one knows what they want, other than random property destruction. It's probable their attack on the bakery wasn't personal. They're new in town too, and people are absolutely terrified of them."

"Random in what way?" Chavali asked. "Are some places burned and others smashed?"

"No." Jaris shook his head. "All of them were burned, but it's one building here and one building there with no clear pattern. The group is small. Maybe a dozen of them, and they lost one in that fire. The survivor already escaped from the guard, and they're interested in a large man with a white horse and a woman with a feather sticking out of her forehead."

"Sounds like you made a whole bunch of friends today," Portia said.

Everyone quieted again as Iker brought a tray full of food. He set out four plates each loaded with plenty of food. This meal involved slices of meat slathered with a thin gravy containing small pieces of unknown vegetable matter topped with small leaves and accompanied by a root vegetable. Two thin slices of plain bread decorated the edge.

That spicy tang she'd noted on entering the room roiled from the plate, distracting Chavali from everything except eating.

Jaris sighed with delight. "This is an qanafe dish, right?"

"It is." Iker set the fourth plate in front of the empty chair. "And it's fresh. I stepped out to the market this afternoon to get it special for you since I know you're only visiting. It would be a crime to let you leave without trying it like this."

Touched by his unexpected and unnecessary effort, Chavali smiled while she cut the meat. "Thank you. That's thoughtful."

Iker answered her smile. "Be sure to try it with a little of everything in one bite. Wave for me if you need anything else." He left them to their food.

Chavali wanted to devour her food as fast as possible. She forced herself to explore the flavor, something she'd done a great deal during her first month as Fallen. Few things there had tasted familiar, and she'd had to work at finding new favorite foods.

This dish could've been made by her clan.

The qanafe spice had a great deal in common with one her clan had grown in wagon rooftop gardens. Perhaps they'd grown a different strain of the same plant or prepared the spice form differently.

She ate to enjoy the food and fill her belly, intending to give Colby a chance to join them before continuing the discussion. Portia seemed content to sip her wine and say nothing. From the way they attacked their food, Sivry and Jaris clearly hadn't eaten in several hours.

When she'd taken the edge off her hunger, Chavali gave up on Colby and started again. "We discovered there's corruption in the guards, which we already knew, but there's also an effort to root it out. And there's more."

Colby entered the room as the words left her mouth. He sat and ate without interrupting.

Portia and Chavali took turns telling Sivry and Jaris about meeting Guyre and the Consul. Both painted Daria as an old friend of Colby's without elaboration on their relationship.

"This city is a mess," Jaris said, shaking his head. "I thought Ket was bad, but this is insane. Are we even equipped to try and untangle it?"

Chavali shrugged. "It is not our job to untangle it. Our job is to make the city livable for Torrel. Which means stable. To that end, I think we want what the Consul wants, which is a strong Riverway Guild and Talons."

Colby paused with a bite of food halfway to his mouth. "How can that be the best option? Shouldn't we want the Guard in control?"

"Sort of?" Portia shook her head. "Consul Shore is Captain Faillit's boss, so she's nominally in command of the Guard. I don't think she's a bad leader, and she doesn't need removal."

"Faillit is questionable." Chavali swished a piece of bread through the gravy on her plate. She handed her second piece of bread to Colby. "I can't decide what I think of her. On the one hand, anyone reasonable should find Nora tiresome as she does. On the other, a number of her people are taking bribes from the Fists. Either she knows or she doesn't, and neither speaks well of her."

"Corrupt or incompetent," Jaris said.

Colby furrowed his brow. "That seems unfair. She has a lot of people to manage. Not knowing some are corrupt doesn't make her incompetent or inattentive."

"I would agree if she had the normal number of guards to manage for this size of a city," Sivry said. "But she doesn't. The Guard is woefully understaffed. They have barely enough patrol officers for a small town, let alone a city with two halves separated by a lake. As far as I could tell, the Guard doesn't even have a single investigator."

Jaris nodded his agreement. "It's even worse than that. We tried to find where an ordinary citizen goes to report a crime, and couldn't. There's a jail and courthouse. Those seem to be the only buildings in the city dedicated to law enforcement in any way. City hall has two Guard offices.

One is Faillit's. The other is for members of the Guard to report to. They have another one of those on the other side of the lake."

At the city hall, Chavali hadn't noticed either of those offices.

"That's..." Colby shook his head and grimaced with distaste. "Criminal. It's worse than criminal. Tiny villages do better than that."

"At least with the Talons," Portia said, "everybody knows the deal. They even do some enforcement on behalf of regular people. More than the Guard does, anyway."

"We aren't here to create a permanent solution," Chavali said. "We should focus on dealing with these Fists and Furies, I think. That will make many lives much better with the least amount of work."

"I agree," Sivry said. "Those are the most toxic elements here."

"Seconded. Thirded?" Jaris raised his glass. "Whatever. Down with the Fists and Furies."

Portia clinked her glass to his. "Colby?"

He sighed. "I don't like it, but none of you have ever steered me wrong before. Except that one time in Ket."

Jaris smirked at him. "You didn't die there, though, did you? No, of course not. That was me."

Chavali laughed.

CHAPTER 10

On the way to their cabins, Sivry put a hand on Chavali's shoulder and nodded for her to stop.

They moved to the edge of the stone path. Chavali brushed against a spray of small flowers on a vine, releasing a citrusy musk into the air. As long as they kept their voices low, the trees, shrubs, and voluminous flowers would keep anyone out of sight from overhearing.

Everyone else trooped onward. Colby glanced at them as if to ask if he should stay or go. Chavali shooed him toward the cabin.

"There's something I want to talk to you about. It's not…" Sivry furrowed her brow and scuffed her sandal on the stone. "There are hardly any elves in Palmia Basin. We crossed the lake and prowled on the other side. Over there, they've got one little enclave of elves. They're insular and don't approve of me because of this." She pointed to the wires between her ears and jaw.

Finally, Chavali had a clear opening to ask about the curious ornaments and nothing to distract her from it. "I admit I have no idea what this means."

"Oh, it's an order thing." Sivry waved a hand in disinterest. "Probably like your beads."

"I doubt this, but if you wish not to explain, I won't pry."

Sivry cocked her head to one side. "You're actually interested?"

"Of course." Chavali nodded and kept the eagerness off her face. Sivry needed sincere interest to want to share, not rapacious curiosity. "I consider you a friend."

"Thanks."

Sivry angled her jaw so Chavali could get a good look at the wires on the left side. Two flexible strands of dark metal formed a two-circle spiral through her earlobe and plunged into her lower jaw about an inch from the spiral. "My order is elf-only. We believe the greatest sin is…more or less, that we shouldn't have let humans outbreed us so much and take control of just about everything through sheer force of numbers. The wires are a marking that I'm not available for breeding. Those who know the order and what it means typically see people like me as lesser."

Chavali had her own reasons for not wishing to breed. Without the specter of her uncontrollable telepathy, though, she thought she would be content to bear children. All the women of her clan had done so, and they'd suffered no great hardship because of it.

Careful not to imply any judgment, she asked, "May I know why would you choose this?"

Sivry smirked. "That's the most polite, nicest way anyone has ever asked me that question. Most of those who have it are barren, diseased, or otherwise incapable. I'm not any of those. I don't like children. I don't want to sacrifice twenty years of my life to raising one. Besides that, I'm just not interested in sex with anyone."

Among clan, no one had ever expressed such a view. As an entertainer, though, Chavali had seen all kinds of proclivities in the hundreds of outsider minds she'd sampled. Sivry's preference was unusual but hardly unique.

"Thank you for sharing this. I'm honored by the trust you place in me."

"You're welcome. Thank you for the respect and lack of judgment. It's refreshing. But this isn't what I needed to say." She frowned. "Not only do I stick out here, I don't feel particularly competent as a mentor for Jaris. He's a very different kind of operative than I was. I served my order, not an individual, and I didn't do information gathering. Not like he did. We don't have a basis of common methodology or vocabulary, and I'm not the right kind of person for this. I get frustrated by simple things with him sometimes."

Unsurprised to hear Aislynn had made yet another dubious choice, Chavali rubbed her eyes. At least they didn't hate each other. "I understand. Do the best you can. If he asks a question you aren't sure how to answer or don't have the patience for, direct him to ask me."

Sivry nodded. "Thank you. I know you have your hands full with Colby, so I appreciate that."

Chavali stifled most of a scowl.

Before she could retort, Sivry patted her shoulder. "You do a pretty good job of hiding it." She leaned close and whispered, "But everyone knows."

"There's nothing to know," Chavali grumbled.

"Of course not." Sivry's mouth twitched. "That's why you bunk with him on missions. And he gives you 'reading lessons.' "

After hearing something so personal about Sivry, Chavali didn't want to snap at her. She did, however, narrow her eyes. "As challenging as it may be to believe, my clan was not literate. He has actually taught me to read. I stay in rooms with him because he is not disturbed by my nightmares."

She couldn't bring herself to tell Sivry the baldfaced lie of having nothing between them beyond friendship. Even her implied denial by omission seemed a trifle rude at this point.

"Of course. Good night, Chavali." Sivry grinned and left her standing alone on the path.

"Everyone knows." Everyone did *not* know, because everyone only heard those irritating rumors. They had no idea what Chavali and Colby had been through, or what they did behind closed doors. But they thought they did.

Wretched busybodies. All of them.

She glared at the flowers beside the path for a short time, then rubbed her face and joined Colby in their cabin.

He gave her space, which told her she needed to do a better job of masking her annoyance in front of him. Colby had no need to see it when she wanted to throttle someone else.

Much later, Chavali woke in the middle of the night, her heart racing from an old, worn nightmare. She lay curled against Colby's warmth with clothing protecting her from his thoughts.

Sleep wouldn't come again soon, she could feel that much. Waking Colby seemed cruel. She slipped out of bed, tucked the covers close under his chin, and wrapped a spare blanket around her shoulders. Tea would help.

As quietly as possible, Chavali stepped into her sandals and left for the main building.

Tiny, twinkling lights marked the boundaries of the walkway. Insects buzzed in a low hum. Though she'd expected the heat to linger through the night, the humidity had dissipated and the temperature had cooled. She almost wanted her boots and a shawl. For a longer walk, she would've gone back to get them.

The back door of the main building proved locked. Apparently, the tavern had closed at some point.

Chavali settled for the next best option at a time like this and headed for the stable. Karias had proven helpful in such situations in the past. She ducked inside the stable and into his stall. The horse lay on the floor with weak moonlight glowing on his side through a high window.

For a moment, she considered not disturbing him and returning to Colby instead, or taking a longer walk. Then Karias lifted his head.

She shut the half door to his stall and sat beside him with her hand on his neck.

::I know Colby is asleep, so he couldn't have done anything stupid.::

"I am awake for no reason."

::Ah. Tell me what's going on, then.::

She related everything they'd discovered about the Fists, Talons, Furies, Consul, and guards. Unlike earlier, she detailed the encounter with Wray.

::Sounds like Torrel's retirement location is a little more interesting than it should be. I trust we're planning to do something about this instead of taking him and running for it?::

"Yes. We intend to deal with the Fists and the Furies. We have already talked Colby into this. I think he gave up with less of a fight than usual because he feels guilty about Daria."

Karias sighed. *::Daria.::*

"A woman so like him it's a miracle they didn't kill each other."

::Yes. And no. She's rather less...dedicated to righteousness, let's say. Regardless, don't let him beat himself up too much. When they parted, he didn't take it too hard. I think, in some ways, leaving her behind when they transferred us came as something of a relief.::

"Speaking of relief." Chavali leaned against his soothing warmth and reveled in it. "I have become torn between two men."

::Is that why Colby keeps having these murmurs of jealousy?::

She snorted. "No. The one who is causing me problems wishes me to keep a secret from Colby and clan, and I have yet to hear a proper explanation why."

Karias's discomfort gave her some satisfaction. *::I....::*

"You have told me you wish to keep him in the dark about your nature to avoid awkwardness, but the more I think about this rationale, the less I believe it's the full truth, or even a real reason. To me, it sounds like the kind of excuse one gives when they wish to hide the real reason."

::This isn't fair,:: he grumbled.

"Fair? Don't growl to me about fairness. The one thing he cherishes above all else is honesty. You've willfully lied to him for years, and you ask me to do it too. We are his heart and soul. His support. His clan. Avoiding awkwardness is not a good enough reason for me to continue to keep your secret."

Karias huffed. *::During a mission isn't the best time to deal with this.::*

Chavali scowled. "I have better excuses than that in my pinky finger. Give me one real, good reason why I shouldn't go wake him and tell him now."

He gave the impression of frowning. *::I don't know how he'll react. He could jeopardize your mission or safety.::*

"I should tell the stablehands to give you nothing but plain oats and water." She crossed her arms and simmered because Karias had a point. Colby already had Daria to handle. Throwing this into the mix might cause him to act like a worse kind of idiot. Especially with how he'd fled the fire's aftermath.

Karias had fled the scene too. Chavali thought over the moments after she'd emerged from the bakery and remembered Karias making an effort to hide. Neither he nor Colby would've felt a need to hide from *her* at that moment. Likewise, the guards hadn't presented any particular danger before or after that moment, so why would he hide from them?

Which left Korrya or her mlinzi.

"What involvement do you have with the Spire?"

::What? I— No. It's not— Look. I just—::

"I see." She pulled away from him, severing herself from his thoughts. "I will give you the benefit of a few moments to collect yourself. Then you will explain to me what I need to know to protect Colby and you from the Spire. If you cannot, then I will go tell Colby what I know. Tonight."

He lowered his head and closed his eyes. The giant horse, fearsome in battle and usually unflappable, acted like a child caught with a handful of forbidden cookies.

Chavali watched him squirm. Then she leaned against him again and held out her hand so he could decide when to make contact.

The soft hair of his chin settled into her palm. *::Thank you for letting me have that short time. I appreciate it. And you're right. I've put you in an unfair position. I'd hoped it would never come up. But then you...::* He sighed. *::Never mind. I'll address both of these subjects at once. Colby served the Spire as a guard.::*

"Did he? I didn't know that. He's never mentioned it."

::I'm not surprised. He was...let's say..."asked to leave" *the Spire long before his death. Because of me, really. Our binding was a mistake. I still don't understand how it happened. Right afterward, though, I was angry and confused.*

One moment, I was a human trying to sneak into a room through a window, and the next, I was a rather large horse in a stable nearby.

I suppose there's genuinely no harm in telling you that I was a spy for Mecalle. My job at the time was to infiltrate the Spire, long term. Lucky me, I was in some kind of wrong place at the wrong moment, and suddenly

I was bound to Colby. Except neither of us realized it.::

Chavali didn't know what kind of story she'd expected, but nothing like this had ever crossed her mind.

She'd assumed Karias had died and returned as a spirit with a flesh form for some unknown yet purposeful reason. He and Colby fit together so well. Like Penny and Marcus. Eldrack and Railan. Herself and Pasha. Any other pair of people who'd spent years working and living together and had learned to anticipate each other. Their rapport had come from time and necessity, not some ridiculous soul mesh, or similar nonsense.

::He felt my anger and didn't realize it wasn't his own. Then he lashed out at his superiors and they sent him packing. I don't believe they knew about our binding. If they had, being the Spire, I expect they would've stopped us both. They're immense busybodies when it comes to magical anomalies. So he left. The binding between us meant I sensed the distance. At the time, I had no idea what it meant. I panicked.

I got loose and followed him. He was crushed by the dismissal and thought the Creator had sent me to show him a truer path. We can't share thoughts, so even though I found this laughable, I played along.

Eventually, I suppose I started to believe it myself. After all, if I choose to believe the Creator has a hand in all things, then I have to believe the accident which bound us had a purpose.::

"And now your true fear is if he knows, he will doubt himself and everything else. It will shake his foundations, destabilize him, and draw you both into dark places." The concern seemed especially relevant after the bakery fire.

::Yes.::

"I understand." Chavali thought through the situation, taking her time while Karias waited. "I think you underestimate him. But I believe I'll wait to explain. I doubt he'll be bothered much by you or your history. By me holding back, on the other hand? This will distress him greatly. When I tell him, I'll have to word it delicately."

Karias whuffed her hair. *::I apologize for the position I put you in. It wasn't fair or right. At the time, I didn't think it would cause a problem.::*

"I accept this apology." She'd fix this. When they returned home, she'd find a way to explain. They could ride someplace secluded so Colby could react however he wished with no one around to witness it.

::Since we're being honest, there's something else I need to tell you. That man with the raven on his shoulder, the mage's mlinzi, is someone I need to avoid. Colby and I both should. Probably also Korrya, the mage.::

"What is a mlinzi? I feel I've heard this term before, but I don't know what it means."

::A kind of elite bodyguard for a mage. Had we not had that accident, Colby likely would've become one. They have special status within the Spire. But that's not why we need to avoid him. I felt a kind of sympathetic attraction to that raven. The magic within me responded to the magic within the bird. I'm quite certain the bird also felt it.::

"And Korrya noticed you. She looked where you hid." Chavali nodded and pondered the situation. Korrya and her mlinzi had some idea of Karias's nature. And...? "Why does it matter if they know?"

::They'll report it to their superiors. Those superiors will want more information. Followers of the Order of the High Path, which is what anyone has to be in order to gain membership in the Spire, always want more information. They believe the greatest sin is willful ignorance.

As they dig into things, they'll realize who Colby is, follow his history, and discover he died. This will put them squarely on the trail of the Fallen. In addition, my body didn't disappear, Chavali. They've had my mysterious corpse all this time. I doubt they failed to take the time to investigate me as fully as possible.::

"Ah. An excellent point. Yes, both of you need to stay away from them. As far as possible." One more thing had to complicate this mission.

Chavali considered asking Colby to return home. Between his moral difficulties, their relationship, and the risk of Spire attention, he posed a number of challenges.

If he left, though, she wouldn't have him to lean on. Aislynn would ask questions. He would feel he'd failed somehow. The request would sound like rejection.

No, she wouldn't send him home. Not this time.

CHAPTER 11

In the dim, pale glow of pre-dawn, Chavali woke to the sound of the stable's outer door shutting. She rubbed her eyes and yawned. When she heard nothing else aside from llama snorts, she knew someone had left.

Perhaps Colby had come looking for her, though she thought he might've tried to join her rather than leave her alone. More likely, someone had come to check on or remove their animal. The stable did have other beasts, after all.

Careful not to wake Karias, she stood and left the stable. The crisp morning air roused her too much to consider trying to sleep again. She returned to the cabin to change her clothes and found Colby still in bed. The peace on his face convinced her to leave him alone. He needed the rest. With luck, he hadn't noticed her absence.

She dressed and slipped into the common room to find tea and breakfast.

Instead, she found a gathering of a dozen people, all dressed like locals.

Torrel and Iker sat among them. Others, she thought she recognized from the bystanders at the fire. The room held the telltale echoing silence of a group who'd stopped talking because of her.

Iker stood. "It's fine," he said as he gestured for Chavali to take a seat with the group. "This is Chastity. She's on our side. You can talk in front of her."

Chavali asked for tea and slid into the chair Iker had suggested.

Anger, frustration, and desperation hung in the air. "Please, continue."

An elder with ink-stained fingers frowned and sighed. "It's time to do something. That's what I'm saying. The guard won't do anything, so we have to."

Iker returned with Chavali's tea and a small plate of bread, cheese, and berries. "I just—" Iker shook his head. "If they come back, I'm terrified they'll kill my mother this time."

"It wasn't so bad before, paying the Talons," another woman said.

"I'm tired of all this." A different man thumped his fist on the table. "We pay our taxes. That's supposed to pay the guards to prevent all this. Why can they afford to do so many things but not protect us or fight fires for us? Don't we matter?"

"Screw them all," a woman growled. "We can protect ourselves. That money we all pay the Fists? We can pool it and hire some real security."

Torrel sighed and held up his hands. "I'm grateful you all came to check on me. It means a lot." He shook his head. "I don't know how to deal with people who start a fire in a random bakery because they can. The Talons, the Fists, and the Guard can't stop these people, so I'm not sure why we think we can." His gaze fell on Chavali. "Chastity, you're new in town, but you helped save my life. I don't suppose you have any thoughts on this subject?"

Caught in the middle of raising a piece of cheese to her mouth, Chavali paused and took a moment to consider what advice would help these people and not hinder her own efforts. "Anger in this room is strong and thick. Which is right and just. You all have many reasons to be angry. But this can make people act without thinking. Before you make serious, impactful decisions, consider the consequences and whether you are prepared to face them."

She flicked her gaze from person to person, wanting them all to feel seen and heard. "The situation you face is not unique to your neighborhood. This is happening all over the city. Which means it is one of large scale. If you resist as a group, there is a possibility the threat will retreat in favor of easier targets. There is also a possibility they will see you as a challenge to be conquered. Without knowing much about these individual groups, I can't say which is more likely.

"My advice in this situation is to do what you can as if to prepare for an emergency before starting any acts of real resistance. Find safe places outside your homes and businesses to hide food, spare supplies, even money, and do it as a group. Rely on each other instead of your government or a gang. Become the local gang, in essence, except one that cares about its whole community, not just itself."

"Or a guild," the elder scribe said. "We could be a neighborhood business guild. Torrel, you should lead it."

"Me?" Torrel blinked at him.

"Yes, you," a woman said. She patted Torrel on the knee. "You've always been a cornerstone around here."

Torrel rubbed his face. "I suppose I have plenty of time on my hands right now."

The group's focus shifted to providing support and encouragement to Torrel. Chavali watched while she ate, pleased to note everyone offered genuine well-wishes. For once, she could enjoy the splendor of a group committed to a singular, positive goal instead of a much less pleasant room full of backbiting crooks trying to step on each other's faces to get ahead.

As the meeting ended and the other business owners trickled out to open their shops, Torrel moved chairs to sit with her. Only Iker remained with them, and he fussed behind the bar, presumably preparing for breakfast service.

"I don't know that I'm equipped for what they want me to do. I don't even have the first clue how to organize the bucket brigade they want to start."

Chavali knew enough about him to provide encouragement rather than discouragement. "The key is not to try to do everything yourself. These others want to help. Let them. Use their skills. Trust them to do their part. This is about all your lives and livelihoods, after all."

Torrel nodded. "I've never done anything like it before, that's all."

He had, but he didn't remember. Chavali thought part of him would make those old connections and figure it out. "Most things which seem complex and challenging are nothing more than a collection of simple tasks smashed together."

Keeping this in mind would guide her mission, also.

Sivry, Portia, and Jaris entered the room. They sat with Chavali and ordered breakfast.

"Where's Colby?" Portia asked.

"Still asleep." Chavali sipped her tea.

Sivry grinned. "Wore him out, did you?"

Chavali rolled her eyes. She had no intention of discussing his problems with anyone outside the clan. Or her own, for that matter. "I would like to speak about these Qanafe Furies."

"I don't know what to do about them," Torrel said. "They're the biggest reason I'm still not sure about this neighborhood guild thing. No one knows where they're going to strike, or why. They just pop up and burn down a bakery for no reason anyone can figure out."

Portia said, "Chaos. That's a tactic meant to cause chaos, which breeds fear. Scared people do things differently from comfortable people."

"If you don't know where they will go, it could be you next. This is what they want." Chavali set down her tea. "I think we should make ourselves a target for them. Not here. I have no wish to cause damage to this inn, or to this neighborhood. We need a plan for this."

Torrel stood. "I have a very strong feeling that whatever comes out of your mouths next is something I'm better off not knowing."

"Probably true," Jaris said. "Do you need anything?"

"No, I'm fine. You've all done more than enough for me already. Plan your trouble and don't worry about me." He gave them a small, friendly bow and left for his room upstairs.

With him out of the room, Chavali told the others about the group the locals planned to set up. "I doubt this fledgling guild will complicate matters for us. They will need time to gain enough notice to be targeted. By then, we should have removed the main problem."

"At least they want Torrel to lead it. That means we're clear to stay, right?" Jaris looked from Chavali to Sivry to Portia.

Sivry smiled at Jaris like she considered him silly. "No one's going to check on us in the middle of a mission. We decide whether to stay or not based upon our opinion of the situation, not whether the mission clearly dictates that we should."

He frowned. "I don't quite understand the point of the mission, then. Why give us one if what they really mean is for us to come and do whatever we want?"

"That's not what she means. Our mission is to help Torrel." Chavali wished she'd thrown the tea in Aislynn's face. If she ever had a chance to do it without endangering paperwork, she would. Aislynn would learn to hold proper mission briefings one way or another. "His safety and well-being is our responsibility. How we discharge this duty is left to our discretion. As is what we consider those words to mean."

Chavali had certainly stretched the terms of a mission a few times.

Finding and dealing with murderers somehow always proved so messy and complicated.

"We have the option to convince him to leave. We also have the option to forcibly extract him. My preference is to leave him here with no serious, obvious threats against him. If we cannot manage that in a week, we'll consider one of the other choices."

Portia and Sivry nodded their agreement.

Jaris sat and thought, frowning at the floor. Chavali sipped her tea and waited. She remembered her first mission as a new agent. No one had needed to explain the importance of the mission to her, but she'd had questions about how the whole thing worked.

After a few minutes, he said, "I don't really feel like I was prepared for this very well."

"How long ago did you wake from death?" Sivry asked.

"Two days before we left for this mission."

Chavali blinked. She glanced at Portia and Sivry, who shared her surprise. "That...is not how Eldrack handles things."

"He didn't let me go on my first mission for a month," Portia said. "I understand wanting to get people out and working, but that's insane. You should've had at least a week to adjust."

"No wonder you're having nightmares," Sivry murmured.

"I'm fine." Jaris crossed his arms and legs.

"You're doing well," Chavali said. "We're not saying otherwise. I'm glad you're here, and your presence is a help to us."

The front door opened and a woman in a guard uniform stepped inside. As she approached and headed straight to the group, Chavali spotted the fake patch on the woman's sleeve. One of Guyre's people, the Talons, had come looking for them.

Chavali offered fake guardswoman a polite smile and nodded to her. The woman stopped beside her.

Leaning close, the woman whispered to her, "Guyre wants you to come meet with him now."

"I see." Chavali didn't jump at anyone's beck and call. "We're finishing breakfast and will visit him shortly."

The woman bit her lip. "I'm supposed to fetch you. Just you."

If Colby had joined them already, he would object. And he would have a point.

Chavali stood. "Very well. But I will bring at least one person for the walk. They need not join me in the meeting. I merely wish to ensure my safety in your unpredictable city."

"Oh." The woman straightened with a relieved smile. "That's fine. Bring two if you want."

Colby would take this news best from Portia. Not that he'd take it well, but he'd accept it from her. Chavali gestured for Jaris and Sivry to join her. "This shouldn't take long."

Portia waved for them to go. "You're right to sneak out before he's up. I'll tell him enough so you can handle him later."

"Thank you." Though she didn't look forward to one more reason to have to "handle" Colby, Chavali nodded and let their escort guide her.

Outside, a light, misty rain pattered on leaves and walls. Damp flower petals sparkled in early morning sunshine.

Chavali had a strong feeling this day would end much worse than it began.

CHAPTER 12

Sivry and Jaris, both playing the part of good bodyguards, trailed behind Chavali and her escort. Chavali feigned interest in the plants while watching the young woman leading her through the city. The girl had a fresh-faced sort of pleasantness about her, as if she'd joined the Talons to see more of the city and hadn't noticed any of its less ethical ventures and tactics.

"Is this kind of rain common here?" Chavali brushed tiny droplets off her face.

"Yes." The girl turned up her face to the sky with a bright smile. "Almost every day. It's why the plants grow so big and fast. That and the fact it never gets cold enough to snow. I really love living here. I grew up on the other side of the lake, and you wouldn't think it'd be a lot different for how close it is, but they get twice the rain over there. My mom would complain about it all the time because our cat hated it so much and she'd just sit in the doorway hissing at the water."

Chavali had found her favorite kind of person on a mission—talkative. "Why did she never move to this side?" From the way the girl had worded her memory, Chavali suspected the mother had died.

"Work. The ferry isn't free. I don't really think that's fair. Even if you have your own boat, they still charge you to dock, no matter how long you stay. They don't charge us, of course, because Guyre made a deal with the Riverway Guild. He's really good at making deals that help us."

This girl, it seemed, would do most of the work for Chavali. She needed only to provide a nudge and information streamed forth like a waterfall. "Guyre is an interesting man."

"He's so amazing," the girl gushed. "He swam into the heart of the mountain. That's upstream! Against the current! He's so strong and amazing, and he met a dragon there."

Dragons only existed in myth. At least, Chavali had never heard of evidence of a real dragon. Strange creatures abounded in secluded places, of course. Dragons, on the other hand, only lived in stories. The idea of a giant, flying lizard with fiery breath was preposterous.

"A dragon?"

"Yes." The girl nodded, her eyes wide with zealous fervor. "A real, live dragon. Guyre wrestled it and won. He follows the Order of Spilled Blood, of course, so he never would've tried to kill it. He still won, though! He cowed the dragon with his skill. It gave him gifts and showed him the truth."

With every new piece of information, Guyre sounded more like a cult leader than a gang boss.

Chavali wished she had an excuse to take the girl's hand. "What truth is this?"

"That we have only one life. There's nothing waiting for us after death. We have to make this time count because this is all we've got." She glanced aside at Chavali. "You don't believe, but you should. He's right. The greatest sin is striving for rewards in the afterlife instead of doing the best we can here and now."

The spirits constantly swirling around Chavali, serving her to further the goals of clan, offered concrete evidence Guyre had either lied or misunderstood whatever he'd found in the mountain heart. Karias's fate also pointed to some other truth.

Souls had to exist for more than the singular purpose of steering a body of flesh through a single life. Otherwise, the mere existence of the Fallen made no sense.

Guyre's idea sounded like any other order's idiocy. None of the notions about death that Chavali knew of could reconcile her relationship with the spirits, and neither could this one. Those who declared the impossibility of knowing struck her as the most sensible on the subject.

So many children in so many orders, all crying out for their Creator's attention, all so certain of their truths. Whatever reason She'd abandoned them, whatever reason She'd forced the memory of it on everyone, Chavali doubted such mindless pandering would convince Her to return.

Still, Guyre's notion, however strange and ridiculous, had some merit. Focusing on the life one lives could promote great works.

"It's an intriguing idea. What do you consider doing your best here and now?"

"Whatever Guyre wants. He's amazing, and he knows so much. I couldn't come up with anything half as brilliant as him if I tried. He's so good at directing everyone according to our talents and making sure we all do a good job."

This girl had allowed Guyre to become the center of her world. Perhaps she'd encountered him shortly after her mother's death and had made him into her idol to assuage the grief.

They reached the building with the fake guards.

The girl opened the door for Chavali with a bright smile. "You should listen to him. He's amazing."

Instead of replying, Chavali nodded and arranged her expression to appear thoughtful.

No one stopped Jaris or Sivry from accompanying Chavali deeper into the building. They followed the girl until they reached the sunken chamber full of curtains and couches. Guyre sat with two of the same women as he had at their first meeting. He lounged, more at ease than before, as if he no longer felt the need to impress Chavali or his other guests.

The middle-aged woman struck Chavali as having a connection to someone else Chavali had already met in Palmia Basin, though she couldn't think of who or how. Perhaps a gesture or cut of clothing had caught in her mind. Once again, she sat like a regal, impassive statue.

Guyre's other guest, the lover, paced behind his chair like a caged animal.

"Thank you," Guyre said to the guide girl with a fond smile. He gestured toward the door. "You may go."

The girl beamed like he'd showered her with praise and bounded up the stairs.

He didn't watch her. "Chastity, thank you so much for coming. Please, sit." Guyre patted the nearest empty couch. "We have much to discuss."

If he chose not to object to Jaris and Sivry remaining in the room, Chavali chose not to mention it. A certain level of paranoia about personal safety could have prevented a few unpleasant situations in the past.

"Thank you for inviting me." Chavali sat.

Jaris remained standing behind her. Sivry sat beside Chavali.

"You've been busy since you arrived." Guyre regarded her with a bemused smile. "Meeting with the consul and chatting up Riverway people. Rumors say you've even gained the notice of the Furies. Quite impressive."

"Making a splash is one of my talents." Chavali arranged herself to appear at ease and in control. She wanted to see how Guyre would react to someone unimpressed with him.

"Clearly." He laced his fingers on his lap. "I'd like to offer your employer a deal."

"I see." Chavali thought a spice merchant would care more about a deal with the Riverway Guild than a cultish gang losing its grip on the city. She gestured for him to go on, though, because what he offered would likely give her an opportunity.

"This is a good place to do business if you know the right people and make the right deals. By now, you're aware the local guards are understaffed and incompetent. My people provide much more substantial security than they can ever hope to offer. While we normally charge for this service, I'm willing to waive those fees for six months if you and your collection of competent operators are willing to help me root out the Withered Fists."

Chavali had to restrain herself to avoid laughing in his face. "If you have such substantial security, why have you allowed the Fists to propagate here? Or, for that matter, the Furies?"

Guyre waved to dismiss her concerns. "The Fists are a band of simple thugs. They pose no real threat. We merely don't have the manpower to fulfill all our obligations and fight them at the same time."

He spoke of obligations as if the Talons had some lofty purpose. As if they didn't spend all their time fleecing businesses and stealing from the docks.

Though they intended to handle the Fists, Chavali didn't see them as the greater threat. "And the Furies?"

The woman pacing behind Guyre stopped and gripped the back of his chair. "No one knows where to find them," she snapped.

Raising a lazy hand to make her stop, Guyre watched Chavali. "They're recent arrivals who don't bother with the docks. Too busy harassing people too poor or pathetic to fight back."

"And yet." Chavali examined her fingernails. She kept them short at the suggestion of her fighting instructor, Eliot, though she still painted them pink to match her feather. "People don't care about the Talons. They care about the Furies. So long as they cause enough fear to choke a goat, you're irrelevant."

Guyre didn't like hearing that. He shifted in his seat. His expression slipped more.

While the woman behind him returned to pacing with a frustrated huff, the second woman, the older one, had almost no reaction. Almost. Chavali noticed a subtle tensing of the muscles in her face and jaw. She otherwise sat silent and motionless as a statue.

People in cults and gangs didn't act like this second woman. She had some other purpose, some other background. Chavali already knew she'd come from elsewhere. Now she suspected this woman had a different agenda than Guyre or his lover and wanted to keep it quiet.

"Could it be that even you fear the Furies?" Chavali asked.

"Of course not." Guyre barked a hollow laugh. "We just don't know where to find them. If we did, we'd do something about them. As you said, they're bad for business."

Chavali decided to call his bluff. "Then perhaps we can draw them out for you. My people can certainly find a way to lure them into the open. Then you can ambush them. We're also prepared and willing to cause some trouble for the Fists. I won't promise rooting them out, but we can reduce their impact." Remembering their cover, she added, "In exchange for taking on this level of risk, we expect a year of waived fees, and we expect you to negotiate with the Riverway Guild on our behalf for the same."

His lover murmured something.

Guyre nodded. "I doubt I can get the Riverway people to go along with an entire year."

Chavali stood. "Then I will speak to them instead."

"I believe I can broker this arrangement with the guild on behalf of the Talons," the second woman said. She had a curiously flat Tilan accent, one Chavali thought she'd heard before in this city.

Everyone looked at this woman. She continued to reveal nothing with her body, using only the most efficient gestures as needed.

"But first, I'd like to hear your plan to lure the Furies into the open."

Smoothing her skirt, Chavali considered what people like the Furies might want.

First, even if they had reason to notice her, they didn't have a reason to target her. She needed to make herself into a target with speed, and offer an opportunity along with it. "I intend to ask around about them in a rather unsubtle fashion while making known that I plan to cross the lake to the other side of the city alone, or perhaps with one other person. Some of my colleagues are capable of disguise."

Guyre jumped to his feet and clapped his hands with greedy haste. "Excellent. They're lunatic enough to fall for it."

"Wait." The second woman held up a hand. "I know you're excited to have these problems handled, Guyre, but this plan is far too simplistic. You'll need to put more effort into it than that. We know they're interested in you. That rumor is swirling around. Interested, though, doesn't mean they'll attack or try to abduct you."

"Anna the killjoy," Guyre grumbled. He crossed his arms and sulked.

"I think she's right," the lover said. "They need to get riled up."

Chavali preferred flexibility, but she could come up with more. "Those rumors prove I am quite capable of making myself intriguing to whomever I wish. From intriguing to infuriating is only a small step."

"You could announce you've found their hideout," Anna suggested.

The lover nodded. "Yes! And that you plan to deal with them, once and for all."

Guyre huffed. He'd lost any semblance of control over the room and hated it. "Act like a Spire mage. Haughty and huffy."

"Good idea," the lover cooed at him.

"Go ahead and use that big man as your bodyguard," Anna said. "I don't think they're stupid enough to think one mage would believe herself capable of taking them all down on her own."

"I thank you for the input," Chavali said with a respectful bow of her head. "These are all rumors I can spread quickly. I have a knack for it."

"Good." Guyre stepped out of his petulance to smile for Chavali. "One year is doable for us." He offered his hand to shake with Chavali.

"A pleasure doing business with you, Guyre. "Before I go, though, I have a question." Eager to know his thoughts, Chavali took it and shook with him.

For now, she didn't want to know about the deal or any plans to double-cross them, or anything of that sort.

His face echoed the smugness of his thoughts as he considered what he could do in a room alone with her. "Oh? Please do ask."

"What did you really discover in the mountain's heart?"

As his thoughts shifted to overpowering rage holding in check tremendous despair, purple crept around the edges of Chavali's vision.

She caught her breath, wishing the spirits could have picked a better time.

"Clarity," Guyre said with a sour frown.

Purple engulfed the world. Chavali wanted to hold back the words. Her mouth opened anyway.

"Scepter draws blood from her loyal beast. Bite the hand as she tempts with a traitorous feast. Seething, reeling, falling, kneeling. Knight of the west sees pain released."

She yanked her hand free and reached for the couch arm.

Guyre gasped. "What was that? Who are you? What does that mean?"

Agony flooded Chavali's head. Someone caught her before she fell to the floor. Confused and distressed voices battered her brain. One voice commanded the others.

Sivry knew what to do. She made everyone else shut up and helped Chavali lie on the couch. Knowing about the pouch Chavali kept on her belt, she called for a cup of hot water. Soon, Chavali's unique, repulsive blend of herbs would chase away the pain.

When Colby heard about this, he'd lecture for days about the folly of leaving without him.

If he'd come, he would've known to sweep her out of the Talons' hideout at full speed. She wouldn't have suffered so long. Whatever else he could think of to express his anger and frustration would pour out of his mouth.

Chavali could hardly wait.

CHAPTER 13

The vile tea forced the pain to retreat, leaving Chavali with fog in her head and the taste of linen on her tongue. Sivry and Jaris, without explaining anything, convinced Guyre and the two women to relax and wait while Chavali recovered.

As she sat up, the rest of the room leaned closer. Their anticipation pressed against her temper.

"It is a warning, delivered by the Creator." She knew the Creator had nothing to do with her prophecies, but preferred not to explain the truth. The clan kept whatever secrets it could. "This warning is intended for you," she told Guyre, "not me. I have no special understanding of the meaning. I am a vessel, not a translator."

"So this is a message for me." Guyre's face flashed with wonder, then he frowned at the floor. "I don't understand it."

This dimwit wanted her to explain it to him.

Chavali wanted him to show up with allies to help fight the Furies. She swallowed several choice insults and sought to make him feel special.

"She can speak only in riddles, the meaning of which can only be deciphered by the recipient. You have the key to unlocking this riddle, Guyre. Only you. No one else has your experiences or wits."

He liked this answer. Guyre puffed his chest enough to notice and adopted a pose of demonstrative thoughtfulness worthy of any lousy stage actor.

"How fascinating." Anna reached toward Chavali. "It happens when you touch someone?"

"Yes, but only once in a while. I doubt it will happen again any time soon." Chavali ignored Anna's hand. "Despite this unexpected event, I see no reason to postpone our deal. Once I have rested, I will arrange my part of the bargain. Someone will bring a message when we are ready to enact it."

Nodding and still deep in fake thought, Guyre waved for them to go.

Chavali stood with Sivry's help.

Anna also stood. "Before you go, may I ask you a few more questions about this unique gift? It—"

"I have no wish to be rude, but I must rest now." Chavali had no need to feign weakness. She let Sivry support her as much as possible. "It's quite taxing on me."

"Another time, then?" Anna flashed her a friendly smile.

"Another time," Chavali agreed.

Jaris led them out of the building.

"Good thing you carry that pouch," Sivry murmured.

"Yes."

"What happened in there?" Jaris asked.

"Something best not discussed in the open." Chavali pointed to an alley overflowing with ferns and flowers.

They sat in a natural nook surrounded by large leaves and fronds. The morning's rain had already slid down stems and dripped to the ground. Heat sapped what little strength Chavali had.

She wanted a dull, quiet room with cushions. Instead, she had a cacophony of flowers shoving their myriad fragrances at her, dogs barking, and damp earth to sit on.

"I occasionally act as an unwilling conduit for accurate prophecies," Chavali said to Jaris. "When the Creator is finished with me, she leaves terrible agony in her wake. As if She must plunge fingers into my mind to do it and Her withdrawal leaves me scrambling to heal in Her wake."

Jaris stared at her in awe.

Sivry jerked a thumb over her shoulder to indicate the direction they'd come. "Don't you usually try to help the target understand what you said? I thought you had a good handle on how these things work. But you told Guyre you're just a vessel?"

"As if I would waste my energy to help that man." Chavali snorted. "A scepter is a symbol of rulership. Consul Shore has revealed to me that she intends to use the Talons until they're no longer of any value, then crush them. This is the basic warning. We all know someone who considers himself a knight and has come from the west. Presumably, Colby will have some hand in his arrest, or perhaps he'll accidentally shield Guyre from attack."

"Or it could be Rowan," Sivry said. "He's a knight, and west of here is a lot of territory. We don't know where he's from."

Chavali waved to dismiss the subject. "Whichever of these two men it refers to is irrelevant. This is the least cryptic prophecy I have delivered in some time. It's of little concern. We have more important matters at hand."

Sivry frowned and twitched her mouth in thought. "It doesn't worry you that the Creator decided to warn that guy, of all people?"

"She may very well choose also to warn Consul Shore if I touch her." Though she preferred the simpler task of reading people by stealing their thoughts, Chavali didn't need anyone else witnessing her curse. Under no circumstances would she touch Consul Shore.

"It's through touch." Jaris raised his hand as if he expected her to shake with him, much like Anna had.

"Yes." Chavali crossed her arms, tucking her hands out of sight. "That is also how my telepathy works. Contact only. I can control neither."

He looked at his hand and blinked. Then he touched his neck. "You said you're a telepath, but I thought it took effort. Visible effort, I mean. When you messed with me in Ket, you did nothing I could see or feel."

Neither Jaris nor Sivry needed to hear about what her gifts truly cost her. Chavali shrugged. "Stealing souls is a more frightening story."

Jaris let out a breath and shook his head. "You're amazing at selling it."

She closed her eyes and leaned her head against the wall. "I have had a great deal of practice. But more importantly, we must create this situation the Furies feel is too good to ignore. I don't trust the Talons to prevent my injury or capture, so we need a plan."

"Colby would probably be helpful for that," Sivry said.

"Yes, he would." Chavali had a thought to check with Korrya. The woman had taken at least one of the Furies into custody, then the guards had lost them. She might want a second chance to catch one or two, and to hold them in her own fashion. "But I wish to speak with the mage Korrya, and Colby is wary of her. I believe they crossed paths in his first life."

"You don't know?" Jaris asked. "Why don't you just ask him and take the answer?"

Chavali thought about how to answer without revealing more than she wanted. "That would be incredibly rude." She opened her eyes to see him with his brow furrowed. "Telepathy is not a tool to use lightly, or as a weapon against those I consider friends and family."

"You used it against me when I was a stranger. Now that I'm on the same team, you won't?"

"Not on purpose."

He rubbed his forehead, twitched his mouth, and finally shook his head. "I've never met anyone with that kind of moral compass. Everyone I've ever known would keep it a secret and use it indiscriminately to gain and keep the upper hand."

Packing a decade of pain and frustration into a short explanation sounded like too much work at the moment.

Chavali also didn't want to talk about the telepath who'd preyed upon her.

She shrugged. "There are more important things than keeping an unfair advantage over my allies."

"All Fallen telepaths follow a code similar to that," Sivry said. "Eldrack made that clear to me early on when I asked about Railan."

Jaris looked at his hand again.

Chavali suspected he'd soon arrive at certain conclusions she preferred not to discuss with him or Sivry. Unlike Colby, she had no need to discuss their peculiar issues with anyone other than her healer, or perhaps clan.

"We should see Korrya." She stood with the help of the wall. "My head will clear by the time we figure out where to find her."

Jaris hovered on the edge of offering help, full of indecision. "Why find her?"

Waving him off, Chavali drew a few breaths to steady herself. "I am about to set myself up to be attacked by a force with unknown capability. It's in our best interest to collect as much assistance as possible."

"Do you really think Guyre will send anyone to set up an ambush to help you?" Jaris asked. "Because I don't think he will. He doesn't gain much by backing us."

Sivry fell into step beside Chavali as they started walking. "I don't think he'll be able to resist the chance to take out the Furies. That woman behind him thinks they're a big problem."

Chavali concentrated on making sure she didn't trip over herself or walk into a wall. The fuzziness in her head had faded enough so she could stand on her own, at least. "I'm not sure if he'll risk any of his people. He does want to remove the Furies. How he and his people treat this opportunity is questionable. They're devoted to this idea of one life and nothing after it. They may not wish to risk themselves."

"I don't understand why anyone would think that," Jaris said. "It's clear we all rejoin with the Creator when we die."

Sivry snorted. "That's clear, is it? Maybe to you. My order is sure there's a veil between this world and the next, and only through death can we pierce it."

"My clan considered it unknowable." This was a complete lie, but Chavali knew Colby and many other people in the world believed it even if her clan didn't. She elected to represent them for Jaris's benefit.

He would have to take the time to re-examine all his beliefs and find ways to reconcile them with his own death. The sooner his mind picked at the problem, the better.

Jaris furrowed his brow and looked at the ground. Good.

"Regardless," Chavali said with a shrug, "holding a daft belief doesn't make them less sentient or dangerous, it merely makes them strange and challenging to predict. Which is the other reason I want as much backup as possible."

"Then we should get going." Sivry patted Jaris's shoulder. "Do either of you know where do we find Korrya? Because I don't."

The answer to that question took an hour to discover. Polite, discreet inquiries brought them to the base of the waterfall feeding the lake.

Several buildings, all sharing the same unusual shape, clustered on a strip of shoreline beside it. Stone covered with thriving moss formed the rounded roofs and sides facing the waterfall. Their rounded angles sent the water sluicing down the stone and back into the lake. Trees and shrubs, trained into a precise thicket, provided the remaining walls.

From this angle, Chavali noticed the mouth of a steep, narrow channel curving around the side of the waterfall with a paddle-tipped wheel on one side and a path on the other. At the base, a metal rod connected to the wheel jutted into a long, low building. The precision of the channel's blank stone walls and walkway suggested someone had carved it, perhaps with magic. Perhaps they used it to haul boats to the top of the waterfall, though she couldn't imagine why anyone would do such a thing.

Along the cliff face, where the water tumbled from a great height to reach the lake, fine, narrow nets hung, tied between horizontal poles. The netting, made of a material similar in shade to both the rock face and water, stood out. She had to stop and stare at them to figure out why. With such a close tonal match, Chavali shouldn't have noticed any of it.

Magic.

"What do you suppose those are?" Sivry asked.

"No idea. She probably knows." Chavali pointed at the building they'd been directed to. "I wonder if you two should hide while I talk to her? I don't think she connected us before."

Sivry frowned. "I don't like leaving you alone. Something bad usually happens."

"Aren't we supposed to protect each other?" Jaris asked. "As a team? Full of people who don't evade each other?"

Chavali snorted. "I leave the choice in your hands. I don't fear a Spire mage and her bodyguard when they're willing to announce themselves as such."

"She has a point," Jaris said. "They aren't being coy about their affiliations."

"I still don't like it," Sivry said. "Chavali is pretty good at getting into trouble."

"If you take much longer to decide, the point will become moot." Chavali crossed her arms while she waited, bemused by their discussion. "These buildings do have windows."

Sivry shrugged. "Let's just go in with her. I think we're fine at this point. Besides, we don't want them to mistake us for Furies."

"Fair," Jaris said.

Grinning at their deliberations, Chavali shook her head and led them to Korrya's home. As promised, they identified it at once by the weathered metal rendering of the Spire's symbol, a pair of entwined spirals forming a tower, hanging on the door.

Korrya's mlinzi opened the door to greet them. He wore a loose vest without a shirt and loose pants, offering Chavali a pleasant view of his muscular chest. She'd seen the tattoo work on his right arm before, and now saw it extended across his right shoulder and pectoral muscle.

His polite interest turned to a friendly smile of greeting. "Chastity, it's nice to see you again. Did you come to speak with Korrya?"

Chavali couldn't remember his name. She had no idea why he remembered hers after such a brief meeting under such distracting circumstances. "Yes, thank you."

He stood aside and let them into the house. They stepped into a cozy sitting room with two plush couches and an armchair. Potted plants hung in the corners with vines trailing to the floor. Light streamed through windows, glowing on the warm wood floor. The raven the mlinzi had carried on his shoulder sat on a simple wooden perch jutting from the wall with its head tucked under its wing.

Without knowing either Korrya or her mlinzi, Chavali liked them. Certainly, the pair had saved her and Colby from a likely death, but also their mingled tastes spoke of comfort without indulgence and an appreciation of simple beauty without snobbery.

A shame she had to keep Colby and Karias away from them both for their own safety.

"Please, have a seat. I'll let her know you're here." The mlinzi shut the door with a soft click and watched while Chavali sat on a couch. Sivry stepped to the window and peered outside. Jaris ran his hand along the back of the couch as if to check for dust.

The mlinzi nodded to them and left through a curtain separating the sitting room from the rest of the house.

Chavali leaned into the couch, finding it as soft and comfortable as it looked.

"Nice view." Sivry pointed out the window. "If you like these trees and ferns. Which I think I've seen enough of to last the rest of my life. I'm fond of the maples where we live. And snow. I like snow."

"Speak for yourself," Jaris grumbled. "I hate the cold. This place is wonderful."

"It's like this year-round," Korrya said as she slipped past the curtain with a cheerful smile. She didn't carry her staff and wore the same light fabrics as the locals with soft indoor shoes. In an intriguing contrast with her casual, plain dress, her light hair lay coiled atop her head in elaborate braids to create the illusion of a crown. Tiny beads peeked through the braids, catching the light at random moments as she moved.

Chavali stood and shook hands with Korrya. In their fleeting contact, she caught nothing more than curiosity about them and their purpose. "How interesting for how high it is here. One expects the mountains to be colder than the valleys below it." She sat as Korrya did.

Sivry and Jaris remained standing, acting like Chavali's guards or keepers. The mlinzi returned and leaned against the wall with a deceptively lazy posture.

Korrya took the couch opposite Chavali's. "Yes. It's one of the reasons I'm here. The whole basin is fascinating. I actually came because of the waterfall, though. It's unusual to find a significant community near one this high, with such easy transportation options."

"May I ask about the netting on the waterfall?"

"Oh yes, it's quite exciting." Korrya's eyes sparkled with enthusiasm. "I'm working on a method to harness energy from the falling water. Anyone can do that with a wheel, of course, but wheels only collect kinetic energy for mechanical uses. With this experiment, I'm collecting magical energy and transforming it to kinetic, effectively making those large, clunky wheels obsolete. There's something quite unique going on here, because I'm not sure this is possible anywhere else in the world. My biggest hurdle at this point is storing and transferring the energy, both of which are challenging to connect to the nets."

The waterfall had magical energy.

Obviously, something here had some kind of magical energy. Palmia Basin sweltered. Cities in the mountains did not swelter.

Once before, Chavali had encountered mages attempting to harness an unusual source of magical power. In that case, the flowers in question had helped werewolves keep control of their shifting.

She wondered what other adaptations the waterfall had caused. Did the waterfall create magical energy, or was it the water itself?

Perhaps the mountain hid secrets it preferred not to share.

"Once I figure that out," Korrya continued, "we'll be able to do amazing things here in Palmia Basin. So many possibilities! Linking it to the boats could provide faster travel without the need for oxen. We could reduce the influence and power of the Riverway Guild, making trade here more affordable. Not that you care, of course, since you're clearly not what you claim."

Chavali blinked at her. The woman had given no sign she'd seen through their story. No one else had questioned it for a moment. She scrambled for an answer to deflect the conversation.

For once, she came up with nothing. That left her with no other recourse than to determine what Korrya already knew.

"Excuse me?"

CHAPTER 14

"Oh come now." Korrya chuckled. "You don't work for a spice merchant any more than I do. You may have fooled everyone else, but you're not behaving like a merchant's scouts. And you certainly aren't the kind of people who do that kind of work. What are you really up to in Palmia Basin?"

The lack of any bite to Korrya's accusation gave Chavali some comfort. That Korrya knew little and guessed much made Chavali want to laugh at herself for worrying too much.

She elected to offer a minimalist version of the truth. "We came to help a friend of a friend who is having trouble with the gang situation."

"Would this friend of a friend happen to be the owner of that burning building?"

Did Chavali have a reason to lie? No. It explained why they'd helped Torrel. "Yes."

"Interesting." Korrya glanced at her mlinzi. Some kind of communication passed between them. "I don't suppose you're willing to divulge who the friend is?"

"No." Now that Korrya knew enough of the truth, Chavali shifted to the reason they'd come. "I will say they prefer my team to leave places in a better circumstance than when we arrived. This is our goal. To that end, we're hoping you're willing to assist us with apprehending the Qanafe Furies. This is why we came today."

The mlinzi cleared his throat. "We've been trying to do just that at the request of Consul Shore since shortly after they made themselves known with a first rash of fires. No one knows where to find them. Even when we do catch one or two, they slip out of the Guard's hands so easily we might as well have not bothered."

Chavali had to wonder if the Guard let these people go on purpose. If Faillit or one of her people wanted chaos for some reason, they had an incentive to allow them to continue to operate. Her people had also already proven susceptible to bribery.

"Have you lost prisoners more than once?" Sivry asked.

He nodded and grimaced. "They're distressingly capable of extracting each other from custody during transport. If we could get them all in one place at one time and capture or kill them all, I think we might stand a chance."

"I believe I can do this," Chavali said. "By making myself into a target. They are already aware of me, so I need only to make clear that I am also aware of them and intend to confront them, then to stage a moment perfect for an ambush."

"And a counter-ambush," the mlinzi said, nodding his approval. "How fast do you think you can get them riled up?"

Chavali shrugged. She didn't want anything to happen to Flower Beds, Iker, or Torrel. That meant moving quickly and decisively. "Before nightfall."

He coughed. "You don't do things halfway, do you, Chastity?"

"No." Chavali also didn't want to come back to this house if she didn't have to. "The ambush point will be a boat crossing the lake from this side to the other."

"I feel it's important," Korrya said, "that I say quite clearly that I must retain the appearance of impartiality as a representative of the Spire. Responding to fires is one thing. Openly participating in an ambush is quite another. That said, we can disguise Rowan well enough to be on that boat with you, and I can happen to coincidentally have decided to take a meal nearby."

Chavali gestured to Sivry and Jaris. "These two will also be in disguise, as will two others."

Korrya raised her brow. "Is one of them that tall man from the fire?

Because I don't think you can disguise him."

"Yes, and this is probably true." Chavali noticed the mlinzi glance at his bird for the first time since they'd arrived. "After his behavior in the fire, I doubt his presence will dissuade them."

Rowan nodded. "Agreed. What's his name?"

She saw no way to avoid telling them. "Colby." Standing, she flashed them a polite smile. "If we are to create this situation, we should go."

"I feel like I've met Colby before," Rowan said. "Do you know if he ever had dealings with the Spire?"

"I don't believe he has. At least, nothing of significance. Are there others here from your order we can ask for help with this?"

Chavali had every intention of asking Colby about his history with the Spire. His version of the story would, no doubt, prove enlightening. Later, though. Prying out that tale would lead naturally to discussing Karias.

"Not that I know of," Korrya said. "We're only here because of the waterfall. I can't imagine what would bring anyone else from the Spire to a place like this. Palmia Basin has no other magical or geographical anomalies. Aside from the weather, nothing about the location or its flora is unusual. There's nothing else to study. It would be boring."

Chavali nodded, pleased she had to manage only two people with a troublesome connection on Colby's behalf. "Then we should go and get to work."

"Of course." Rowan opened the door for them. "I'll meet you and Colby on the docks this evening."

The three of them trooped out of the house.

Jaris turned back before the foliage blocked their view of the house. "I feel like I missed something with that last exchange. Why did he want to know about Colby?"

"Colby is kind of hard to miss," Sivry said. "He's not forgettable. That guy probably met him somewhere."

"Probably. It's not important." Chavali waved for them to take a different route back to Flower Beds. "You should both go and work on your disguise for later. I'll return to the inn and explain to Portia and Colby."

"I know better than to argue with you," Sivry murmured. "We'll meet you at the docks later."

"If you see a good opportunity, gossip about a foreign woman with a feather on a quest to find the Qanafe Furies. Embellish as you see fit, but do not mention the inn." Chavali waved to them, confident Jaris and Sivry had enough skill to drop such information in a way that would help rather than hinder.

The pair turned down a street while Chavali continued on her way. She strolled, watching for places to return with Colby at her back while she planted rumors and caused trouble.

Dogs, chickens, and children chased each other up and down the streets. When she passed a road lined with market stalls, the clashing aromas of scented oils, herbs and spices, and fresh fruits lured her down the street.

She'd seen other permanent markets like this one in places with similar weather. Unlike those areas on the southern shores of Mecalle and South Cascain, Palmia Basin never had to worry about hurricanes or high waves roiled by storms at sea. As a result, most stalls consisted of one or more rugs, four poles, and a large piece of cheap fabric over the ends of the poles to provide shade. Some offered their wares on wooden racks, others on trays or platters on the ground.

Chavali passed several stalls, ignoring the questions and sales pitches hurled at her. She stopped when she found one carrying only qanafe in all its forms. As befitting the agent of a spice merchant, she inspected the powdered seeds and purchased a small quantity.

While tucking the pouch into her pocket, she caught sight of someone swaggering. She turned to see them and noted five people with the sash belts of the Withered Fists moving as a unit. The one in the center walked with the confident assurance of a tyrant surveying her fiefdom. Around them, people kept their heads down.

Watching them would provide her valuable information. The Fists needed to be dealt with as much as the Furies.

Turning her attention to the next market stall, she pretended interest in chicken feathers and feet. The cluster of Fists swiped fruit along their way. They shoved people who didn't get out of their way fast enough.

Chavali swooped in and aided an old woman they'd knocked to the ground. The spirits swarmed through their skin contact to deliver the elder's thoughts.

::Those kids need a beating. If I had the strength, I'd deliver it.::

People feared the Furies. They merely felt powerless against the Fists. Torrel's neighborhood guild likely had the ability to keep the second kind of threat in check.

Unless they had a deal with the guards. Chavali saw two guardsmen greet the gang members like friends. They shook hands, patted each other on the back, and laughed out loud. One Fist tossed a piece of stolen fruit to one of the guards.

No wonder someone like Wray had earned so much hate from his fellow guards. Chavali knew she'd just witnessed a payoff with the fruit as a tip. From the faces around her, the locals all knew it too.

She wanted to do something. The impulse surprised her, because she didn't know these people and owed them nothing.

Colby's sense of justice had infected her.

Of course, such brazen corruption had frustrated her before, but not with this churning sense of betrayal. These ordinary people wanted to survive and have simple comforts. They deserved guards willing to help ensure that.

Yes, the guards infuriated her the most. Gangs happened anywhere. Corruption happened among the powerful everywhere. Guards normally stood as the common folk's line of defense against this kind of thing.

Chavali had a thought to use these traitors for her own ends. To do that, though, she needed to know more about them. Following them would take time she didn't have. Besides, Colby had probably worked himself into a froth by this point.

She'd scoffed at the notion the two of them shouldn't work together anymore. Perhaps she needed to reconsider.

With an annoyed huff, she paused at a market stall while the two guards continued on their way. The elder woman running it sat on a woven rug, surrounded by bins holding onions, garlic, and a few kinds of starchy roots.

"I've heard," Chavali said, choosing her words with care, "about a group called the Qanafe Furies and I wonder—"

The woman shushed her. "Don't say the name so loud."

Chavali had expected this kind of response. She frowned as she inspected an onion, though, playing a part. "Why not? I don't fear them."

"Then you're a fool. Go away. Don't bring them here."

She made a show of shrugging like she thought the woman silly, and left. The first seed planted, she debated staying out in the city to do more of this. The longer she spent letting people see and hear her prodding about the Furies, the sooner they'd come for her.

Except she needed Colby with her. She'd paused here to avoid him.

"Coward," she muttered to herself. Again. This man forced her into the least comfortable positions imaginable. And she let him do it.

Squaring her shoulders, she marched herself to the inn. Along the way, she paid attention because she needed to. An Agent's job demanded it.

She could not pause long enough to barge into the shop she noticed under siege by Fists.

They outnumbered her and she didn't have backup. Killing any of them could bring unwelcome scrutiny or cause her arrest.

Flower Beds appeared long before she wanted to see it. The cheerful front door to the common room loomed. She skirted around the large building in favor of the cabin she shared with Colby. He had no reason to wait there. By her reckoning, Colby would sit with Portia after eating. They could even have plunged into the city together, looking for their own information.

She unlocked the door with her key and stopped in the doorway. Where she'd expected to find an empty space, she instead discovered Colby. He lounged on the bed, reading a book. He'd changed his clothes and combed his short hair, but hadn't shaved. The stubble would feel rough on her cheek yet soft on her fingertips.

A desperate desire to flee and seek out simpler problems warred with an equally powerful desire to slip between him and his book.

His quiet lack of reaction gave her no guidance for which to choose.

At some point, he'd stepped into her blind spot. She'd lost the ability to read him without fail. No one else had ever done that to her. While she could still gauge him most of the time, he'd developed an uncanny knack for confounding her at the worst possible moments.

Without looking up from his book, Colby asked, "Get into any trouble?"

"This depends upon the definition you use." She shut the door.

He glanced at her over his book, then turned the page and focused on it again. "I found this in the common room. It's a collection of local stories. There's a lot of insight here, into the history of the city and its layout. Have you heard anything about the mountain's heart yet?"

"I have heard it holds a dragon." Chavali stepped out of her sandals and left them by the door. She could spare whatever time he needed to take.

"There's no such thing as dragons."

"I agree."

"I'm glad there are actual things we can agree on."

She resisted the urge to sit with her back to him. Cowards did such things. "You're angry."

Colby sighed and set aside his book. "I'm not." He held out a hand for her. "Not much, anyway."

Chavali stared at his hand from across the small room. He always gave her so much space. Years of wishing for the freedom he offered made refusing to take advantage of it seem petty and childish. She climbed onto the bed and sat beside him. Leaning her head against his shoulder, she refrained from touching his bare skin.

He leaned his head against hers. "It's hard to be angry with you for following a lead and taking two people as backup. Especially for that particular lead. Why didn't you wake me when you left, though?"

Portia had done a better job of explaining than Chavali had expected. "I slept poorly. You don't deserve to suffer because I do."

"Whether I deserve it or not isn't important. What you need is important. What I can help you deal with is important. You know you can wake me to sit with you while you recover from a nightmare, Chavali, and yet you never do."

"I don't need that from you." She cut herself off before she told him Karias had helped her more than once. The words hovered on the tip of her tongue, wanting to break loose.

If this kind of moment happened again, she would accidentally tell him before they returned home. "It's better for everyone if I—"

"I don't care about everyone."

Chavali's chest warmed and she wanted to say something stupid. Lifting her head, she met his gaze with a smile. "Then I will say it's better for *you* to sleep."

He leaned close to kiss her. They didn't have time for that.

"I do need your help to pick a fight."

Colby sighed. "Of course you do." He kissed the tip of her nose with contact so fleeting the spirits didn't have time to collect his thoughts. "Who are we picking a fight with and why?"

"The Qanafe Furies, to make people happy."

"Right." He gave her a look she knew well, one that demanded more information before he accepted what she said.

"Certain specific people. Torrel, for example. Iker. Also Korrya. Perhaps others."

"Korrya." Colby sat up and put his feet on the floor. "Why mention her?"

This subject carried a great deal of peril. Chavali slid to the edge of the bed and chose her words with care. "She will help us, as will her mlinzi. You and I will move through town, stirring up trouble with them while several forces mobilize to take advantage of the two of us presenting ourselves as a target. Sivry and Jaris are already working on a disguise. Portia will also need to do this. The two of us are terrible at blending, so we won't bother trying."

He nodded. "That's a terrible plan, but it's better than anything else I've got to deal with them."

Hoping to lighten his mood, she said, "At least it won't happen inside a building."

"Oh? Where are you planning for us to be ambushed?"

"On a boat."

She laughed at the look on his face.

CHAPTER 15

Once she knew the plan, Portia headed into the city to find a disguise. Colby, wearing his armor and sword, collected Karias and met Chavali in front of the inn. They strolled through the city, making no effort to seem unconnected.

At every opportunity, Chavali asked about the Furies and intimated she wished to challenge them. People warned her off, tried to dissuade her, or called her crazy.

As a final piece to the puzzle, she boldly claimed she knew they had a hideout on the other side of the lake and meant to challenge them today.

By the time she and Colby reached the docks in the lazy heat of late afternoon, Sivry and Jaris had found someplace to perch near the passenger ferries. Their disguises worked well enough to keep Chavali from noticing them on first glance. She didn't see Portia or Rowan at all, though she did recognize Korrya taking a seat in a cafe on the water's edge.

Colby pointed to a ferry barge. He made an effort to extend his arm so everyone watching would see it. "I think that's big enough for my horse."

The square, flat-bottom boat had enough space for a small army, which suited Chavali's purposes. Railings lined the four edges, with a single hinged gate on one side for entry and exit. She nodded and headed for it, taking care to appear focused on it as if she had nothing else in mind.

As they walked, she caught people tracking their movements with a distinct lack of subtlety. Chavali didn't recognize them as Talons, but figured they'd dressed to blend. Guyre had some small amount of sense within his madness. Perhaps a few had worn their fake guardsman uniforms and pretended to patrol.

They approached the man taking passengers for the barge. A woman and two men boarded before them.

The barge man looked over Karias with a raised brow. "Can you control that horse?"

"Yes. He's well-trained. When I tell him to stay still, he stays still."

Chavali could imagine Karias's offense at the suggestion he might bolt or overturn the boat. The thought made her smother a grin. To assuage the barge man's concerns, though, she paid him double the fee he asked for the crossing.

Three crewmen handled ropes and directed the two dozen passengers to keep certain areas clear. Chavali thought the boat could hold another dozen more without feeling crowded. People had room to sit together and set down sacks or baskets.

They gave Karias plenty of space, which meant Chavali could act her part without worrying about a stealthy knife between her ribs.

Colby made a show of ordering Karias to stay still in the center of the boat. Karias made a show of strict obedience. Chavali produced a fat, thick berry of a local type she'd purchased in the market. The horse inhaled it off her palm.

::This is why I don't complain very much about how you have such an amazing penchant for tying him into knots. So thoughtful under that irritating façade.::

Unable to respond directly, she gave him a sideways glance.

::Of course, half of the reason you're tying him in knots is my fault. Do you have another?::

Chavali produced a second berry. Karias whuffed it off her hand.

"Don't spoil him," Colby said.

::Never mind him. He uses that word, but it doesn't really mean what he thinks it means.::

"Is it not one piece of fruit for each leg?"

::Clearly, the clan has the best rules.::

Colby rolled his eyes. "No."

Karias nudged Colby's arm and gazed at him like a begging puppy.

::I think you should distract him so I can have another. Wait. Do I smell...what is that? What else do you have in that amazing bag at your side? You sneaky woman. How did I not notice you buying all these things?::

"He's a horse, Chavali. He may be smart for a horse, but that doesn't change the fact he can only digest so much of this stuff. The apples I know you give him when I'm not around are fine, but he's never had these things before."

One member of the barge crew closed the gate while the other two untied the ropes holding the barge in place. Set adrift, the boat glided across the lake's smooth surface without bobbing or rocking.

"What about this?" Chavali produced a radish with the greens still attached.

Colby huffed. "Save it for later."

::Such a cruel master. Pass it to me when he's not looking. If you don't tell him, neither will I.::

Still holding the radish, Chavali asked, "Are you sure? He's a very large horse."

"Yes, I'm sure."

"You poor thing." Chavali tucked the radish into her bag. She watched Colby with a suppressed grin and rubbed Karias's nose. "You suffer so much."

"I have no doubt he's forgotten what suffering is like with you and the kids around."

Karias whickered. *::I remember standing in pouring sheets of rain while you hid inside your tent, Colby. We didn't have a feed bag, so I got grain in a bucket, the frigid water overflowing before I finished. My hoof stuck in the mud and sucked up a rock, and I froze for a day because no blanket could keep away the chill in that mess.::*

He painted a picture vivid enough to make Chavali shiver despite the heat. She kissed his nose in shared sympathy. "Don't listen to him. I know you work very hard for us."

::But I will admit that I do have a rather pleasant life most of the time now. He hasn't tried to run me into the ground more than a handful of times since becoming Fallen, and one of them was for you.::

Colby rolled his eyes and huffed again.

The barge floated toward the ferry line, remaining stable as it passed other boats. Two of the crew held large hooks attached to ropes while the third pushed them toward it with a long pole.

Chavali shifted her attention to the rest of the people on the barge.

She knew that group of three watched her with excessive interest. The other pair over there were Sivry and Jaris. Portia had not joined them on the boat, which didn't surprise Chavali. Rowan stood at the bow. The remaining seventeen people on board concealed their motives and interest well enough to keep her from deciding who they all represented.

She slipped her hand into Colby's, wanting to know his thoughts on the subject of their true intent here. "We could all use less suffering. Like today. This ride is pleasant."

::If I were prepping this ambush, I'd wait to spring it until we neared the halfway point, then I'd cut the ferry line if possible, or this barge's hook lines if not. Karias is the biggest target, and I think I've given the impression of a bodyguard well enough that they'll go after us before targeting you. They might use fire again, but it won't be hard to use the fact we're surrounded by water to minimize that danger.::

He considered a variety of options for dousing flames on the boat. Each centered around a different approach the Furies might take.

"The weather is warm for my tastes, though." She nodded to him and thought about what kinds of illusions would work well in this situation.

"Agreed." *::Hopefully, our enemies will reveal themselves soon. Stay close so I can keep track of you.::*

Nodding again, Chavali let go and stretched her arms. When she relaxed, she settled her hands on her hips. This put one hand close to the hilt of the dagger at the small of her back.

The smooth, calm ride passed with the screech of birds, the ripple of water, and the murmur of voices.

As they neared the halfway point of the ride, she wondered if the Furies had failed to take her bait.

Anyone present could have accidentally tipped them off to the force they could expect to encounter. Perhaps they preferred to attack at random.

They might balk at facing Karias. If they preferred fire, water might dissuade them.

Someone squawked with surprise at the rear of the boat. As Chavali turned, she heard a splash. Shouting filled the air. The barge wobbled as people rushed toward the splash and the captain tried to stop them.

She slid her hand to her dagger. This kind of small chaos likely signaled the start of the attack.

"Steady," Colby murmured. "Don't let it distract you."

Though Chavali watched the front end instead of the commotion at the rear, she couldn't tell who cut the rope for the first ferry hook. The front end of the barge swung to the side. Chavali staggered to keep her balance. Colby steadied her with one hand while drawing his sword with the other.

The barge sloshed sideways.

Chavali stumbled away from Colby and Karias.

Chaos erupted. Screams, shouts, and the clangs of sudden combat filled the air. One moment, people milled, confused. The next, Colby dodged a dagger aimed at his gut. A man knocked Chavali to the deck with a fist to her side. Karias kicked someone behind him. People with blades leaped from a boat traveling in the other direction. They used grappling hooks to swing from the ferry lead to the barge.

Chavali drew her dagger as she rolled to her feet. In her experience, she didn't belong in the thick of a battle so sprawling and confused. She had to judge friend from foe in a split second, and had no idea how to identify any Talon allies they hopefully had in this mess.

The man intent on her, though, she could fight.

She watched his shoulders and face, as Eliot had taught her. Once he'd explained how people move in combat, her training in body language had helped her a great deal.

He rushed her. She slid aside and stabbed with her dagger. The steel teeth of her spiral blade scraped across his upper arm, ripping a ragged hole in the thin fabric of his sleeve. He yelped and clutched the minor wound.

Chavali's blade drank the blood it drew, leaving no spatter or spray.

"What is that thing?" he gasped.

Taking advantage of his distress, Chavali rammed the dagger into his side. The man gurgled and spasmed with pain.

She yanked the blade free. He fell.

Chavali spotted Sivry using a wire garrote to slice through a woman's neck. At her back, Jaris kicked a man over the railing.

Rowan hacked off a man's arm with his thick blade. Colby fared well against two men at once. Karias kicked another woman hard enough to send her flying into the water.

Dull pain exploded across Chavali's thigh. She turned and wobbled backward to discover a man taking another swing with his staff. He'd disguised himself as an elder, using the stick for support.

She dropped to one knee and ducked under his next swing. Karias shoved him sideways.

Chavali shoved off her uninjured leg, leading with her dagger. The blade grazed the man across the side, tearing open his shirt without drawing blood.

Karias reared onto his hind legs. The barge shuddered. Chavali and her opponent tumbled to the deck with a thump, a grunt, and a groan.

Karias brained someone, cracking their skull open with a hoof.

Tepid water sloshed across the deck and over Chavali. Metal clanged against metal. Someone growled. Feet and legs splashed.

Chavali's dress clung to her body. Her attacker sputtered and slapped the water, pawing the deck with his empty hands. Her sandals slipped as she tried to stand.

He pounced on her. She flailed with her dagger. He squealed.

As with the other man, the dagger's first bite distracted him enough to leave an opening for the second. Chavali slashed across his neck.

He gurgled and slumped, pawing at the wound. After a moment, his blood stained the thin layer of water around him.

Her dagger glowed as she sat up and surveyed the battle.

Though competent, these people had none of the skill or magic she expected of the Qanafe Furies. Only three Furies had magically repelled fire in a burning building. Mention of their name inspired terror in ordinary people.

These men and women bore much more resemblance to common

thugs than creeping nightmares.

Chavali doubted the Talons would attack her in this situation. Had the Withered Fists come in disguise to fight?

A thick metal spike, as wide as Chavali's waist, punched through the barge from below.

Wood cracked and shattered. Water sprayed in every direction with enough force to shove Chavali to the railing. Splinters stung her cheek and arms.

Karias screamed. Several voices cried out in surprise, shock, or pain. Wood cracked. Heavy things splashed and thumped.

When Chavali opened her eyes again, she saw people crawling out of the water and onto the barge. One, she recognized as the Fury man who'd survived the bakery fire but not escaped until later.

Another eight, all dressed in those same fine linens with embroidered mushrooms, emerged with him.

One woman rose from the water as if she stood on a platform. She was the one who had seen Chavali in that bakery fire, and had escaped it.

Despite her rising from the lake, no water clung to her. She dressed in the same tailored, embroidered shirt and pants as that night in the fire, with the addition of several short blades strapped to her arms and thighs. Her dark hair splayed around her head as if she remained underwater, and she scanned the scene until she stared directly at Chavali.

Chavali met the woman's steely gaze, this time with the certainty she'd stirred a nest far more dangerous than expected.

This floating woman waved both hands with a flourish. Flames sprang from the water's surface and whooshed onto the boat.

Ropes of burning water rose and darted in, snapping like angry snakes. Chavali leaped to the side to avoid one. It slammed into the deck, missing her by scant inches.

Fire spread as the rope fell to join the water. Sheathing her dagger, Chavali scrambled to her feet.

Flames licked to the sky in opaque sheets taller than Karias. Heat radiated from the fire, proving its reality. Chavali ran to Rowan, the only other living person she could see. She wanted to call out for Colby or Karias but didn't dare focus attention on herself.

"I didn't expect this," Rowan said as he raised a hand in a warding gesture.

"Neither did I." Chavali had no defense against normal fire, let alone these strange, water-burning flames.

"Stay close. I'm doing what I can until Korrya gets here."

The flames leaned away from Rowan as if a cocoon surrounded his body. Chavali slipped behind him. His bird dropped out of the sky to land on his shoulder. It cawed.

Rowan nodded. "She's delayed, but guards are on their way."

"Colby, don't panic," Chavali murmured, wishing she could make him hear it.

A thick band of water wrapped around Chavali's waist from behind and yanked her off her feet. She plunged backward into the water.

Nothing she could see dragged her into the depths until the light failed.

CHAPTER 16

Thrashing against her unknown captor, Chavali clawed at the water. After everything she'd suffered through, after all the nightmares and pain, drowning seemed a particularly inane way to die.

Bubbles spiraled around her, tickling her flesh like feathers. Rushing water deafened her. Burning pressure built in her chest.

The lake hadn't seemed this deep.

She scraped at the rope around her waist. Her fingers passed through it to no effect.

Had this same fate taken Colby? She wanted to see. Every direction felt like up and down and sideways all at once. Even if she broke free, she didn't know which way to swim.

How did water burn? Such a useless question to consume her at a time like this.

Her body refused to let her hold her breath any longer. Though she tried not to, her mouth opened and she sucked in dark, silty water. She choked and gagged. Whatever held her refused to let go.

And now, she would die again. The spirits would do what they did the first time. Whatever that had been. They hadn't told her a story about the experience.

This time, they had no chance of a reprieve, and neither did she.

Fear fled her as certainty of death took hold. She wondered what would happen if someone found her body and burned it.

The water pressed close, wrapping her in a gentle embrace. She remembered her mother holding her close as a child. Once upon a time, her father had carried her in his arms. Young Chavali had tripped and scraped her knee, and Papá had scooped her up, giving her the calm assurance of complete safety.

She refused to regret anything. Blaukenevs did not succumb to such pettiness. Instead, she wished she could have had more time.

With Colby. With Eliot. With Biholtz. With Danel, Haizea, Portia, Kelly, Marcus, Penny. With everyone who had come to mean something to her.

Light, velvety caresses kissed her outstretched hand in the darkness. Strong fingers gripped her wrist and held her.

The spirits rushed to leave her, as if someone had cut a gaping wound in her belly and they would spill forth from the hole. She drew her knees close, curling into a ball. Holding onto them might only last a few scant seconds, but she would take every moment she could.

The Seer of the Blaukenev clan did not give up without a fight. She would not willingly allow the spirits to leave her care.

No matter how much hardship they caused her, she had fought, bled, and died for them, and she would not relinquish those souls to anyone but the next seer.

"Guide." A woman's voice, low and commanding, echoed in her ears.

Someone had called her that before. A madman in Harbor City had seen the spirits around her as dark butterflies and had pledged his life to his queen, the Guide. To Chavali.

Water flowed in and out of her as freely as air. She breathed it, tasting life and death.

"You have forgotten your purpose, Sorgeya."

Her purpose had always been to serve the clan, to safeguard its secrets, to teach the children, to choose a successor, to make the sacrifice, to hold the spirits. Chavali had done all these things. Even now, she did all these things.

When she opened her mouth to speak, to deny this baseless accusation, the water kept her silent.

"She calls. Can you hear it? Listen to Her voice."

Chavali heard nothing. Vast, yawning emptiness filled her ears.

"If you want your heart's desire restored, you must listen. You must heed Her call. And you must answer."

Before Chavali could wonder what this meant, her body punched through a barrier as hard as a sheet of wood. Then she slapped against stone. Water heaved out of her lungs.

"Chavali!" Portia knelt by her side and rolled her onto her side. She patted Chavali's cheek. *::We thought you were gone.::*

Gagging on bile and water, Chavali batted feebly with numb hands at Portia to cut off her thoughts. She sucked in ragged, raw breaths, unable to get enough air.

"Karias!" Portia called. She didn't know anything more about him than Colby, but she did know he responded to his name.

As Chavali wheezed, her throat stinging and her head throbbing, hooves thundered to her side. Karias whinnied in alarm. He pressed his nose against her face.

::Colby is missing. I can tell he's moving to the mountain, upriver, which makes no sense. Why did they take him? What do they want? What do I do? The lake is too deep! I can't run like that, and I can't swim that well!::

Chavali shoved against his head. "Stop." She rolled to her side and spat again. Her arms and legs prickled as feeling returned to them. "What did you see?" she said to Portia.

"The fight broke out on the barge. As I moved to get into range to help, another fight broke out on the docks. I wound up in the middle of a gang fight. Talons and Fists. You did your job too well. Everybody knew you were going to be here. By the time I could spare some attention for the barge, it was burning with blue fire reaching ten feet into the air. The guard has some boats out now, looking for survivors in the water."

"Sivry and Jaris?" Still too weak to sit up, Chavali stayed on her side.

Portia looked up and scanned the area. "Picked up. Rowan is with them. They're on a boat together, and it's headed this way."

"That was a surprising end result for your plan, Chastity." Korrya stepped into Chavali's field of view. "I can honestly say I didn't expect you to rile up the entire city's crime elements. I think we even had some independent actors involved in this mess."

Karias stomped his front hooves hard enough to crack stone. Portia and Korrya flinched.

"You haven't asked about Colby yet," Portia muttered.

"I already know about Colby." Chavali braced her arms against the ground and sat up. "Get supplies. We need to travel upriver."

"Are you crazy?" Portia took her by the shoulders. "You almost died, and you want to get up and go now? You need rest. We all do."

"We will have time to rest on the boat." She took a deep breath, intending to stand.

"I can't let you do this." Portia pushed against her. "You can't go running after him right now. It has to wait. He has to wait."

"I'm fine," Chavali snapped. She could handle burning water, losing Colby, and nearly dying if people would not harass her about any of it. Later, she would unpack all of it. Now, they needed action. "If you don't want to come with me, then don't come with me."

"Where's Colby?" Daria stepped into view. Just the person Chavali needed.

"He is in danger, and I need assistance to rescue him." Chavali held up a hand, hoping Daria would take it.

The woman didn't disappoint. Daria grabbed Chavali's hand and yanked her to her feet. *::I don't know what to make of you, but I'd do anything to help Colby.::* "What do you need?"

Portia stepped between them. "Chastity, this is a bad idea. You're not thinking clearly."

Karias whinnied a frustrated war cry.

"You're not helping." Portia jabbed a finger at the horse.

"Neither are you." Daria shoved Portia out of the way. "If Colby's in trouble, then I'm going to get him out of it. Either help or step aside."

"What are you going to do?" Portia poked Daria in the chest. "Shout at the river until it yields? Punch it?"

"I don't know," Daria said. "But I'm going to try, which is more than I can say for you."

Chavali knew Portia had a point. She could tell by how long it took to stop swaying on her feet.

Stepping between Portia and Daria, Chavali held up her hands and used both women for support. "I understand," she told Portia. "If I thought waiting would put him in no greater jeopardy, I would wait. But we must leave as soon as possible. I know how hard sailing is on you. I won't hold it against you if you choose to stay."

For the first time, Portia took Chavali's hand and forced thoughts at her. She'd known for some time how Chavali's telepathy worked, yet had never sought contact before, even in useful situations. *::This is why you shouldn't go on missions together. If you kill yourself chasing him because you couldn't be bothered to take care of your needs, you haven't done him any favors. I know how much he means to you, and I know how much you mean to him. Take a few hours, at least, to change into dry clothes, eat something, and rest. Please. I'll come with you regardless, but I'm begging you to be kind to yourself.::*

"You're too much like my sister," Chavali murmured.

Portia let go of her hand. "I'm still taking that as a compliment, no matter how you mean it."

Chavali nodded and turned to Daria. "One hour." They could spare that long, she thought. The sun would set behind the mountain by then, giving them a cool night to recover from this disaster. "Find us a boat, big enough for Karias, that will take us upriver."

"I'll get some gear too. One hour." Daria clapped Chavali on the shoulder, knocking her into Portia, and jogged down the docks.

"Karias can take me back to the inn," Chavali said as she regained her balance. Only now did she notice she'd lost her sandals in the water. The wet stone heated her feet, which helped nothing. "You fill in Sivry and Jaris. There's a market nearby where you can get food. I don't know how long we'll be on the boat, or wherever we wind up. Plan for a few days, I think."

Portia gave her a boost to climb into Karias's saddle and handed her the key for the second cabin. "Bring our stuff. We'll have a boat, so I'll plan for a week. And I won't forget food for Karias."

The horse had swirling, fear-laced thoughts, all pushing for haste and hurry. The thread connecting him to Colby pulsed with distress.

"I can send Rowan," Korrya said. "He can help."

Chavali struggled to think through Karias's maelstrom of panic. "This is not your fight, and I would not choose to deprive you of your bodyguard when people such as these are riled up."

Portia glanced from Korrya to Chavali and back. "It would help us more if you could keep a watch for our return. We may need a healer for Colby." She paused. "And we'll want to know what really happened here and how it affects the city. Our employer isn't going to like this report unless it's thorough."

Korrya nodded and didn't seem upset. "I understand. I'll see what I can learn, and I'll see about having a watcher set up for your return."

"Thank you," Chavali said.

Portia patted Karias's flank and rushed to go meet the boat. Karias took it as a sign and lurched into a run. They galloped through the city. By the time Karias reached the inn, Chavali no longer dripped. She changed her clothes, put on her boots, collected everyone's belongings, and told Iker to rent out the cabins if he needed to. They'd return, but she didn't know when.

She handed over a few extra coins to make sure Torrel had a place to stay, to keep the horses safe in their absence, and to get a sausage roll. While waiting for her food, she noted Torrel approaching her from the stairs.

"You're leaving?" he asked, sounding conflicted about it.

"Temporarily. We have an emergency to tend elsewhere."

He nodded. "When you get back, I want to show you something I found under the bakery. I didn't know it was there, and I'm not sure what to make of it."

In Chavali's experience, unexpected things under buildings tended to cause trouble. "Is it a passage?"

"No. I...I'm not sure how to explain it." He frowned. "I covered it up so you could get a look at it without anyone disturbing it first."

Under other circumstances, such a curious find would have drawn Chavali's full attention. She wished she could spare the time to investigate. "Good thinking. We hope to return in a few days, but it may take longer.

Keep an eye on it, but don't risk yourself for it."

"No, I wouldn't. I'm just hoping someone can tell me what to do about it."

"Remind me when we come back."

"I will." He gave her a small smile. "I'm really grateful to all of you. I've been helping Iker here, and we've talked about me taking over part of the kitchen duties instead of going back to trying to run a bakery." Leaning close, he murmured, "And I'm kind of taken with him, truth be told."

Wishing she had time to enjoy the moment with Torrel, she forced herself to smile. "I'm glad. Sometimes the worst things that happen to us lead to the best things, yes?"

"Yes, I suppose so."

Iker returned with a lump of bread on a small plate. He flashed a smile at Torrel. The baker melted enough for Chavali to notice as she took the bread.

"I'll see you again soon. Take care with yourselves." Her arms full of backpacks and a sausage roll, Chavali left the inn and hoped she would see it again with Colby by her side.

CHAPTER 17

The man piloting the small boat taking them upriver, a stocky, squinty gentleman with a face weathered by the elements more than age, muttered to himself constantly about drowning, angering spirits, and other such nonsense. Chavali caught the dark looks he flashed at everyone when he thought they couldn't see or wouldn't notice.

Like many boat captains, he'd seen their fate on the ferry barge, and the fate of that craft. Daria had performed a minor miracle in getting him to take them on the journey in the first place. The fee he'd demanded with a craggy snarl could've paid for a week's stay in a lavish resort.

Portia sat at the bow in the dim twilight, relieving her stomach into the river, with Sivry keeping watch over her. Daria sat with them, trying to convince Portia to try a neverending litany of herbal remedies she hadn't brought to soothe her sickness. Jaris rested against the left side railing, watching Chavali as she leaned against the other side.

Karias and all four oxen plodded up the path on the left side of the channel to the top of the waterfall, dragging the boat against the swift current.

Wooden and metal wheels tipped with paddles mounted on the right side of the channel creaked and clanked as the water pushed them. Metal rods connected them in a line. At the bottom of the channel, a final rod passed into a long, low building on the shore.

The whole contraption had the feel of a highly complex mill. Using the channel for some kind of industry made sense, especially when so few people seemed to use it.

They had some space on the boat, but not enough to feel alone anywhere. Chavali could nudge Jaris with her boot if she had the energy to shuffle five or six feet closer.

Beside the captain, his helper lay on the deck, sleeping so she could steer the boat through the night. She shared his build and had the same hawkish nose, leading Chavali to believe they were related. Her younger features, even relaxed with sleep, showed the beginnings of the same sun-kissed wrinkles.

With nothing but wheels, rock, and her companions to watch, and the temperature growing steadily more pleasant, Chavali dozed. She woke when they reached the top of the waterfall under a starry sky in crisp, cool night air.

The captain and his helper moved all the animals onto the boat. Karias settled himself in the center, in front of the resting pen for the oxen. Chavali wanted to help but couldn't muster the energy to do more than take off her boots.

They'd had a long day.

Soon, two oxen plodded on a treadmill inside a pen at the rear of the boat. The other pair lounged in the resting pen, waiting for their turn propelling the boat. The craft had a small space below for cargo, where they stored food for the oxen. Other than an open deck, it boasted a solid railing around the edges, a series of hooks hanging along that railing, and several lengths of rope hanging with the hooks.

Chavali nodded off again as the boat bobbed upriver in the dark. When she woke at the first hint of dawn, she watched the sky brighten with no idea how far they'd traveled or how much further they had to go.

She sat up, yawned, rubbed her eyes, and leaned against Karias.

He looked peaceful and calm.

His thoughts roiled with a desperate need to get to Colby.

She remembered the last time the two had become forcibly separated. In Ket, she'd first discovered he had thoughts of his own when Colby had gone missing. That time, he hadn't displayed this level of frenzied drive to find him.

Perhaps the speed or distance, or the manner of his removal, had caused this. The difference could even relate to Colby's induction in the clan, or a dozen other events.

Trying to find out struck her as an exercise in frustration. Until Karias calmed down, she could learn nothing of value.

The captain's helper piloted the boat through a narrow valley while the captain slept. Foliage grew so thick along the shores they could barely see tree trunks. Vines draped into the water, flowing downriver as far as their roots would allow. As the sun climbed the sky, it baked Chavali more and more. Sweating made her feel grimy without helping her stay cool.

Judging by how frustratingly slowly they floated past the thick plant life, this boat moved half as fast as the one that had brought them to Palmia Basin. Their journey would take far longer than she'd prefer.

Chavali would have plenty of time to fret herself into a froth like Karias. She tried to focus on simple things, like breathing and not melting.

Everyone else woke eventually and shared food. They had little to say to each other. Words seemed like too much work in such abysmal heat. Daria managed to get up and use a bucket to douse everyone who wanted it. The steam it caused, especially on Karias's back, amused Chavali enough to giggle like a twit. It helped. A little.

As the afternoon crept into evening, the heat eased and Chavali perked up. She watched the thinning trees as they passed and enjoyed the occasional glimpses of other peaks in the distance. She spied goats bounding across rocky slopes, large cats lounging on shaded tree branches, and sizable raptors gliding overhead.

Portia still lay on her side, probably wishing for death, but Sivry and Daria chatted amiably about boats and dockworkers.

Jaris moved to Karias's other side, leaning against him to talk to Chavali over his back.

"I have some questions," he said in a low voice. Perhaps he lacked the energy to speak louder, or perhaps he didn't want the others to overhear. Chavali was too tired to care which. "Sivry is my mentor, and I know I could ask her, but you've got a different perspective than her. Besides, you kind of got me into this."

She nodded, expecting him to ask about the mission.

"This, what we're doing right now? It isn't part of the mission, so how do we justify it when we report? Or do we not mention it? Is there a lot of wiggle room for that?"

He'd surprised her. She struggled to focus her wits lest he wheedle secrets out of her. If he'd recovered his sharpness and used it against her, she needed to find hers also. "This is part of the mission."

"Rescuing a member of our team isn't really covered under investigating a specific problem." The way he watched her mirrored the way she watched him.

Born to a different life, Chavali might have become the same kind of spy as he.

"I disagree."

"Of course you do. You're in love with him."

She pursed her lips, annoyed he'd noticed with so little effort. Had they chosen different room arrangements, perhaps Jaris wouldn't have picked up on it so swiftly. Not that he should've paid attention or cared.

Why did everyone want to know? So many questions, all the time. When she didn't answer them, they made up their own answers.

If she kept thinking along these lines, she thought she might hit him for no reason. A team leader shouldn't do that, and neither should a friend. She rubbed her eyes and banished all thoughts of this irritating subject.

"This is not why I disagree," she said after a pause she knew had stretched too long. "I believe you worked alone before?"

"With a superior, but yes."

"We do not work alone."

He frowned at Karias's back. Chavali wondered how, with his clear skills, he'd missed such an obvious point.

"This is about taking care of your team," he said, his words careful and the pauses between them long. At the end, he sounded like he couldn't decide if he meant it as a question or not.

"I will put it a different way." She recalled something Eldrack had told her. "Fallen are a finite resource. We do not have legions, we have around one hundred and fifty. When one is lost, there may or may not be another to take our place. The process used to bring us back is perilous and difficult, and cannot be undertaken on a whim. Also, it can only be done once for any given person.”

Understanding bloomed on his face. “It’s not that this is part of this mission, it’s part of every mission. An implied part.”

“Yes.”

“But this does necessarily make our actual mission harder to accomplish.”

Chavali shrugged. “Perhaps. Considering who took Colby, it’s possible his abduction will take us closer to our goal. In a roundabout fashion.”

“Right. Of course.” He rubbed the fine hair on Karias’s flank. “For someone so emotionally attached to him, you’re awfully calm.”

If only he knew the irony of saying that with his hand on the horse. Chavali wanted to praise Karias for not pitching the man overboard. “Would I accomplish something by displaying my distress?”

“You’d seem more approachable. Less remote.”

She snorted. “For all that I am unapproachable, here you are.”

“True enough.” He echoed her grin, then let it fade. “You’re not worried about him?”

“I am most assuredly worried about him.” Of course, she didn’t worry much. Karias at least knowing where to find him kept her from fretting. “There is no way for me to get there faster, and there is nothing else I can do but sit and keep his horse company. As such, I am doing everything within my power at the moment. Knowing this keeps me relatively content.”

Jaris paused as Portia made rather loud retching noises. He took a few deep breaths and shook himself with a grimace. “Where did you get that dagger you use?”

The abrupt change of subject irritated Chavali only because she hadn’t expected it. “There’s a smith in the tower who made it for me. His name is Kiron.”

“I’ve never seen anything like it. Why did you ask him to make that?”

“I didn’t. He made it without asking my opinion beyond how heavy it should be.” In truth, he’d asked her one question, regarding what she felt a blade should do for her. The answer she’d given—slitting throats—had no place in a conversation with those she barely knew.

"Huh." Jaris drew his dagger and held it up.

Chavali knew little about weapons and couldn't say if he had a nice one or not. One side of the ten-inch blade had a sharp edge and the other didn't. Eliot could've spoken to the quality.

She imagined Colby would take it, turn it over in his hand, and return it with a one-word comment. The one time he'd picked up her dagger, he'd noted the hilt was too small for his hand. Which made sense, as Kiron had designed it for hers. Colby hadn't said anything else about the weapon.

Colby didn't teach her fighting for a reason. He used a large, heavy blade and his fists. And when she'd first met him, of course, she'd avoided him. The oaf had irritated her beyond reason with his ridiculous sense of honor and addiction to honesty.

She recalled an argument between them about the subject of honor in a carriage. The exchange had marked a moment when they'd connected for the first time as something other than two agents forced to work together.

"Does he do that for anyone?"

Jaris's question shook her loose from her thoughts. He wanted to know more about Kiron, as any reasonable person would. "He manages his own time. Ask him if you'd like something. Much of the tower works this way."

He sheathed his dagger and sat with his hands resting on his knees. Something about the pose spoke to discontent, though Chavali couldn't guess why. "Do you remember anything from...you know, between?"

"No. The time is lost to me." She did remember one thing, but he had no business hearing about clan secrets.

"Sivry doesn't either. So I'm wondering what it means that I do?" He fidgeted. "You're a telepath. Can you get into my head and figure it out?"

The crass boldness of asking her to reach into his head and solve a mystery for him made her want to slap him. "No, I cannot. I can try to help you discover the root cause, but dealing with it should be between you and your healer. Even so, I am not the best choice for this, and on a mission is a terrible time to try it."

"Sorry." He hung his head. "I didn't think it was a big deal."

"It may not be, but I won't take the chance, especially when we are outside the tower. Minds are delicate. Tampering with yours carries risks, for both of us. Even mere observation is not a simple matter of looking around. Accidental influence is surprisingly easy to cause."

She'd once spent hours combing through Colby's memories to find damage caused by someone else.

The task had taken weeks, and she'd made mistakes. In truth, she didn't know with absolute certainty she'd found every single instance of meddling. Did he allow the fire to defeat him because of his death, or because of something more sinister?

Perhaps she needed to take the time to delve into his mind again. When they returned, she'd speak to Railan about it. A much stronger and more experienced telepath, she might have some insight, or might have the time to check on him.

Chavali put a hand on Jaris's arm, careful to keep his sleeve between them. "Talk to your healer about it. She can determine if you need intervention or not. And if she's not sure, she has superiors with more experience who can help make that decision."

He nodded, accepting her advice. "Are all the healers women?"

"Yes."

"Isn't that weird?"

She shrugged. "It depends upon how you look at it."

"How do you look at it?"

Only recently had Chavali learned how they created the miracle of returning life to the dead. The information had changed her perspective on her own healer, Kelly. Jaris didn't need to know yet. He needed to settle into his role as Fallen first. "Healing is a rare, special gift from the Creator. It makes sense to me that She would bestow it upon those made in Her image."

"If it's so rare, how are there so many in the tower?" He sounded sullen, though he didn't look it.

She chuckled at him. "You're in such a hurry. But I understand. As a spy, your job demanded you collect information as fast as possible. Missing something could mean serious problems." Leaning close, she whispered, "The Fallen will not betray you if you make a mistake."

She nudged him with her shoulder and smiled. "Remember why we're here. To help a man who no longer serves among us and has no memories of the Fallen at all, for no reason other than loyalty to our own. You're part of something special, a family with so many members we can't possibly meet them all.

"I won't suggest you'll get along with everyone. That's ridiculous. But we're all on the same side, and we all know it. When we get back, spend some time in Cloverdale, and in the tavern. Sit in the dining hall and watch people. Talk to your healer. Find someone to spar with. Ask questions. Think about the answers."

Jaris sighed and rubbed his face. "I would've liked to have the chance to do all of that before going on a mission."

Chavali would've liked not to deal with someone so raw and new. But she wouldn't say so. "Eldrack wouldn't have sent you so soon. You're doing fine, though. You are having nightmares, you said?"

"Yes. Sivry claims that's normal."

"It is. They will recede. Your mind will adjust."

"I feel like... I don't know." Shaking his head, he huffed, the sound full of exasperation and frustration.

That feeling had defied explanation for Chavali, also. The sensation settled in the belly and demanded attention without explaining what it wanted. In hindsight, she knew she'd lashed out more than she should have. She also knew she hadn't surprised anyone by doing so.

"I do want you to know I'm grateful you decided to bring me back. It's better than being dead."

"It's also worse, in some ways, yes? I remember when I first awoke. I understand."

He blinked and glanced at Portia and Sivry, then back to Chavali. "All of you are so competent and self-possessed, it's easy to forget you all went through this too."

"Thank you."

Jaris nodded and fell silent.

Chavali did the same. She stared at the strip of clear, darkening twilight sky between the treetops and rock walls, refusing to engage with Karias's thoughts, and hoped they found Colby soon. Despite her words to Jaris, Colby's forced absence left her struggling to breathe around an ache in her chest.

Had she no idea of his condition, she doubted she could ignore it half so well.

CHAPTER 18

In the middle of the night, Chavali's nightmare concluded with her remaining alive during her dismemberment by squirrels wearing hats and vests made of keys, as it had a thousand times before. This particular dream never woke her anymore. She'd reached the point of boredom with its macabre performance.

Therefore, she woke for no apparent reason. Overhead, stars crowded the strip of dark sky visible between the banks. Mild vibrations rumbled in her chest.

As much as she enjoyed the cushion Karias willingly provided, she'd elected to sleep flat on her back again to avoid touching him. The tremors didn't come from him.

She noticed unexpected stillness of the air. Something seemed wrong about the unmoving view of the stars.

Too much silence crowded her.

Water should have lapped against the side of the boat. No one made breathing noises. The boat didn't creak.

Chavali sat up and saw the captain's helper fussing with the oxen in dim lamplight, though she couldn't hear any of it.

After a few moments, she realized they'd paused to swap the animals so one pair could rest while the other continued to carry them upriver. The view seemed wrong because they'd anchored near the shore.

Movement at the railing attracted her attention. A large, white shape glowed softly on the far side of the boat. With every passing moment, the white thing withdrew from her.

When she'd closed her eyes to sleep, Karias had lain beside her. She'd moved far enough to avoid his body heat. With the breeze created by the boat's movement, she'd left only a foot of space between them.

Karias was not on the deck. The white thing over there, withdrawing at a slow, steady pace in utter, unnatural silence was Karias.

This made no sense. Chavali rubbed her eyes and tried again.

Scanning the deck, she accounted for Portia, Sivry, Jaris, Daria, and the captain, all sleeping. The captain's helper latched the pen holding the active oxen. Two exhausted oxen lay in the second pen in front of it.

"Portia!" She couldn't hear her own voice. Chavali sprang to her feet, their impact on the deck eerily silent, and charged for the shore. On her way past Portia, she kicked the mage's shoulder.

Karias's body disappeared.

Portia rolled onto her side and opened her mouth yet made no noise.

Chavali rolled her body over the railing. Her bare feet splashed in warm, ankle-deep water to land on knobby roots.

Frogs suddenly croaked in the night. Insects buzzed and chirped. Water lapped.

Bright light flared overhead, bathing the trees and shrubs in a harsh glare. An unknown elf man froze, his eyes wide with surprise. Two women, also unfamiliar, stopped in the light.

Karias lay on the ground before them, his body engulfed by a net of fine mesh. Chavali had awakened because these people had the gross audacity to try to steal Karias.

One woman carried a metal staff and wore chain armor. Dark ink climbed out of her collar on her left side to run up her neck and around her ear on her half-shaved head. A hawk sat on her left shoulder. She took a step to stand between Chavali and Karias with her staff held ready. Everything about her bearing screamed her status as a bodyguard for the other two. With the tattoo and bird, Chavali suspected she served as a mlinzi.

The other woman wore far too much loose, flowing clothing for practicality. Her medium hair reached her knees and danced in a light breeze Chavali couldn't feel. She held no obvious weapons, only the rope attached to the net containing Karias.

Either the net or something else held the horse immobile and silent.

Their elf had long hair braided down his back and wore a fine, embroidered jacket tailored to his narrow frame. His teeth bared in a snarl for Chavali, he reached into his pants pockets with both gloved hands.

Heedless of what she stepped on, Chavali rushed them. She knew she couldn't stand against three people trained to fight, and she didn't care. Without Karias, she lost Colby. In every way imaginable. He would never recover.

If they kept Karias alive, Colby would do anything to rescue his beloved companion sent by the Creator.

She drew her dagger and screamed at them. The mlinzi leaped forward to meet her. Her hawk screeched.

"Stay back. This isn't your—"

Chavali crashed into the mlinzi. They hit a tree together. She slashed her dagger and tore cloth. The mlinzi grunted and flung her to the side. Dull pain thumped Chavali's lower back as she hit the ground.

One of Portia's shimmering darts streaked at the elf and slammed into the air a foot in front of his chest. The impact showered the area with bright sparks and knocked him against a tree trunk.

Sivry and Jaris rushed over the boat's railing, weapons out and ready. Daria followed them, bellowing a war cry.

"I'd know that dart anywhere," the elf growled as he straightened. "Portia, you coward! Come out and fight me to my face."

"I'm not as stupid as your face, Narryn!" Portia called as she closed the distance.

"Narryn?" Sivry bellowed with her own, less friendly fury.

"Sivry?" Narryn sounded confused more than anything else. He raised his hands, each holding a crystal.

Chavali gasped for breath as she forced herself to her feet through the pain in her back. Later, when she hurt less, she'd marvel at the fact Sivry and Portia somehow knew—and hated—their horse thief.

She hoped the others could handle the mlinzi, because she had no ability to harm that woman.

"All of you back off!" the woman abducting Karias shrieked in a high-pitched voice. "We didn't come here to hurt any of you."

Daria charged the mlinzi. Sivry lunged past them to attack Narryn. Jaris followed Sivry. Portia flung another dart into the fray.

The abductor woman shut up and dragged Karias deeper into the trees.

Chavali launched herself at that woman. She stumbled over the roots, grimacing with every step. The sounds of battle faded as she narrowed her focus to the abductor and Karias.

When she reached Karias, Chavali lunged and stabbed through the net. Her blade screeched against the material. With a great heave, she snapped one thread.

"No!" The abductor squealed. "Sien, help!"

The net parted as if Chavali had slashed it in half. Karias flopped out, limp and unmoving. His eyes rolled with wild panic. He wore a strange bridle she'd never seen before.

The abductor squawked and fell backward, still holding the net.

Something hit Chavali from behind so hard she flew forward. Chavali raised her arms in time to let them take the brunt of her impact with a twisted, gnarled tree.

She heard a crunching snap. Sharp, burning pain engulfed her right arm. Her hand wouldn't release her dagger.

She stumbled back a step. The tree slid sideways. No, she slid sideways. Staggering to the side, she watched the mlinzi fight off Daria while standing over the abductor. Karias lay on the ground, not helping.

Chavali knew she needed to sit and rest. Instead, like a fool, she fought through rising nausea to Karias's side. There, she knelt beside his head and tried to lift her dagger. The arm didn't work. It hurt too much.

Pain had never stopped her before. She wouldn't let it hold her back when Karias needed her.

She gripped her own wrist with her uninjured hand and used it to cut the bridle.

"Stop," the abductor whispered.

As with the net, as soon as she ripped through one section of the bridle, it failed.

Karias surged to his feet. Chavali fell over. Her head hit something solid. She blinked rapidly, trying to stay awake. The world spun. Karias trumpeted and whinnied. People shouted and screamed. Her heartbeat pounded in her ears.

For some reason, she smelled the rich, earthy ink Eldrack always kept in a well on his desk. Aislynn used pens with their own reservoir. They had a more acrid tang.

She tasted blueberries.

Sivry crouched in front of her. "Chavali?"

Chavali blinked at her. "What?"

"She's conscious," Sivry told someone else. "And hurt." She touched Chavali's hand.

Pain screamed through Chavali's entire arm. Her mouth fell open but no sound came out.

Sivry's thoughts gnawed at Chavali's mind, revealing she couldn't tell how much agony she caused. She tugged the dagger loose.

Chavali thought Sivry had sawed off her hand. She wished she could fall unconscious. The spirits buzzed in her mind, refusing to allow it.

"I'll carry her." Daria scooped her up without the gentle tenderness Colby would use.

Every step Daria took jarred. An eternity of torture later, she laid Chavali on the boat.

Sivry crouched over her and checked her injuries. Finally.

"I wish someone had, just once, mentioned Narryn was in town," Portia snapped, every word clipped and short.

"I would've liked to know that too," Sivry grumbled. Through unintended contact with Sivry's skin, Chavali heard a stream of curses, most disparaging Narryn and his fertility.

Daria patted Karias. "Got history with him, huh?"

"You might say that," both women answered at the same time.

"No one knew," Chavali said. She sounded vacant to her own ears, like a disembodied voice floating on a breeze. At this point, she felt like one.

"Korrya should have. She's Spire! He's Spire!" Portia stomped her foot and growled. "I hate the damned Spire. There's a reason I left it, and he's a big part." She stalked to the boat, looking for a target for her anger. "And you!" she shouted at the captain's helper still sitting on the boat. "How much did he pay you? I ought to throw you overboard!"

The effect dampening sound on the boat had apparently lifted. Perhaps it had fled with its master.

The woman covered her face. "I'm sorry," she whimpered.

"Sorry isn't good enough!" Portia screamed.

Their captain stood between them, his hands up in surrender. "This is my sister. I don't know what she did, but please don't hurt her."

"Stop her," Chavali mumbled.

Sivry nodded and handled Chavali's arm. "Jaris won't let her kill anyone, so don't worry about that."

Pain nearing the level she felt after a prophecy surged through Chavali's arm. Her vision blanked with white. She couldn't breathe.

::Damn. It's broken.::

"This will hurt," Sivry said. *::A lot.::* "Maybe we should go back and get you to a healer?"

"No." Chavali gasped for breath. "Colby."

"Of course." Sivry grinned. *::If I distract you, this won't hurt as much.::* "I don't want to be the one who frees him from whatever situation he's in. That's your job."

"Karias." Chavali had nothing to treat ordinary pain. She never carried such herbs. Why would she?

"He's fine." Sivry thankfully broke skin contact to gingerly move Chavali next to the horse.

When she turned her head, she could see Jaris standing with his hands up to ward off Portia. The captain shielded his helper from them both. Daria leaned against the railing with her arms crossed, waiting for a chance to pursue more violence.

Whatever Jaris had said, he'd calmed Portia enough to stop shouting. She glared over Jaris's shoulder at the helper.

"You'll refund the fee for this trip, of course," Portia growled.

"I can't." The captain held up his hands and bowed his head. "I'm sorry. As soon as you left to get your supplies, the Riverway Guild swooped in. Like vultures smelling blood. I owe them money because someone damaged a pier last week. They pinned it on me because I was docked there at the time. I tried to get the Guard to help me refute it, but they blamed me for it too. What little I have left is for the docking fee when we return. If we don't pay that, they won't let you ashore."

"That doesn't account for the bribe she accepted." Portia's anger had faded in the face of his story. She pointed at his sister without heat behind it.

"Your foot is bleeding," Sivry murmured. "It's pretty bad."

Chavali rested her uninjured hand on Karias's back. Later, when she hurt less, Chavali would react to the captain's plight. For the moment, she could barely think straight.

::I don't know what he did. When I woke up, I couldn't move.::

"How much did they pay you, Finna?" the captain asked.

Finna dug a handful of coins out of her pocket and offered them to him. "The guild and the guards take so much. I saw the money and..." She covered her face again. "I'm sorry. She said no one would get hurt. They just wanted the horse."

The captain frowned. "We're not so poor we need to consort with horse thieves."

Sivry tore a strip of cloth from the hem of her dress, and another from the hem of Chavali's. "Breathe, Chav—astity."

Chavali laughed. She couldn't help it. Chavastity, indeed. Laughter bubbled out of her mouth. The moment Sivry jerked her arm, she stopped and blanked.

::Don't pass out,:: several voices urged in Chavali's head. They shifted to a swirl of different ideas, merging into a cacophony she couldn't track.

"It's set," Sivry said. "Help me bind it. And tie up her foot before she bleeds to death."

Jaris leaped into action, taking his thoughts with him.

"Keep Karias calm. I'll get some water," Portia said.

Another of the voices disappeared, leaving her with Karias and Sivry thinking over each other. Both worried about her, about Colby, and about Narryn returning with a larger force and better tactics.

Jaris returned. Daria told the captain to get the boat moving again. Sivry focused on wrapping Chavali's arm. Then her thoughts stopped because she stopped touching Chavali.

::I should've awakened when the boat stopped.::

"Karias," Chavali said. "This isn't your fault."

Portia draped a cool, damp cloth across her forehead. The dark outline of trees framing the stars moved.

::I'm glad you're aware enough to scold me. I don't think this attack was my fault, or your fault, or anyone else's fault other than those three people. But I do regret not keeping a watch tonight. I could've rested more during the day and stayed awake all night. Now hush or they'll figure out you're talking to me. Get as much sleep as you can. Broken bones are serious when there's no healer around.::

"Maybe we should go back," Sivry said. "She can't fight like this."

"If you have enough money," Daria said, "the guild has a healer."

"No." Chavali closed her eyes. She drifted in an ephemeral world. "Keep going. I'll be fine when I need to be."

"Stubborn as always," Portia muttered. "We'll keep going. But we're going to keep a watch. We have no way to know if Narryn will track us along the way or go back and set up an ambush for our return. I'll sit up first."

"I wouldn't worry about that," Sivry said. "My brother is many things, but persistent isn't one of them."

Chavali blinked at Sivry.

"Really? Your brother?" Portia snorted. "I know him because I had to work with him a few times for the Spire."

Sivry nodded and sighed. "Now that he knows I'm here, he'll run away like the little brat he is. He'll whine to his masters about how his savage big sister was there and foiled his mission to steal a horse. By the end of it, they'll think I'm twenty feet tall and breathe fire."

Portia chuckled. "Did he know about you?" She used a thumb to covertly indicate a slash across her throat.

"No. None of my family knows."

Though she wanted to hear more, Chavali drifted to sleep, secure in the knowledge that her friends would watch over her.

CHAPTER 19

Chavali lost time. Twice, Sivry woke her long enough to make her drink water and try to eat tiny bites of bland porridge. Otherwise, she slept. When she finally breathed in the air and didn't fall back asleep, she murmured a wordless protest at the deep ache in her arm and the lesser ones in her back and foot. Too-warm sunshine baked her body.

She opened her eyes to a strange, light-colored fuzziness. The ground gently rocked beneath her with a chorus of slow, creaking groans.

No, she still rode on a boat. There, she heard Portia groan. Chavali turned her head toward the sound and the fuzzy thing moved oddly. Someone had covered her face with a cloth. Her hand rested against Karias.

::This is worse than sitting in a cramped stable while you and Colby get into trouble.::

Karias had calmed a great deal despite the undercurrent of Colby's distress remaining constant. They knew he still lived. That had to be enough for now, and Karias had apparently accepted this.

Daria lifted the cloth from Chavali's face. "Welcome back. Portia is miserable by the railing again. Jaris is sitting with her this time. Sivry is napping."

::They've been taking turns staying with you, and also keeping watches at night.::

"Do you want to sit up?"

Chavali lifted her head a fraction of an inch. The effort made her dizzy. "No. Not yet."

Daria nodded and offered her a tiny gob of unknown substance.

"Eat. This stuff will get you going again." She showed Chavali the rest of a block of food she couldn't identify. "We'll take it slow." She dropped the bite into Chavali's mouth.

It tasted and crunched like berries, nuts, and coconut held together with honey. Chavali took her time chewing, finding the effort draining.

"When we first met, I figured you were all some sort of specialized mercenary team. Colleagues and not much more. Then that fight happened, and you all acted like losing Colby was the worst thing that could happen, which isn't how mercs behave. I know. I've met plenty. I mean, Colby's never been like that, but we all do what we gotta to stay fed, right?"

She dipped the mouth of a skin into Chavali's mouth and poured a splash of water. Following it with another piece of food, she gave Chavali no chance to respond.

"Now that I've been around you guys for a couple of days, and that fight, I'm getting a really different feel for what you people are. Is there actually a spice merchant? Because I don't think there is. I think you're out here for some other reason."

::I'd let her ramble,:: Karias suggested, *::and see if she ever arrives at some kind of point.::*

"Knowing Colby, which I do, I'm betting you all work for one of the Orders. It's clearly not the High Path, because that's the Spire. Portia said Narryn works for them. One of their mages wouldn't try to steal Karias if you worked for them. That's stupid. I know they fished gutted bodies out of the lake, and Colby would never go for 'no killing,' so you can't be Spilled Blood. Strong Arm is possible for Colby, but not the rest of you. Sivry and Jaris fight like sneaks."

::Her observations are as blunt as I would expect of her. I recant my previous suggestion. Interrupt her before she lists and discounts every single order she's heard of. I'm not sure if it would be wise to tell her anything, but you can tell her not something.::

"Not an order," Chavali said as Daria stuffed another bite into her mouth.

"Huh." Daria gazed to the side for several long moments. "I think I believe you. It tracks with the differences between you. So you're all from different orders, I guess. Which means you either really do have a spice merchant, or you work for a government. Or maybe a wealthy woman pretending to be a spice merchant to cover up what she's really into."

Chavali didn't want to talk about it, so she changed the subject to one she wished to discuss even less. At least it didn't involve the Fallen, though, or clan secrets. "Colby said you were lovers."

"For a while, sure. We served together in the Grippan Guard." Daria smiled. "That was a really good time in my life."

Of course she remembered him fondly.

"Then he got promoted and transferred. The officers all liked him because he followed orders, had his own horse, and could improvise without disobeying. They also liked how he repelled corruption so hard the other women and men straightened up around him."

"This sounds like him, yes."

"See? That's what I mean." Daria pointed at Chavali's mouth, then stuffed another bite inside it. "That smile. You're not just casual co-workers or teammates. The lot of you are close. Good friends, practically family. And the way you charged off to save his horse? Are you courting him?"

Yet another person had seen through her. This time, Chavali chose to forgive herself. Pain and weariness had rendered her incapable of maintaining a fiction of distance. Colby's absence had affected her more than she wanted to admit.

Portia was right. They had no business working missions together anymore.

"You don't have to say it. I can see it on your face." Daria splashed water into Chavali's mouth and fed her another bite. "I admit I'm kind of disappointed. I kind of had this idea we might try it again. Him and me, we worked well together. And I haven't clicked with anyone else since. I'd kind of given up on finding someone. Then Colby drops into my life again."

Those words gnawed at Chavali's belly. She wanted to hit Daria, or hiss and spit at her.

She wanted to lay claim to her property.

Taking a deep breath, Chavali forced away the urge. Colby had every right to handle this in his own way and his own time. If he wanted to chase

Daria, she had no right to stand in his way. Such a betrayal would strike hard, like a knife to the heart.

Making him miserable would also hurt her.

::I think you should tell her how you feel. The real version. Unvarnished and plain. Daria wasn't terrible for Colby, but she wasn't good for him either. They had fun. Shallow fun. Nothing about her touched him on the level you do. Despite how diametrically opposed you can be on some subjects, I don't think he could find someone better suited to him than you. And I doubt you could either.::

Chavali already knew Karias liked her. She hadn't realized he endorsed her as a match for Colby. As far as she'd understood, he accepted, allowed, and didn't resist. His approval and backing gave her a certainty she hadn't known she craved.

Something inside her cracked, or maybe it healed.

All this time, she'd thought she wanted privacy. People always wanted to know things, and she held close her duty to keep secrets. At some point, she'd allowed the definition of "secret" to encompass everything in her life.

Karias had swept that aside.

Bracing her good arm on the deck, she tried to sit up. Daria lifted her shoulders and helped her lean against Karias. The woman mercifully failed to cause any skin contact. Chavali settled with her splinted arm resting on her lap.

The food had helped a great deal. She took another bite of the block and chewed it, watching the gnarled roots and underbrush pass at a snail's pace. Colby would ignore the scenery in favor of keeping vigilance over the river ahead.

"I love him."

Until this moment, she hadn't said as much to anyone except Colby. She hadn't bothered to restrain herself much in front of clan, so they knew without needing to hear anything concrete. Those Fallen who knew them well had guessed.

Speaking the words gave them a certain strange gravity, a kind of finality she didn't expect.

At the same time, they lifted her on incomprehensible wings.

Some part of her soared over the treetops to hear those words chime in her ears with her own voice. This bold combination of sounds issuing from her throat rang out in challenge to an uncaring world daring to keep them apart.

She felt a bizarre desire to stand outside the tavern in Cloverdale and scream it until everyone heard and knew.

::I have rarely heard anyone say so much with so few words.::

"You really mean that." Daria blew out a breath like she needed to release something weighty.

"Yes. Without hesitation or reservation."

"I'm kind of embarrassed to have thought about rescuing him and having that triumphant moment." Daria ducked her head. "I may be kind of daft, but even I can see you've got something much stronger than I could ever imagine, let alone have with anyone."

All concern about Daria attempting to present herself as some kind of rival for Colby's affections disappeared. "Perhaps you search in the wrong places."

"Could be." Daria flicked her gaze from place to place, looking anywhere except at Chavali.

Not wanting to add to the awkwardness, Chavali kept her attention to the shoreline. "I'm grateful to have met you, Daria."

"Are you? I'm not sure why. Seems like meeting me has put some friction in your life. And maybe in mine too."

"Yes. The necessary kind. When everything is easy and right, nothing is resolved. We sit where we are and never reach for more. Stagnation is death, the enemy of progress and growth. Contentment is a terrible place to be. Challenge is the blood of life. Each new mountain we climb leads us to the next. Those who settle in a valley lose something. They lose the spark. Life becomes routine, day after day passes with nothing better in sight. Apathy creeps in. The body plows on while the mind dies."

Daria blinked at her. "What order do you follow?"

Chavali shook her head with a small smile. "A small one you've never heard of." Smaller than Daria could imagine.

"Are you taking adherents? Because that's the most amazing thing I've ever heard someone say."

"It's not so hard an idea to live by on your own." She reached with her good hand and touched Daria's shoulder. "Take a risk you fear and see what happens. Try not to harm anyone while you do so. Help someone if you can. This is easy to remember, yes?"

"I suppose so." One corner of her mouth quirked up. "I can tell what he sees in you. You're really different from him on the outside. And really the same on the inside."

::She's right, you know.::

"That's why I didn't work with him, I guess. We're the same on the outside and really different on the inside."

::I know you don't see it that way, but it's true.::

Chavali had no response. She wanted to argue, yet had no reason to do so. Yes, they fit together. No one needed to analyze it. "Thank you."

Daria nodded in perfunctory acceptance. "You know how to take care of horses?"

"Yes. I grew up around them." She patted Karias's back. "We have come to an accord wherein I am not stealing his master and he is not snapping at my hand when I offer him forbidden foods."

::You don't happen to have any treats, do you? Because no one will stop you right now. If we're going to look on the bright side, that's the best I've got.::

Daria chuckled. Chavali had a feeling she would guffaw if not for her disappointment regarding Colby. "Good. Do you have brushes? Because I can do it for now. You probably shouldn't."

"In Colby's bag. If you bring mine also, I have a few treats left for Karias."

Karias turned his head to see her with both eyes. *::My favorite person ever.::*

"He's always known that word." Daria patted Karias's neck as she stood to fetch the packs.

"My favorite horse ever," Chavali murmured.

CHAPTER 20

As the sun slipped out of sight for the day, the river narrowed and thinned. The boat moved even slower in the swift, steep current. Their oxen had to switch more frequently.

By the next morning, they barely moved, despite the best efforts of the beasts.

Overnight, the shores had shifted from trees to low-growing shrubs clinging to near-vertical rock faces. If she had both arms and feet in good order, Chavali thought she could climb, swing, and crawl from place to place. For a while. Not for as long as they would probably have to do it.

The sides of this cleft otherwise had no paths or other options.

"I hoped we could get all the way up," the captain said. He shook his head. "This might be as far as my team can bring you. My oxen won't last much longer at this pace."

Daria leaned over the side. "It's too deep to walk, and the current is too fast to swim."

"We did not come this far to give up," Chavali grumbled. "Does anyone have other options?"

Portia, lying on the deck like a limp rag, lifted one hand. "I can help with magic, but only if I can see the propeller."

"You're awfully weak for swimming here," Sivry said. "Even with a rope around your waist."

::I can try using the treadmill. I'm capable of keeping up a gallop for some time at need.::

Trying this sounded better than half-drowning Portia. Chavali said,

"We can put Karias on the treadmill."

"That's the horse, right?" The captain scratched his beard. "He'd have to do it alone. The oxen work in a pair because they can walk at the same speed. I can brake one belt, though, so he can just walk on the other."

Chavali nodded her understanding. "There is no harm in trying."

The captain squinted at Karias. "If he's got as much muscle as he looks like, it might work. We'll have to anchor so we can switch him in, and I'll need help watching over the resting oxen." He nudged Finna awake and told her the plan.

"Daria," Chavali said, "guide Karias into position. Sivry, do whatever the captain needs an extra two hands for. Jaris and I will help with the oxen."

The captain swerved the boat to the side of the river to anchor it. Chavali stumbled. Jaris caught her. Sivry and Finna used hooks with ropes to catch scrabbly shrubs. The boat strained against the hooks. Roots snapped on their chosen shrubs.

"The anchors won't hold long on this stuff," Finna said.

With Chavali and Jaris's help, the captain urged the oxen pair off the treadmill. They tried to enter the second pen. When that didn't work, the animals shuffled toward the gate to leave the boat. Chavali didn't need their thoughts to understand the confusion the oxen faced. She cooed and clucked to urge them to the center. Jaris patted their haunches to guide them.

Karias hurried onto the treadmill, careful to give the appearance of Daria controlling him.

"Ready to release the hooks!" the captain called out. He switched the lever to turn off the propeller brake for Karias's treadmill.

With a whinny of surprise, Karias lowered his head and trudged forward. His hooves moved the treadmill fast enough to give the ropes on the hooks some slack. By himself, he managed the same as the oxen pair. But nothing more.

"Gonna have to go faster than that!" Darias smacked Karias's flank.

The slap jolted him into a trot. His effort jerked the boat into motion.

"Release the hooks!"

Sivry and Finna yanked their hooks free.

Chavali watched Karias strain against the treadmill. His muscles bulged. Even without checking his thoughts, she read him well enough to see he needed help.

Abandoning the resting oxen to Jaris's care for the moment, Chavali hobbled to Portia's side. "What can you do to help?"

"Easiest would be to modify the propellers so they work more efficiently. After that, I can sort of enchant the space around them. Give them an aura, more or less." Portia rubbed her forehead. "Anything else, I'll have to think about."

"Karias won't be able to maintain his pace for long under these conditions. I think he's working as hard as a gallop with Colby on his back in full armor."

Portia sat up and covered her face. "I'll need a rope with a secure knot around my waist and a signal to pull me back out of the water. And probably one to stop feeding the rope so I don't wind up in the propeller. Let's not do that. I only need to see it."

"Or we could stop the boat and hoist the back end out of the water," Sivry said. "Karias rests, you work without fear of drowning, and we can take whatever time we need."

Chavali turned to regard the aft section. "How do we get the boat up?"

Sivry raised a finger. She opened her mouth to speak, then shut it. "Good point. I don't know."

Checking on Karias, Chavali asked the captain to anchor the boat anyway. The horse could take a break while Portia figured things out and gathered herself for the effort.

"The water is clear here," Chavali said. "Do you need to go out of our sight to get the propellers in your sight?"

"Maybe not." Portia gripped the railing and pulled herself to her feet. "Creator bless, I'm starving and too ill to eat anything at the same time." Keeping her hold on the railing, she shuffled to the boat's rear.

"At least you're not puking up water." Sivry grinned at her.

Portia glared.

"She does have a point," Chavali said. "You would be dead already without this small kindness on the part of your stomach."

"I just want to stop feeling this terrible!" Portia leaned over the railing.

Sivry held onto her. "I'm not saying it isn't excessive. I've never met anyone as sensitive to this as you. By now, you should've gotten used to it."

Portia straightened enough to slump against the railing. "I think I can see enough by trailing behind the boat. It should be moving while I work, I think. Even though that's much more dangerous. Then I'll know right away if I'm helping or hindering, and we won't lose any more time."

"I'll get Daria to help set it up. Don't fall overboard, because Chavali can't catch you." Sivry left them.

"She's right. This is ridiculous." Chavali held out her hand, offering Portia the opportunity to explain without saying anything. "You should be better by now."

"I've always had a problem with seasickness, as far back as I can remember." Portia sat on the deck. She waved off Chavali's hand. "I'm not wild about riding inside wagons either. If Eldrack had assigned this mission, I seriously doubt he would've sent me."

"He sent you to Harbor City. The best way to reach it through the Creator's Towers is by boat."

"That's true, but I think he had a specific reason why. Besides, we didn't have to use a boat to cross any part of the city." Portia stretched her hand over the side, letting it hit the water. "Does it seem like it's getting hotter the higher we go? Because I think the heat might be making me sick more than the boat at this point."

"It does, yes. I don't quite understand the climate here. Palmia Basin shouldn't be as warm as it is, and the higher we get, the cooler it should get."

"Magic. It's always magic. Something in the water, probably. Which means something at the source causing it. Why does it affect me so much? Korrya seems fine. Narryn certainly didn't act like anything hampered him, and he's from the north. All of you are fine too."

Chavali shrugged. She knew little about how magic worked. Everything she could do came from the spirits. "Perhaps whatever treatment the city applies dilutes it. May I ask how you know Narryn?"

"I don't really want to talk about it. Maybe when we get home and I've had a dozen solid meals." Portia pointed across the boat. "Sivry and Daria are ready."

Not offended, Chavali provided what support she could by limping beside Portia while she shuffled. "I didn't imagine that you hate each other, yes?"

"No, you didn't imagine that. Real, genuine hate. In both directions." She glanced at Chavali. "We never had a romantic relationship. It was just work."

"I would be surprised if you had. You have far too sensible a head for that. Certain unnamed exploits notwithstanding."

Portia grinned. "Thanks."

Chavali stepped out of the way to watch. Daria anchored the rope. Sivry tied it to Portia's waist with a complex knot.

"Are you sure you're up for this?" Sivry pulled the knot tight one last time. "Because we could let you sit for a while on what passes for dry land around here. Eat something. Get your strength back."

"Tempting." Portia took a few steadying breaths. "No, let's get it over with. Whatever I can do to get us to Colby faster, I'm going to do it. He deserves the best we can do for him."

Jaris had the captain and Finna release the boat and get Karias moving again.

Sivry and Daria helped Portia climb over the railing. Daria looped the rope around the railing, then held it across her back and looped it around her hand. With Sivry helping, Daria lowered Portia into the water.

Chavali wanted to do something more useful than watching. They didn't need her help. No one needed her to do anything at the moment. Even if they did, she couldn't do it. Besides her useless, throbbing arm, her back still hurt, her foot demanded rest, and her head wanted her to sit.

Karias whickered at her. She took small steps to reach him, then laid her hand on his shoulder.

::I want you to know this is much harder than it looks and I'm burning myself out here, even with that break. My weight is doing most of the work to make my hooves catch on the treadmill, but I still have to place

each one correctly each time. There's no possible way I can go faster.

Also, I don't think I mentioned it yet, but Colby isn't moving anymore. I'm sure of it. This happened shortly after you broke your arm. We're getting closer. The—::

The boat gained speed with a lurch. Karias raised his head and strained less. Their forward progress returned to normal, as it had been at the beginning of the journey.

::Whatever Portia is doing, it's working.::

Daria pulled Portia high enough from the water to see her head. Sivry knelt and held her arm.

Portia gasped for breath. She took a moment to look around and smile with satisfaction, then nodded toward the water. "I can do more."

"Are you sure?" Sivry asked.

"Yes. This isn't hard, it's just...no, I take it back. This is hard. The magic isn't the hard part, though." She grinned. "Maybe I should stay like this until we get there, because I feel pretty good right now."

Daria laughed. "I think that's the thrill of facing death by drowning."

Watching them reminded Chavali of watching clan. Then as now, she'd often stood on the periphery of whatever happened. That sense of exclusion annoyed her this time only because she wished she could do something to make the task easier. Everything didn't have to revolve around her or her struggles.

At Portia's request, Daria lowered her again. Chavali watched with her hand still on Karias's neck. His thoughts dwelled on wanting to react quickly if Portia managed another burst of speed. Sivry leaned over the railing again, watching Portia.

Karias stumbled. The boat lurched. Chavali staggered into the fence around the treadmill pen.

Sivry swore and dove overboard. Daria fell backward, her hands full of slack rope.

CHAPTER 21

Somehow, Chavali reached the back of the boat first. She leaned over, already extending her arm, and discovered Sivry hanging from a hook on the back of the boat by one hand. In her other hand, she held the snapped end of the rope attached to Portia.

"I think she's unconscious!" Sivry hauled on the rope.

How Sivry had caught her, Chavali had no idea. Nor did she care.

"Get out of the way, Chastity!" Daria barreled into the situation. She leaned over, took the rope, and hauled Portia closer.

Chavali groaned as she took Sivry's hand and helped her climb back onto the boat. The strain affected her entire body. Everything pulled apart, tearing her in half.

Finna rushed to help Daria get Portia onto the deck.

Sivry took Chavali by the shoulders and eased her to the deck. They sat together, both gasping for breath.

As soon as Portia lay still, Finna checked her mouth. "She's breathing, and I don't see any blood."

"She might've knocked her head," Sivry said. "I'm not sure how the rope broke."

Picking up the snapped end of the rope, Finna frowned. "This is the kind of break that happens from wear. But I inspected these ropes myself a few days before this trip. If we had one ready to fray, I would've noticed it."

"That assumes we trust you," Portia croaked.

Relief flooded Chavali. She hadn't realized she worried so much until she didn't have to anymore. So much worry, so much concern made her lump it all together and lose track of it.

Finna hung her head. "I'm sorry. I really am. She just offered so much money, and we've struggled for a long time." She raised her head. "But I would never, ever sabotage this boat. It's all we have. Neither of us is going to learn a new trade at this point."

Chavali wished she could get up. Her foot throbbed like the wound had reopened. "We understand. Portia is not truly angry at you."

"Isn't," Portia grumbled as she rolled onto her side with Sivry's help, making Chavali chuckle. If she could manage to make a joke, Portia would recover.

"Do you rotate your ropes?" Jaris asked.

Finna nodded. "Yes, every three days."

Chavali understood what Jaris asked. "When they boarded to steal the horse, one of those three people must have weakened the two ropes used for the anchors so she could make sure we couldn't chase them. Except I woke earlier than she expected, so the pressure on the ropes didn't last as long as they expected. Then you swapped the ropes for the anchors, and Daria chose one of them by chance. That means you have another damaged rope waiting to snap under pressure."

Jaris nodded. "I think so, yes."

Covering her face, Finna shook her head.

"Try not to be too hard on yourself." Chavali patted her shoulder. "Had you refused or interfered, she likely would've done something worse. No one died, they didn't get the horse, and I will heal. In the end, this has turned out as well as it could, and now we're moving at quite a clip. Do what you can to inspect the ropes and find the other weak one so it doesn't cause a problem."

"I'll help." Jaris offered Finna a polite smile. "We can loop each rope around the railing and pull on both ends for a little while. Eventually, one will break."

Chavali restrained the urge to whine about her pain while Sivry helped Portia to the front of the boat. Daria and Jaris both tested the ropes with Finna. They pulled until one snapped.

Unable to help, she sat with the two loose oxen, watching Karias trot on the treadmill with his head high. Though he had few facial features to express it, she thought he enjoyed the opportunity to work off some of his frustration.

When they returned from this rescue, Narryn might attempt to take Karias again. Why? Karias had suggested the Spire might've wanted control over him, but not the reason.

His condition had come about as a result of spying on the Spire. On that day, he'd stumbled into something capable of ripping a soul out of a human body and shoving it into a horse.

The obvious conclusion left her jaw hanging open. Somehow, the Spire had discovered a means to move a soul from one body to another, perhaps only from a person to an animal. Even with that caveat, the implications staggered her. One could achieve immortality, of a sort.

Karias served as a perfect spy, aside from his size. A mouse with human intelligence, assuming it also gained an extended lifespan, or could be moved from mouse to mouse, would have even fewer limits.

Or a raven, like Rowan's. Or a hawk, like that other mlinzi's.

Without Karias's accidental intervention, Colby would've become a mlinzi, which meant he would've eventually gained that same sort of bonded creature. His honor would've demanded a willing subject, and his style would've called for a bird of prey, or perhaps some sort of dog.

Yes, he would've preferred a dog.

She imagined the Spire asked the elder mages to volunteer for the duty of continuing to serve as an animal. Given the choice, who wouldn't take another chance at life? Every Fallen knew the difficulty of turning down that option.

Their bodyguards carried tomes of wisdom and experience in the form of innocuous creatures. Perhaps a full, proper binding allowed the pair to communicate with a specialized form of full telepathy. She hadn't noticed Rowan speaking to his bird, after all.

Perhaps she could help Colby complete the binding.

With that capability, the pair could become much more terrifying in battle.

How to accomplish such a thing, she had no idea. Between Portia,

Penny, Eldrack, Railan, Karias, a few healers, and herself, she thought they could discover an answer of some kind. This meant she'd have an offer to present as a gift when she revealed Karias's nature to Colby.

Considering the likelihood he'd see her withholding this information as a betrayal of sorts, she'd take any boon she could get.

The boat picked up speed at an alarming rate. Chavali blinked until she could grasp their situation.

They'd reached a lake the size of the entire city of Palmia Basin. Sparse, struggling plants, many creeping along the rocky ground, covered a sharp, steep slope forming a pocket valley. Snow-capped peaks poked above the ridgeline in the distance.

Some of the oppressive heat dissipated, lowering the temperature noticeably. Karias kept running, propelling them across the still, serene waters fast enough to buffet them with a strong wind.

"I'd say we're here," the captain said. "Now what?"

Chavali stood and hobbled to Karias. His sides heaved and he needed a rubdown. "Slow down and tell me where to go," she murmured as she rubbed his nose.

He blinked and slowed to a walk as he looked around. *::I seem to have stopped paying attention to anything except running toward Colby.::*

She'd done the same with her own thoughts. "You're fine. Catch your breath."

::Colby is ahead and down. If I had to guess, I'd say head for the ominous bulge of rock with the dark, gaping maw of doom on the other side of the lake. He's presumably in a cave connected to it by a submerged passage. Anything less would be incredibly unlikely.::

Of course they took him someplace like that. Stifling a snort, Chavali pointed for the captain. "Take us to the other side."

The captain nodded and kept the boat sailing straight.

They slipped across the smooth, glassy lake under weak sunshine. In the center, a light breeze stripped away the heat long enough for Chavali to sigh in relief.

::Whatever we find, if there's any possible way for me to fit, I'm coming with you.:: Under his coherent thoughts, he struggled to control his

frantic need to reach Colby as soon as possible.

"I know." Chavali didn't need to experience his panic. She had her own.

Colby hadn't abandoned them on his own. He couldn't swim to the top of this mountain without help. The party responsible had either wanted him for some reason, or had taken him as bait.

Chavali already had at least one nemesis with a reason to lure her into a trap. Colby had a new one in Narryn. Others could exist for either of them.

She wanted to do something. Pacing wouldn't solve anything. Neither would trying to swim with one arm. Karias pushed them forward at a good clip, one which gave her no honest reason to complain.

As they left the center of the lake, the breeze faded. Heat wrapped Chavali in a damp blanket more unpleasant for having had a break from it.

The captain had to stop short of sailing through the shadowy opening Karias had pointed them toward. A lip of bleached stone jutted through the water's surface like a tooth-studded jaw. Checking to either side, Chavali noted they couldn't land elsewhere and reach the opening without getting wet. They might as well land at the mouth.

"Have the horse stop," the captain said. "Finna, get ready to anchor."

Chavali pretended to relay the command. Karias stopped. The captain pulled the treadmill brake and handled the rudder. Finna picked up a hook and readied to use it. Sivry picked up the second hook and held it so she could pass it to Finna.

A figure climbed from the water onto the lower jaw of rock. As soon as the newcomer had a steady perch, they raised their hands in peace.

In the bright sunshine glaring off the water, Chavali had to squint to see them.

Sivry, standing at the bow, turned back. "It's one of those Furies! I think it's the leader."

Karias's distress gave way to rage. *::I'm going to tear her apart.::*

"Easy. She has power in the water." Chavali planted her fist on her hip, ready to slip it to her dagger's hilt. "And I believe she operates at the whim of another. Or, at least, she has some greater calling than her own interest."

::She took Colby.::

"To bring us here, I suspect. And now, we discover why." Chavali led him out of the treadmill pen to the ship's bow at a slow, stately pace. Leaning against him helped spare her foot. "Don't screw this up like Colby would."

Taken aback by Chavali's command, Karias lowered his head to break contact.

The woman wore the same embroidered outfit she had for the bakery fire and the attack on the boat. This time, she lacked her collection of blades. Water still refused to drench her, leaving her dry despite having climbed out of the lake.

As Finna used the hook to keep the boat from hitting the rock, Chavali met the Fury woman's gaze from twenty feet away. "What do you want?"

"You." The woman held out her hand to Chavali.

Her voice had been the one to scold Chavali while she floated in the lake, neither breathing nor drowning.

"The mountain calls for the Guide who wears the feather. The traveler who has stepped beyond and returned with the future. The—"

"Yes." Chavai raised a hand. Daria, Finna, and the captain had no need to hear everything about Chavali described in minute detail. Portia, Sivry, and Jaris had no business hearing some of it either. "I recognize myself in this description. What do you want with me?"

Finna found purchase for her first hook on the rock and took the second.

The woman gestured inside the mouth. "I am Vimarica, a host. Your man is there, safe for now. Harming me will not return him to you. Only venturing into the mountain will secure his safe release. This is the will of the mountain and the waters, not me."

This moment didn't surprise Chavali, except that she'd expected a fight. She peered into the darkness, seeing nothing other than water. "Do I need to bring supplies? Must I venture inside alone?"

The second hook caught a rock. Finna and the captain shifted the boat closer so Chavali and Vimarica no longer needed to shout.

"We don't go beyond this pool." Vimarica gestured to the water inside the mouth. "But we won't stop anyone from joining you as you plunge into the mountain's depths. The mountain itself may." With a shrug, she again extended her hand toward Chavali. "I only know what the mountain allows, so I can't say if you'll need supplies. If you have something that won't suffer for getting wet and won't slow you down, bringing it shouldn't cause a problem."

Chavali nodded and set the heel of her injured foot on the boat railing.

Portia pushed against her arm. "You're not seriously going to just hop over the side and dive into a submerged mountain at the suggestion of someone who tried to kill you?"

Vimarica put a hand on the boat's railing beside Chavali's foot and pulled the craft closer. "I swear on my life that if you do not attack us, we will not harm any of you while we all remain here. Everyone is welcome in the pool. Its waters are refreshing in unexpected ways."

"I have done much less rational things for the benefit of those I care for." Chavali gripped Portia's forearm, avoiding skin contact. "This time, I do it for Colby. Next time, I would do it for you."

Karias whinnied a battle cry, startling everyone, including the lounging oxen. He charged the bow. Portia yanked Chavali to the side. The horse leaped over the railing and flew over the lower jaw to land in the pool with a great splash.

"Fine," Portia grumbled. She helped Chavali climb over the railing.

Vimarica helped Chavali from the other side. Chavali jumped into the pool feet-first. Her head plunged under the surface, wrapping her in a cool, pleasant embrace.

Then the pain in her back, foot, and arm exploded and she cried out underwater, unable to think anything coherent.

CHAPTER 22

A strong grip on the back of Chavali's dress hauled her to the surface. She couldn't stop shrieking and kicking from the intense agony. The pain continued to worsen until it rivaled that of a prophecy many times over. As far as she could tell, someone shoved white-hot, barbed spikes into her arm, foot, and back, and charged them with lightning while scraping them across her bones over and over. Even with her eyes closed, her vision flashed with white.

Then it stopped.

Chavali gasped for breath in a sudden, bizarre absence of pain. She lay on her side, curled and clenched on a shelf of rock near the surface with cool water lapping gently against her body. Her head rested on something soft and warm. Everything smelled damp and earthy, like leaves rotting on a forest floor.

She opened her eyes and discovered Portia looming over her, holding Chavali's head in her lap. As her body relaxed, her hand brushed Karias's damp nose.

::*That was exciting. Let's not do it again. Ever.*:: His head rested on the ledge with his body submerged.

"Welcome back," Daria said. "Again." She sat on the ledge beside Karias, swishing her legs in the water and rubbing behind Karias's ears.

"She said the water can heal injuries," Portia murmured, "but it's not gentle."

Pushing off one arm, Chavali took help to sit up. Her body felt better than it had in some time. Portia untied the wrap holding her arm immobile. Chavali flexed her hand and arm, finding them whole and unharmed. Her back also felt fine without stiffness. She removed the binding on her foot and discovered a notable lack of injury.

"Not gentle." Chavali snorted. "I'm glad I'm healed, but I'd prefer not to go through that again."

Light flickered on the water rippling inside the dim cavern. Overhead, reflections played across a jagged rock dome. Shelf mushrooms clung to the rock in sporadic clumps. Aside from the mouth they'd entered through, she saw no other exit.

"Where am I supposed to go?"

"Let the water guide you," Vimarica said, her voice echoing through the cavern. She remained standing at the mouth.

"That doesn't sound suspicious or anything," Portia muttered. "Just jump in, you'll be fine. Never mind the giant sharks, or the current that'll suck you into oblivion, or whatever else might lurk down there."

Chavali smirked and petted Karias's face.

::*There's a passage underwater. It's just below this ledge and to the left. I'm standing on stable rock right now. Horses aren't the most capable swimmers when fully submerged, but what I lack in fins and gills, I make up for in muscle. If you hold onto my neck, I'm confident I can pull you faster than you could go on your own. Any time we can find air to breathe will help me tremendously. It's quite challenging to hold my breath for any length of time while exerting myself.*::

"We should get moving." Chavali let go of Karias to slip her body into the water. "Sivry and Jaris are not coming?"

Portia shook her head. "I don't trust the captain not to leave us here. And I definitely don't trust these Fury lunatics." She pursed her lips and looked away. "And I'm not going either. I saw something. In the water. I... don't think the mountain wants me to come with you, which sounds stupid." She returned her gaze to Chavali. "I'm not willing to risk it, especially with how bad my seasickness has been."

"I understand." Chavali knew well how mystical visions and prophecies could affect people. She smiled at Portia, hoping she didn't feel like a failure for this. "Daria?"

Daria shrugged. "I didn't see anything, and I feel pretty good right now. I'll come."

"Then we have nothing else to do but swim. I think I see a passage there." She pointed in the direction Karias had indicated.

"What about the horse?" Daria asked as she slid off the ledge.

"He has led us this far. I believe he can take us to Colby." Chavali wished she had some way to make this easier on Karias. At least the force of his need to reach Colby would see them through.

Portia squeezed Chavali's shoulder. "Let him take the lead, then, and stay close to him. Good luck. Come back with Colby."

"Be here when we return." Chavali patted Karias's neck underwater and pointed to the cave.

::I have to admit that maintaining this fiction can be somewhat annoying at times.::

Karias took a few short breaths, then a few deep breaths. With her hand still on his neck, Chavali timed her own breathing with his. The moment before he submerged his head and pushed off the rocks, she ducked under and wrapped her arms around his neck.

::I was right. This is tiring already. Let the tunnel be short.::

Kicking her legs to help, Chavali shared the same hope. They found a narrow, dark hole in the rock. Karias dove into it and turned to propel himself along the side with his hooves. He focused his thoughts on moving without breathing.

His head broke the surface as he worried about air. Chavali surfaced with him.

Water, glowing with plenty of light, lapped at a small hill of smooth rock with a gap in the wall on the other side. Karias would have difficulty ducking under the low wall over the passage, but they'd find a way if needed. The rough, glittering walls and ceiling offered enough room for him to stand, at least.

Colby lay on his stomach halfway up the short rise. He shivered and breathed with a wheeze.

His arms ended a few inches below his shoulders.

The cave reminded Chavali far too much for her tastes of that one in

Ket where she'd also rescued Colby from a lunatic. She wondered if whatever directed Vimarica had pulled the scene from her mind and tried to duplicate it.

This entity had, perhaps, missed the part later when Chavali had killed the woman responsible.

She rushed to Colby's side. She tried to roll him and discovered he still had his arms. They stuck into the rock, anchoring him in place. As she pulled on his sleeves, then his arms to no effect, Daria climbed out of the water and hurried to help.

"Let him go," Chavali snarled. "I'm here. Whatever you want, I won't do it until he's free. Do you hear me?" she shouted at the chamber. "Free him and I'll cooperate!"

Karias trumpeted a war cry and kicked the wall with his hind hooves. Stone cracked and his shoes chimed.

Daria lifted Colby's leg. "It's just his arms. That's something." Slipping her hands under Colby's chest, she tried and failed to lift him.

Chavali touched Colby's cheek, covered with nearly a week of stubble, and discovered he dreamed. His thoughts swirled around fire and loss, failure and death. She snatched away her hand and tried to think.

He never suffered nightmares when sleeping with her, and her own had mostly receded in potency with him by her side. Haizea, on the other hand, still had occasional vivid nightmares about her parents, fire, and the sensation of Chavali's death. Rousing her from one took a physical shock.

She slapped Colby hard enough to hurt her hand.

Colby's eyes snapped open and he sucked in a breath. The rock shuddered and cracked. Daria pulled Colby free. Where the rock had trapped his arms, the holes filled in with a burbling swish, as if made of sand or water.

He coughed and gasped. Daria set him on the ground. Karias whinnied. Chavali watched, unable to do anything.

"We've got to stop meeting like this," Colby rasped.

Knowing he meant that for her, Chavali wiped the tears she wished would stop falling. Jaris had asked her how she could maintain so much detached calm, and she didn't know anymore.

Colby sat up and rubbed his cheek. "Trust Chavali to know when to deliver a good slap."

She wrapped her arms around him and didn't want to let go ever again.

"I'm fine, Chavali." He hugged her close.

Karias bumped his head against Colby's back.

"I thought her name was Chastity."

Colby grunted. "Sorry," he whispered to Chavali. Louder, he said, "It's a long story."

"It doesn't matter right now." Chavali sniffled and drew back to touch his cheek. "I would like very much if you could stop letting yourself be stolen and brought into dank caves."

::If Daria wasn't around, I'd kiss you.::

"We can leave now, can't we?" Daria asked. "That passage wasn't too bad."

"If we can, we should get out of here," Colby said. He shifted as if he intended to stand.

Chavali clung to him, wanting to sit for a minute and savor his presence. She shouldn't have willingly left him behind for half a day. Any moment, someone could snatch him from her. She needed to stop working missions with him, but how could she leave him behind? How could she watch while he left her behind?

Daria nodded and hurried into the water again.

Karias bumped Colby again.

Colby rubbed the horse's jaw. "I know. We're going to work on the fire thing." *::Will you help me deal with that fear?::*

"Of course." Chavali kissed him because she could.

"The hole—" Daria began. She coughed and looked away while Colby broke off the kiss. "Sorry. The hole is closed. We'll have to find another way."

Of course the mountain wanted Daria with them. Chavali sighed and leaned her forehead against Colby's shoulder. "There is a rather obvious option." She pointed at the low-ceiling passage.

Colby kissed the top of her head, then pulled her to her feet as he stood. "I'm sorry about this," he said to Daria, clearly meaning Chavali. "I would've liked to have a chance to—"

Daria waved him off. "Chastity, or I guess Chavali, and I had a good, long talk about it. I get it. You've got someone else, and she's pretty amazing."

Chavali smiled at her, grateful the woman didn't want to cause trouble. The moment still felt awkward, though. At least they could leave her behind when they left Palmia Basin for good. "Thank you. And we have a problem. How do we get Karias through there?" She pointed to the passage.

The horse clopped across the uneven rock. At the passage, he laid on the floor next to the edge and wriggled. As he'd done underwater, he set his hooves on the wall and used them to help direct himself.

"I've never met a horse like yours, Colby." Daria crouched to watch Karias squirm across the ground. "He's plain uncanny sometimes."

Colby chuckled. "He is." He crawled behind Karias, giving him a gentle shove every few steps.

Chavali followed him, able to walk bent over instead of crawling.

Daria brought up the rear, also on her hands and knees. "Is it Chavali or Chastity?"

At this point, Chavali thought she could trust Daria with small secrets. "Chavali. This name was deemed too exotic and memorable for our duties, so I use Chastity while working."

"Sensible. I realize it was accidental that I found out, but I'm honored you're willing to trust me with that explanation."

"Chavali is twice as sensible as either of us," Colby said. "Maybe both of us put together."

Glancing back, Chavali rolled her eyes for Daria's sake. Daria grinned.

"You know, this blue glow from the water is awfully familiar. It reminds me of those flowers in that small town." Colby huffed. "And you would've thought of that already if you could see color. It's the same shade of blue, even."

"Interesting," Chavali said. She needed to speak to Eldrack about these connections. If she thought Aislynn could help, she...would still not discuss it with her. Out of spite.

The report from this mission would have a great many omissions. When Eldrack returned, Chavali would discuss the missing pieces with him.

Karias rolled to his hooves in a new chamber. The wide cavern had a shallow ring of more glowing water between the edge where they emerged and the center. Another passage left the chamber on the other end.

The center, a circular rise about twenty feet across, boasted a healthy fungus colony cushioning a creature Chavali could only describe as a dragon.

Folded wings with darker lines for bones laid across its back, a long tail wrapped around its body, and dark, slitted eyes stared at them. Spotted light-colored horns spiraled from the back of its head.

This dragon didn't have scales. Instead, it had smooth flesh. This skin substance also made up the horns and claws.

"But there's no such thing as dragons," Daria murmured.

"I agree with you," Chavali said, also keeping her voice low. "Yet that looks dangerously like a dragon."

"It's not moving," Colby whispered.

As if prompted by him, the dragon shuddered and swelled. It contracted.

Darkness spewed from its mouth and nostrils to fly at them.

Karias jumped in front of everyone. Chavali turned and covered her head. Colby and Daria both stepped in front of Chavali to protect her.

The darkness smelled earthy and damp, like old leaves rotting on the forest floor after a long, soaking rain. Tiny specks settled on Chavali's hand.

"What is this stuff?" Colby said. He turned over his hand.

Chavali noticed her eyelids drooping. She blinked rapidly, trying to focus on her hand. If she could get to the water, she could wash it. The dirt would go away. This mattered for some reason she couldn't comprehend.

Daria raised her head. "It smells kind of strange."

"Chavali what are you doing?" Colby took her arm.

Karias sneezed.

Chavali stared at Colby's speckled hand without comprehension. Thinking demanded so much effort. Did the ground tilt to the side? She reached back to find the wall. Everything tilted more. She lay on her back without understanding how or why.

Colby frowned at her.

She passed out. At least, she thought she passed out.

CHAPTER 23

Chavali floated in dull, blue-gray murk. Around her, long strips of brown, tree-like kelp waved in a gentle current. Fish in every color of the rainbow darted through the window of a small house nearby. She stood near a fence meant to keep cows or sheep contained. No goat would've let such a simple barrier stop it from wandering as it pleased.

Seeing color meant she'd fallen into one of her usual nightmares. Knowing this, she relaxed to let it happen. She recognized this scene. The bodies would come, the sense of someone chasing her, and many other things.

"Where am I?"

Confused by clear words from an unexpected source, Chavali spun. She recognized the woman as Daria, yet she appeared as a giant made of weathered, scratched copper. Crusty flakes of orange clung to her uneven green flesh. With every movement she made, she creaked like metal scraping together.

Daria's appearance made Chavali look down to see herself. Excessive amounts of red-brown hair floated around her, somehow avoiding her line of sight no matter how she moved her head. Her flesh had turned alabaster, marbled with irregular blood-red veins and crusted with sparkling crystal. Tiny, dark butterflies fluttered in circles around her, forming three loose rings. Instead of feet, she had goat hooves covered with purple scales.

Colby appeared in front of her, large like Daria. Liquid sunshine formed his flesh. Flickers of fire streaked across him in random places and at random intervals, like clouds following no true weather pattern.

"Why are you here? This is my nightmare." Chavali reached for him and found his skin yielded to her touch, as if he truly held no more substance than light.

"You have a nightmare like this?" Colby's hand swished over hers, unable to make contact.

Daria turned over her hands. "I'm sure he could get into your dreams without much trouble. Me, though, is weirder."

A fourth person glimmered into sight. Like Colby, golden light formed his flesh. Unlike Colby, he seemed solid. Instead of fire, dark script of some unknown language flickered across his flesh, folding in and out of sight too fast to attempt to read. The silver horse's tail and full head of hair gave him away, to Chavali at least.

"Karias?" This nightmare made even less sense than the usual ones. Chavali had endured them for a decade, and knew what to expect. Even when someone had meddled with them, they'd still followed the normal patterns.

Karias blinked rapidly. "Yes? What's going on?"

Chavali took Karias's hand, grateful she could touch one of these men. "I don't know. The scenery is from one of my nightmares, but all of you are not."

"Definitely strange." Karias squeezed her hand.

"Wait." Colby held up a finger. "I don't understand. Why are you shaped like a person and not a horse? And also why are you talking like a person? Is this real?"

Karias held up both hands to ward off Colby. The script flowing across his skin clustered on his palms, then sped up his arms. "I can explain this." He glanced at Chavali and back to Colby. "Some of this. I can explain about me. I have no idea with the underwater scene here."

Colby settled his golden, glowing gaze on Chavali, full of accusation. "You're not surprised by him."

Chavali sighed. She didn't have words to soothe his feelings. Not for this. It should have waited until she did.

"Of course you're not surprised." Colby frowned. "You're a contact telepath. Every time you touch him, you share his thoughts. You've known for a while. And you never said a word." He sounded so hurt, as she'd expected from him when he learned this truth.

"It's my fault. I begged her not to tell you." Karias took Colby's hand and held it between both of his own. The two men could interact. Did that mean something, or did it merely represent the binding between them? "Keeping secrets is what she does. It's the fiber of her being."

"But why?" Colby tugged his hand free and crossed his arms. Every inch of him screamed discomfort and distress. The free-flowing flames wriggled across his skin, flickering with the sting of betrayal.

Karias hung his head. "She found out in Ket. The last time she had to rescue you in a cave."

At the time, Chavali hadn't found Karias surprising. She'd deduced the horse had much greater intelligence than he pretended.

"I asked her to keep it to herself. I thought..." Karias shook his head. "I thought I knew better, I suppose. There are very real dangers if people find out about me, which we've already experienced here. I wanted to protect us both."

Colby said nothing. Tension curled him tighter and he glowed brighter.

Chavali noted Daria watching this exchange with a furrowed brow and a frown. Tiny flakes of orange and brown rust broke off her body and flickered out of existence every few moments.

"Explain it all," Chavali urged. "He should know the whole truth. Even if it shakes him to his core, he should know."

"How long has she known the rest of it?" Colby jabbed a finger at Chavali, refusing to look at her.

"A few days. It came up on the boat here because someone from the Spire tried to snatch me. I've been mysterious yet helpful."

"This is true. I assumed he bore some relationship to the—" Chavali glanced at Daria. She waved a hand through her butterflies, disturbing the rings. "To these." The butterflies fluttered together again.

"What are those?" Daria asked.

Chavali shrugged as if she didn't know. "Butterflies."

"Why would someone from the Spire try to snatch you?" Colby

asked. Confusion caused his glowing to lessen.

"I gotta admit," Daria said, "I don't understand why anyone would put that much effort into stealing a horse, even if he is a person inside."

Karias rubbed his face. "Because the Spire did this."

Either Karias thought Colby could make all the leaps necessary to figure it out, or he couldn't make himself spit out more than one fragment of the story at a time. Chavali suspected the latter as more likely. If anyone knew Colby well enough to gauge his comprehension, Karias did.

"It was a mistake." If someone had to say the unpleasant thing, Chavali would do it. Her duty to clan demanded she not shy from the awful truth, even for a loved one. "The binding between you was an accident. Karias didn't want to destroy your foundations. He knew you think the Creator forged this binding on purpose, with a plan for you. I also know you think this. That it is your blessed duty to carry out justice in the Creator's name.

"When I first discovered Karias, I saw no harm in keeping his secret. We barely knew each other, and you had lived in blissful ignorance for years. Neither of you belonged to my clan, and both of you had equal weight in my mind. I certainly wouldn't have discussed it at any time during that mission in Ket or its immediate aftermath. Then it became one more secret to hold onto, and this, I consider routine."

She sighed. Karias holding back made no real difference. He hadn't been able to communicate with Colby until Chavali came. Chavali was the only one who could truly hurt him by omission

Colby looked at the silty ground, not meeting her gaze. He listened, and he heard her, but he had nothing to say. Not yet, anyway.

"When I inducted you into the clan, I knew I needed to fix this, but I didn't have a good chance to speak with Karias about it. Then Aislynn sent us without a proper briefing. Portia suffered on the boat. The bakery burned. You relived that fire." Chavali snapped her fingers with increasing speed. "One after another, these things rushed us. That morning you woke alone, I had gone to the stable to speak with Karias, as I have done many times before, and we agreed I should tell you because it bothered me to keep holding this back. When we got home and you could rage at your healer about my horrifying betrayal."

"I thought I'd imagined that you were talking to Karias," Daria murmured.

"No, you didn't," Karias and Chavali said together.

Lost and confused, Colby kept staring at the ground with his brow furrowed.

"I take the keeping of secrets quite seriously." Chavali watched the kelp strands wave. They rippled as if something had thumped the ground. "Divulging one is a grave matter, not to be done lightly."

"Agreed," a deep, echoing voice said. Everyone checked their surroundings for the source, so Chavali knew they'd all heard it. "Secrets are quite serious." The sound carried the weight of many voices, many lives all working together.

Like the spirits serving the clan through Chavali. If anything could make the spirits speak the same words at once, they would sound like this.

Darkness approached from the distance. Karias stood in front of them as if he still had a large horse's body and could shield them all.

"I want to talk about this more," Colby said. A sword of blazing light appeared in his hands and he stepped in front of Chavali.

"Of course." Chavali tried to touch his shoulder. Her hand swished through him again. "It is because I love you that I have found keeping this secret increasingly uncomfortable."

"If you don't forgive her," Daria said as she also stood in front of Chavali, "I'll have to crack your thick skull against a rock." She held a jagged blade of matte steel marred by rusting patches.

"Bring the Guide before me." The shape resolved into a dragon.

Except it wasn't a dragon. Chavali squinted in disbelief at a massive cluster of mushrooms arranged in the shape of an enormous dragon. Thousands of mushrooms of different types clustered together, giving it a mottled, scale-like appearance in brown, red, and white. Long stems created the illusion of claws, horns, and fangs. Its "wings" rested against its back and the "tail" streamed behind it in a straight, unmoving line.

"Guyre's dragon," she whispered. Did each mushroom represent a soul? If it did, Chavali knew she'd encountered a cluster of spirits at least as weighty as her own clan's.

"Stay out of sight," Karias muttered.

Colby and Daria closed ranks with Karias, putting all of them between Chavali and the dragon as an impenetrable wall of muscle.

Touched by everyone trying to protect her, Chavali smiled at the backs of her protectors.

Then she swam upward. They couldn't stop this force with mere bodies and blades. "What do you want with me?"

"That's the opposite of staying out of sight," Colby grumbled.

"Is she always like this?" Daria asked.

"Yes," Karias and Colby said.

Chavali ignored them.

The mushroom dragon lowered its head close to her. "You are the last of your kind. This is tragic. Once, there were five, and now you are alone. I weep for the loss."

Certain this creature meant her no true harm, Chavali kicked forward and touched her hand to the dragon's snout. "There are four of us born of clan blood, and I have added several more. I am not the last of anything."

Thoughts didn't flood her. Given their surroundings, this seemed reasonable to Chavali.

The dragon *tsked* at her. "No, there is only one of you. The rest are lost. Once, five shared the destiny, making it easier to bear. Now you must suffer the full weight on your own."

This dragon knew something and spoke around it, mimicking the frustrating behavior of the spirits. She doubted she would get a straight answer from it. "This doesn't help me. I do not lose my burdens by hearing about them or speaking of them."

"Too true. I will show you." The dragon waved a claw to indicate they should all look to the side.

A hooded figure, glowing with the brightness of a thousand suns, swept away from them. In their wake, tiny figures fell to their knees and wailed in despair with tiny, pathetic voices. The figure stopped and whirled.

"Begone from me!" Their voice boomed with enough force to create ripples in the water. Chavali felt the wave as a stinging slap to her entire body.

"We already know the story of the Creator leaving," Colby said. "Everybody knows that. We're born knowing it."

Despite possessing this memory like everyone else, Chavali had never truly believed it.

Something about the vision rang hollow and false. Among her clan, they shared this feeling yet rarely spoke of it. Once she'd become the seer, Chavali's sense of this as a sham had increased.

Indeed, Colby's statement had carried an unexpected note of disbelief just now.

Joining clan had given him this sense of wrongness, but he had yet to settle into it.

The vision skipped forward. The Creator clapped Her hands together and raised them to the sky. In front of Her, a shimmering curtain of all colors rose. Those figures who ran at it burst into flames when they reached it.

Everyone also knew contact with the curtain caused death by immolation. Those who'd tried it had screamed while they burned for a precious few seconds, then turned to ash.

The wall grew smaller and the figures disappeared until they could see the shimmering curtain enveloped a massive portion of the globe, closing it off from all angles. Beyond it, an unknown shape blotted the stars.

"Behold the void," the dragon rumbled. "It comes and this world is unprepared. We are unprotected victims for its hunger. Nothing can stop it. Nothing but the Creator. There is no hope if you do not fulfill your destiny. Only you, who have died and been reborn, last of the Guides, Queen of Madness, and scion of cowardly heroes. This is your path."

Chavali raised an eyebrow. She didn't believe a single word of this nonsense.

This bundle of spirits masquerading as a fungus dragon told her things she already knew, called her silly names she'd already received from others, and wanted her to embrace some idiotic quest.

She could've delivered this delusional drivel to someone else with half the theatrics and twice the impact.

Turning away from the unimpressive spectacle, she asked, "And what is your part in all of this?"

"I have no part in it. This threat will not affect me inside the mountain. The world will remain when the people are gone."

The dragon turned and lumbered away.

"Coward," Chavali snapped.

"Pragmatic," the dragon said.

Chavali snorted. Another queer mission, another cryptic being stepping in the way to cause problems. The mushrooms had no answers, only fearmongering.

Her vision faded to black and she blinked in the cavern once more. "No," she said. "I'm pragmatic. You're truly a coward."

CHAPTER 24

Daria sat up and stared at Chavali, wide-eyed. She opened her mouth, yet failed to make any sound.

Chavali lay on the rock, shoving the self-important mushrooms out of mind in favor of Daria. The woman had learned far too much in that short time.

Depending upon how much she understood, she potentially knew the most important secret of the Fallen.

They couldn't leave her in Palmia Basin. Not with this much information. Whether she grasped all of it or not, the Fallen would consider her a liability.

Colby sat up beside her and took her hand. *::I have half a mind to stomp on that mushroom colony. We have to walk past it anyway.::*

"While I share the sentiment, it is presumably an important part of the ecosystem here. Destroying it would likely cause catastrophic damage to Palmia Basin." She took his help to sit up. "This was supposed to sound like a reason not to do it."

Colby chuckled. *::The sooner we get out of here, the sooner we can talk about this whole Karias thing.::* He tugged on her hand to help her stand.

"If that's supposed to make me hurry, we should work on your ability to motivate people." She stood with him.

He grinned and pushed her damp hair off her face. Karias stuck his head over Chavali's shoulder and looked up at Colby, reminding her of a puppy worried about punishment.

Colby let his hands dangle at his sides. "Everything just feels weird now."

Chavali rubbed under Karias's jaw, not sure what to say.

::*This is also something I worried about. Please remind him that I still occupy a horse body, and this horse body still probably shouldn't have as many treats as you give me.*::

"Can it feel weird while we get out of here?" Daria asked.

Chavali nodded and led the horse to the water ring. "I have hopes that, with help from the clan, and perhaps Railan, we can complete the bond between you so you can communicate directly. Until then, I can bridge the gap, so to speak."

::*I suppose that's a necessary preamble.*::

Frowning, Colby splashed into the ring. Chavali expected to also splash into the water. Instead, the surface supported her weight. She stepped onto the pool. Karias's first hoof and both Daria's first steps splooshed like Colby's had.

"That's really..." Daria cocked her head to the side and stared at Chavali's feet.

::*Apparently, the mushroom dragon wants you to feel special. Fungus with that much ego could probably find a way to support you, and only you.*::

"Agreed." Chavali shrugged for Colby and Daria's benefit.

The effect gave her enough extra height to stand taller than either Colby or Daria as they waded through two feet of water. Karias seemed more appropriate for her size. The unexpected view amused her. Perhaps she'd find a box to put her at Colby's eye level and use it once in a while for a change of pace.

"Karias wishes me to remind you that you're still right about the amount of treats he should have. Yelling at me for giving them to him is still the proper approach. I think this might be unfair."

Colby said nothing and kept wading through the pool without letting Chavali see his face. What she could read from behind suggested he needed to think. Later, he would want to talk. Then he would settle into some new version of normal.

Everyone passed the dragon-shaped mushroom in the center without disturbing it. Chavali considered this an admirable display of restraint.

::This would've gone much smoother at home. But at least we don't have to fake it around him anymore. Or Daria.::

"Yes."

On the other side of the ring pool, everyone else stepped out of the water. Chavali lost her height advantage. The world seemed lesser somehow because of it. Yes, she'd try getting a box or standing on a chair from time to time.

They trooped through the passage on the other end of the cavern to find another glowing pool. No one hesitated. Karias pulled Chavali again. Colby and Daria swam behind them. This time, the passage ran quite short. When Karias and Chavali surfaced, they discovered Portia still lounging on the shelf, waiting for them. Vimarica sat on the lower jaw of the cave mouth.

"Go in peace," the woman said. She gestured through the mouth to the boat waiting beyond it.

Chavali swam across the pool and climbed onto the rock. Colby and Daria would have much more luck helping Karias than she. "I wish to make clear that abducting someone to get to me is not a tactic I approve of." She jabbed a finger at Vimarica. "The next time you want to come for me, you come for *me.*"

Vimarica pursed her lips. "I do as the mountain bids." She coughed. "But I'll remember that."

"See that you do."

"Sorgeya." Vimarica reached a hand toward Chavali but didn't touch her. "I suggest you conclude your business in Palmia Basin as soon as possible."

"This is my plan, yes." Chavali turned her back on Vimarica. The mushroom dragon had a plan for the city and wanted Chavali out of the way. Either it preferred she not meddle, or it wanted to avoid harm coming to her. Perhaps both.

She, of course, considered dealing with Vimarica and her people as her business. If not for the declared and honored truce, this moment would have become a battle.

With Sivry and Jaris's help, Chavali climbed onto the boat. She hurried out of the way and held onto the railing. The effort to get Karias onto the boat took six people and rocked it enough to frighten the oxen. Once Karias laid on the deck and Finna removed the anchor hooks, the captain urged one pair of oxen to work.

Portia sat by the railing with Sivry on the right side. Daria sat on the left with Jaris. Chavali guided Colby to the bow. They sat together with their backs to the railing and she leaned against him, facing Karias. The horse watched them in return.

Despite the glaring, oppressive sunshine and smothering damp, she relished Colby's warmth. That he provided it without hesitation spoke to his desire to truly forgive her. She closed her eyes and savored the moment.

As they crossed the lake, he said nothing, and she didn't touch his skin. They hit the refreshing patch in the center swiftly. The heat on the other side of that area stifled as much as it had the first time.

At the cleft where the lake tumbled into the river, Colby wrapped an arm around Chavali and covered her hand with his.

::I didn't see anything on the way up. Didn't even know I was going up.::

He wanted to avoid anything weighty. Chavali could tell by the guarded edge to his thoughts.

::Did you know this river was originally called the Path to Tortured Miracles? It was in that book I found at the inn.::

This described Chavali's opinion of the pool's healing effect. But they didn't have the luxury of time to dawdle on simple matters. The trip back to Palmia Basin, sailing with the current, would take far less time than the trip to the peak had. They could arrive as early as the next morning.

"You need to understand that someone from the Spire tried to take Karias. I don't know if Korrya had any knowledge or involvement, and am torn about whether to confront her or not. I do know they will try again. Portia is familiar with one of the mages who tried to abduct him, so we are certain they work for the Spire. Karias has suggested it would be prudent for you and him to avoid contact with anyone from the Spire as much as possible."

::I'm really confused about Karias.::

"I know. I can feel your distress on the subject." Apparently, he wanted to talk about it despite not wanting to talk about it. "Had that mushroom incident not happened, I would have found a way to explain after this mission. I had already made that decision. Keeping this secret from you was not my preference."

::I remember the day he found me. Clouds parted and he stood in a ray of sunshine. His coat sparkled, and so did his hooves. I thought....::

Colby pictured the moment. Chavali had seen the memory before without knowing Karias's side of the story. Understanding more of the context made this vision feel nostalgic instead of real. He'd idealized it, turning it into a kind of mythological event. In his mind, the Creator had reached from beyond Her wall and delivered a horse perfect for him so he could do Her work.

"You thought you'd earned the attention of something greater than yourself. You thought you'd gained a special purpose. And now you feel this must be a lie. Everything you believe must be a lie. Which is the worst horror of all, because it means you have willingly lied to yourself about something you consider foundational for several years. The evidence of your eyes and ears becomes suspect. Did this thing really happen, or did you imagine it?"

::I suppose you understand lies much better than I do. I didn't mean that. Yes, I did, but not like it seems.::

"I know. Hear me when I say this, Colby. A bizarre, freak accident bound you and Karias. This does not mean it didn't happen for a reason. The reason is unclear and defies our ability to understand, but it is there. Why you? Why not the person next to you, or ten feet away? And why that horse? The stable certainly held several others. Yet it bound you to that horse with that soul inside it."

::You mean that if it had truly been a complete, undirected accident, the binding could've tied us to a lesser horse, or even something else, like a sparrow or a housecat.::

"Just so. And I will tell you something else. Among clan, what you have is unique. There are no stories of any soul bound to another in any true fashion. We have stories of people bound by love, hate, vengeance, pain, duty, and many other things, but not a true binding of souls. Nothing with animals, either. The goats are not special in that fashion. They are symbolic."

::The spirits?::

Chavali waved off the question. "This subject is more complex. If they're bound to anything, it's the feather, not me."

::What would happen if someone took it from you?::

"This is not a good place for me to explain such things. Ask again when we have true privacy."

::That's not what I want to do the next time we have true privacy.::

She rolled her eyes. "Stop this line of thought, please."

He let go of her hand, which she considered a mercy. Resting his chin on top of her head, he sighed. "I'm sorry. You can't blame me for thinking about that. I know you need time and slow steps, and I'm fine with that. The best thing to do whenever I veer in that direction is to stop touching me."

Chavali wished all problems could resolve themselves so easily. "I will take this request as confirmation that I am forgiven."

"I always believed Karias was exceptional. I knew he could understand what I said because he acted like it. You say you have a treat and he's there, waiting for it. Call his name, he comes. Tell him to search for something, he finds it. That's beyond training. It's intelligence. But I still thought of him as a horse. With horse wants and needs. Horse thoughts. Not human wants, needs, or thoughts."

She laid her hand on his leg. "Now you're having many conflicted thoughts about what you've said and done to or around him. There is some embarrassment. And much frustration and jealousy that you can't know what he says but I can."

His chest rose and fell with each breath he heaved instead of responding.

"He is not and has never been upset with you for treating him like an animal. You had no way to know. With your and his permission, I will explain all of this to Penny and Railan, and perhaps Portia. We will work together to complete the binding so you may speak *with* him instead of *to* him."

"Portia?"

"She is a mage of considerable skill." Chavali noted that, for the first time, she saw Portia eating on a boat. Bathing in the pool had, perhaps, helped her a great deal, at least for this journey. "And I have considered asking her to join the clan already. She would make a good addition, and I like her. All the clan elders would have to agree, and then she would also."

"It's funny that you liking her is the last thing you put on the list, as if it doesn't matter much."

"On the contrary, it's astoundingly important. I merely think it not particularly moving as a reason for others."

He kissed her cheek. *::I happen to think it's the most important reason you could offer. In my experience, you're an excellent judge of character.::*

"You may be somewhat biased."

Wrapping his arms around her again, he held her close. "Maybe."

She reveled in his embrace, content to ignore the world while the boat careened down the river.

CHAPTER 25

Chavali woke in the early hours of the next morning with her head on Colby's shoulder, breathing in his scent. The sun provided only a dim glow to the east and a light drizzle slicked everyone and everything with damp.

The growing roar of a nearby waterfall goaded her to sit up. They'd almost reached the channel to Palmia Basin's lake already.

She hated to wake Colby. He slept on his back with no tension or concerns. Neither of them had any idea what to expect from this day, but she doubted they'd have much time to sit in idleness. If she could let him steal a few extra moments of peace, she wanted to.

Karias stirred and whinnied to wake everyone. The captain tipped the boat into the channel while the others mumbled and yawned. Colby hadn't even sat up yet. He grabbed whatever he could reach to steady himself, which meant Chavali.

She smiled to make sure he knew they faced no danger, and held onto the railing. He hadn't come up with them and had no idea what to expect.

The boat flew down the channel with the captain and his sister working together to keep them from crashing into the walls. They reached the bottom swiftly. Momentum carried the boat halfway across the lake before the captain needed to urge the oxen to work again.

"Is that smoke?" Jaris asked. He pointed at the north side of the city.

In the midst of buildings and trees, a dark cloud pushed against the light rain, swirling and spreading outward.

"Yes," Sivry said.

Chavali noted a raven circling them as the captain returned to his berth at the docks. It dove to the ground, calling her attention to Korrya and Rowan approaching. The bird landed on Rowan's shoulder. Korrya waved aside a Riverway representative.

"I'm going to check in," Daria muttered to Chavali. "I'll be around if you need me."

Chavali nodded to Daria. "We have greeters," she told the others as she set her hand on her hip, near her dagger. She noted an appropriate amount of tension among the rest of the group. Colby stood beside Karias, confused, determined, and ready to launch into action.

He may have had conflicted thoughts about his horse, but he still knew how to fight while riding Karias.

"Welcome back," Korrya said with a light bow as she passed Daria on the dock. She held her staff, using it like a walking stick.

Rowan took an inconspicuous step to the side, putting him closer to Colby and Karias.

Chavali had asked them to watch for their return. They'd honored her request.

Whether she'd regret this or not remained to be seen.

"Thank you."

Daria slowed significantly and watched the meeting.

"I've been asked to take the horse into custody for the Spire." Korrya smiled, polite and friendly.

Not certain why Korrya would say such a thing so bluntly or make this attempt without more manpower, Chavali took Colby's hand.

His thoughts danced across the wide open docks, mapping escape options.

"Naturally, Colby is invited to join us. I wouldn't be so unpleasant as to separate you, unlike some people."

Portia jabbed a finger at Korrya. "Why didn't you tell us Narryn was here?" she growled. "He almost killed Chastity."

Korrya raised both hands in surrender. "I didn't know until yesterday. He delivered his request to detain the horse in his usual grumpy fashion, extracted a promise from me to help, and left like the ass he is."

"I didn't know there were any mlinzi operating independently," Rowan said to Colby, "but I'm guessing they've rethought that stance."

::I didn't know that either.::

Chavali wanted to roll her eyes. Rowan obviously meant Colby, yet Colby didn't realize it. She squeezed his hand to keep him from talking. "Before you perform this duty, we would appreciate hearing about the state of the city in our absence."

"Yes, of course." Korrya beckoned for them to follow. "Let's get out of this rain and have tea. I'm sure there's no chance Colby and his horse would ever manage to slip away while we're chatting. The pair of them are so large. It's impossible. Rowan would never allow that to happen, not even while assisting one of your number who's clearly not at her best."

Suddenly, Chavali liked her a great deal more.

"No, of course not." She waved for Daria to move on. They didn't need her help at the moment.

"Here, let me help you, miss." Rowan offered his assistance to Portia. "You look like you might need it."

Sivry, Portia, Jaris, and Chavali exchanged glances. Chavali nodded toward Sivry and Jaris, then Colby. She couldn't say for sure that Sivry understood, but Jaris did.

After patting Colby's hand, she let go and shooed him away. Between Sivry, Jaris, and Colby, she expected they could come up with Flower Beds as a place to regather.

"Is Narryn still in town?" Portia grumbled. She leaned on Rowan despite needing no help whatsoever.

"No. He tasked me with collecting the horse and had to leave for some other errand."

Chavali smirked and walked with Korrya. If Sivry had the right of it, her brother's mysterious other errand revolved around licking his wounded pride. "We'll try not to distract you too much."

Korrya grinned and opened the door for them. "Oh, goodness. Rowan, you've lost them already." She sighed. "So careless."

"My apologies. This woman is exhausted. She needs the help."

"Of course. When you have a chance, go see if they've left any clues for their whereabouts. But not until you have a chance. We do need tea, after all. I don't want either of these women to catch a cold. They're soaked to the bone."

Portia snorted as she sat on Korrya's couch. Chavali sat beside her. The small room and its tidiness felt so strange after so much time on an open boat deck. She sighed in appreciation for the lovely cushions, a luxury she'd missed for the past few days. Qanafe hung in the air, teasing her with the promise of that tea Korrya had offered.

Quite pleased with herself, Korrya took the chair opposite them.

"I'm glad I'm not the only one with that opinion of Narryn," Portia said.

Korrya rolled her eyes. "I can't explain how there's anyone who doesn't share it. But there are a few in the Spire who respect him. Keep that in mind."

"This is good to know. What can you tell us about what else has happened?" Chavali asked.

Rowan handed warm mugs of the delicious local tea to Chavali and Portia. He hadn't heated the water much, allowing them to drink without fear of scalding.

"The Qanafe Furies have burned down at least five more buildings," Korrya said. "That smoke on the north side this morning might be number six. There could be others I don't know about. They're quite capable at it. Only one building is destroyed. Even when they share walls with other structures, the fire stays contained."

"None of the targeted buildings appear to have anything specific in common," Rowan added. "They have different purposes, shapes, sizes, locations. Both sides of the lake. It seems random. Like everything else they've done."

Chavali doubted they selected their targets at random. The thing in the mountain undoubtedly guided them. It clearly had a plan, though she didn't understand it or have any brilliant ideas for decoding it.

"What did you find at the top of the mountain?" Korrya asked. "I've heard a number of rumors, but haven't attempted the journey myself."

"There's a lake which appears to have some magical properties." Chavali shrugged and looked to Portia. Sending Korrya up to meet the mushroom dragon struck her as a terrible idea.

"None of us are much for studying that kind of thing," Portia said. "You'd probably find it fascinating if you can get up there. I recommend taking an overland approach. The river is treacherous and we were lucky. The Creator smiled on us."

Though Chavali didn't think the Creator deserved any credit, she nodded. "It was certainly not a pleasant journey, and I doubt you'd find it worth the effort. The area is curious, not wondrous or miraculous."

Nodding like she understood, Korrya gestured for Rowan to speak next.

"Even though you didn't ask," Rowan said, "I kept an eye on your baker friend of a friend. He was arrested for murdering a guardsman yesterday, which I find farcical. The man is harmless. And yet, I have no ability to investigate, as they won't tell me the name of the dead man. It's none of my concern, apparently."

Chavali frowned into her tea. "Thank you for watching over him. Did you happen to inspect the bakery in our absence, or see him doing so?"

Rowan and his raven both cocked their heads in the same fashion to regard her. "I noticed he strolled past it at least twice. Why would you ask?"

"It was his livelihood," Portia said. She waved off his interest.

More than ever, Chavali wanted Portia in the clan.

She set her half-empty mug aside and stood. "We should go so you can begin your investigation into the horse's mysterious disappearance from your custody."

"One last thing, Chastity." Korrya stood with her. "It's become clear there's something questionable going on with the Guard. I'm not sure what Consul Shore is up to, or if she's even aware of it. For all I know, she's playing some kind of dangerous game to get corrupt officers to expose themselves. What matters is that members of the Guard are taking liberties they haven't before, and others, like the Riverway Guild and what's left of the Withered Fists, are taking advantage of it. You should watch your backs."

"Thank you. We appreciate the warning." Chavali waited for Portia and followed her out the door.

"That was interesting," Portia said once they'd put some distance between them and Korrya's home. They passed two- and three-story homes smashed together in tight clusters with fan-leafed trees flanking them like sentinels.

"I'm pleased to know she's an ally," Chavali said with a nod. "The news about the Guard is troubling. It suggests Faillit may have some plan she's preparing for."

"Such as...?" Portia raised her brow.

"I don't know." Chavali shook her head. "I need more information. What are the guards specifically doing or not doing? Where? Some window into whatever Faillit wants would also help."

Portia nodded. "It's always nice when you admit you're not all-knowing."

Chavali snorted. They laughed together.

At an intersection where they needed to choose whether to return to the inn or not, Portia asked, "Do you want to fetch the others first or go check on Torrel? I don't believe he murdered a guard any more than Rowan does."

"Of course he didn't. We should go find Torrel first. The others will only get in the way."

Portia smirked. "You mean one person in particular."

Chavali snorted. "Obviously. We have to bluff our way into a prison. He's terrible at this. Jaris or Sivry might be an asset if we had to sneak. In my experience, sneaking isn't necessary. I can talk my way in."

"You've certainly done it before," Portia said with a nod. "I'll wait outside."

Discreet inquiries brought them to a two-story jail squatting near the building where Chavali had met Nora and Consul Shore. Guards stood at attention outside without blocking the inexplicably open doorway. More guards patrolled the rooftop and a narrow strip of balcony around a second floor with a curious lack of windows or vents.

Chavali had seen better security at bars and fish shacks. Unless the inside boasted some unexpected obstacle, she'd have no trouble extracting

Torrel.

She handed her dagger to Portia, then breezed inside with an air of belonging.

Two steps inside the door, a guard checked Chavali for weapons in a tiny cubicle of a room. She waved Chavali deeper inside without asking any questions.

Stepping through the doorway blasted Chavali with stagnant, damp heat like a brick to the face. She gasped at the sudden change. Only magic could've created such a discrete difference from one room to the next.

She'd found her obstacle.

Despite pristine white walls, the room stank of sweat and desperation. Six additional guards posted beside three doors seemed unaffected by the wretched place. Two of them sniggered, presumably at Chavali's reaction to the conditions.

A number of benches holding two men and a woman in the process of completing forms on clipboards. One struggled with the forms. All three wore loose clothing of rough fibers, worn in places and patched, and no sandals.

Petitioners suffering from such gross poverty at the jail suggested Palmia Basin imprisoned those who failed to pay fines and fees. The boat captain's story about owing money to the Riverway Guild for a crime he hadn't committed spoke volumes about the real priorities of the Guard.

In some places, authorities tried to keep their jails empty. In others, they preferred full. Palmia Basin looked like the latter.

"Are you here to see a prisoner?" asked a bored, uniformed man behind a fine-mesh screen with a small access flap. He sat at a desk in a small room with an open door behind him. Papers in neat stacks covered his desk. The barrier meant Chavali had no options for touching him.

Chavali leaned a hand against the rough wall to steady herself and flashed him a polite smile. If she could function with a broken arm, she could function in appalling heat. "Yes, please. His name is Torrel."

The man ran his fingers down a page of neat lettering in rows. "There's no Torrel here."

Such a curious thing to say when she knew she'd find him here. She decided to take a leap based on Korrya's information and see what happened. "Is that what you want me to tell Guyre?"

He blinked and peered at her. "Excuse me?"

She smirked and inspected her fingernails. "He sent me to try some... unusual forms of persuasion. Did you not get the notice?"

"No." He frowned and searched among his papers.

"That's not my fault. He said he sent it ahead. This was supposed to be taken care of so I wouldn't have to waste time."

Raising his hands in defeat, the man huffed. "It wasn't."

Chavali had no need to feign annoyance. "My services are not cheap. Guyre is covering my fee as a favor for the captain. Either let me through or be responsible for turning me away."

She'd flustered the poor man. He pawed over his papers, muttering, "How hard is it to send a notice?"

"Fine. It's on your head." She whirled to leave, expecting him to call her back.

As if on cue, he only let her take one step toward the exit. "Wait." He yanked open a desk drawer and snatched a small block of wood from it. "Here. Take it upstairs." He shoved the block through the access flap and pointed to one of the doors.

Chavali took the block and nodded to him. On two sides, the number seventeen had been burned into the wood.

She crossed the room with as much haste as she could muster and showed the block to the guards at the indicated door. One checked the block. The other opened the door to a narrow flight of stairs.

At the top, she showed the block to another guard. This one took it from her and escorted her down a shadowy, sweltering hallway lined with cages. Each numbered cage afforded one person enough room to lie on the floor or stand. They had small toilets built into the walls and buckets of water hanging inside the doors. Several cells held prisoners, all lying on the floor of their cages.

Some kind of sickly sweet flower smell tried and failed to cover the aromas of vomit, urine, and sweat. Combined with the heat, Chavali wondered how many prisoners died before release or trial.

They stopped at seventeen. Torrel lay on the floor with his back to his cage door. His sweat-soaked pants and shirt had rips and dried blood stains.

"I'll be able to see you the whole time," the guard said. "If you try to pass him anything, you'll get your own cell."

"I understand."

At the sound of her voice, Torrel turned his head, then rolled onto his back. Hope flickered in his eyes.

Chavali crouched and stuck her open hand through the bars. "I am not here to release you," she murmured as the guard left them. "Not yet, anyway."

He took her hand. His thoughts ran torpid and half-formed. The heat had sapped much of his energy and will to live. Something confusing and disjointed about his basement reminded Chavali she needed to check on it. Perhaps it had a connection to everything else.

"Thank you for coming," he rasped.

"I'm sorry we were gone when this happened. Now that we're back, I need to know what happened so I can fix it."

"You can't fix this." He remembered the involvement of an unexpected person. Someone Chavali recognized too.

"Don't be ridiculous. How do you know Wray?"

While he tried to swallow so he could speak more, his mind showed her what she needed to know. Wray had come to see him. They'd talked. The conversation flowed through his mind without catching.

Chavali got the gist. She wanted to strangle the consul for letting the guard get out of control.

"Never mind." She squeezed his hand. "I will free you. Trust me to do this. Destroying corruption is my job, and you will not be a casualty. Drink water. Survive. Do not give in. Can you do this for me?"

Torrel didn't know if he could manage it. The heat made him want to die.

"Can you do it for Iker?"

At his name, Torrel met her gaze. His despair faded and determination stepped to the forefront. "For Iker." *::Dear Creator, watch* *over him. I don't know if we're right together, but I'd like the chance to find out.::*

She helped him to his knees so he could drink from his bucket. "I will protect Iker and his inn. You will walk free from this place and see him again. I swear it on my soul."

"Thank you." *::You have a strange job, Chastity. Ten years ago, I might've volunteered for something like that.::* "Creator watch over you."

"And you." Satisfied he'd take some care with himself, Chavali let go and hurried out of the jail. She took care to school her expression for the gentleman behind the mesh so he'd think she'd succeeded.

She met Portia outside and headed for the inn. "We need to collect the others, then I would like very much to speak with Consul Shore."

"The consul? Why?"

Baring her teeth, Chavali glared at the road ahead. "To tell her she's an idiot."

CHAPTER 26

Anger roiled among the group. They sat in the common room, filling a booth in the back. Few other customers populated the room, and all sat on the other side of it. That handful of people ate swiftly, fear pressing on their shoulders.

Once Chavali explained the conditions at the prison and Torrel's situation, Colby wanted to storm the jail and destroy it. Sivry, Jaris, and Portia exercised more restraint, but they clearly agreed.

"*Why* he's there is the worse crime," Chavali said over a meal she needed but didn't want. Eating took time they didn't have.

She waved to Iker to bring more tea. After suffering for only a few minutes in that jail, she couldn't drink enough liquids. "The Talons tried to shake down the area businesses. Torrel took the lead and stood up to them with everyone behind him. The next day, guards showed up and assessed fines for ridiculous offenses."

"The fines are harsh," Iker said as he refilled Chavali's tea. His voice warbled with tension and distress. "We can't afford ours. It's twice as much as the Fists ever demanded. They want even more to release Torrel." He stumbled over the man's name and sniffled. "I don't know what to do."

"Don't pay it," Portia said. "Definitely don't try to pay even part of it. None of you should. We're going to sort this out."

Iker's hand shook. His eyes watered. He spilled a few drops of tea on the table before righting his kettle. "Before someone gets killed?"

Chavali touched Iker's sleeve, certain he cared the most about one particular someone. "If the Guard, the Talons, or the Fists wish to kill, they will do so regardless of what money is or isn't handed over. This is no longer about greed. It's about power and control. We will do everything in our power to free Torrel and you both from this blight."

Nodding, Iker swiped his sleeve across his face. "Please save him." He fled the table for the back room.

Colby radiated rage. Jaris and Sivry wore similar grim scowls. Portia pressed her lips into a thin line and tapped her fingernails on the table.

They needed to step away from all the anger to work effectively. Chavali frowned because she had more news, and it wouldn't help.

"Wray, our one honest guardsman who Torrel is accused of murdering, is not dead." She replayed Torrel's memory to refresh the details. "He's hiding. Wray met Torrel because Torrel did what any of us would do. After the guards came to do the Talons' dirty work, he spied on the guards. Wray discovered him while also spying on those guards and they met later to share information. Someone followed, Wray hid, and Torrel wouldn't reveal his location."

"So they arrested him to get him to talk," Colby growled. "Since Wray is hiding, no one can refute his murder."

Chavali sipped her tea. "Quite. He will not talk. At this point, the consul is either blind or directing this corruption. I would very much like to know which and deal with it accordingly."

"This city is so screwed up," Jaris said. "You walk in and it looks like paradise. Then you stay for a few days and discover it's the opposite."

"Shouldn't we find Wray?" Colby asked. "They can't hold Torrel for the murder of someone who's alive."

Sivry shook her head. "At this point, it doesn't matter if Wray is dead or alive. They'll lose Torrel's paperwork, stage an escape attempt to foil, or just kill him outright and dump the body because he knows too much."

"I agree," Chavali said. "Shore may be a Spilled Blood adherent, but not everyone is." She laid a hand on Colby's arm to keep him from leaping out of his chair to vent his outrage. "Wray needs to remain hidden for now to keep both men alive." She pushed away the remains of her food and stood.

Portia held up her hands. "This is terrible and we need to get Torrel safe and cleared. Is storming to the consul and demanding it the best option?"

Colby picked up his sword and strapped it to his back. "I trust Chavali's opinion of how to attack this problem."

Chavali gestured for the group to get moving. "If the consul is unaware, then she becomes our ally. If she's running this madness, we go now to confront the source instead of wasting our time by squabbling with her lackeys."

"And if she has us arrested?" Portia asked.

"We resist," Colby growled. He stormed out of the room, ready to rain fire on anyone in his path.

Portia leaned close to Chavali as they headed for the door. "You know I just want to make sure we're doing the right thing?"

"Yes, and I appreciate it."

Outside, they collected all the horses to hasten their travel across the city. Chavali rode with Colby. For the first time, she could explain their destination to Karias without needing to hide it. She did keep her voice low to avoid alerting Portia, Sivry, and Jaris to his intelligence. For Colby, though, she no longer needed fiction.

Releasing this secret lifted a burden. She wanted to turn around and tell him other secrets and other fictions she'd used to protect the clan.

He didn't need to know so many things, yet she wanted to share them with him anyway.

Pondering this alien impulse kept her quiet for the short ride to Palmia Basin's city hall. She'd confided in her sister once in a while, though less so as they grew up. Becoming the seer had set her apart, even from her truest friend. No one else had ever earned that much trust from her.

Colby would never betray her secrets. He might tell a close friend about his feelings, but he wouldn't reveal anything important or dangerous. She should've known that before.

She leaned against him and took his hand. "When we get home, I would like to sit and speak of uncomfortable things."

::When you put it like that, how can I refuse?::

With a grin, she kissed his palm. "You cannot. This is an order from your seer. Refusal is therefore not one of your choices. You could try to avoid me for a while, but once I become determined, this is impossible."

Colby chuckled. Karias whinnied his amusement.

::Tell me what Karias has to say.::

She let go of Colby's hand to touch Karias's neck.

::He's taking this remarkably well. Much better than I expected.::

Under no circumstances would she tell Colby any such thing. "He believes he has underestimated your resilience and would like to apologize for letting his fear prevent him from seeing your true inner strength."

::That is not at all what I said, you manipulative wench.::

Instead of responding, Colby grunted to acknowledge her.

They turned the corner, putting the city hall and its decorative plaza in sight. Gentle breezes through the shady tunnel of foliage kept the heat at bay. Locals traveled on foot in both directions, some with dogs or llamas bearing loads. An elder woman sitting in front of a shrub festooned with large blossoms offered crumbs to a collection of noisy, fat squirrels and birds.

The double doors leading into the building stood open. The first time they'd visited, Chavali remembered two guards had flanked them and opened the doors for them. Perhaps some circumstance had called them elsewhere.

::Something seems off.:: His ears flicked back and forth.

"Karias believes something is wrong?"

Colby shifted behind her. He drew his sword. "There are no guards."

"And?" Chavali didn't see this as a cause for alarm.

::I hear fighting. We're charging into the courtyard.::

With no further warning, Karias sped into a gallop. The other three horses followed him through the doors and into the courtyard. They slid to a stop among the statues.

Guards battled on the stairs with their backs to the courtyard, fighting others on higher steps. Chavali couldn't see their enemies above the knees. Clanging metal echoed off the walls. Shouts and grunts rang out. A portrait fell from the wall with a crash and tumbled down the steps, spreading broken glass. Someone screamed upstairs.

Colby leaped off Karias's back and rushed the fight.

"Who are they fighting?" Portia asked as she clambered off her horse.

Chavali slid to the ground, watching for some hint. If these guards fought other guards, they didn't want to kill the honest ones.

"Fists!" Colby bellowed.

With that one word, Sivry and Jaris rushed forward to join the battle. Karias circled Chavali, Portia, and the horses, checking in every direction.

Chavali stayed with Portia. She didn't need to rush the front line and break another bone.

The Fists on the stairs fell under the combined assault. Colby led everyone up the stairs. Chavali and Portia followed at a sensible distance, keeping watch behind them.

At the top, half of the door to the council room hung from the top hinge. Debris from broken chairs littered the floor around the central table and spilled into the hall. Far too many people for the size of the room clashed with swords and daggers in a messy, chaotic melee.

They shouted and grunted. Metal clanged. Papers flew. The coppery taste of blood hung in the air.

Colby plowed inside with Sivry and Jaris on his heels.

Two men, one a uniformed guard, bled on the floor outside the room, both either dead or unconscious. Among those still fighting, Chavali recognized Captain Faillit and the one young woman who'd stuck out and asked an annoying question. She could tell a tight cluster of people sheltered under the table at the far end.

As Chavali and Portia the doorway, an explosion rocked the building. Chavali's ears thrummed and rang as she stumbled to the side. Debris blew into the council chamber from the back wall. Portia tumbled into her and they hit the wall. Dust puffed through the door. Chavali covered her mouth and nose with a sleeve. Portia did the same. Both coughed anyway.

The blast had not harmed Colby. Chavali repeated this to herself. Chunks of wall or table, or whatever else the explosion had flung, had not hit him. Sivry and Jaris were also fine.

If she believed it hard enough, she would make it true.

Portia pointed at the hallway leading around the council chamber.

Chavali nodded and followed her with a hand on the wall to keep herself steady. The ringing in her ears faded. Noise from the battle murmured in the distance, muffled by the wall. She straightened as she recovered from the blast and hurried in Portia's wake.

They turned the corner to the hallway behind the council chamber and paused. Dust clogged the corridor in a thick cloud. Portia waved her hands once as if she held a large fan, forcing air past them. The dust swirled as it dispersed deeper into the building, revealing minimal debris.

The explosion had blown a hole into the council chamber without damaging the office behind it.

Portia rushed to the hole. Chavali drew her dagger and followed. At the hole, Portia collided with a man in a guard uniform wearing a scarf around his head and holding a bloody dagger. Both fell with grunts.

Chavali crouched to check on Portia and grimaced at the stench of fresh death. The downed guardsman lunged at them. Chavali shoved her blade at his head. Though he flinched, the spiral knife slashed across his eye and cheek, drinking from him.

The man screamed and clawed at his face. Chavali stabbed him in the chest.

He gurgled and collapsed. Beyond him, the council table blocked her view of the rest of the room. She saw legs and a few weapons. Colby kicked someone in the knee.

Closer at hand, three messy bodies lay on the floor. The stink of skewered guts and blood came from them. Slimy, bloody ropes of intestine covered one woman's limp body. Another rasped her death rattle from a slashed throat. The third fell limp from a wide gash in her chest.

Consul Shore had died much too fast for Chavali to do anything about it.

Portia took her hand and tugged. *::If we're seen, they'll accuse us of murdering all four.::*

Chavali nodded and crawled backward until they cleared the hole. She scrambled to her feet and they dashed around the corner. Pausing to catch their breaths in the empty hallway, Portia and Chavali exchanged glances.

"Was that a guard or a Fist in a fake uniform?" Portia whispered.

"Or someone else entirely? I don't know. It doesn't matter. Shore is dead. Who killed her is irrelevant. Someone will seize power now, and I wish to know who." Chavali cocked her head to the side. "The battle is winding down. We should be seen again."

Portia nodded. They rushed back to the chamber's front door. The noise had faded to moans of the injured.

Still acting like a protector, Chavali leaned around Portia to peer inside. The dust settled more with every passing moment. Several more bodies lay on the floor. Colby checked a corpse. Sivry tied a small bandage around Jaris's arm. Several guards remained standing, tending to each other's wounds. They'd taken no prisoners.

Captain Faillit stalked to the rear and crouched when she reached the bodies. Through the decreasing haze, Chavali thought she saw the captain's mouth twitch with annoyance at discovering the dead man in the guard uniform.

"Consul Shore is dead," Faillit announced to the room. "As is her secretary."

Only a few people seemed upset by this. The young woman covered her mouth and turned her back on the captain. Two other members of the council remained standing. One let out a strangled sob. The other lowered her head and touched her hand to her heart.

Of the guards, most seemed both unsurprised and unmoved. Two blinked in stupid shock.

Faillit stood tall. "I hereby invoke emergency powers to assume control of the city, as accorded in the Palmia Basin charter."

"Now we know who wanted her dead," Portia murmured.

Chavali also considered this action swift and specific enough for suspicion.

The young woman staggered out of the room. As she caught her breath, Chavali realized who the young woman resembled. Anna, the older woman in Guyre's company, bore a curious similarity, not in facial features or build, but in carriage and accent.

The same person had trained both in some collection of spy-like skills, or perhaps the older woman mentored this younger one.

"Your spice merchant hires capable people," the woman said as she scowled and wiped her narrow blade clean. "I'm glad you were here for myself, at least. The one man, the smaller one, saved my life."

Chavali nodded. "A shame he couldn't do the same for Shore. I didn't catch your name before?"

"Tam." They shook hands. *::Shore was a valuable ally. This will make everything harder.::* A flicker of surprise slipped across Tam's features so fast Chavali almost missed it. She ended the contact swiftly and with no option for Chavali to continue it. "Excuse me. People need to know about this." She hurried down the stairs.

Somehow, Chavali suspected Tam had noticed her telepathic intrusion and fled from it.

Shore had selected an interesting councilor in Tam.

CHAPTER 27

Chavali flashed a discreet thumbs-up at Sivry, trying to indicate she and Portia were fine, then tapped below her eye. She needed to get Colby out of there without signaling their connection to Sivry and Jaris. Faillit may not have seen it, and keeping her from noticing sounded like a good idea.

Sivry nodded and stopped checking in her direction.

"Lieutenant, do you recognize any of these bodies?" Faillit asked.

"These two are known members of the Withered Fists, ma'am."

The exchange struck Chavali as off somehow. Though she could see neither Faillit or her lieutenant, she had a suspicion they might have planned it.

"And you work for some kind of merchant, don't you?" Faillit asked.

Chavali had a feeling she knew who Faillit meant. She stepped into sight. "A spice merchant, yes. We were passing by and noticed the fight. It's our habit to assist city officials when under attack."

"That's a dangerous habit, but we appreciate your help." Before, Faillit had paid her little attention. This time, she studied Chavali for several seconds. Her gaze flicked to Colby, who stood under her scrutiny. "You can both go."

Colby kept his mouth shut for once. He nodded to Faillit and left the room without glancing at Sivry or Jaris.

Stifling her surprise at his perfect reading of the proper behavior she needed from him, Chavali gave Faillit a polite bow. "I'm sorry for the loss of your leader. The city is undoubtedly poorer for it."

Faillit nodded and flicked her wrist to suggest Chavali should get out of her sight. "Lieutenant," she said as Chavali turned and took the stairs down with Colby and Portia at an excessively slow pace, "since we know the Fists have been bringing in fresh members, I want the docks shut down for a few days. We need to assess and deal with this external threat."

"Yes, ma'am." The lieutenant saluted and hurried down the stairs past the trio.

At the bottom of the stairs, they collected Karias and Portia's horse. Colby still stayed quiet as they lead both out of the courtyard. He helped Portia onto her mount before climbing onto Karias's back and pulling Chavali onto his lap.

Chavali noted a guardswoman watching them through the open double doors. Karias clopped up the street. The guard followed.

With her on foot, they could lose her if they wanted.

Chavali considered their options. If Captain Faillit wanted to know where to find them, she could get that information one way or another. For the moment, Chavali preferred to make any information gathering as annoying and challenging as possible.

They could take the guard on a scenic tour of the city. If she didn't tire, or found another guard to take on the duty in her stead, this accomplished nothing.

She leaned forward. "Karias, we're being followed. Speed up, lose them, and take a few side streets."

He acknowledged her request and shifted to a canter. Colby held Chavali close and said nothing. Portia's horse kept pace with Karias, following on his heels.

Karias led them down one street, then another. He followed a wide loop and backtracked. When he slowed again, Chavali recognized the neighborhood. The shops on the ground floor and apartments above had a particular style of gingerbread trim. Likewise, the flowers had a particular shape.

"Take us to the bakery. Torrel worried about something strange in the basement. We're almost there anyway."

Karias turned down Torrel's street.

"We should regroup with Sivry and Jaris," Colby said. "Jaris was hurt in the fight."

Chavali shrugged. "It will take only a few minutes, and is likely trifling. Better to get it over with than to have to trudge over here again later. I can take a look while everyone else waits outside."

"I'll go in with you," Portia said, "to check for magic flavors of weird."

Karias stopped in front of the burned out bakery. Aside from the windows and door, the facade remained intact. Streaks of soot decorated all the edges. Plant life sprouted from cracks and crevices in the charred floor and walls. Through the gaps, Chavali could see the display cases had broken, their glass littering both their shelves and the floor.

Colby climbed down and helped Chavali to the ground. Through his hand, she caught his disjointed thoughts and gathered he needed to think about that fight before discussing it or the likely fallout from it.

She left him behind to duck under a beam across the front doorway. With Portia right behind her, she picked her way through the damp front room.

Ants and flies swarmed in clumps amidst the sooty glass, rock, and wood debris. The wooden floor creaked underfoot. They moved slowly to avoid spots where they might break through.

"I suppose you can answer yes or no questions," she heard Colby mutter to the horse.

Portia nudged a pile of broken ceramics. "I expected it to smell like burnt things, but this smells like..."

"Rot and earth, yes. Curious." Taking care not to dislodge more than necessary, Chavali pushed another fallen beam aside. Mushrooms with stems as thick as Chavali's neck ringed a hole in the floor as if they'd climbed from it. Shelf-like fungus clung to the walls. The plants seemed to strive toward the ceiling without trying to leave the building through the hole in the back wall.

She and Portia stopped and stared at them.

"This must be a new development," Chavali said as she approached the nearest. "If Torrel had seen this, he would've said there were giant mushrooms in his back room, not something curious in his basement."

Portia crouched beside one with a wide cap and examined it without touching. "There's something weird going on for sure. Did the mushroom dragon in the mountain look like these?"

"If that's red and orange, then yes, some of its parts did. It was made of several varieties. Considering the Furies burned this bakery, odds are quite good these are related to it."

"Maybe we should get the others before checking the basement."

Chavali peered into the darkness of the hole to the basement. More stems stuck at odd angles, some with feathery fronds and others with multiple thick sprouts. She thought they might cushion a fall. "This seems wise."

She turned and saw Colby looking up the street and waving to someone. Horses' hooves clopped on the tiled street. As she reached the front door, Sivry and Jaris joined him.

Sivry leaned down to peer inside the building. "We stayed long enough to introduce ourselves to two of Wray's friends. Everyone else there was highly questionable. Why are we here? Jaris happened to notice Colby and Karias as we passed the street."

"There is something quite curious in the back room, and I think we should all see it." Chavali beckoned for them to follow. "Did you discover anything else?"

Jaris and Sivry dismounted and followed.

"Stay," Colby said. Then he coughed and mumbled something as he joined them inside the structure.

"The guard I talked to," Sivry said as she swatted flies around her head, "said Faillit claimed she'd interrogated a captured member of the Fists and discovered they had a plan to meet with Consul Shore to assassinate her. After the fight, this guard isn't so sure she believes that."

Jaris poked the remains of a limp, charred curtain with her dagger. "There were no Fist bodies near Shore. One of the questionable guards spit at Shore's corpse. Faillit took something from the dead guard near Shore and stuffed it in her pocket. I think it was cloth."

Chavali exchanged a glance with Portia as she reached the back room again. "This was the man who killed Shore."

"Why would Faillit want Shore dead?" Colby asked.

Portia shrugged. "The same reasons anyone else might. Power, lust, or greed."

"I would bet on power," Sivry said.

"Seems like a safe bet." Jaris blinked at the fungus. "What makes mushrooms grow this big this fast?"

"I doubt it's natural." While the others entered the room and inspected the mushrooms, Chavali pondered what Faillit stood to gain. According to Nora, Faillit had supported Shore. In turn, Shore had appointed Faillit to lead the Guard.

She thought of Tam and Anna, acting as outside influences. The Fists also came from the outside.

Perhaps she tried to overcomplicate things. Some matter of simple policy may have divided Faillit and Shore, leading to a kind of impasse. Bit by bit, decision by decision, Faillit had wound up hating Shore over it and convinced she had a better solution.

She liked this simple, human reasoning. Anyone could take small steps without realizing the path she traveled until far too late. Once mired in a pit of sinking sand, she grasped at any rope, no matter how despicable.

"I think we should take a look below," Colby said, distracting Chavali from her thoughts, "but maybe try the stairs instead?"

"They're under this." Sivry tapped a pile of debris with her boot. Part of the trapdoor showed at the edge of the mess. "If we clear it off enough to use it, the place might collapse."

Colby sighed. "I'll go first. Portia, can you give me some light?"

With a flick of her wrist, Portia conjured a glowing globe and dropped it into his hand.

Chavali wanted to stop him. He often barged into danger, both known and unknown. But he had all the skills necessary to do so. On missions, his entire purpose involved taking this kind of risk. She snapped her mouth shut and watched without a word while he stepped over large mushrooms and lowered himself into the hole.

Someone had to go first. Why did that someone have to be the man who'd stepped into her heart?

Mushroom flesh snapped. Colby's head cleared the floor. He dropped out of sight, leaving them with a dim glow to mark his location.

He swore with a sense of disturbed awe. "Uh, I think you should all probably see this. I have no idea how to explain. It's even weirder than the dragon."

Chavali, Portia, and Sivry exchanged glances. Jaris shrugged and climbed down. The women followed.

When Chavali saw the basement, she agreed with Colby's assessment. Torrel's shelves and stores lay scattered in broken piles atop the freshly churned earth. The smell of rot and damp earth hung thick enough to choke on.

One of the people she recognized as a Fury from the fire had been buried to his chest in the packed earth, with both arms free.

Thin, light-colored fungus sprouted from the back of his skull, as well as his eyes, nose, mouth, and ears.

The dozens of tendrils twined around his neck and arms, snaked across the ground, and plunged into the cracked skulls of eight other bodies. Each of these people wore ragged, unkempt clothing suggestive of poverty. More of the shelf-like fungus grew from the joints of their emaciated bodies lying on the ground.

"With everything happening in this city, no one even noticed these people missing," Portia murmured.

"They were undesirables." Chavali crouched beside one and used the hilt of her dagger to try to lift its head.

As soon as she touched it, the body twitched. Chavali flinched and backed away. The Fury at the center moaned.

"I think you woke it up," Jaris whimpered.

"I'll bet fire is really good against fungus." Portia raised her hands and flung a ball of flames at the Fury.

They grew. The mushroom tendrils thickened and snaked along the floor, reaching toward Chavali.

"No bet," Sivry said.

Everyone drew weapons. Colby slashed his sword in front of Chavali. Pieces of fungus flopped to the ground.

"The ones overhead didn't like that either," Jaris said.

Above, the mushrooms swelled to block the hole. The bodies wobbled to their hands and knees. As the first one lifted its head, Chavali saw more fungus spilled from its eyes, forming light-colored ruffles that waved in the air.

Colby stabbed one of the bodies. His blade sliced through with ease, spilling dark, drippy ooze to the ground.

The body didn't notice. It kept rising. They all kept rising.

"Cut the lines?" Chavali pointed to the Fury. "Maybe it's controlling them." She backed up until she reached Portia.

With a nod, Colby ripped his blade through the thing, cutting it in half. The dark muck spattered everywhere. He grimaced in pain as he hacked the tendrils on the Fury's left side, cutting off three bodies.

"Don't touch the black stuff," he ground through a clenched jaw. "It burns."

They kept moving. All eight continued to lurch toward the group. Even the halved one reached with both hands and dragged itself to reach them. Its lower half lay inert on the ground, at least.

"Any other bright ideas?" Colby hacked the half-body at the neck to leave a head on the ground with waving fungus ruffles. The arms slowed and subsided.

"They don't seem dangerous," Jaris said, "just creepy and persistent."

Colby beheaded another of the bodies and slid back to evade the sludge. The neck burbled like a sluggish fountain. Its body wavered and collapsed. The head bounced on the ground.

At least this made them easier to contain.

"My blade is not good for this task," Chavali said as she shuffled toward the wall.

Jaris held up his small dagger and moved with her. "Neither is mine."

Sivry darted close to a body and slashed at its neck. She kept her other sleeve in front of her face and jumped back to avoid any spray.

Portia swiped her palms together. In front of her, two thin arcs of energy sliced through a neck.

One body lurched at Chavali. She dodged into another. It seized her shoulders and mashed its ruffled fungus at her neck. Where the fungus touched her bare skin, lines of agony seared her flesh.

::SPREAD, SPREAD, SPREAD....::

Its single-minded drive threatened to swallow her. She couldn't think past it or push it away. This thing wanted to pry her flesh apart and implant spores in her blood.

Fresh, hot pain spritzed her cheek in tiny pinpricks. Someone yanked her to the side. She stumbled and fell. The relentless beat of its determination ceased.

Chavali stopped screaming, unaware of having begun, and gasped for breath.

Jaris squatted in front of her. "Are you all right?"

"No," she whispered.

Behind him, the others stomped and stabbed heads. Colby showed rage against two of them at once.

The Fury moved. Behind his head, a pair of legs covered in thick, clear slime wriggled out of the body. His torso followed, then his arms and head.

He appeared to have generated a new body somehow.

Before Chavali could find words to warn everyone, he leaped at the wall and passed through it as if it had no physical substance.

She blinked.

:: Wake up, Chavali.::

The voice in her head came from everywhere and nowhere. It sounded like Colby, and it also didn't. Nothing made sense.

Colby filled her vision. "This doesn't look bad, but you screamed like it was killing you." His hand cupped her cheek.

"He melted into the earth." The words sounded insane as they passed through Chavali's lips.

"She's in shock." Sivry tapped Colby's shoulder and pointed upward. "Carve up some fungus and let's get her out of here."

"I'll take a sample so I can figure out how to kill it," Portia said.

"Maybe Korrya will have some ideas too."

Colby and Sivry hacked through the mushrooms above. Chunks of fibrous flesh bounced on the ground. Chavali watched a quivering mass the size of her thigh without comprehending what she saw.

Her mind felt numb or stunted, like she needed to sit and stare at a wall for several hours to crawl out of a daze.

With Colby's help, Chavali wobbled to her feet. He lifted her to Sivry, who pulled her out. Chavali hadn't noticed Sivry climbing out first.

She barely registered the ride to the inn. Without Colby holding her in place, she would've fallen off Karias's back.

CHAPTER 28

Tea helped, as did food. Once she'd eaten, Colby took her to their cabin. He scrubbed her neck hard enough to make her whimper. When he finished, he used a soft towel to inspect her skin without pushing his thoughts at her. She saw smears of blood when he tossed it aside.

Sitting in the warmth of his arms on their bed gave her an anchor. That she needed one made no sense to her. That voice had drilled into her mind, smothering and devouring. She hadn't known such a thing could happen.

"It stunned me," she said after a long, empty silence broken only by the soothing regularity of Colby's heartbeat. "The voice in my mind. That mushroom thing. It had a singular need, and it projected a persistent drumbeat of that need so loud I couldn't handle it."

"Like when your ears ring after an exceptionally loud noise?"

"Yes. This is a good comparison."

Colby kissed her cheek. *::I was starting to worry it might've caused more permanent damage.::*

It had wanted to. The fungus had wanted to turn her into another host. She'd seen what it meant by spreading. Whatever had spawned it wanted all people to become hosts.

The dragon in the mountains had spawned it. She knew that. They all knew that.

She should have let Colby and Daria destroy the mushroom colony when they had the chance. Now they faced an infestation of fire-loving fungus bent on murdering everyone to turn them into mindless slaves.

The dragon had a peculiar plan to save the world.

At least they'd prevented it from spreading for a while. Those heads would take some time to find a way to leave Torrel's basement.

Chavali shivered as she considered the possibility it had embedded spores or tendrils in her body. "Are you sure it left nothing behind? And no one else was infected?"

"Yes." He pushed her hair off her neck and ran his fingers over the injury.

She winced at the mild sting he caused.

::I may have been rougher than necessary to make sure. We all scrubbed anyplace the burning ichor touched us to be on the safe side.::

"Good." At least they'd stopped its progress for the time being.

He kissed her neck then stopped touching her bare skin. "Portia is trying to figure out how to best damage the mushrooms. Sivry and Jaris are helping her with that. Karias is in the stable."

She heard the hitch in his voice and wouldn't pretend she hadn't. "You are conflicted about this final thing. And yet, he is still a horse with horse needs."

"But he's not."

"But he is." She shook her head and shifted to settle deeper into his embrace. Weariness dragged at her. Her eyes wanted to close, so she let them. "He is a person's soul inside a horse. He is not a horse-shaped spirit or a person transformed into a horse. He still needs to eat like a horse. He is still much too large and unwieldy to stay anywhere other than a stable. He still has hooves which require care and a notable lack of thumbs."

Colby sighed. "I wish I'd known from the beginning."

"Are you sure?"

"That I would rather have known I was riding a person all this time? Of course."

She mulled over what Karias had said about his state of mind when it had first happened. "I think this is not as true as you want it to be. Karias was angry and confused when it happened. He didn't see the incident as a sign from the Creator, but rather a punishment. Had you known his feelings on the subject at the time, I doubt you would have become the man you are today. I'm quite fond of this man, and so I see it as all to the good."

He didn't answer. Even without touching him, she could tell he sank into his thoughts. No further words from her would help at the moment.

Warm, comfortable, and safe, Chavali fell asleep. She dreamed of bipedal mushrooms marching relentlessly toward her instead of a usual nightmare. The visions, though disturbing, let her sleep until Colby woke her with an accidental brush of his first slow thoughts of the day.

By the time they sat in the inn's common room, waiting for breakfast with Portia, Jaris, and Sivry, Chavali felt she'd slept better than usual. The world seemed clearer.

No other patrons had come in, so they sat at a table in the middle with room for Colby to stretch his legs.

Iker brought a tray to serve everyone. Chavali recognized the defeat in his shoulders and the miserable, fake cheer he wore.

"Has something new happened since we retired last night?" Chavali asked as Iker set a plate in front of her.

Her stomach growled at the aroma of qanafe-spiced roots and vegetables with eggs and juice.

"There's been a declaration of emergency." Iker set out the plates with slow, deliberate care. "Anyone on the streets today is subject to questioning by the guards. I've already been questioned because I went out to buy eggs. The guard who harassed me said they're conducting a city-wide search for members of the Withered Fists." He hovered on the verge of tears as he poured tea for Chavali. "He also said they're planning to empty the prison so they have enough space to hold the gang members."

"Empty," Colby said with a curl of his lip. "Are they sending the prisoners elsewhere or executing them?"

Iker sniffled. "I don't know."

Chavali stabbed her food. Her pleasant mood disappeared. "Captain Faillit is taking swift action. She will more likely choose execution. It's faster and offers fewer opportunities for mishap."

"But they arrested Torrel to make him talk," Jaris said. "Executing him is counterproductive."

Portia shook her head. "If she's willing to search every single building in the city, she may not care about what Torrel knows anymore. They'll find Wray eventually."

Sivry laid a hand on Iker's arm, offering a small measure of comfort. "Are executions public?"

Tears slid down Iker's cheeks. "I don't know. We've never had them in my lifetime."

"Because there is a tradition here of the leaders following the Order of Spilled Blood," Chavali said, remembering her conversation with Nora. It felt like it had happened a lifetime ago. "But Faillit is Strong Arm. She'll have no problem holding executions. Announcing Torrel's would serve her well as a gambit to flush Wray. Staging it publicly will also help her in this, so we can expect some warning about it."

"We can't leave him there," Colby said. "Or whoever else might be wrongfully imprisoned. If they have one innocent man, it's likely they have others."

"I agree with you." Chavali wanted to jump to her feet and rush to throw open the prison gates. She suspected that impulse came from wanting to soothe Colby's anger. "But we cannot go storm the jail without a plan. Likewise, we need to know what Faillit intends to do. Are the Talons involved? What about the Riverway Guild?"

"I'm with Chavali here," Portia said. "I don't want to rush the prison to find out the Talons are keeping watch. I also don't want to free people who actually committed serious crimes."

"We do need to free Torrel, though." Sivry patted Iker's hand. "Maybe you shouldn't listen to the rest of this."

Iker nodded and wiped his face. "Please save him."

"This is our most important priority," Chavali said. After Iker left the table, Chavali met Colby's gaze. "But we will not pursue it blindly or stupidly."

Colby huffed, then nodded his agreement.

"What's our second priority?" Jaris asked.

"Stopping Faillit," Portia said. "Which means we need to know what she wants."

"And that's because we want to keep Torrel here, right?" Jaris asked.

"Would we do that otherwise?"

He didn't want to challenge the goals, Chavali thought. He wanted to understand them.

Chavali wrapped her hands around her tea mug. She glanced at Colby, who frowned at his plate while eating. Portia and Sivry both looked to her.

All the more experienced Fallen seemed to think Chavali had the answers. Perhaps they merely thought she could explain it best.

"It would depend upon a great many factors. Suppose our intent here centered on discovering and punishing Torrel's murderer. In the course of such an investigation, we uncovered all this corruption and chaos.

"In such a case, dealing with this much danger and difficulty would seem excessive. We could reasonably perform our duty and leave the city to its fate. But we have to consider if we've riled up new enemies for the Fallen or personal enemies who can track us. With Colby's abduction, for example, I would recommend we evaluate that particular danger and determine if we can eliminate that threat. Do you see? It is not so simple as if this, then that."

Jaris nodded as he finished chewing a bite of his breakfast. "I think so. We have a lot of leeway to use our own judgment. I'm not used to that."

"Eldrack trusts us," Sivry said. "The organization is built around trusting its agents."

"Thank you for explaining," Jaris said.

"You're welcome." Chavali turned her attention to how their problems had multiplied with Shore's death. They still didn't know how much Shore had known or authorized.

She shook her head. It didn't matter anymore. What Faillit wanted to accomplish mattered.

"Today, I think we should split up again. Colby and I will never blend, so we will stick together and focus on the Talons. I believe Guyre will consent to speaking with me. You three, find out anything and everything you can regarding the Fists, Riverway, the guards, and the prison. If there's an execution scheduled or announced, we need to know about it. Meet back here at midday."

Everyone nodded. Chavali stayed behind to finish her breakfast while Portia, Sivry, and Jaris left. Colby sat with her.

He tapped his fingers on the table, showing his eagerness to leap into action. "We won't be able to talk them into releasing Torrel."

"Agreed."

"We'll have to attack the prison."

"Probably." Chavali took a final gulp of her tea, set it down, and stood.

"We should do that right away, then. The longer we wait, the bigger the risk we're taking with Torrel's life."

"I agree about the risk." She led him out of the building and to the stable. The morning rain had passed and not yet evaporated, leaving everything damp and glistening in the sunshine.

"Good." Colby stepped inside to saddle Karias.

Chavali followed him and rubbed Karias's nose. "I don't agree we should attack immediately. If we're presented with an opportunity, we should take it. Until then, every moment he remains alive in that jail is another moment we don't have to hide him. The conditions are brutal, and I hate leaving him there to suffer. I would hate more for the guards to kill him in the escape, or for us to stumble into another piece of intrigue with him in our custody. This is why I want more information first."

::Do I get to hear the rest of what's going on?::

"Excuse me, Karias. I'm used to trying to find circumspect options for relaying information to you." She explained what they knew.

::I agree with your assessment. We don't know what kind of magical protections the jail has, nor do we know how many guards are there currently, or whether they have any unofficial backup.::

Chavali repeated this for Colby. At some point, she would grow weary of acting as a messenger between them. The relief of releasing this secret would have to wear off first.

So strange to feel that relief. Revealing secrets more often made her worry. Sharing this with Colby had such a queer effect. She wanted to stop and pick apart the curious sensation to understand it.

Later, when they returned home, she would speak with Kelly about it.

"We should find Daria and enlist her aid. You do understand we have to bring her home with us, yes?"

Colby frowned as he climbed onto Karias's back. He held out a hand to help Chavali. "Why?"

"She knows enough to become a problem." Chavali took his help and settled in front of him. "About you and about Karias, and possibly about me. The greatest concern is Karias. But I don't think Princess Aislynn needs to know about him, so perhaps we should tell Daria about the Fallen so we have a better excuse to bring her back."

Colby sighed. "You're right."

"Yes."

He snorted. "See about explaining it to Railan instead. You said she'd be a good person to help with the binding anyway. I'm sure she can approve bringing in Daria based upon knowing too much."

"This is a good solution."

"Thank you." He kissed the side of her head.

She leaned against him and wished for a great many things that would never come to pass. Some power had chosen a cruel path for them. Hating it felt righteous. And pointless.

Better to enjoy the moments she could have than to curse the ones she couldn't.

"Karias, we need to visit the Talons. And use haste. They cannot question us if they can't stop us."

The horse leaped into action and galloped up the street.

CHAPTER 29

Karias slowed to a walk when they reached the street with the entrance to Guyre's domain, having encountered no serious resistance. Those others who ventured into the streets hurried, their faces drawn taut with fear and worry.

::Do you want me to go straight to the door?::

Chavali considered doing exactly this. Colby could remain with Karias. If anything came up while she spoke with Guyre, he could burst in to rescue her, which would appeal to him.

Except she also wanted to see the area first. If it swarmed with guards or any other group, she wanted to know about it before going inside. "Walk past, then drop me off out of sight."

"Drop you off?" Colby refrained from touching her skin. She could still tell she'd irritated him, though she couldn't say why. "Did you bring me so I'd have something to do?"

Karias gave her the impression of smirking.

Chavali huffed. "Don't be childish. I brought you to keep watch."

"Childish? You think I'm being childish? How many times has charging alone into a dangerous situation almost gotten you killed?"

At least bickering made them seem distracted and irrelevant to any watchers. "Fewer times than you."

Colby grumbled under his breath while they passed the Talons's door and kept going. Two nearby guards sniggered at them but didn't move to intercept. In fact, they harassed no one, suggesting they assumed anyone who'd reached this part of the city must have already faced questioning.

"The last time you accompanied me to speak to Guyre, you made things more difficult. Do what you're good at and let me do what I'm good at."

"I'm good at protecting you," he snapped.

"Yes, you did an incredible job on the barge."

::Settle down, Chavali. He's prickly about something and you're making it worse.::

"Fine. Go handle everything yourself. I'll be over here, doing nothing because I'm useless."

Karias stopped out of sight of the door.

"Stop sulking." Chavali restrained the urge to slap him. "I don't know what's bothering you—"

"You don't? I thought you knew everything."

She'd never heard him mock someone before, especially not her. He'd shown her exasperation, anger, and many similar sentiments, but not this kind of derision.

Perhaps he'd suffered an unsettling nightmare, or needed to gripe more about the Karias secret. The second made a great deal of sense. Thinking back to what she'd said in the stable, she'd shoved it in his face, in a manner of speaking. She'd refused him the right to attack the prison. He had likely also dredged up the memory of watching her with Jaris, and fifteen other things he found somewhat frustrating.

In the moment, he hadn't reacted much to any of those things. Then she'd given him an order he didn't like. Everything had rushed in.

No wonder he wanted to pick a fight.

They didn't have time to deal with his insecurities. Later, she would have to defuse all of this. For the moment, she needed to make him stop and get the job done.

She twisted to face him and found the scowl she expected. Swift and sudden, she kissed him. "Thank you for playing along. This distracted those guards perfectly. I'll return shortly."

As she slipped off Karias's back, Colby stared after her, blinking stupidly.

::That...was brilliant.::

Hurrying away and around the corner, she missed anything else Karias had to say.

Though she had no real skill with blending in, she knew how to match the behavior of those around her. Like everyone else, she hurried with her head down. Furtive glances ahead let her see Anna stepping out of the Talons's door before she arrived.

This woman definitely matched Tam. She'd noticed it in the council chamber after the battle, and remembered it upon seeing her. Chavali knew these two had some other objective or intent than the Talons, the guards, or anyone else. What they wanted, she had no idea. Interacting with them more would help.

Anna hadn't noticed her, so Chavali followed at a discreet distance. As far as Chavali could tell, the woman never saw her. She appeared to have a destination in mind and strode toward it with purpose.

Chavali followed her into an unexpected grotto-like oasis of calm. Stone paths crossed from one side to the other of a wide space covered with springy moss and festooned with flowers and buzzing with insects. Trees lined the outer edge to create a living fence holding back the city and its noise and smell. In the center, water sprayed from a statue of a woman holding flowers to sprinkle into an irregular pond with fish the size of Colby's thigh darting under floating flowering plants.

Under other circumstances, Chavali would've liked to stroll through this sheltered retreat with Colby. As long as he didn't want to argue with her.

Three steps into the park, Chavali no longer saw her target. She checked in every direction, wondering if she'd missed Anna bending to pick up some object or passing behind a tree.

"It's lovely, isn't it?"

Apparently, Anna had noticed her after all.

Chavali crossed her arms and nodded, not bothering to glance at the woman standing beside her. "Yes, quite. Have you brought me here for a reason?"

Anna chuckled. "It's a pleasant place to chat where the guards tend not to interrupt. We haven't been properly introduced. I'm Anna. It's nice to meet you, Chastity." She offered a hand to shake.

Taking her hand, Chavali flashed a polite smile.

This woman had seemed so casual in her stroll to the park. She'd undoubtedly led people on such chases before. Clearly, her work had given her cause to notice followers and use them.

Anna had also clearly pursued this mysterious work for many years, and Chavali wanted to know about it.

"I hope Tam is well," Chavali said. "She seemed fine after the fight, of course, but injuries can sometimes reveal themselves later, yes?"

Anna's thoughts during the brief contact revealed her surprise Chavali had connected her with Tam, as well as flashing to a symbol Chavali knew.

Tam and Anna worked for the Continental Trade Syndicate. The same organization responsible for deaths and disaster in Eagle Falls and potentially harboring some small blame for Harris's death had stepped into Palmia Basin.

"She was roughed up a bit, but not seriously harmed. Tam knows how to take care of herself. A shame about Consul Shore, though. She was able to exert a moderating influence over the various elements here. Her deft hand will be missed." Anna showed no sign of remorse, feigned or otherwise. Either she hadn't known Shore well, or she'd worked toward the consul's death.

"Indeed. But this is not what you wish to discuss."

"As perceptive as expected." Anna nodded her approval. "I know who you are, Chastity. I know you were in Eagle Falls, and I know you happened to visit Harbor City in North Cascain around the time of that distressing news about Princess Bricene. I wonder if you've heard she slipped out of custody and escaped?"

Chavali refused to allow herself to betray surprise at this revelation. She shrugged. "The matters of royalty are not of particular interest to me. What do you want?"

"I want to help you." Anna set a hand on Chavali's shoulder, not touching any bare skin. "We have the same goals, you and I."

Far less savory people had put their hands on Chavali in far less innocent places. She gave Anna no reaction to the contact. "Which goals are these?"

"Palmia Basin is spiraling into chaos. You want to protect the common people, the ordinary folk who bear no blame for this mess."

Though this skirted Chavali's intent, she nodded her agreement. If the Syndicate believed Chavali and her fellow agents nothing more than foolish do-gooders, she could work with that. Further, if Anna believed Chavali thought the same of her, all the better.

Anna stepped closer, turning the conversation intimate. "We both know this place needs outside help. I have a small contingent of armed specialists waiting for a signal. As soon as I give it, they'll be here immediately."

People arriving "immediately" interested Chavali. She knew the Syndicate had performed research into teleportation, as had the Order of the Creator's Path. In Harbor City, the order had sold dust for it. Perhaps the Syndicate had discovered another method. "And what stops you from giving this signal? Surely the situation here is dire enough."

"It is, but the various factions are still too strong." Anna removed her hand. She gazed at the pond as if they spoke about trivial matters. "I have a noble willing to relocate here and take control of the city until the dust settles and the Tilan government intervenes, but she can't challenge Captain Faillit. She has no standing here, and Faillit has too many supporters. Likewise, my specialists can only handle threats up to a particular size, especially on short notice."

Chavali crossed her arms and raised an eyebrow. "You want my people to challenge Faillit? If we considered this feasible, we would have done it already this morning."

"Have you considered asking Korrya?"

That Anna knew Chavali had a connection to the Spire mage didn't surprise her. They hadn't hidden anything after the barge attack.

"She may prove willing to assist with this." Chavali nodded, projecting the notion she gave it some thought. "It is her home, after all. But it's not yours. What do you gain from interfering here?"

"What do you gain?" Anna smiled like she knew a secret.

"I am saving lives." As much as she hated revealing what she knew,

Chavali decided she had to in this case. "You, on the other hand, are here for the Continental Trade Syndicate. Their purpose is not about saving lives."

Anna's smile broadened. "I see the rumors about you are true. The Syndicate isn't so different from your spice merchant. We currently have no operations in Palmia Basin and would like to change that. Like you, Tam and I have been attempting to determine the best angle of approach. This whole disaster has ruined several months' worth of work laying a foundation."

The woman seemed honest in the same way Chavali seemed honest —she spoke truth by virtue of omitting many details. Chavali wanted to know more.

They didn't have time for that.

Guards could discover Wray at any moment. Faillit could decide to execute Torrel at any time. If anyone chose the path of rebellion, Torrel could be killed in an attempt to storm the prison. Any of a dozen other things could become worse, including the Furies's fungus domination plan.

"I can see this is tempting yet suspect to you." Anna leaned closer. "The Syndicate is not interested in governance. We're interested in trade. Once the situation is stabilized, Palmia Basin will hold elections for a new consul. Some residents will choose to leave. We'll be here to purchase their property for a fair price so they can leave with coin in their pockets to set up new lives elsewhere. That's all.

"We're not going to steal their homes or businesses, and our presence will include an interest in true law and order. Gangs and similar groups are counter to our purposes. Trade doesn't flow where the criminal element is strong."

Chavali doubted everything Anna said would prove true. Chavali also had no better options. Five Fallen plus Daria and Karias couldn't handle the Talons, the guards, what remained of the Fists, and the Furies's bizarre plan to grow mushroom people. They needed backup, and Anna had it.

"Very well. I believe we are more likely to succeed with your help than without it. Do you have a plan?"

"Nothing concrete. Tell me where and when you want my specialists and they'll be there. I think this should happen swiftly. The longer we let the situation deteriorate, the harder it'll be to deal with."

"Agreed." If Chavali made a plan for battle now without soliciting input, she would annoy Colby. She didn't want that. Not over something within his area of expertise. "I await more information from my people. How can I contact you once we've crafted our plan?"

CHAPTER 30

Chavali attempted to find Colby and Karias after leaving Anna. She doubted Karias would have abandoned her, or allowed Colby to do the same.

When she didn't find them where she'd left them or nearby, she elected to return to the inn on foot.

As she hurried down a shady street filled with trees hiding small cottages, a man barked at her.

"You there, the woman with the feather! Stop."

She stifled a sigh as she obeyed. He needn't have specified "the feather." No one else wandered the street.

When she turned, she saw a man in a guard uniform by himself, jogging toward with his hand on his sword hilt. Until this point, she hadn't seen any guards working alone, but who knew what orders Faillit had given and for what reasons. If she faced a Talon instead, she had no idea why he'd stop her.

"What's your business in this neighborhood?" He stopped in front of her, his square jaw set in gruff irritation.

Busybody guards had nothing better to do than harass people walking around. She pouted at him. The patch on his uniform looked genuine.

Letting her accent run thick, Chavali said, "I am lost? I come here with my husband on his horse, and we argue. He leaves me behind. Now I must find our inn by foot, but I do not know the way." She faked the edge of tears for him and took his hand for support.

::Looks an awful lot like that woman we're supposed to watch for, but she sounded like a dangerous warrior, not a weepy twit.::

A random guard watching for her meant either one of Wray's friends or one of his enemies. Chavali had planned to con him into letting her go. Instead, she wanted to know more.

She kept his hand in a tight, desperate grip. "What do I do?"

::I can take you in. If you're that woman, I get a bonus. If not, I get recognized for keeping my eyes open.::

"Come with me." He smiled. It didn't reach his eyes. "I'll help you get your bearings."

"Thank you. I always trust guards. Such good people."

His thoughts shifted to hunger for recognition from Captain Faillit.

Hoofbeats pounded on the road. Chavali stumbled into the guard on purpose to keep him from noticing the large white horse charging them from behind. She apologized loudly. He hated her.

At the last moment, Chavali hopped to the side. Karias shifted enough to miss the guard by inches. Colby kicked the guard in the face.

The guard squawked and crumpled.

"What were you thinking, running off like that?" Colby reached for Chavali.

She grinned and took his help to climb up. Karias lurched into a gallop again as she settled on his back.

::Congratulations. You confused him so much he forgot what was bothering him, and then you sent him into a froth of fretting. Fortunately for us all, the clan binding means I can track you without much effort now. Which I did as soon as he stopped acting like a complete idiot and let me. Yes, he knows I'm a person now, but that doesn't override all his experience and reflexes.::

In other words, Colby had acted like himself. Chavali laid her hand on Colby's thigh, uninterested in trying to talk to him while Karias ran through the city at full speed. She didn't want to hear his thoughts either.

::Whenever you're done helping him pull his head out of his ass, I want you to facilitate a conversation where we talk about how hard he can pull my reins. It will involve threats about dumping him on his head.::

Chavali snorted. They reached the inn as she shook her head. Karias slowed in time to avoid crashing through the stable door.

Colby took her hand and helped her climb down. *::I expect an answer.::*

"Are you my Papá now? I followed an unexpected lead. There was no danger."

He landed beside her, hitting the ground hard. "How could I have known that?"

She pointed to the ground between them and kept her voice down. "You're supposed to trust me."

"I want to." He sighed and rubbed his face. "It's hard when you keep pushing."

Since he'd softened his tone, she did the same. "I have always pushed. I will always push. Pushing is what breaks the wagon free of the mud." She stepped close and wrapped her arms around him.

"Please don't leave me behind." He settled his chin on top of her head and held her close.

"Don't ask me for promises I can't make. You know this has to be our last mission together."

He grumbled under his breath. "I don't have to like it."

Chavali could've stayed like this all day. But they had things to do and lives to save. "Portia and the others will return soon. We have much yet to do today."

Nodding, he pulled away. "I'll leave the saddle on Karias and join you in a minute."

"Tell him, not me." She pointed to the horse and left Colby to sort himself. She needed tea to settle her nerves.

On her way to the common room, she saw Sivry jogging up the road. Chavali waited for her at the door and opened it for her.

Inside, the otherwise empty space held a woman who radiated contained violence like a predator. She wore a sleeveless shirt allowing them to see the wiry muscle on her arms. A straight wooden staff leaned against the chair beside her.

Iker poured dark liquid into a goblet for the woman and she thanked him. "That's them." He pointed at Chavali. "Some of them, anyway."

She nodded and beckoned for them to join her. "I'm Mara. I believe you know my husband? Rather strong, law-abiding gentleman in uniform too noble for his own good?" She had a rich, earthy voice and an infectious smile.

Chavali returned the smile and sat at her table. Wray had mentioned his formidable wife. "Sounds familiar, yes. I'm Chastity. Is he here?"

Mara pointed up. "He says he needs help. You have no idea how rare that is."

Colby walked in.

"I have some idea," Chavali said.

Sivry laughed.

At the door, Colby paused and waited for someone. Jaris slipped inside with Portia right behind him.

"This is all of us." Chavali stood. "Iker, if you could bring lunch upstairs for us, we would appreciate that."

Iker handed her a mug of tea and promised to bring up food soon.

Mara led the group to a small room with Wray inside. He sat on the narrow bed, wrapping his hand with a bandage. His hair dripped and he wore clean clothes, perhaps for the first time in a few days.

Wray sagged with relief. "Oh, thank goodness."

"This has been quite a day," Portia said, "and it's only lunchtime."

"Agreed." Chavali stepped inside the room behind Mara.

Mara sat beside Wray and took over the duty of wrapping his hand. Portia claimed the chair at the small desk. Jaris and Sivry stood side-by-side against the wall in front of Wray. Chavali leaned against the door, holding it shut.

Colby shook hands with Wray, then sat on the floor. The two men had a lot in common. Under other circumstances, they would've become friends and stormed the corrupt together.

The room felt both cramped and cozy. A small space didn't seem overfull when Chavali liked all the people in it.

"I'm so glad to see you," Wray said. "Do you have a plan to get Torrel out of that jail?"

"I have been pondering the problem and believe I have an idea." Chavali clasped her hands and hoped they didn't expect too much. "It's not a plan, but it's something."

"Captain Faillit needs to go," Wray said.

"Yes," Chavali said. "I have no proof to offer, but suspect Faillit had Consul Shore murdered so she could seize power. Too much of her immediate reaction seemed prepared, and the murderer was highly suspicious."

"A shame we didn't get a chance to question him before killing him," Portia said with a sigh.

"You killed Shore's assassin?" Wray looked from Chavali to Portia and back.

Mara nudged him with her shoulder. "You have good taste in allies."

Chavali watched them together. The pair had an easy camaraderie. Whatever had brought them together kept them close. "I believe it was one of Faillit's men."

"As expected," Sivry said, "they're blaming it on the Fists."

"Of course they are. To do otherwise is to suggest weakness." Chavali shrugged. "Faillit didn't see us near Shore and had no other reason to suspect us, so she placed the blame where it would solidify her power. Members of the Withered Fists murdered Shore. The suspects were killed when Faillit burst in to protect the consul, or something of the sort. A few guards, including Shore's true murderer, sacrificed themselves heroically trying to save her. This is all quite reasonable and logical."

Wray squinted at her. "I'm glad you're on our side."

"Yes, this is fortunate."

Iker knocked on the door and passed plates into the room. He'd prepared a selection of cold finger foods for all of them. When he left, Chavali sat on the floor with her meal, balancing the plate on her lap.

"I had a hunch," Sivry said, "so Jaris and I checked other recently burned buildings. Mushrooms everywhere. We didn't get into the basements, but saw enough to feel confident the Furies aren't small scale. There are at least ten of those sites. Maybe more."

"The fires are feeding the fungus," Portia said. "It makes them grow and mature faster. My experimentation has revealed that hard liquor with a fair amount of salt will kill them."

"Most kinds of fungus release spores, yes?" Chavali recalled the dragon-shaped one in the mountain doing so. "What will the spores for this type do?"

"Infect, probably," Colby said. "That's what you said they want. Releasing spores would be much more efficient than the method that hits eight people at a time."

Sivry whistled. "Ten sites means eighty people. If each one can release a bunch of airborne spores..."

"They are a much more serious danger than we thought," Chavali finished for her. "At the same time, we must also handle the Fists and Talons. I have access to extra muscle and can get Korrya to help, but we need to prioritize our targets before we can determine the best course of action and summon what assistance can be mustered."

"Not all the guards are corrupt here," Wray said. "I can get able-bodied people with some notice too."

Chavali nodded and ate a few bites while she continued to listen. Ideas bounced in her head, waiting for some critical piece of information she didn't yet have.

"At this point," Jaris said, "the Fists only have a handful still standing. They're done. If any of them want to stick around, they're going to keep their heads down or join the Talons."

Portia drummed her fingers on the desk. "Speaking of the Talons, they're working with Faillit. She's got them bolstering the guard presence all over the place. They're wearing their uniforms and doing the job. That job happens to involve breaking into homes and businesses to loot and take prisoners. It's not happening everywhere, but it's definitely happening."

"We need to divide their forces," Colby said. "An attack on the prison to free Torrel will bring all kinds of defenders. If something else happened elsewhere, attracting attention, we'd have a much better chance of success."

Looking at Colby caused pieces to click into place. Chavali had an idea. He would hate it, but she doubted he could do better.

"Did anyone hear about executions?" Chavali asked.

"Yes," Portia raised her finger. "I would've mentioned it right away, but I worried everyone would rush off without thinking or hearing the rest of the news. Faillit has scheduled Torrel's public execution for tomorrow at noon. He'll be hanged in front of the jail."

Wray stood. "We have to go get him right now."

Portia flashed a look at Chavali. "Case in point."

Mara wrapped a hand around his arm and tugged him back down. "Don't be an idiot," she murmured.

"Indeed." Chavali held up a hand to stop Colby, who'd also started to rise. "Stop. We have to wait for a time least likely to involve alert guards or staged drama. Faillit expects you to rescue him," she told Wray. "That is her intent. She wishes to trade him for you. Which we will do, but not in the manner she intends."

Colby sat again, his gaze thoughtful and not focused on her. "Wray, what's the fastest you can get your allies together for an attack?"

"A few hours, maybe." Wray glanced around the room and also sat. He frowned at his sandal. "I'm not sure how many I could round up by nightfall, but I think I could get everyone by morning."

Chavali nodded. "Based upon what I have seen of Faillit, she will not be easy to dupe. Portia and Colby, go with Wray and Mara. Assault the prison at dusk. The rest of us will provide a distraction to split her forces and attention. I will need Karias, and you must wait in hiding until dusk. Faillit cannot see you getting into position. Collect Daria and get her to bring whatever Riverway people she is willing to trust."

Wray, Mara, Portia, and Colby stood, all nodded. Wray's relief and determination flashed across his face.

"What kind of distraction?" Colby asked.

She hesitated to tell him too much. If he knew the details, he'd try to stop her. "The flashy kind. This is my expertise."

He crossed his arms. "You won't fool Guyre."

"Not by doing the same as I've done before, no. Sivry, Jaris, and I will work together. Our efforts will surprise everyone." Had he not so recently displayed his concern and vulnerability, she would've found his objection insulting. Instead, she considered this an outlet for his insecurities and let it bemuse her. "This is what I do. Go do what you do."

Better to have him questioning her abilities than sniping and griping.

"I just—"

"Worry, yes. No one is plunging alone into danger." Chavali stood to open the door for them. "You'll need to map out the prison and lines of approach. This will take time."

He hesitated, then he sighed. "Watch over yourselves."

"I expect the same from you." Chavali flashed him an affectionate smile. She could tell he wanted a parting embrace or something of the sort. Reuniting afterward suited her preferences more.

Portia took Colby by the arm and led him out of the room.

Wray bowed to Chavali with his hand on his heart. "May we all meet again after." He took Mara's hand and led her out of the room.

"Agreed." Once she shut the door behind them, Chavali let out a breath of relief. She'd half expected Colby to wrench his arm free and rush to express his love or something similarly foolish and dramatic.

With her biggest distraction handled, she turned to the task of creating one for Faillit. "Jaris, I need you to deliver a message. Sivry, I have a whisper for you to spread. I also intend to see Korrya. Come. I will explain."

She beckoned them closer and laid out her idea.

CHAPTER 31

Chavali sat on the couch in Korrya's living room again, enjoying the small luxury of a soft cushion while watching the raven on its perch. The bird put on a good show of indifference. She couldn't decide if she wanted to prod it to interact or not.

Keeping it unaware that she knew it had human intelligence seemed safer. As with the Fallen, the Spire might well prefer its secrets held close.

On previous visits, Chavali hadn't noticed the subtle Spire symbol in the pattern of the wood floor. Korrya's home had a different ambiance at different times of day. In the afternoon, without light streaming through the windows as it did in the morning, the sitting room projected cool and calm.

"That's a bold plan, Chastity." Korrya sat with her hands clasped in her lap, also watching the bird. Her hair draped over one shoulder in a ponytail of thick curls.

Rowan stood to the side, alert yet relaxed. He'd accepted Chavali as a dangerous person who presented no threat to Korrya or himself.

"The situation here is dire. I admit I'm averse to putting you in the position of justifying your inability to restrain the horse. Unfortunately, I see no other good option. Many terrible options also exist, but I prefer to avoid disaster when possible, especially for those on my side of a conflict."

"Are you sure you're not being a bit of an alarmist?" Korrya asked. "Things sound bad, but they're changing fast. If we stand by and do nothing, the new status quo that emerges may be better than you expect."

"This seems unlikely to me. For the sake of argument, suppose I do nothing." Chavali started with the most critical piece. "An innocent man, my baker friend of a friend, will die. Once Faillit has consolidated her power, she has no reason to keep him alive, and plenty of reason to have him killed.

"Faillit will then have to decide how to deal with the Talons. She may elect to keep them on the payroll as extra guards. In this case, a gang full of criminals becomes part of the law enforcement in the city with police powers and no recourse for citizens. If, instead, she chooses to turn on them, the conflict will engulf a sizable portion of the city and affect many ordinary people.

"Speaking of those ordinary people, Faillit has closed down the docks. I believe she intends to starve out the Riverway Guild. This means she will leave the docks closed until Nora concedes to Faillit's demands, whatever they may be. In the meantime, ordinary people who rely upon trade are stuck. Faillit may even interfere with transport across the lake. I would. Dividing the city will make it much easier to pacify."

Korrya held up a hand. "I'm sorry about your baker. That's clearly something in need of attention. I can probably help secure his release. The rest of it, though, will resolve itself in time. Assaulting two parts of the city at once seems excessive to deal with it. Besides, my experiment is showing some excellent results, and if I wander off, I could miss tweaking it at the right time."

Chavali could relate to Korrya's point of view. If not for Colby's influence, Chavali would likely feel the same. Aside from Torrel, she owned the people of Palmia Basin nothing.

"I understand. But I haven't told you about what the Qanafe Furies are actually doing. They've created a method to infect people with a fungus that circumvents their brain and keeps them going under its control." She had a feeling Korrya would respond to a mystery better than grim predictions about the city's conditions. "How this infection functions is something I cannot explain. Studying such things is outside my expertise."

"How interesting." Korrya gazed at the window, clearly considering her options.

"Portia was able to determine the fungi are best affected by some kind of liquor and salt combination. She did so with only a small sample. Once the main threat is removed, studying a portion of one should present no great danger.”

Korrya made a thoughtful noise. Chavali knew she had the woman hooked, though she couldn't say how heavily Korrya would invest.

“Rowan, go with Chavali for the distraction. I’d like to take a look at one of these mushroom infestations, then I’ll head to the prison and see what I can do to prevent the need for a fight there.”

“If you don’t mind my saying so,” Rowan said with a respectful dip of his head, “I think you’d be better off using a disguise and helping the attack. I don’t like what Faillit is willing to do for her power. I think we need the Tilan government to step in as soon as possible, and I doubt you can convince anyone to release Torrel into your custody. He’s charged with murdering a guardsman, which is no small crime.”

“These aren’t Spire concerns,” Korrya said.

Rowan smirked. “That’s why you should wear a disguise.”

Chavali realized part of Korrya’s reticence came from not understanding the depths to which Faillit had sunk. “Torrel is charged with murdering a guardsman who is not dead. This guardsman is a whistleblower in hiding who wants to expose Faillit’s complicity with corruption in her ranks. Additionally, Faillit arranged for Consul Shore’s murder and has blamed a group of conveniently dead members of the Withered Fists for it.”

“Those *are* Spire concerns,” Rowan said. “We shouldn’t stand by and watch while a tyrant seizes power.”

“Very well.” Korrya stood with a sigh. “I’ll check on these mushrooms, then join the attack on the prison. My skills aren’t particularly battle-oriented, but I’ll do what I can.”

“Thank you,” Chavali said, meaning it. She also stood. “Before you go, will you help me craft my illusion? My perception of color is skewed, so I require outside assistance to make fully realistic people.”

Korrya’s eyes lit up with pleasure. “I’d love to. I don’t think I’ve ever met an illusionist with a visual impairment before.”

“I was not born with this problem.” Chavali raised her hands and threaded her fingers through the spirits. With her coaxing, they conjured an image of Colby around her body.

She didn’t need to see it to craft small details. Chavali knew the lines of his face, the way his shirt hung just so, and how his muscles flexed when he walked.

The people she loved always made the best illusions.

Rowan stroked his chin, examining the image obscuring Chavali's body. From the inside, she saw a thin, flickering outline. She needed to see through it, but she also needed to know if someone disrupted it.

Korrya nodded her approval. "I'm not sure why you think you need help, Chastity. That's a remarkable rendering."

"It looks good to me," Rowan agreed. "I don't think anyone will see through it if you maintain it properly."

"Then we should go." Chavali had expected to need to shift the colors. She'd never managed a proper rendition of a person on the first try before. After a great deal of practice under the tutelage of Fallen agents she knew, she could handle objects, especially if she could access someone's thoughts.

Her illusions of people, on the other hand, tended toward green or pink.

"Don't forget to duck when you use the door," Rowan said as he retrieved his raven. "A shame Colby will manage to slip his horse right out from under my nose. Again. Can you affect your voice?"

"No." She closed her mouth. She had to think the words she wanted the illusion to say instead of speaking them. "But I can create sounds." Instead of her own voice making the words, Colby's came from a spot about a foot above her mouth.

They wouldn't appreciate the nuance of how his voice rumbled around the edges. Neither would they care about the way he breathed.

Chavali thought she could keep up this particular illusion through almost anything.

She layered in the soft jangle of his armor, the creak of his boots, and the swish of his pants. The sword hanging on his back made a tiny rattle. When he turned his left arm just so, his elbow cracked so quietly she often missed it.

Korrya reached toward her and pulled back without touching the outline. "I don't know what you just changed, Chastity, but that's among the most realistic illusions I've ever seen. It's hard to convince myself it's fake."

"Thank you," Colby's voice said. "The practice is grueling. I'm happy to know it's also worth it." Before becoming Fallen, she'd only produced obviously fake images to accompany stories.

Three months of intensive practice, tucked into stolen moments, had given her the tools to do so much more.

Trying to do this particular task with anyone else as the subject, though, she expected would fail.

"Let's go cause some trouble," Rowan said as he opened the door.

Chavali ducked the illusion through the door. She had to concentrate to keep all the parts moving naturally.

Outside, Karias turned to see her and froze. He whinnied, the sound full of confusion and no small amount of distress.

"It's Chavali," she murmured as she closed the distance. "I'm wearing an illusion." Touching him with her hand meant contorting to both reach the correct height for Colby and not break the outline. She couldn't conceal herself if she broke the outline.

::I can't express how incredibly confusing it is to smell you and see him. You've grown a great deal as an illusionist.::

According to her teachers, Chavali could fool other senses with her illusions, such as smell. She hadn't yet tried. Mastering this much had taken all of her attention so far.

More immediately, she had to get onto Karias's back without help and without breaking the illusion. She rubbed Karias's nose and thought about the challenge. By the time Rowan returned from collecting a horse from around the side of Korrya's home, she had an answer.

"Whatever we do," Chavali said, "I believe I must stay on the horse's back for the duration."

"That's reasonable." Rowan stepped into his saddle's stirrup. "If one of us needs to get down, I'll handle it."

Chavali made Colby nod, then clambered onto Karias's back. As expected, she couldn't lift her knee high enough, Colby's leg pressed into Karias, and her arms stuck out while she pulled herself up. Once seated, she settled everything into place and arranged her skirt to let her bare calf touch Karias.

Colby's longer legs meant Chavali's real ones couldn't reach the stirrups. His longer arms meant she had to lean forward to hold the reins.

Maintaining this fiction for a long period of time would wear her down. One afternoon and evening seemed reasonable.

"You're good now," Rowan said.

"Thank you," Colby's voice said. "Shall we?" The illusion gestured down the road.

::Your command of his voice gives me shivers. Let's not tell him about this, because it'll probably mess with his head.::

If not for Rowan's presence, Chavali would've retorted about how well keeping secrets from him had worked. She noted the undercurrent of Colby's mood through Karias's bond as bored anticipation. He'd most likely moved into position already and now waited to attack. No one had given him any serious trouble or Karias would've felt it.

Good.

"Where are we headed?" Rowan asked.

"Wray said he would meet me at Teristial Park. Do you know where that is?"

"No," Rowan said, following Chavali's earlier instructions, "I don't think so. We'll have to ask for directions."

"I'm surprised you haven't run across it in all your time here," Colby's voice said.

::I think I get the idea. I'll see if I can find us a guard or two as we wander through the streets. They all smell like corruption, so it won't be hard.:: Karias turned his attention to the scents around them, trying to pick out people in the open among the flowers and animal odors.

"Korrya is primarily concerned with the waterfall. I don't have much cause to investigate the city."

Certain Rowan would continue to play along, Chavali focused all her attention on maintaining the illusion. Colby would wait until dusk, Anna's people would show up, and Wray would succeed in contacting his allies.

The whole effort had many opportunities for disaster, but Chavali thought she'd planned well enough to mitigate them.

Guyre would come. He had to. The bait, even if he recognized it as such, would lure him. She knew how prophecies affected people.

Unlike others, Guyre had already experienced meddling from that idiotic dragon, which made him twice the target.

He lacked the capacity to resist an opportunity to discover how the Knight of the West might see pain released.

CHAPTER 32

Chavali and Rowan rode through the city, stopping to ask for directions more than once. The guards didn't question them, presumably in deference to Rowan. As Chavali had requested, Rowan participated more than once in a short, purposely overheard conversation wherein he asked how Colby had become a knight and Colby's voice discussed his service to the crown of Shappa on the western coast.

They took wrong turns, stopped for a bite to eat, and urged their horses to walk at a slow pace. As the sun sank lower, they neared the park.

To Chavali's surprise, Wray had selected the same place Anna had used to stop and chat with her. He'd said it would seem appropriate for meeting someone trying to hide from the guard.

In the fading glow of twilight, the grotto revealed a new side of itself. Among the mosses in the cracks between the pathway stones, tiny pinpricks of soft light glowed, enough to see the walkway. Light sprayed with the water from the fountain to dissipate when it returned to the pond's surface. Clusters of flowers along the tree fence also glowed, forming swirling shapes without relying on color.

One man sat on a bench with his back to them. Chavali saw no one else.

Karias took two steps into the park. *::We're not even close to alone. People are thick in the shrubs and trees.::*

"Watch yourself," she whispered to Rowan.

Rowan didn't respond, but she knew he'd heard her.

With only a brief pause, Karias continued into the park. Rowan's horse fell into line behind him.

"Your friend is late," Guyre said, glancing over his shoulder.

"Friend?" Rowan asked. "I don't know what you mean."

Guyre chuckled as he stood. "Was it a ruse so Wray can sneak out of his hiding hole?"

Chavali had Colby glance backward as if to order his horse to charge out of the situation. Several men and women in guard uniforms crept out of hiding to block any escape. Among them, two stood out as regimented and precise like genuine guards.

Until she'd seen Talon members and guards together, Chavali hadn't realized they stood and moved with such obvious differences in bearing.

Once they'd revealed themselves, more stepped into view all around. Talons and guards surrounded them in numbers too large for the real Colby and Rowan to handle on their own.

"Who's Wray?" Rowan twisted in his saddle and projected some concern.

"A troublemaker." Guyre grinned. "Much like yourselves. Both outsiders. Both convinced you can solve all our problems. Both working for meddling women. Korrya interferes with power she doesn't understand. Because what else would a mage do? Always caught up in their studies, never concerned with the things that actually matter.

"Chastity walks into my city. My city! She brings a knight." He gestured to Colby like he might a disfavored dog or piece of art. "This man!" Guyre raised his arms, stretching them to the sides, and turned around on the spot like a showman. "He's the knight who will release us all from our pain!"

As if cued, the Talons and guards laughed.

"Did you consider that might mean I'm here to kill all of you?" Colby's voice asked. The real Colby would never say such a thing.

These people didn't know the real Colby.

Guyre's face twisted into a mask of rage. "You can try." He stabbed a finger at them. "But I have more than enough allies to make quick work of you. Even the dragon in the mountain is on my side! It showed me the truth. There is only one truth, and it's mine to safeguard."

Chavali said nothing. If Guyre wanted to waste time making speeches for his people until her reinforcements arrived, she would allow him to do so. Nothing he could say would change anything.

"What's more, I've defeated those who defeated you." He pointed at Colby again, this time with a mad grin. "Those Qanafe Furies are as pathetic as I thought. Obsessed with some stupid quest to spread mushrooms, as if that can stop anything. Fools! My people, we slew two of them and put their leader into jail because we are the chosen ones, not them."

::He what?::

Chavali's breath caught. She couldn't hear what Guyre said next over the roar of panic in her ears.

The leader of the Furies, a woman who could burn water, languished in the jail where Colby waited to attack. If someone who didn't recognize her found her first, they'd release her. She'd use fire.

Fire would force-grow another mushroom. The jail held prisoners, locked inside cages where they couldn't escape. They would make excellent fodder for another of those root clusters.

Vimarica must've allowed her own capture.

Without Karias and herself there to prevent it, Colby stood little chance of survival against that.

::We have to go help him before he gets into the situation that will kill him. Which we both know he will.::

She heard an echo of Colby's defeated whisper as he'd prepared to die in the fire raging in Torrel's bakery. Soot and sulfur filled her nose. Everything crackled and popped in her ears.

Guyre stopped his ranting and squinted at Chavali. His eyes widened.

"Chastity," Rowan hissed.

Chavali blinked away the memory. The outline of her illusion had disappeared. She'd let it fail. Flames wreathed her body instead.

"You," Guyre said, his voice filled with wonder. "You're..." He leaned toward her. "Who are you?" he whispered.

Someone grunted. Something heavy hit the ground. Guyre snapped his head aside in time to see a Talon hit the ground next to another, both bleeding from fatal neck wounds.

"Attack!" Guyre shrieked.

Instead of launching himself at whoever murdered his people, he ran at Chavali.

::I'll get us out of this mess as soon as I can. Hold on and stab people as needed.::

Chavali drew her dagger. Since she no longer had a fiction to maintain, she laid her other hand on Karias's neck. His thoughts helped her move with him.

Karias kicked his rear hooves. Chavali braced. Bone crunched. He pivoted and reared onto his hind legs. She held onto the saddle. Guyre backed off.

Within moments, the park erupted with screams, shouts, grunts, thumps, and metallic clangs. Rowan leaped off his horse and slapped its flank. The poor creature shrieked and ran. He danced with his blade, fending off several attackers at once.

Chavali slashed across a woman's face. Karias kicked.

"Chastity!" Guyre screeched.

She didn't care what happened to him. If he survived this day, whoever took charge tomorrow would have him hunted. Like Karias, her attention focused on dodging, attacking, and getting out of the park.

Between one eyeblink and another, two dozen armed men and women appeared with their weapons ready. In the dim gloom of dusk, they gave the impression of a troop of ghosts.

Chavali waved to them and gestured all around.

A woman barked orders. The Syndicate force rushed into battle with a confident war cry.

Karias maneuvered himself toward a park exit too slowly for both their tastes. Rowan stuck with him and Chavali.

The undercurrent of Colby's mood riding under Karias's thoughts shifted. As promised, he'd waited until dusk. Chavali recognized the feeling of anticipation breaking in favor of action.

She hoped forging the rest of the bond between Colby and Karias would allow them to communicate better over distances. If only Karias could warn him. If only she had the skills of a full telepath.

With one more kick of his hind legs, Karias backpedaled into the street.

Rowan's raven screamed a war cry and swooped through the battle. Its talons raked a woman's face and scalp, ripping away flesh and hair.

"Take me with you!" Rowan hacked through a man's gut and reached for Chavali's hand.

Chavali reached for him. They could use the extra help against a Fury.

His thoughts centered on the mechanics of getting into the saddle while Karias moved, the fight flowed on, and Chavali already sat in the saddle. He used the stirrup and flung himself onto Karias's back. As with Colby and Karias, his thoughts included an outside connection to someone else.

Unlike Colby, Rowan had a full telepathic bond with his raven. Chavali could tell from the complexity of the second line. These two beings shared their thoughts as easily as breathing. Their souls had become entwined on a level far exceeding Colby and Karias's.

He let go of Chavali's hand and wriggled to settle into the saddle with her. Karias turned and galloped up the street. Neither of them held the reins. Rowan set a hand on her hip.

Glancing back, Chavali saw the raven flapping to catch up.

If she wanted to, she could ask him questions. In the moment, while they charged through the city, he might not guard his tongue. She'd have to bounce from one topic to another to keep him from noticing.

She turned and leaned toward him. "Your bird is curious."

He smirked. "About as much as Colby's horse."

"Will the bird do most anything for treats?"

Rowan laughed. "Yes, especially from Korrya."

::I don't know where you're headed here, but it's a dangerous path you're walking. I trust you, but be careful. The more he learns, the more the Spire knows.::

"Then I agree. They are the same kind of curious. Is it common for a mlinzi to fall in love with his mage?"

"Uh." He coughed. "No, not really."

"Don't worry. It's not obvious."

"Thank you?" He raised a hand. The bird landed on his fingers. Rowan pulled the bird close, helping it keep its balance until he sheltered it behind her body. "Is Colby your mlinzi, or Portia's? I thought he was independent at first, but he's not, is he?"

Karias swore in her mind.

The Spire knew Portia. In her first life, Portia had belonged to it. Chavali knew this from talking to her. Bad enough they had confirmation of Portia's continued existence. Chavali had no idea what attaching this new status to her would cause.

Chavali could deny Colby's status as a mlinzi, but then Rowan would see Karias as an enigma to prod. They faced the possibility of a more concerted effort to collect Karias. If, instead, she claimed him, they might shift their tactics to information gathering.

Considering Korrya and Portia's opinions regarding Narryn, she suspected this new information might discredit him somewhat. On the subject of Karias, at least.

"Mine." The Spire knew little to nothing about Chavali. They didn't even have her real name. Her status as an unknown would, hopefully, goad them in a better direction. She and the Fallen could both handle questions about her.

"But you're not Spire."

He could, she expected, confirm this with minimal effort.

"No. Neither am I the Spire's enemy."

"So he's not actually a mlinzi. That's interesting. What order do you work for?"

Colby's thread flashed into panic. Ahead, dark smoke billowed above the trees in a sudden, giant spurt. A deep, thrumming pulse beat against Chavali's ears and chest.

Karias swore. So did Rowan. Chavali patted Karias's neck, knowing he didn't need her to tell him to go faster.

They turned the next corner and discovered flames licking the sky and belching smoke where the jail had once stood. Even from a few blocks away, Chavali could feel the intense heat.

Rowan's bird streaked ahead. Karias charged the massive inferno. Plants near it shriveled. Charred bodies and debris lay strewn across the ground in a wide arc around the building.

Karias slid and hopped to a halt before the heat stole Chavali's breath. The intensity from twenty feet away reminded her of standing a few feet from a bonfire. It roared like insatiable hunger.

Portia rushed to Karias with Daria on her heels. "I didn't start this!" Portia shouted over the noise. "It blew up from the inside! We took down the defenses, then everyone stormed inside. I stayed out as part of the team watching our escape." She grabbed Chavali's leg. "A lot of our people are still inside. All the prisoners, so far as I know. Colby's in there."

Chavali stared at the blaze, feeling Colby's helplessness.

She had no way to stop the fire and no way to reach him.

CHAPTER 33

Rowan leaped off Karias's back. "Where's Korrya?" His raven cawed and streaked up the road, away from the fire.

"I don't know," Portia said, looking around. "She hadn't shown up yet when Colby gave the word."

Daria growled and smacked herself in the head with her open palm. "He thought timing was more important than waiting for more people. I should've gone in there with them."

"Stop it." Portia slashed through the air. "This isn't your fault."

"Vimarica was inside," Chavali said. Her voice sounded numb and stupid. "She started the fire."

"What moron put her in there?" Portia shook her head and raised a wine bottle. "Never mind. Blame won't save anyone. I've got this and another bottle of mushroom-killing solution."

"We had more soldiers." Daria pointed down the road, toward the docks. "Wray led a charge against a handful of corrupt guards and maybe some Talons who responded to the fire. I'm not sure where the Riverway Guild stands on all of this, but we definitely don't like Faillit shutting down the docks. If Colby hadn't gone inside, I would've gone with Wray."

Korrya ran toward them with the raven flying beside her. "I can put out the fire! But it's really big! It'll take me a bit."

Rowan rushed to meet her. He checked her for injuries.

Oddly, Colby's state shifted from helpless defeat to determination. The change—and Korrya's arrival—shook Chavali out of her own stupor.

::He's doing something on his own. It's a positive something. He

was so upset after the bakery fire. Maybe he needed that push, and some time, to finally get over this.::

Perhaps he'd also needed to fight with her to prove to himself he remained a separate person with separate wants and needs. These things didn't seem related, but in his mind, he could've connected them. She'd rescued him a few times over the past months, after all.

"We need to meet him halfway." Chavali wriggled off Karias's back and waved to Korrya. "Make me a path!" She took Portia's bottle. "Does anyone else have more of this?"

"Jaris and Sivry each have two bottles." Portia pointed at the inferno. "They're also inside."

"This way." Chavali squared her shoulders and marched toward the fire.

"She doesn't wait," Korrya said as she hurried to follow.

Daria responded, "Nope. Won't hide either. Not even when you ask her to."

In a wave before Chavali, the fire retreated. Fingers of flame strained against the force of Korrya's magic. Soot marked every surface. The area smelled shocked and smoky.

Behind her, the sandals of several people following her slapped the ground.

"Hey, back off," Daria snarled at someone.

Chavali ignored everyone in her wake and strode through the blackened doorway. Three burned people lay on the floor, making mewling noises. They hadn't died in the fire or blast. Without a healer, they wouldn't last much longer.

She could do nothing to help them, so she moved on. The door to the cells upstairs remained intact. She laid a hand on it and found the thin wood warm to the touch.

"What in the name of the Creator happened here?" Captain Faillit led a group of guards into the central space from the outside, far too late to do any good. She held her sword ready.

"You attempted to hold a Qanafe Fury here," Chavali said. She turned the handle. The door fell toward her. She backpedaled to let the door fall to the ground, charred on the inside. A crispy, still-burning body fell with it. Dark, smoky dust puffed with the impact, filling the air with the stench of scorched meat.

The walls in the stairwell had already suffered fire damage. Chavali rushed inside, certain she'd find Colby at the top.

"Get out of my way," Korrya snapped at someone.

At the top of the stairs, more fire fled from Chavali. Mushrooms in different shapes covered every surface. She saw Vimarica rise, dripping with slime. The body she'd left behind remained burning. All the cages lacked their doors. Twisted heaps of metal lay further down the hallway.

As Chavali watched, uncertain what to do, Vimarica straightened and flexed her hands. She grinned, thick ooze dripping in slow motion from every inch of her new body, including her eyes. The mushrooms on her original body swelled with every passing moment.

Captain Faillit pushed past Chavali. "Prison break!" She rushed Vimarica with her sword drawn.

Chavali stumbled and tripped to the side as more guards shoved past her. Rowan stepped from the stairs to reach Chavali and help her to her feet.

::...never hear the end of this. Korrya's going to rant about Faillit for —::

Rowan saw something Chavali didn't have time to process. He yanked her into the stairwell. She didn't resist.

Behind them, Chavali thought she heard a great wind blow, yet she felt nothing. Several of the guards made noises of disgust.

"What is this stuff?" one man asked.

"It won't brush off," a woman said.

"Get back here!" Faillit shouted.

Chavali and Rowan leaned at the same time to see what had happened. The fungi on Vimarica's body had deflated. Dark spots, each the size of Chavali's thumbnail, settled to the floor. They must have blown into the air like the dragon's spores had in the mountain.

Spots covered Faillit and her guards. They grimaced and tried to wipe off their tongues and hands. Faillit continued to try to fight Vimarica. All the spores slid off Vimarica's body with the slime.

"Don't touch them," Chavali murmured. She waved to keep Daria and Korrya from approaching.

"What do they do?" Rowan asked, also keeping his voice down.

"I don't know, but it won't be good." She suspected similar spores had caused the mushroom infestations of those poor people in the basement, though she had no idea.

Based upon the quantity of spores, each Fury body could easily infect dozens. They'd probably started with eight in each of those buildings to avoid discovery.

Vimarica laughed and leaped through the wall like the other Fury had.

Korrya moved closer to them. Lingering fire in the hallway disappeared.

Faillit cursed and rubbed her eyes. "Why do I itch so much?"

Several guards muttered their agreement.

Colby rounded the corner at the far end of the hallway. He carried Torrel slung over his shoulders. Soot streaked his face and clothing, and he wore a fierce, determined grin of victory.

He hadn't let his fears hold him back. Perhaps he still needed time not to suffer that first, irrational surge of panic in the face of fire, but she knew he'd battled it and won. He'd overcome it once.

He could do it again. Especially if she helped him deal with it later.

Chavali desperately wanted to rush to greet him.

She waved for him not to go any further. No matter how much she wanted to kiss him, she wanted much, much more for both of them to avoid the spores. He stopped.

Faillit dropped to all fours and coughed at the floor. Her guards did the same. They seemed to want to vomit, yet nothing came out of their mouths but noise. Like cats trying in vain to hack up hairballs, they shuddered and rasped.

"Is there anything you can do for them?" Rowan asked.

Chavali shook her head. "Without knowing what the spores truly do, no. If they become mushroom people, we can apply this solution to kill them." She held up the bottle.

"I don't want to watch any of this," Korrya said, sounding queasy.

"Let's get out of here," Daria said. She helped Korrya retreat.

Faillit groaned. Her eyes burst, spattering the floor with wet goo.

Feathery fungus snaked from the sockets. The flesh on her hands bubbled. More mushrooms flowed from her ears and nose. She screamed.

Her guards shared her fate. Their voices echoed in the blasted space until they cut off. Fungus tendrils spewed from their mouths.

Colby caught Chavali's gaze through the fungus nightmare, then ducked out of sight again. He showed determination and disgust, but not fear.

Chavali tugged on Rowan's sleeve to get him to follow her down the stairs. If the second floor had another exit, she wanted to find it. They could make one if necessary.

Portia rushed inside as Chavali and Rowan reached the ground floor. "Vimarica is headed that way." She pointed at the wall.

"The lake is that way," Rowan said. "So is the waterfall."

Chavali pointed at the far corner of the second floor. "Colby is trapped upstairs. We need another exit for him."

Portia nodded and ran outside. Chavali followed her. Outside, Karias planted himself beside her. She laid a hand on his neck.

::He's not panicking. He's relieved. I think he knows you're getting him out of this one way or another. I'm so grateful we don't work alone.::

With a sweeping hand gesture, Portia conjured a thick dart and punched it through the outer wall on the upper floor. She followed it with a second and third, making the hole bigger with each impact.

As she did so, Korrya and Rowan ran outside and kept going.

Chavali saw no sign of Rowan's crow, though she didn't care about it at the moment. "Colby!" she called, hoping he could hear her. "Can you get through this way?"

Sivry slipped through the hole to stand on the balcony. It creaked under her feet.

For a moment, Chavali stared stupidly at Sivry. She'd forgotten anyone else existed.

Her focus had narrowed to Colby. In a different circumstance, this might have killed someone. If she needed yet another clear indicator that she couldn't work with Colby anymore, she had it.

Within a few minutes, a team of people, including Jaris and several guards, moved a collection of former prisoners and injured guards to the ground.

Colby, the last one out, lowered himself and jumped the last few feet to reach the ground. The already damaged balcony collapsed as he did so. He coughed on the dust as he retreated from it.

Daria thumped him on the back and nudged him toward Chavali.

"She's at the waterfall!" Rowan shouted. "I think she's trying to use Korrya's netting!"

"What?" Stopped in the act of hurrying to Colby, Chavali squinted at Rowan. "Use it for what?"

"I don't know?" Rowan beckoned for her to follow him. "Make spores faster? Or bigger?"

Karias stopped beside Chavali. Colby, on his back, took her arm and lifted her. They raced toward Korrya's home.

"But how could that happen? How could she use the netting... designed to capture magical energy..." Chavali blinked and cursed her own stupidity. "...to power a magical process."

Given enough power and time, Vimarica could produce enough spores to blanket the city. If the spores could survive submerging, they could flow down the river and infect the other cities and towns on its banks. Bizarre mushroom fish might spread the spores even farther.

She held up the last bottle of mushroom killing solution they had. "Vimarica is too powerful for the three of us."

"We need to do something to make things more even," Colby said. "She's not invincible. No one is."

As they neared the waterfall and Korrya's home, Chavali saw Vimarica floating in the air beside one of Korrya's netting installations. She couldn't have figured out how to use it yet, or she would have already.

"Such as? She can fly. Breathe water. Repel flames. I don't think taunting her will work. This is my best skill in a fight."

"What are your other skills in a fight? I can swing a sword from

Karias's back, which is a powerful tool."

Chavali turned her palms up and stared at them. "Crippling telepathy? Illusion?" She drew her dagger. "I can stab things?"

"Did you know the blade is glowing black?"

She examined the weapon, careful not to stab either of them while jostled by Karias's swift pace. It seemed no different than usual to her. "No."

"I've seen it glow red before, but not black. I think you should stab her and see what happens."

"I have to get close enough first." Chavali pointed at Vimarica, still floating beside the waterfall. "I think she will object."

::I hate to interrupt this amusing conversation, but there's at least one more at the top.:: Karias turned and raced along the water's edge, headed for the channel to the top.

Chavali glanced up. She counted three heads. Four Furies against the three of them sounded like exceedingly poor odds. With luck, Portia would arrive in time to assist.

Chavali doubted they'd have so much good fortune.

CHAPTER 34

Karias thundered up the channel's path. As he neared the top of the cliff, Chavali heard Vimarica exclaim her victory. She'd connected to the netting.

Someone cried out in pain.

"Keep them busy," Vimarica said.

"They're distracted," Colby whispered. "Can your illusions screen us long enough to get close?"

"Yes." Chavali could do that. She'd done something like it before. As long as no one scrutinized her work too carefully, she could mimic their surroundings to keep them hidden.

To keep the colors close to natural, she kept her hand on Karias's neck so his thoughts could guide her. "Be silent."

As she wove the image, the faint outline flickered into life. Her illusion told a lie, one that disavowed their presence.

Karias reached the top. Vines and shrubs thick with flowers clung to the uneven, slick surface of rock. A fifteen-foot wide channel allowed a torrent of water to slip over the edge and plummet to the lake.

Near the edge, four of the Furies sat in the channel. The water reached their chests, and they let their arms drift with the current. Tiny fungus threads writhed in their hair like hungry worms.

Another stood with her back to the Chavali, Colby, and Karias. She raised her cupped hands above her head as if performing a ritual.

Two more Furies watched over the cliff's edge. One fired a bow. The other made gestures similar to those Portia employed to create destructive fires.

Vimarica floated with her head and shoulders visible above the water's edge, concentrating on a task at the height of her waist. Chavali guessed she connected to the last of Korrya's nets.

::My hooves will not be quiet on this rock. There's nothing I can do about that.::

"Let me down," Chavali whispered. "I will handle the standing one. You charge."

Colby helped Chavali to the ground. Dagger in hand, illusion pushing forward, she ran. Within moments, Karias pounded past her, his hooves clacking on the stone.

The archer looked up and squinted in their direction.

Chavali leaped at her target. She plunged the dagger into the woman's back with all her strength. The woman made a short, sharp squawk of surprise and pain.

Karias charged the two combatants. Colby cleaved the archer's head and left arm from his body. The two pieces wavered for a moment, then pitched over the cliff.

When Chavali ripped her dagger out of her victim, the blade began to hum in her hand. She felt more than heard the tiny vibration.

Her weapon wanted more. If Chavali could manage it, Vimarica would provide.

When the woman fell, she dropped a dark ball. Chavali scooped it off the ground before it could roll into the water. The thing squished like a sponge. She stuffed it into a pocket to douse with the solution later.

The mage shrieked and raised her hands to ward off Colby and Karias.

Vimarica snapped her attention to Chavali. Chavali met her gaze. They glared at each other for a heartbeat.

Chavali took a step. Vimarica raised her hands. Fire grew from the water before Vimarica.

Karias whinnied his outrage.

One of Portia's darts slammed into Vimarica's back. The attack distracted her. Without direction for a moment, her burning water dumped over the edge.

If Chavali understood correctly the process currently unfolding, Vimarica intended to use the burning water to cause the fungus spores to bloom faster. By pumping power from Korrya's nets into the process, she would increase the effect in some fashion.

This meant the people sitting in the water presented the greatest threat aside from Vimarica at the moment.

She pointed for Colby and Karias to direct them at the helpless targets. At the same time, she leaped into the water and waded as fast as her legs could manage.

"Why are you fighting us?" Vimarica raised burning water in a cocoon to protect herself from Portia. The fiery egg hovered at the far end of the waterfall. "We aren't your enemy."

If at all possible, Chavali always wanted an enemy to talk. Sometimes, she stabbed them while they did so. Other times, like this one, she engaged with their madness.

Despite how much she wanted to stab that woman through the heart with the dagger in her hand, Chavali had no problem buying time for Colby to spear her instead.

"Why do you think this?"

"We all want the same thing. Release from the void. Together, in perfect harmony with nature, we can find this release."

"You're part of it," an unexpected voice said. Chavali blinked and discovered Guyre crawling over the edge of the rock face on the other side of the water channel. A shallow cut marked his face and he favored his left leg. "You're part of it!" he screamed.

As Colby stabbed his sword through the skull of the first seated Fury, Guyre leaped at the flaming shield around Vimarica.

"It took everything," Guyre wailed as he embraced the flames.

With each passing moment, Vimarica's flame shield flickered less and Guyre screamed more. Guyre's sacrifice drained her defenses. Even with access to Korrya's netting, Vimarica couldn't maintain the flames.

Chavali hurried to reach them. She thought she knew why Vimarica didn't use the netting to power the flames.

She used it for another purpose.

As the fiery shield lost its opacity and Guyre lost his voice, Chavali saw Vimarica cupping her hands. She held another of the dark, spongy balls. Tiny worm-like tendrils sprouted from it.

Vimarica shoved the ball into Guyre's mouth. She let her shield collapse. Guyre gurgled and fell. Flames shot from Vimarica's hands to engulf him.

Chavali leaped off the edge of the waterfall and crashed into Vimarica.

She couldn't stab Vimarica like this. She held the dagger tightly, worried about dropping it, and clung to Vimarica's back.

The woman smelled revolting, like burning meat and hair.

"I do not seek release," Chavali said.

"That's a shame." Vimarica's hand patted Chavali's thigh.

While Chavali shifted to get an angle to stab Vimarica without falling, Vimarica raised the dark, spongy ball from Chavali's pocket.

"We could've been allies. I could've helped you bear your burden. I still could. Imagine the Last Guide in communion with the Last Guardian." Vimarica held the ball in both hands.

Her interest piqued by the idiotic titles, Chavali wriggled for a better grip with her legs around Vimarica's waist. Her dagger wanted blood, but Chavali wanted to make sure she knew what she'd dealt with.

Eldrack would need to know, after all.

"Help me imagine this," Chavali murmured. "What does it mean? Who is the Last Guardian?"

Tiny spots glowed on the surface of the dark, writhing ball.

In no way would Chavali allow this nonsense to continue until Vimarica attempted to make Chavali eat that thing.

"You met the Last Guardian in the mountain. When the emptiness comes, we will be safe because the Guardian will hold us close. Then our spirits will fly free while the masses are smothered."

Zealots all sounded the same.

Chavali had no need to hear more. She stabbed Vimarica in the side. Though she would've preferred to target the woman's heart or brain to assure death, any part would work.

The dagger roared in Chavali's ears. Vimarica stiffened in her grip. For the first time in her life, Chavali watched a soul leave a body. Wisps of dark smoke streamed from Vimarica's eyes. The smoke roiled and twisted toward the dagger's hilt. Once it touched the blade, she felt it use the dagger as a conduit.

Vimarica's soul joined the spirits of the clan.

Later, when she had time, space, and Railan by her side, she would determine if Vimarica presented a danger as the spirit of Pale once had.

She also needed to speak with the man who'd forged her dagger. He'd never mentioned it could do anything like this.

For the moment, Chavali fell into the lake with a corpse. She plunged into the water hard enough to fully submerge.

The dark ball floated free of Vimarica's limp hand. They would need to douse it with Portia's liquor solution. Chavali snatched it as she sheathed her dagger.

A hand closed over her wrist. The spirits swarmed across the link. Guyre's face, with tendrils of fungus protruding from his eyes, nose, mouth, and ears, filled her view.

The cluster of spirits from the mountain sighed into her mind. "My disappointment is weighty." An immense dragon made of mushrooms ambled into sight.

Though she didn't see the dragon in color this time, Chavali again no longer felt the need to breathe. The spirits gathered and became visible, forming spiraling circles of butterflies around her body.

"My scale is too small to bother measuring it," she said.

The dragon stopped in front of her. It laughed. "Your tongue is sharp, Guide. But your time has passed. It's too late. No one will survive, and so, I have taken the mantle of Guardian. I will protect the lost souls until it is safe to return."

Chavali swallowed a snort. No wonder the thing had such sloppy, blunt methods. "May I ask what you are? I have never encountered a being such as yourself."

"I am the Last Guardian."

"Yes, I heard you." She waved it off, choosing the treat the thing as an equal. "Besides this. Did you spring from the enchanted water, or did the enchantments in the water spring from you?"

The dragon shifted its head, pondering the question. "I'm not sure. My first memory is of the taste of blood and the crunch of bone."

Her best guess from this description suggested the water had some other source for its magical effect. At some point, a fungus spore had landed near the lake at the top of the mountain and sprouted, perhaps in that pool with the jawline of rock.

Someone had reached the top, discovered the water's healing properties, and spoken of it enough to goad others into making the trip. Colby had said the river had a name about tortured miracles.

Whatever chain of events had led to the mushroom's awakening and soul-stealing had resulted in no one returning from such journeys anymore.

With no one telling tales of miracles, people stopped making the trek. The world moved on. People forgot.

She wondered if there might be an abandoned and forgotten overland path to the summit. Perhaps Vimarica had stumbled across it while on some errand.

Such matters could wait, though. If she let this pompous, self-appointed savior of all continue to exist, it would try again to save the world by murdering all the people in it.

Despite her distaste for some specific individuals in the world, she preferred it filled with people.

To have Colby, she would endure a thousand idiots. For Biholtz, Haizea, and Danel, she would suffer a thousand enemy telepaths. In the name of Marcus, Penny, Kelly, Eliot, Patrick, and others yet to become clan, she would unseat a thousand corrupt nobles.

Chavali pressed her hand to the dragon's nose. Nothing happened, of course. She hadn't expected anything to happen. The dragon made the rules for this space, and it only wanted to talk.

Unfortunately for it, she had experience with arrogant asses, and also with spirits.

"I regret we cannot come to an arrangement," Chavali said. "Such power as we could command together... There is much potential to oppose the void."

"There is," the dragon agreed.

Chavali sighed, echoing its initial disappointment.

For several moments, neither spoke.

"Do you...have some alternative proposal to safeguard this world?"

She stifled a smile of victory. "I believe we should commune to determine how well our power can mesh."

The dragon would immediately think of trying to overpower her. It would see the possibility of absorbing her and the clan's spirits into itself. The idea she might have a way to use this against it would never occur to it. Why should it? It had never met anything able to rival its power. Even knowing Chavali had killed Vimarica, it couldn't imagine true defeat.

"Yes, of course. This is wise. We can hardly plan without knowing what we're capable of."

Chavali nodded. "Reveal yourself to me and we will fashion a partnership the likes of which shall shake the foundations of the world." She pulled back her hand and let her posture show her openness and expectation of glory.

Doing its part, the dragon opened its mouth.

She tried to act surprised when it snapped its jaws shut and swallowed her.

CHAPTER 35

Mushrooms pressed close. Chavali recognized them as individual spirits. The souls worked together to create the body of the dragon. The sentient fungus in the cavern guided them.

If she thought for one moment its death could've come with something so simple as Colby stabbing it, she would've indulged in regret. He would've gladly carved up that ridiculous mushroom in the mountain.

More than likely, such an attack would've drawn them all, including the spirits of both the dragon and the clan, into a metaphysical conflict. Daria and Colby lacked the skills to prevail in such circumstances. Karias might have more ability as a kind of spirit himself.

Chavali would've had to deal with it when it already knew her intent. The dragon wouldn't have entertained the possibility of working with her because it would've known she wanted to trick it.

She landed in a stomach of sorts. The small chamber afforded her enough space to stand and turn around.

"My apologies, Guide." Its voice rumbled all around her. "You will give us the power to carry out the necessary work. I regret the pain you will suffer, but this is a necessary sacrifice."

"Pain and sacrifice are my constant companions." She plucked a mushroom from the wall and crushed it in her hand.

The dragon grunted. "What are you doing?"

Dark smoke seeped through her fingers and to her dagger. Like Vimarica's soul, it used the blade to join the clan.

"Entertaining myself while I wait for my demise." She snagged two more mushrooms, one with each hand, and crushed both.

Two more souls for the clan.

The dragon rumbled without words. The chamber shook. "Your resistance is annoying yet futile. You're an ant prodding a giant with a stick."

Chavali agreed. She wrapped her arms in the butterflies and used souls to fight souls.

As if she held two whips, she flung her arms to the side and in wide circles.

The butterflies lanced through the mushrooms, slashing them and releasing the trapped souls.

"Do not despair," Chavali said. "As clan, these souls will have a freedom you refuse to grant. I will safeguard them as is my duty. They will add their stories to our traditions. We will learn from them, not force them into obedience."

The dragon roared its pain and anger. "Stop! Please! You'll ensure the void's victory. We must work together to bring back the Creator! She will only return once all the sinners are gone."

Snapping the whips through the mushrooms again and again, Chavali ignored its pleas. Nothing would make a difference to the demented fungus.

More and more souls funneled into the clan. The chamber shrank. Water showed through between the mushrooms. Chavali's butterfly whips grew in length.

"Maybe I made a mistake." The dragon's voice gained a dissonant edge and backward echo as if the remaining spirits tried to break free of its imposed hegemony.

Chavali smirked at its attempt to prevent her from taking all its power. "Yes. You made a grave mistake." She cracked her whips one more time. They burst into a flock of dark butterflies dense and vast enough to devour the ocean.

"Maybe there's still hope." It spoke as a single voice, as if it stood beside her.

She plucked the last mushroom and held it between a thumb and forefinger. "There is always hope."

The butterflies returned to her and settled into a cloak draped around her body.

"You are truly the Last Guide. A force your ancestors would fear. I will think on this. Should we meet again, I hope we can be allies."

"Perhaps." Chavali closed her hand around the mushroom and crushed it.

She opened her eyes in bright light from one of Portia's globes.

Once again, she lay on the ground by the water's edge. At least this time she didn't cough up anything.

Colby sat beside her with his hand on her shoulder. Water dripped from his hair. Portia sat on her other side. Rowan, also drenched like Colby, crouched on one knee at her feet, keeping watch in other directions. Daria, Sivry, Jaris, and Korrya each stood nearby. Anna also lingered, watching everyone.

The two men had jumped into the water to rescue her. Chavali wanted to laugh at the idea, but had more important things to worry about.

"Was Guyre's body recovered?"

"Yes, we caught it," Portia said. "Vimarica's too. All the Furies are accounted for, and we got the spore seed thing in your hand. Everything's been doused and destroyed."

"I'll make sure all the fire sites are dealt with," Rowan said.

"Torrel?"

"Is fine." Colby took Chavali's hand and helped her sit up. *::I was worried. Not as worried as other times, but still worried. Karias is fine. He's on his way down the slow way. He balked at jumping off the waterfall.::* "Wray is also fine, and so is his wife." He expressed concern about Chavali's condition and stopped touching her skin.

Korrya met Chavali's gaze. "I have so many questions."

Chavali chuckled. "No doubt." Poor Korrya would learn little of what she wanted to know. "I'm not sure I can illuminate most of what happened. My goal was to end it, not study it. At this point, the fungus threat is over. If any Dragon Talons or Withered Fists remain, they will not be troublesome. The Guard is likewise no longer a threat. I believe we have accomplished more than our spice merchant intended, though I'm glad for it.”

With Colby's help, she stood. "At the moment, we need rest. Then we need to return to our employer and report. This area now seems safe enough for trade expansion.”

"Can you stay at least long enough for tea?" Korrya asked.

"I will see how I feel in the morning. If we're ready to leave then, I will see about explaining what I can in a letter.”

Korrya nodded, her disappointment clear. "That's something, at least.”

Leaning on Colby for support, she turned to make the trek to the inn. "Daria, come with us, please.”

"I'll tell her," Colby said.

"If you wish.”

"You need the rest.”

Chavali snorted. "As if this has ever stopped me." She looked past him to the Syndicate woman still nearby. "Anna, I expect you to honor your promises.”

"We will." Anna nodded to her with wary respect. "We're still not your enemy.”

Though Chavali nodded as if she agreed, she muttered, "We'll see.”

They took their time walking through the city to reach Flower Beds. Chavali allowed Colby to fuss over her and help her into bed, then he left to speak with Daria. She fell asleep long before he returned.

Her nightmare shifted this time. Where all of the bizarre visions normally left her feeling a sense of inevitable dread and defeat, this one followed a skewed path. For the first time in many years, she woke with an odd flicker of hope.

Colby woke as soon as she stirred. They took their packs to breakfast before leaving. Portia, Sivry, and Jaris joined them as their food arrived.

"Korrya's not the only one with questions," Portia said. "You went into the water with Vimarica. Colby and Rowan fished you out long after you should've drowned twice.”

Chavali shrugged. She held a mug of tea in both hands, savoring the scent. When they returned home, she would have no more of this unusual blend. Buying some to take with her would only postpone the inevitable.

"The fungus being is tied to the enchanted water."

Everyone leaned close, expecting more.

She shrugged again. "There were more important things to discuss than how it allowed people to breathe underwater."

After she left another silence, Portia prompted, "Such as?"

"Its erroneous belief that mushrooms are superior to humans?"

As expected, this answer satisfied no one.

Colby shook his head with a grin. "By now, we should all know better than to expect her to explain everything once the problem is solved."

Portia rolled her eyes and huffed.

Sivry laughed.

"That's not fair," Jaris said with a huff, "but I understand. What happens now?"

"We check on Torrel once more and return home." Chavali nodded to the man as he wobbled down the stairs with the aid of the railing. "I will make the report for us, as I have trained them to accept what I give and not beg for more."

Colby chuckled as he stood and helped Torrel complete his journey to the table.

"It's hard to believe how much recovery I need after spending only a few days in that hole." Torrel's voice shook, yet Chavali heard the strength underneath. He would be fine in a week, perhaps two. "Thank you all for... for everything. I'd be dead a few times if not for you folks."

Iker served more food. He let his hand linger on Torrel's shoulder as he asked for his order.

Chavali forced herself to eat despite a lack of hunger. Once a few bites landed in her belly, she devoured the rest with abandon. She enjoyed the presence of friends and loved ones, and laughed with them as they recalled particularly amusing pieces of the mission.

When they finished and stood to leave, Chavali remained to speak with Torrel one last time.

They clasped forearms. "I wish to give you this." She handed him the remainder of the team's travel stipend for the mission. They'd used a great deal of it, but a few coins remained.

He blinked at the pouch in his hand. "I can't accept this. You've given me too much already."

"If you won't accept it for yourself, accept it for your new neighborhood guild. Consider it an investment from an outside party interested in its success. And if this still doesn't sit right, accept it to acquire the proper clothing required to present yourself as a candidate for consul of the city."

Torrel's mouth fell open. "I don't—"

"You do. And you would make an excellent leader for this city you love and know so well." She patted his shoulder and smiled at him. "Consider it, at least. They will undoubtedly hold elections soon, and you have many people willing to lend support if only you ask."

She leaned close. "Start with Iker. Consider Wray for Guard captain and Mara as a councilor. Good fortune, Torrel. I hope you never need our help again."

"Me too. And you too. Have a safe journey home, wherever that is."

On her way out, she waved to him. Outside, she found Daria waiting.

"I'm not wild to leave this place behind. At least I'm going where you guys are, I guess. Colby said it's all really secret so he couldn't tell me much until we get there."

"This is true. Thank you for not forcing us to knock you over the head and abduct you."

Daria laughed, loud and brassy.

The others brought their horses, saving Chavali from having to follow up that remark. On the docks, no one harassed them. Few members of the Riverway Guild showed themselves. Boat captains loaded and unloaded their goods without inspections.

They hired the same man and his sister who'd taken them up the mountain. He charged them a pittance because they'd saved him so much money and grief by undermining the Guild, the Talons, and the guard.

Portia sat at the bow as they floated downriver and didn't throw up even once.

CHAPTER 36

They arrived in Cloverdale soon after, in a pleasantly cool midmorning with puffy clouds chasing away the tail end of a passing light rain. As they passed the clan's farm, Chavali considered asking to stop.

If she did, she'd delay reporting to Aislynn for as long as she could get away with it. Eventually, the princess would send a servant to fetch her. Those poor souls had enough to do without running out to the farm to drag reluctant a Fallen agent to tend her duties. Chavali had already promised to handle the report.

Karias brought them past all the farms, through the town, and to the warm, straw-filled stables behind the tavern. The others handed over their borrowed horses to stablehands for care. Portia draped an arm around Jaris's shoulders and promised to introduce him to some of the staff. Sivry strolled out behind them.

Colby unbuckled and removed Karias's saddle. Chavali rubbed the horse's nose while Daria stripped off his bridle.

::Would you please ask him to let the stablehands tend to me? I think he needs more time to process all of this about me, and scraping my hooves isn't going to help.::

Chavali nodded. "Leave it for now," she said to Colby as he stared at the brushes with his back to her. "He'll be fine."

"I don't..."

"Colby. There are others who can tend to him, and we need to take Daria to meet Railan. They won't let her inside without us."

Daria glanced at Chavali, then nodded like she understood. "You did say you'd show me around and introduce me to the lady in charge."

Karias sighed. *::At least he waited until after the mission to truly act dumb about this. I suppose that's some kind of blessing. Sort of.::*

"We'll come back to check on you later." Chavali kissed Karias's nose and let go of him to step to Colby's side.

For once outside of clan, bedroom, or a mission, she took Colby's hand. She expected the moment to feel awkward and conflicted. Instead, she wished she'd done it sooner. That impulse to shout about him from rooftops returned.

::What...?:: Colby lifted their hands and stared at them.

"The time for discretion has ended. Come. We need to bring Daria inside." She tugged on his hand and pulled him out of the stall, bemused by his scattered, slow thoughts as he stumbled in her wake.

::Are you sure?::

"Quite."

::Why now?::

She rolled her eyes at him and grinned, pulling him through the door and into the sunshine. "Are you going to walk with me, or do I need to drag you into the tavern?"

He pictured her trying and failing to haul him across the ground by the arm. Some of his confusion faded in favor of a growing smile. His expectations, though, stayed low. He thought she intended to let go when they reached the tavern door.

"I'll help if you need it," Daria said. She spoke briefly to a stablehand, presumably making sure someone tended to Karias, and followed a few paces behind Colby.

He glanced at Daria. "That sounded like a threat."

Daria grinned broadly. "It was one."

Chuckling, Colby squeezed Chavali's hand and fell into step beside her. *::She's really not bothering you in the slightest?::*

"No. I have much more useful things to worry about."

They rounded the corner of the building and crossed the cobblestone square in front of the tavern at the heart of Cloverdale.

Clover's Tavern and the buildings around it had exactly nothing to mark them as unique or interesting. Such a stunning lack of memorable qualities, Walt the bartender had once told her, was a purposeful choice made many years ago.

They didn't want random travelers leaving with the thought to tell others about the place where they'd paused, other than to mention it didn't have an inn or especially good food. He'd paired it with the suggestion she not try the cookies no matter how delicious they looked.

::Thank you for this.:: Colby meant her willingness to take small steps toward openness. He showed his acceptance of her expected intention to let go when he opened the door.

Colby released her hand to reach for the door handle. Chavali held on and wrapped her other hand around his.

He blinked at her. *::What are you doing?::*

"Leaving discretion behind, as I said. Would you like me to open the door for you?"

For a long moment, he stared at their hands. His smile grew.

She hadn't realized how much it would mean to him that she no longer wished to hide her feelings for him and no longer demanded he do the same.

Colby pulled open the door and walked inside with her.

Like the outside, the inside had no intrigue about it. Tables and booths filled the space around a bar. Walt, a tall, spindly man with at least as many secrets to hoard as Chavali, nodded to her and Colby. The smell of polished wood, strong beer, and fresh coffee defined the end of a mission.

In a stroke of luck, Railan sat at the bar, leaning against the back wall where she could see everyone and everything passing through. The door to the back room and the Fallen tower opened, letting in the biggest gossip in the entire tower and his healer wife.

Sean noticed them. His entire being glowed with delight.

Chavali couldn't have chosen a better, more annoying moment to prove her determination to Colby.

Walt raised his brow as he looked past them.

Obviously, they still had Daria with them. "She's with me," Chavali said.

::*Railan is right there. I'll take care of Daria. You go report to Aislynn and I'll see you afterward.*:: Colby released her hand again.

"Please mention I'd like to speak with her about telepath matters later." After a brief moment of hesitation spent thinking about how much her behavior would please Sean, she beckoned for Colby to lean closer.

When he did, obviously expecting her to whisper some other request, she kissed him.

His surprise faded swiftly. ::*You never do anything halfway.*::

Sean ruined the moment by squealing with excitement.

"I'll come to your room," Chavali murmured.

As she turned to leave, she noted Railan watching with her brow raised so high the creases concealed some of her scars.

"Sean," Chavali said to greet him as she breezed past.

Sean vibrated with enough glee that Chavali almost felt bad for leaving Colby in the same room with him.

Almost.

She descended through the tower with haste, eager to get the stupid report out of the way. People she knew gave her a second glance after returning her wave as if they'd never seen her happy.

Perhaps they never had.

The loss of her clan had weighed heavily on her when she first awoke. That grief hadn't left her, but it no longer hunched on her shoulders, pressing her down with every passing moment.

Life moved on. Love wandered in.

For the first time since that loss, her heart didn't ache. She felt full and light, and ready to face anything.

Including Aislynn.

Chavali opened the door to Eldrack's office and breezed inside. Aislynn jumped with surprise, scraping a line of ink across the page in front of her.

"Is it really too much to ask that you knock?" Aislynn picked up her paper and regarded it with a scowl.

"Yes." She still wanted to throw tea in Aislynn's face. Startling her and ruining one of her documents served as a second-best option. For now. "The mission was successful. Torrel is safe and his tormentors have been dispatched." She didn't bother to sit because she had no intention of reporting much more detail than this.

"Good." Aislynn daubed at her paper with a hand towel. "Have a seat."

"No, thank you. I'll stand." Chavali set her hands on the back of the chair indicated.

Aislynn huffed. "You don't need to be contrary for the sake of being contrary. It doesn't help anything."

Chavali shrugged, not caring in the slightest about Aislynn's opinion. "The mission would have gone smoother had we known more about Palmia Basin prior to leaving. Or had we known more about Torrel, his peculiar situation, or a dozen other pieces of information you withheld. Meeting with his handler would've helped tremendously.

"The team was not appropriate for the mission either. Jaris should not have gone on a mission so soon after waking, and Portia spent more time throwing up on boats than anything else. Sivry is an elf, and Palmia Basin has few other elves. She was also not a good choice to mentor Jaris.

"In addition, we were forced to bring back a woman who learned more than we'd like about the Fallen and is too competent to ignore. Railan is already aware of this and dealing with it."

She wondered if Aislynn would've heard about Bricene, the North Cascain princess, going missing. Regardless, she had no reason to mention the Syndicate's involvement. The fewer openings Chavali offered, the better.

Aislynn dropped her towel and leaned back in Eldrack's chair. "You said the team was inappropriate, but only mentioned three members. Why shouldn't you have been there?"

"I am highly adaptable, but I do object to you selecting a mission leader. This is not the most efficient or positive way to organize a Fallen team. We are not royal spies."

"Mmhmmm." Aislynn nodded and acted casual. "And why shouldn't Colby have been there?"

Seeing the obvious trap, Chavali shrugged again. "The city has very few horses. Like Sivry, he stood out more than usual because of his mount." Daria didn't count. Any Fallen agent could accidentally encounter someone from their first life on a mission.

"Not because you're sleeping with him?"

Chavali raised an eyebrow. "If by 'sleeping' you mean 'having sex,' then you, like many in the tower, are misinformed. I expect better information gathering skills of someone from a royal court, let alone a keeper of spies."

She hesitated over how to word her request regarding him. For Eldrack, she would've explained in as upfront a manner as possible.

This princess didn't deserve that frankness, but she still needed to know. "However, I am quite fond of him," Chavali said, "and it would be wise not to pair us for missions in the future."

Aislynn smirked at her. "I see. Then I suppose this next mission is your last one together." She patted a closed folder on her desk.

Chavali blinked twice before she determined Aislynn was serious. "No. Send someone else. We both require more time between missions than half a day. Every agent does."

"Sadly, you don't even get half a day." Aislynn clasped her hands over her stomach and shifted her smirk to a smug grin. "You and he are expected in Todan as soon as possible to present testimony as witnesses in the matter of Eldrack's competence. The king had hoped you'd show up a few days ago, so haste is appreciated."

For Eldrack, Chavali would suffer the lack of her clan. She stifled a great deal of her thoughts on the subject, though she let through a flat glare. "Where do we report?"

As expected, Aislynn didn't give her a folder, a copy of the summons, or any other documentation.

Chavali restrained herself from slamming the door as she left the room. At least she'd have Colby with her.

Maybe they'd even bring Eldrack home.

EPILOGUE

One could tell a great deal about the king's opinion of a prisoner by the type of cell they occupied. Robin nodded to the guard in Shappan royal livery as he opened an ordinary wooden door. Inside, he discovered a room worthy of a backwater noble.

The front room held a couch and chairs around a low table, all upholstered with common materials in neutral tones. Charcoal pencils and paper lay on the table. One shelf on the wall held a dozen books. Beside the door, a wooden pitcher and cup sat on another shelf. The guards could open a panel in the wall to access the shelf. They probably used it to deliver meals.

Another door stood halfway open, offering a glimpse into a bedroom with similar decorating. He saw another, much larger bookshelf full of many more books and several potted plants with lush greenery. Robin noted a distinct lack of glass or other materials prone to creating sharp edges. Even the pencils lacked a serious, stabbing-capable point. In a pinch, one could smash the furniture to create a stake or makeshift spear, though the wood looked thick enough to resist most efforts.

"Hello?" Robin noted the click of the lock behind him. They afforded their prisoner a great deal of comfort, but not the luxury of potential escape with a visitor. "Eldrack?"

Based upon his inquiries about Eldrack, he hadn't expected the man who stepped through the door, drying his hands with a white towel. He could've fit among any collection of bureaucrats or scribes with no effort. Middle aged with a slight paunch, graying brown hair and hazel eyes, he had that elusive everyman quality so many thieves relied upon to escape justice for their crimes.

He wondered what could have defeated that kind of armor to land Eldrack in this situation.

"I don't believe we've met." Eldrack extended his hand with a friendly smile and approached Robin.

Unable to resist his overture, Robin shook his hand. "Robin."

Did he imagine it, or did Eldrack recognize him based upon his name? Lauryn had announced their impending marriage already, and she was the Queen of North Cascain. Eldrack might get news of that type. The king of Shappa clearly held him in some regard.

"Please, sit. I'd offer you refreshment, but I'm afraid there's only one cup and I've already used it today." Eldrack gestured toward the chairs. "The accommodations are pleasant, but somewhat restricted."

Robin smiled and took one of the chairs, charmed by Eldrack in some way he couldn't explain. Something about him screamed openness and empathy. In Robin's experience, such persons often proved more perilous than those who exuded mystery or danger.

He sent an initial probe into Eldrack's mind as he sat. To his great surprise, he met resistance.

"What brings you to me today?" Eldrack made no indication he'd noticed the attempt at intrusion.

A telepath with that significant of a defense would notice. No matter how well trained in the art of controlling their face, that telepath would always betray it somehow. Robin himself couldn't keep the muscles around his eyes from tightening.

"I have some questions about a certain individual I believe you may have met."

Eldrack gestured for him to proceed. "I'll tell you whatever I can, Robin."

Certain someone else had set up the defenses in Eldrack's mind, Robin pressed against them. His efforts applied a fine needle against tightly-woven cloth, wriggling and boring relentlessly inward. Still Eldrack offered no sign of noticing.

"Thank you. First, I'd like to relate a story of sorts, so I hope you'll indulge me?”

“I’m certain your time is more valuable than mine at the moment.” Eldrack gestured, polite and comfortable. He sounded for all the world like he’d rather be nowhere else than listening to whatever Robin had to say.

Robin nodded his gratitude. “Like many people, I’ve done my best to work toward Reunion. I’d like to think my efforts are more serious than most. I’ve spent a great deal of time investigating one type of unexplained event or another, looking for patterns and clues. A keyhole must have a key, right?

“Roughly two years ago, I heard a rumor about a woman working as part of a troupe of traveling entertainers who’d accurately predicted the location of a missing child. Her directions were vague and cryptic. Entirely unhelpful. After the fact, though, once they took the time to think about it, her instructions matched the situation perfectly.

“Naturally, I assumed it was a fluke. On the way into town, maybe she’d seen an area where children played outside of their parents’ sight and figured she could suggest the location without saying it outright. But I like to be thorough, so I sent someone to investigate and try to find this woman.”

His attack slipped into Eldrack’s surface thoughts. He didn’t care about that. Not much, anyway. Instead of pausing to catch or examine any of it, he pressed onward.

Whoever had constructed the outer defenses had done an excellent job. They paled in comparison to the inner shielding. Robin blinked, pausing his story to marvel at the impressive wall around Eldrack’s memories. The feel of it spoke of his own order, the Strong Mind, though he didn’t recognize the patterns as the mark of anyone he’d ever met. Likely, they’d done it many years ago.

“It took Yliana the better part of a year to find the correct traveling band of entertainers. She approached the woman and managed to trigger a curious manifestation of the Creator’s power. The words Yliana brought back to me didn’t strictly make sense. ‘Eyes of blue. Taken from you. Mountain view. Dreams askew. Burning through.’ It sounds like a load of rubbish, doesn’t it?”

One tiny probe against the massive fortification in Eldrack's mind sent Robin mentally reeling. If he tried to break through, he risked destroying the information he wanted. Even if he could get it, he stood a better than even chance of leaving Eldrack a drooling idiot. People would notice the difference.

The amount of effort it would take to break through would prevent Robin from wiping the guards' memories of his visit. They'd tell their superiors. The King of Shappa would learn about Robin.

No one could learn about him.

"It's quite a ridiculous riddle, yes," Eldrack said.

Robin abandoned any hope of rifling through Eldrack's memories to focus on his surface thoughts.

::Did it refer to you, Robin? Your eyes are, after all, blue.::

Yes, Robin had considered that. In retrospect, he thought it referred to Yliana's ultimate fate.

"I laughed it off at first. Like so many other rumors, this one had proven a waste of time. In the back of my mind, though, I mulled over the words every so often. Yliana had reported a curious transformation in the woman's demeanor along with the riddle, and her bodyguard had explained the woman sometimes saw things that didn't make sense until after the fact. She should go home and think about how any of the things mentioned might apply to her or her problems, either directly or metaphorically."

::I hadn't realized you were that particular Robin. How interesting.::

Eldrack's thought, cleaner and better structured than Robin expected from an untrained person, suggested he'd at least heard some account of the fate of the clan. Those three children had, after all, been taken from the telepaths he'd entrusted them to. If Eldrack knew the whereabouts of the teenage girl, Robin wanted to discover it.

"If that gift proved real and true, even if it required a great deal of decoding, imagine how much time and effort could be saved by knowing in advance which leads to follow and which to ignore. I believe the Creator wants Reunion, Eldrack, do you?"

::A curious question.::

Eldrack's mind pursued several options for how answering that question would turn out. He followed the paths much too fast for Robin to catch all of them, but a flash of Chavali caught his attention.

The flicker showed an image of her draped in white cloth with only her face exposed. She lay on a slab, her skin a deathly blue-gray and her eyes closed. The pink feather and its surrounding tattoo gave her away.

"Yes, I do." Eldrack seemed so harmless and pleasant, yet he'd recovered Chavali's body for some reason. What did this man do for the king?

No one Robin had asked knew. He'd find other people to ask.

Robin nodded his satisfaction. "I decided to investigate for myself. When I found the clan, a task which took me some time, I met her and determined she did, indeed, possess this incredible gift. When I attempted to secure her cooperation, she became unstable and killed herself."

::That's an interesting interpretation for your actions. I wonder if you believe that fiction? No, you're an accomplished liar, just like Chavali herself. You know what you did.::

Robin stifled the frustrating urge to respond to Eldrack's pointed thought by defending himself. He'd learned to quash that years ago. This infuriating man had no right to provoke it.

"That must have been disappointing," Eldrack said.

"Yes, quite," Robin said.

"I'm not sure what it has to do with me?"

"I was led to believe you've met this woman. Her name was Chavali."

Eldrack betrayed nothing with his expression. He appeared mildly confused. "I can't imagine why anyone suggested such a thing." *::We can probably blame that Pale woman for this. Who knows what she did before Chavali exorcised her spirit.::*

Robin caught himself after he'd blinked only once. Even if he accepted the possibility of exorcising spirits, Chavali had died several months before Kirena. One dead woman couldn't affect another dead woman.

"The source of this information had no reason to lie to me. She may have been mistaken, though. Another source has suggested Chavali had a sister named Chastity and they look very similar."

"I've never met a Chastity." ::*The next time I see you, Chavali, we'll have to discuss using multiple fake names. One, it seems, isn't enough. We should also finally discuss a disguise, no matter how little you think of hats.*::

The next time...

Not only did he know Chavali and Chastity to be the same woman, Eldrack clearly expected to see her soon.

He didn't expect to see her corpse, he expected to see Chavali, alive and capable of engaging in conversation.

Robin had seen her dead. He'd watched helplessly as she bled to death faster than he could prevent. Her heart had stopped, and her thoughts had drained to nothing. She'd died knowing she'd beaten him by defying her nature.

Chavali had *not* tricked him. She hadn't played dead. If he'd had any question at all about her condition, he would've taken her. Wounds could be healed, even grievous ones.

Someone working for the king had a way to bring back the dead. He doubted Eldrack had involvement until after the fact. Most likely, he kept records involving the subjects and their activities.

He clasped his hands in his lap so Eldrack wouldn't see them tremble. "Are you sure? She's quite distinctive. Unusual olive skin tone, pink feather sticking out of her forehead?"

Eldrack held up his hands, both empty. "I'm sorry to have wasted your time, Robin."

::*In a way, I hope you meet her again. She's a great deal more formidable than when you first encountered her. And that's saying something.*::

Robin thought enough time had passed that he needed to wrap up this meeting. The longer he spent, the more effort he'd have to spend to deal with it. Beyond that, he had no idea how long he could truly maintain a facade of dispassion.

His dearest prize, a precious gift from the Creator, lived. Some power had granted him a second chance.

Chavali wouldn't escape him again.

"You haven't." He stood and shook hands with Eldrack. "Now I know Kirena sent me to you because Chavali is alive. That's worth a trip to Todan."

Even as Eldrack realized what had happened, much faster than most people would, Robin stole the man's still-forming memory of this event. He stunned Eldrack and guided him to lay on the couch. In a few minutes, he'd recover and remember nothing.

Staring down at him, Robin grinned like an idiot. He couldn't crack into Eldrack's mind, but he had enough to go on. The last time he'd searched for Chavali, it had taken a year to find her, and he'd botched it by not understanding his prey.

This time, he'd lay a trap so elegant and perfect she'd have no choice but to cooperate. She'd see her possible second death as a failure instead of a success.

The sooner he started, the sooner he'd have her in his hands, working for him instead of against him.

He tapped the minds of the two guards outside to remove their memories of his entrance and get one to open the door for him. With a bounce in his step, he slipped out of the building and into joyous sunshine.

Before he left Todan, he'd find someone with more information about Eldrack, take it, and follow wherever it led.

ABOUT THE AUTHORS

Erik Kort abides in the glorious Pacific Northwest, otherwise known as Mirkwood-Without-The-Giant-Spiders, though the normal spiders often grow too numerous for his comfort. He is defended from all eight-legged threats by his brave and overly tolerant wife, and is mocked by his obligatory writer's cat. When not writing, Erik comforts the elderly, guides youths through vast wildernesses, and smuggles more books into his library of increasingly alarming size.

Lee French is a *USA Today* bestselling author living in Olympia, WA with two kids, two bicycles, and too much stuff. She is an avid gamer and member of the Myth-Weavers online RPG community. In addition to spending too much time there, she also trains in taekwondo, has a nice flower garden with one dragon and absolutely no lawn gnomes, and tries in vain every year to grow vegetables that don't get devoured by neighborhood wildlife.

She is an active member of the Science Fiction and Fantasy Writers of America and a Municipal Liaisons for her NaNoWriMo region.

Thanks for reading! If you liked this book, please take a minute to post a review of it wherever you buy your books.

www.tangledskypress.com